Jonathan Griffiths

Walking the Dog

Suburban Tails

WATER PUMP

PRESS

Water Pump Press
14 Railway Parade
Newport, Melbourne
Australia 3015

Cover design and typesetting by
Jamrag Productions, Newport, Victoria

Printed and bound by Griffin Press, Salisbury South,
South Australia

First published 2014

National Library of Australia
Cataloguing-in-Publication data:
Griffiths, Jonathan 1956 –
Walking the Dog

1st Ed

ISBN: 9780987116017 (pbk)

A823.4

To Gemma

Our friend and companion, 1992-2006.

You taught us that dogs are people too.

The phrase *dog owner* is misleading. The relationship between Man and Dog isn't master and slave. It's more of a partnership. Man offers food and shelter. Dog offers companionship, exercise, the opportunity to wander your neighbourhood and much more.

A man with a child is called a father. What's the word for a man with a dog? A woman with a dog? A child with a dog?

Our language is sadly lacking,

author with dog

Acknowledgments

The following stories have been previously published:

The Tart	Sleepers Almanac #8	2013
Within these Walls	The Other Side #6	2005
A White or a Red	The Other Side #3	2003
Rabbits	The Other Side #2	2002
Words	The Other Side #1	2001

Walking the Dog

WALKING THE DOG is a series of interconnected stories with the narrative arc of a novel. These stories can be read individually or sequentially.

Set in the immediate neighbourhood of the Parker family, in Melbourne's western suburbs, *Walking the Dog* tells tales of love, family, friendship, voyeurism, infidelity, jealousy, mortality and dogs.

It's only in the last couple of years that I've walked a dog. It's only the last couple of years that I've owned a dog. I'm not a doggie-person. I don't particularly like dogs, and our dog is no exception. But there's something very soothing, almost therapeutic, about strolling with a canine companion. Sometimes I walk in the mornings, sometimes in the evenings, and when I have time, both.

We used to walk in the wastelands, over the railway lines, where the dog could chase rabbits to her heart's content. With my infant son hanging in a sling on my chest, we'd set off for adventures – dodging stinging nettles in the spring and snakes in the summer. The dog would chase rabbits and I'd discover interesting bits of junk. Gemma loves chasing rabbits. She's a kelpie/pointer cross and when I mention that to doggie-people they nod their heads understandingly.

But when the council started putting down baits, we moved to the streets.

There are no rabbits to chase but there are other benefits. I enjoy watching our neighbours going about their suburban lives – seeing what they have for breakfast and dinner, what they watch on TV, how they keep their gardens, when they mow their lawns and do their washing.

I've always been tall and always had an inquisitive nature, a dangerous combination. By the age of eight I could easily see over a four-foot fence, and as an adult, at six-foot-five, there aren't many fences I can't see over. Not that I'm a Peeping Tom or anything; I just like to glance as I walk past.

An Open Gate

I often write letters to our local paper, to complain about the council, the trains, or the refinery – and they publish a few – but I use the pseudonym Mister Walker, to maintain my anonymity.

Once we reach the end of our street, we can turn left over the railway crossing, pass the horse paddocks and head down to the bay, or we can follow the railway lines to the oil refinery – but there are no houses those ways.

I often let Gemma decide our route – although this has got me into trouble on a few occasions.

Gemma turns right; a good choice.

As we pass the second house, the purple one – number sixty-three, I laugh to myself. Just after we moved here, they put a door out on their nature strip. *Free to good home*, they'd scrawled on it. That'll come in handy I thought and carried it home. Eighteen months later it still hadn't come in handy and Michelle, sick of seeing the purple door leant up against the side of our house, persuaded me to get rid of it. *Sorry, my wife says I don't need it after all*, I scrawled on it and put it back. I wonder what they made of the return of the prodigal door.

Number sixty-nine is gathering together more junk for a garage sale – they have one every three or four months. Their front door opens and the smell of bacon and eggs wafts out. The woman of the house brings out a bag of garbage and I nod to her.

'Having another garage sale?' I ask.

'Yes,' she yawns. 'On Saturday.'

'I'll come and have a stickybeak.'

'You do that.'

'I will.'

I expect that one day I'll discover the purple door there – scrubbed clean of all notations.

Michelle would stay and have a fifteen-minute chat but I like to keep on the move when I'm walking – and unlike Michelle, I'm not much of a conversationalist.

As per usual, the doberman at seventy-five jumps onto the roof of their car, trying to leap over their eight-foot fence. If I had a dog like that I'd park on the street. Gemma ignores the barking and banging, and the sounds of buckling steel.

I admire the progress on the extension at number eighty-one. There seems to be a young couple living there now but the old man's car is still parked outside. They're sleeping in the front room, the young couple. The son or daughter of the old man, perhaps. Not much of a likeness, though. Gemma wees on their gatepost. Now that the nights are getting colder, they let their dog sleep in their room and it leaps at the window as we pass, twisting the curtains into knots. The young woman gets out of bed, in her nightie, to shoo the dog out and straighten the curtains. I nod to her and she yanks the curtain across. I see they've painted the bedroom walls. Nice colour.

After we cross the road, where the new townhouses are, Gemma turns into the school grounds and I let her off the lead. I imagine our son, Christopher, will go to this school, but that's a few years off yet – he's only just turned one.

The townhouses have back gates that open into the school grounds and at the third gate, which is usually open in the mornings, sits Gemma's friend, a border collie. The woman that lives there often lounges against the gatepost in provocative poses, wearing only a nightie and dressing gown, whilst sipping a coffee or munching on a bowl of muesli. *The Tart*, Michelle calls her. However, she seems nice enough; she's about my age – late thirties. We nod to each other and sometimes exchange a few words. I haven't seen her for a while though.

Generally Gemma and the collie leap at each other and race around in circles, but today their meeting is subdued, almost formal. The collie goes through its gate, into its backyard, and Gemma follows. The collie goes through the back door of the townhouse, and Gemma follows. That's unusual; she's never done that before. I wait, expecting her to trot out any moment.

'Gemma,' I call. No response. 'Gemma!' I call again, louder.

A faint female voice seems to answer me, but I can't be sure – it's so quiet.

I go through the gate; the backyard is tiny, and all brick. No wonder she leaves the gate open for the dog.

Standing at the door, I call 'Gemma!' again.

'She's in here.' The voice is so quiet I can't be sure that I'm not imagining it.

'Hello,' I call.

'Come in.'

I tentatively enter, almost knocking my head on the light fitting. I could never live in a place with ceilings this low. The kitchen is very tidy – too tidy – it's like a display home. I think she lives alone.

'I'm in the bedroom,' the woman, *The Tart*, almost whispers. 'Come in.'

I pass the bathroom, which is also spotlessly tidy, apart from a bra hanging from the shower rose. Why do women do that? A faint smell of disinfectant and vomit drifts into the hallway.

At her bedroom door, I can hear Gemma's tail beating against the bed. The collie whines softly. I feel like an intruder, or some sort of stalker. But I remind myself that I've been invited.

'Come in,' the woman whispers again, more urgently.

I push her door open, slowly, wrapping the fingers of my left hand around the door, to most prominently display my wedding ring. I clear my throat before entering her boudoir. I have the uneasy feeling that she's on her bed, wearing very little.

With the doona only covering her legs, she's sprawled diagonally across her queen size bed. She looks like death – even in her flimsy negligee. Worse than death. Her skin's grey and dull, like something a snake would slither out of. She looks as if she could go at any moment. Her hand drapes over the side of the bed, weakly stroking Gemma. There's a bucket beside her bed, with half an inch of watery vomit in it.

'Do you want me to call an ambulance?'

She gives the slightest shake of her head.

'Family? Is there anyone I can call for you?'

'No. I'm fine. My sister will be over later.'

'Anything I can get you?'

'A glass of water, thanks. And my pills.' She nods towards the floor.

I pick up the pills she's dropped on the floor – *Voltaren*, a painkiller I think – and hand them to her, then take the empty glass from her bedside table, which is stocked like a pharmacy shelf: *Prednisone, Celebrex, Tramol,* all prescribed to a Ramona Lobados – sounds Spanish.

I take her glass to the kitchen, fill it from a jug in her fridge and return it to her bedside. She nods appreciatively and tries to sit up. I help her up and push pillows behind her. She smiles weakly, then winces with the effort of pushing two pills from the packet. She pops the pills into her mouth and I raise the glass to her lips. She takes the glass from me with shaking hands, asserting her independence like a one-year old child. She spills half the glass on her bedding and drops the pill packet on the floor again.

I pick up the bucket from beside her bed and tip its contents down her toilet. I find the bottle of disinfectant in the cupboard under the washbasin and rinse out the bucket, before returning it to her bedside. She nods a thankyou.

'Is there anything else I can get you?' I ask. 'Something to eat?' She doesn't look capable of eating but I don't know what else to say.

She shakes her head.

'Are you sure you don't want an ambulance? You don't look well.'

'No. I'm fine. I'm okay. This is the body's natural response to chemo.'

Then she slumps further into her pillows as if the effort of speaking has drained every last joule of her energy.

I nod. I don't know what to say.

She says nothing either. She tries to smile. I grin like an idiot, then adopt a concerned expression. I don't want her to think I'm laughing at her.

I'm acutely aware of the sounds of the dogs, panting and wagging their tails.

'Nice dog. Does it need feeding?'

She shakes her head. 'My sister feeds her.'

'What's her name?'

'Ivy.'

Ivy? Is that the sister's name or the dog's name? Strange name for a dog.

Ramona closes her eyes. *Thump, thump, thump*, goes Gemma's tail against the mattress. *Huh, huh, huh*, goes her breath.

I feel the need to say something more. Have you been here long, I long to ask, but it's a stupid question: I already know the answer and she's far too tired for small talk. But why did she ask me in? She wants more than just her pills and some water and her bucket emptying.

'I'm Peter. I live nearby.'

She nods. 'I'm Ramona.'

'Ramona Lobados. Is that Spanish?'

She shakes her head.

There goes that conversation.

'The treatment, the chemotherapy,' I venture, 'What's it for? What's wrong with you? Some kind of cancer?'

She nods. 'Non-Hodkins disease.'

What sort of answer is that?

'That tells me what you haven't got – what isn't wrong with you. So what is wrong with you? If it's not Hodkin's disease then whose bloody disease is it?'

She laughs – actually laughs, a couple of quick, quiet chuckles. 'I've been saying that to my doctor for years.' Then she closes her eyes and drifts off. She drops the glass on the floor. Water spills onto her carpet and Gemma laps it up.

Shit, I've killed her. Killed her with my stupid joke.

I pick up her phone and dial triple zero. 'I'm okay,' she croaks and I hang up.

She opens her eyes. 'I'm okay,' she repeats.

Thump, thump, thump – huh, huh, huh – tick, tick, tick. I look at my watch. I need to get going.

'I'll get you some more water.' I retrieve the glass from under her bed, take it to the kitchen, get a fresh glass from the cupboard over the stove and refill it from the jug in the fridge. When I return to her bedroom, with her drink, she's sitting up – looking relatively healthy.

'You're looking better.'

'Good. I always try to look my best.'

She leans forward, hugging her legs, flattening her breasts against them, accentuating her cleavage.

'I have to go.'

'Maybe you can come around later.'

'I don't know.'

'Please. I need to know what's going on.'

I nod at the television in the corner of her room and the unopened newspaper on her bedside table.

'I don't care what's going on in the world,' she croaks. 'I want to know what's going on around here, on my doorstep. I want to know who's screwing who, who's buying, who's selling, who's renovating – who's got a new car.' She slumps back into her pillows.

'Number eighty-one's putting on an extension.'

'Up or out?'

'Out, at the back, but I think they might go up as well. There's a young couple staying there.'

'Yes, Mister Richardson's stepdaughter – she's a pretty girl, isn't she?'

'Yes.' How does she know she know the old man's name? How does she know his relationship to the girl?

'They were doing up the front room, last I saw,' she says.

'Yes, they've painted it a gorgeous blue.'

'You've been inside?'

'No, I've only seen it through the window.'

She smirks.

'I wasn't trying to look through their window. I just glanced as I walked past.'

'Whatever you say, Peter.'

I look away, embarrassed. She thinks I'm a pervert. Her – lying around half naked and inviting strange men into her bedroom – with her tits practically bursting out of her negligee. She's got a cheek!

She giggles. 'I'm sorry.'

I glance at my watch. Shit, I've been here for half an hour. I'm usually only out for twenty minutes. I'll be late for work. Michelle will be worried. 'I've got to go.'

I clip Gemma's lead to her collar.

She grabs the lead. 'Come back later. The door will be open.'

'I don't think my wife would approve.'

'I'm not after your wife's approval,' she snaps.

'My wife thinks you're a tart,' I blurt.

She looks at me, totally stunned.

'I'm sorry, I didn't mean to say that.'

She laughs. 'No, don't apologise, you've made my day. It's been a long time since anyone's called me a tart. I used to sing in a jazz band, years ago. My male fans would often tell me how sexy I was – but their girlfriends all said I was a tart.'

'You're still sexy,' I tell her, trying to coax Gemma's lead out of her clutches.

'No my sexy days are long since gone.' She hums a couple of notes then bursts into song. *Those Were the Days my Friends*, she sings and her dog howls accompaniment, continuing for a few bars after she stops. She lets go of the lead as I stare at the dog in amazement. I take the opportunity to bolt.

'I've got to go, see you later.'

She tries to grab the lead but isn't quick enough – I'm out of her bedroom door like a rat up a drain pipe. I've got no time for long goodbyes.

'Come back and see me again,' she whines after me. 'And don't tell a soul that I'm sick – please. It's bad enough without everyone knowing. Please – promise me….'

But by then I'm out of the backdoor and out of earshot. I sprint out of the school grounds and across the road, past number eight-one – Mister Richardson's place – and past the doberman before it can let out a single bark.

What a strange woman – she'd rather be despised for being a siren and a succubus than pitied for being an invalid.

I suppose I should go back and see her tomorrow, check that she's all right, and reassure her that her secret's safe with me.

When we reach the end of our street, I slow down. What am I going to tell Michelle?

Maybe I'll tell her about the dog. And maybe I'll take Christopher with me next time. He'd love her dog.

I generally walk the dog to the school up the road, these days, casually checking out the neighbours as we pass. But I'd noticed that for a few days there had been workmen drilling in the wastelands across the railway tracks. Two or three utes, with portable drilling units on the back, parked in different spots each day. They must have drilled a dozen or more holes. What were they looking for?

We turned left over the railway crossing, past the pipes running from the refinery, then turned left again along the dirt track that followed the pipes past the horse paddock. Gemma found a friend to play with, Ramona's dog, Ivy. Why was she out on her own?

'Ivy! Ivy, come here,' I called. She ignored me. 'Ivy!' Stupid bloody name for a dog, no wonder she wouldn't respond. Then I spotted Ramona, sitting on the pipe. I made my way across and sat down beside her. 'Hi, you're a long way from home.'

'Tell me about it. I'm exhausted.'

'You're looking well. You're in remission?'

'More like intermission. It won't last long.'

'Do you want me to drive you home?'

'I'm fine, Peter. I just need to rest a while.'

'Okay.' The dogs ran around madly, leaping and barking. Further away I could see the utes, drilling for something. What? The closest was only a hundred meters or so; I wanted to quiz the men, but I didn't want to leave Ramona on her own. 'You look cold.'

'I am cold.'

'Borrow my jacket.' I took it off and put it over her shoulders.

'Thanks.'

Then I was cold.

'The train tracks have been such a psychological barrier to me. Today, finally, I had enough strength to cross over the rails. But I'm not sure I can make it back.'

'I can give you a lift.'

'Just sit with me a while.'

'Sure.' I nodded at the utes, 'What do you think they're doing?'

'I don't know.'

'Drilling for oil?'

'Possibly.'

'Have you heard of fracking?'

'Jesus, Peter. It's a long time since I've done any fracking. I've almost forgotten what it feels like.'

'Hydraulic fracturing. It's nasty.'

'No, never heard of that.'

'They pump fluids, at high pressure, into deep crevices…'

'Yeah. That's the fracking I'm talking about. I haven't been fracked for years, Peter. I miss it. Miss it terribly.' She looked at me with such sad, lonely eyes that I wanted to hug her, but thought better of it.

'I'm not explaining it well. Look it up. Google it. It poisons the water and releases toxic gases. If they're fracking around here we could all be dead from cancer in a few years.'

'I'll probably be dead from cancer by then anyway.'

'Sorry. That was tactless.'

'That's okay. So you'll investigate what they're doing?' She nodded at the workmen.

'Absolutely. I'll question them, grill them, drill them. Ring their company, ring the council, write to the paper…'

'And will that made any difference?'

'Probably not.'

'Walk with me, Peter. Walk me home.'

'Sure.' I helped her up. She was very unsteady. Her place was only a few hundred meters away, but for her that was a long way. We clipped the dogs onto their leads; I held both and Ramona took my arm as we shuffled back towards the road.

'You know what I think, Peter?'

'What's that?'

'I think they're testing the soil for contamination. You know this place used to be a tip?'

'Yeah.'

'If the soil's clean, they could rezone this land as residential and build a thousand townhouses. Someone would make millions – billions.'

'Maybe.'

We had to wait for a train before we could cross the tracks. Ramona leant her head on my chest. I hoped Michelle wasn't looking out of the window, although the train would block her view. 'You're so tall, Peter. So funny. You're my ideal man.'

'I'm married, Ramona.'

'No one's perfect.'

Her hair smelt like strawberries.

'It's a lovely shampoo, isn't it?' she asked. How did she know I could smell it?

The train passed and we crossed the tracks and made our way up the road.

'It's a wig,' Ramona said. 'My hair's long gone. I'm not sure it's coming back.'

'I'm sorry.'

'Don't be sorry. Technically speaking it is my hair. But don't tell a soul – and especially not Michelle.

'Why shampoo a wig?'

Ramona just laughed. She pointed over the fence of number sixty-one, 'Their lawn does really well, what's their secret?'

'I don't know.'

'See if you can find out.'

'Okay.'

I generally keep up a decent pace while I'm walking, but I discovered that at Ramona's speed I could take in much more. The lawn was gorgeous, almost like the surface of a pool table.

Outside number sixty-three she asked, 'What do these two argue about all the time? I hear them at it almost every time I pass. But I can never make out what they're saying. Have a listen one day. See what you can make out.'

'Sure.'

At sixty-five she had to sit on the wall to rest.

'Can't we keep going, Ramona? We're almost there. I'm cold. I'm running late. Michelle will be worried.'

'Let her worry. It's not every day I go out on a date.'

'It's not a date.'

'Put your jacket around both of us. Or go home and grab another jacket. Your place is just around the corner, isn't it?'

'How do you know that?'

'I just know.'

How would I explain to Michelle that I needed another jacket? Best to stay put. Wrapping the jacket around both of us was actually quite warm, but it put me into uncomfortably close contact with Ramona.

'Back to the fracking, Peter. Are you well fracked?'

'That's a very personal question, Ramona.'

'I'm a very personal person, Peter. And you didn't answer my question.'

'I'm sufficiently fracked, thank you.'

'Good. I'm not. I need a man in my life, Peter. And if it's not you, then who?'

I nodded in the direction of Ramona's. 'Mister Richardson. He'd be up for it.'

'I'd like someone with full bladder control.'

'I think he just spills his tea. His hands shake a lot.'

'I want someone under forty, with a sense of adventure and a good sense of humour. You are under forty, aren't you?'

'I'm thirty-eight.'

'The ideal age. Someone tall who likes dogs.'

'I don't like dogs that much.'

'Even someone who'll tolerate dogs, if they're young enough, tall enough, and live locally.'

'How about my twin brother?'

'Perfect, send him around.'

'I'm joking. I don't have any siblings. How about my next door neighbour, Dave? He's young, he likes dogs…'

'And he's tall?'

'No. He's about your height. He's very handy with his hands though, that's got to count for something.'

'He likes opera and fine red wines?'

'I doubt it.'

'I suppose he smokes?'

The dogs began to bark and pull on their leads. 'Only rollies.'

'And he drinks beer?'

'Never more than half a slab at a time.'

'Not my type, Peter. You'll have to do better. See who you can find.'

'Sure,' I replied, before I'd even noticed that I'd agreed to everything she asked for. The dogs were getting very restless and so was I. 'We need to keep moving, Ramona.' I stood and helped her up. I draped my jacket over her shoulders and again she took my arm.

'You could carry me, Peter. Carry me like a bride over the threshold.'

'I'm not carrying you, Ramona.'

As we walked past number seventy-five the doberman leapt crazily on the roof of their car, slavering and barking at a thousand decibels. I'm sure he could leap over their fence from there, but he never does. He just jumps on the car. Its roof creaks and groans as the metal dents and rebounds. I imagine one day it'll just collapse.

'He must have such a great view from up there. I hate tall fences. They block out so much. You're so lucky, Peter, being so tall.'

'Sometimes it's a curse.'

'I wish I had that curse. I want to get a periscope installed at home, twenty feet tall, able to swivel in all directions, and tilt to whatever angle's required. With a zoom lens. Then I could look over everyone's fences. I'm sure the technology's available but I can't get anyone to do it. They all claim it's a breach of the neighbours' privacy.'

When we got to number eighty-three, Ramona said she couldn't walk another step. 'You'll have to piggy-back me.'

'Come on, you can do it Ramona. It's only another forty meters.'

'Come on Peter, you can do it. It's only another forty meters. I only weigh sixty kilos. Maybe less.'

So I squatted down and she climbed on. She really was very light. It was no trouble at all to carry her. She held my shoulders and I held her thighs. They felt soft yet firm at the same time. She has great legs. She snuggled against me and blew on the back of my neck.

'Stop that or I'll put you down.'

She giggled. Then as we passed eighty-five she instructed me to slow down. 'Wow, I've never seen in there before. I love that light fitting. And those geraniums are gorgeous. Why do they keep them hidden?'

'I don't know. Maybe they like their privacy.'

Just then Mister Richardson walked past, smirking. 'Beautiful morning isn't it?' he asked.

'Yes,' we both answered.

I dropped Ramona at her door and she let Ivy in. I looked at my watch. I'd been out for almost an hour. 'My jacket, please.' She handed it over, and as I was putting it on she threw her arms around my neck, stood on her tiptoes and kissed me on the lips.

'Thank you, Peter, for a lovely date.'

'It wasn't a date,' I said, more to myself than to her, as I wiped the lipstick off.

'Next time can you bring flowers?'

'No,' I replied as I turned to leave. 'Next time I'll bring my wheelbarrow.'

Words

I've always enjoyed the flexibility of sentence structure our language offers, allowing, with appropriate punctuation, such a huge range of possible configurations.

But once our son, Christopher, started to talk, I realised how much can be communicated in sentences of just one word.

'Down,' he says and I put him down. 'Door,' he says, and I open the door.

Amazing. No syntax, no grammar, no plurals, no adverbs, no adjectives and no prepositions – but he can say so much in one word or, on the odd occasion, two.

'Dog,' he says, when we see a dog, whose name he doesn't know. 'Plane,' he says, when one flies overhead, and 'Train,' when one rattles past.

'Dave,' he'll say, pointing to our next door neighbour.

'Yes, Dave's home.'

His consonant sounds aren't always distinct – a horse, for example, is generally a *sauce*, our dog Gemma is referred to as *Nemma* or *Memma*, and the dog from the house behind us is known as *Ex* – but his vowel sounds are generally very clear.

'Truck,' he says, when we pass one on the road, although sometimes it's *chuck*.

'Truck,' he continues to say, until we acknowledge it. 'Truck. Truck. Truck.'

'Truck,' we say, and he's appeased until he sees the next one.

As we frequently drive along Francis Street, Yarraville, which, much to the displeasure of the many residents displaying *No Trucks* signs in their windows, is a major truck route, this is a frequent exchange.

Sometimes Michelle or I accidentally say fuck in his presence, and he repeats it. *Duck*, we say, correcting ourselves, and he repeats that instead. 'Duck. Duck. Duck,' he said the other night, pointing at the plaster ones on our hallway wall. I didn't know he knew what a duck was.

Another of his favourite words is *stuck*. 'Stuck,' he says when I strap him into his car seat, or his highchair. 'Yes,' I say. 'That's the whole point of them, you're meant to be stuck.' But he doesn't understand, it's too many words.

The other night I was carrying him around the backyard and didn't notice a branch protruding from our apricot tree. 'Duck,' he said, as I knocked him into it.

Duck? Did he mean duck? As in *bend your body quickly*. Or did he mean stuck? Or did he mean something else again? Was it instruction, statement or complaint? Verb, participle or expletive? All three, I suspect – and in just one word.

I took him to the supermarket yesterday; he trotted along beside the trolley grabbing his favourite foods off the shelf and dropping them in.

'Juice,' he said, as he dropped it on top of the avocados.

'Cheese,' he said, as he dropped that on top of the juice.

'*Biggit*,' he said, as he dropped two packets, one in the trolley and one on the floor.

Maybe he just can't pronounce esses, that's why he doesn't pluralise.

A little girl, twice his age, smiled at him and he followed her for an aisle and a half, until I retrieved him. Then he wanted to push the trolley, very slowly, until he saw the little girl again and trotted off after her. Sometimes he gathered items that we didn't want: disinfectant, bleach, condoms and jam. I had to put these back on the shelf. It was so much easier when he was younger and was happy to just ride in the trolley.

He tried to name each item he collected but wasn't always correct.

'Juice,' he said, dragging a five-litre bottle of engine oil halfway down the aisle.

'No. Not juice. Oil,' I said, finding myself using his sentence structure.

'Juice,' he repeated.

'Not juice.'

'Not juice?'

'No. Oil.'

'Oil,' he said, and tried to lift the bottle.

'Back,' I said.

'No.'

'Back,' I said, more sternly, pointing at the shelf where it belonged.

'Back?'

'Yes,' I replied and he dragged it back up the aisle.

Words

I wonder, sometimes, if I'm limiting him by speaking at his level. His sentence structure is entirely appropriate for a one-and-a-half year old, but should it not develop further, it could seriously limit his career options in adult life.

A different little girl walked past with her mother, smiled at him and off he went.

I guess it's all right to speak on his level sometimes, because on other occasions I string together more words in one sentence than he could possible unravel and comprehend, so maybe it's not such a bad thing occasionally.

Eventually we reached the checkout, where he fondled chocolate bars. I opened the packet of *biggits* and gave him half of one. By the time I'd paid for our groceries and packed the bags into the trolley, he'd had three and a half. Also I'd retrieved him twice more from the supermarket sirens, put a dozen chocolate bars back on the shelf and, in desperation, had dropped him by the Blind Society's plastic dog, which he patted affectionately.

'Dog,' he said.

I slid a fifty-cent piece into the dog's head.

'More,' he said.

'More coins?'

'Coin.'

I handed him a twenty-cent piece, which he dropped into the slot.

'More.'

I handed him more coins, in diminishing denominations, and

they all disappeared into the dog's head.

'More.'

'No. No more.'

'Coin?'

'No. No coins. Car. Come on mister, we're going to the car.'

'Key.'

I gave him the keys and we made our way back to the car. Several times as we crossed the car park he tried to wrestle his hand free of mine, but I held tight until we reached the safety of our car. I opened the front passenger door and let him climb in.

'Door,' he said and I closed it. No sooner was it shut than he locked it – fortunately I'd given him the house keys, not the car keys, I'm on to his tricks.

I loaded the shopping into the boot and tried to persuade him to get into his seat. 'Seat.'

'No.'

'Into your seat, Christopher.'

'No.'

At what age do they learn to say yes?

'Dog,' he said, changing the subject, pointing to a pointer in a nearby car.

'Yes, dog. Let's go home and see Gemma.'

'Nemma.'

'Yes, Nemma. You get in your seat and we'll go home and see Nemma.'

He climbed in and I fastened the buckle. 'Stuck,' he said.

'Yes, you're meant to be stuck.'

Once home, he helped me to carry the shopping in, then instructed me to open the door, allowing Gemma in.

'Memma,' he said, as he gave her a big hug. He patted her head and stroked her fur, looking for the coin slot. 'Coin,' he said.

'No, no coin. Gemma's a real dog, not a money-box dog.'

'Gemma, dog.'

'Yes.'

'Coin?'

'No, you can't put coins in her head, she's a real dog. The other one is just a means of collection for the Blind Society, to fund the training of guide dogs for blind people – oh, I don't suppose you know what blind is do you? Well, imagine if you close your eyes, so you can't see anything – then you don't open them.'

'Gemma, dog,' he said, leaning against her. 'No coin.'

'Yes. Gemma, dog.' I couldn't have said it better myself.

Peter's away for the night and the house feels empty. Not that he does a lot when he's here. He parks himself in his comfy chair, submerged deep in the upholstery, with his elbows and knees protruding at acute angles and his head hidden behind a newspaper. He'll sit there for hours, barely moving, tut-tutting alternately at the paper and the television.

Meanwhile Christopher goes crazy. He's taken to pulling his nappy off after dinner, shouting, 'Don't need nappy! No poos! No wees!' and running through the house pulling out toys, clothes, pots and pans, books, shoes and CDs faster than I can possibly put them away. Our dog, Gemma, loves it. She prances in his wake, delighting in the chase, tripping me up each time I get close to Christopher with a nappy.

'Don't need nappy! No poos! No wees! Oops!'

Inevitably, each evening, there's a mishap of some sort – usually on the bedding or the couch. I sometimes wish he'd shit all over Peter and his bloody newspaper. But he never does and I'm not convinced Peter would even notice.

At some stage the washing machine goes on, the dog goes out, and I throw my hands in the air and scream. That's Peter's cue. He slowly straightens his limbs, folds his paper, places it on his chair, turns off the television, takes Christopher by the hand and leads him to the bathroom. And sanity returns.

Toilet, teeth and story proceed in an orderly fashion and Christopher sleeps like a baby. Or sleeps how they say babies sleep. I suspect the author of that saying never had children.

By then I'm exhausted. I usually drop off soon after Christopher, but I don't sleep well. Peter stays up for hours, fiddling: fixing taps and hinges and broken toys. Not that he's a home handyman by any stretch of the imagination. But he likes to tinker. He'll spend hours trying to fix some crappy knickknack that you can pick up from Bunnings for seventy-nine cents and not be bothered a bit if all his efforts come to naught. If he's not tinkering, he's parked at the computer for the night, searching the internet for the meaning of life, writing letters to the local paper, or just playing games for hours on end.

I'll wake sometime during the night and hear him at it. I can always tell when he's playing, by the rhythm of his tapping. 'What are you doing?' I call.

'Writing my memoirs,' he'll reply, guiltily.

Then, at some stage, when I'm fast asleep, he'll slide into bed next to me and drop straight off. I usually wake soon after that. I can tell how long he's been asleep by the tone and the volume of his snoring. Like waves crashing against rocks as the tide rolls in then recedes. I find it oddly reassuring.

But not tonight: Peter's away.

Christopher generally sleeps fitfully when I've put him to bed. He tosses and turns. He snuffles like a hedgehog, talks in his sleep and wakes two or three times. But tonight he sleeps like a log. Gemma too is oddly silent, while the world outside rages.

Peter, for all his faults, seems to keep the outside world at bay. But he's away and the media's warning of gale force winds.

While the Cat's Away

The wind, trying to fulfill its role, whistles; our trees strain at their roots and the trains thunder past with monotonous regularity. But in here it's like a morgue, a vacuum, a void. I miss the reassuring sounds of human activity: the snores, the tapping and the tinkering. I miss Peter's presence.

My sister and I shared a bedroom for ten years. We bickered and sniped over music and lights and windows and curtains: I want it on, she wants it off. I want it open, she wants it closed. I've got to study, she wants to sleep. Our four brothers shared the room next to us. They shouted and fought and banged and crashed, and Mum would bustle about half the night, washing and vacuuming, cooking, sewing and ironing, like a thing possessed. It was bedlam. But once I closed my eyes, I slept like a baby.

I can't sleep tonight. The house is too still and my mind too active. I make myself a coffee and log onto the internet, to connect to the busy outside world. I never know what to look for but that doesn't matter – it's a way to generate noise in an empty house. I find crochet patterns and recipes, suggestions for living a more fulfilled life and then I stumble onto an internet introduction site, a sort of on-line singles bar. I wonder what kind of people visit a site like that. Is it just the swinging cyber-singles, or is it ordinary people like me? People who are bored and frustrated and think that surely there's something better than this, out there, somewhere.

While the Cat's Away

My fingers tap keys and click the mouse, and I find myself searching the site by gender, age group and sexual orientation. Again I wonder about the users of this site. What motivates them? What are they lacking and what do they expect to find?

Not that I'm looking for anyone. As far as husbands go, Peter's one of the best. I don't want an affair – that would be way too sordid. And I'm not after sex, with man, woman or beast. I don't know what I'm after. I don't know what it is I'm missing. But I'm curious. Is there something wrong with me? Am I missing some vital ingredient – like a cake without flour which comes out of the oven flat and lifeless? I feel like a flat cake.

With little thought, I key in the selection criteria: Gender: female; Age: thirty-five to forty; City: Melbourne. And there, in front of my eyes are screens and screens of women. Hundreds. Hundreds of women like me.

I narrow the range to women aged between thirty-five and thirty-six, in Melbourne's west, and there's only a page and a half. The first woman even looks like me. The same mousy coloured hair, in the same bob. She's got my double chin and my glasses. Shit! They really are my glasses – they're exactly the same. She probably got them from the same optometrist.

Sexybabe, she calls herself. She doesn't look that sexy to me. She's 5'2" of *average* body type – which seems to mean *a* little plump. God, she does look like me. She's looking for excitement and adventure from a man who's kind and courteous. Seems an unlikely combination. In my experience, kind courteous men tend to live dull, predictable lives.

The next entry, *foxychick36*, looks a little like me too. Most of them do. Almost all of them have names that could belong to Benny Hill's bevy of buxom beauties but bodies that don't quite match up. What would I call myself if I registered as a member? And how would I describe my body type? Slim? Hardly. Athletic? Perhaps. Average? I think that's the best fit.

Before I even notice what I'm doing I've registered. I've called myself *PlumpMouse*. That should scare off any prospective suitors. I add a photo – a frazzled, frumpy, pre-menstrual snap that Christopher took. That will certainly scare them off.

I'm just dipping a little toe into the water. I'm not after a bite, or even a nibble.

I go back to the crochet site and print off a couple of patterns as justification for my time on-line, then brush my teeth, again, for probably the third time, check on Christopher – who's still sleeping soundly – and go to bed.

I wake a few hours later and look in on Christopher again. He's so still that I have to check that he's breathing. Is he sick? I touch his forehead but he doesn't feel hot. The wind howls and the windows rattle. Gemma gets up and we pace around the house, looking for boogey men.

The computer whirrs and hums. I forgot to turn it off. As I'm about to shut it down an email pops up. It's from the dating site: *PlumpMouse, Sexybigboy would like to contact you.* Oh my God! An email to my personal address – <u>our</u> personal address. Peter could be logged on right now. 2.35am, he probably is. He could be reading this at the same time as me, wondering who the hell *Sexybigboy* is. He'll know who *PlumpMouse* is.

I delete the email. God, what have I done?

I open the dating site. I need to work out how to unsubscribe. Another message pops up, it's from *Sexybigboy* again. *Hi, I see you're on-line. Can't you sleep either?* God, his photo is disgusting. He has eyes like a pig. He's wearing a leather G-string and has breasts like Dolly Parton, with a ring in one nipple. He has the figure of an overripe DNA molecule. I can see where the *Bigboy* comes from, but *Sexy?*

Shit, that will be another email. I need to delete that one, too. No sooner have I deleted it than a third email arrives, from *Sleek_n_trim*. I flick back to the site – he's as old as my father and as thin a rake. He has ratty teeth and a lecherous leer. I'm not game to read what he's written.

Then the phone rings. It's almost three. No one rings at this time. How the hell did they get my number? I pick up on the second ring. I don't want to wake Christopher. I hold the receiver to my ear and say nothing.

'Hello?'

'Peter. God, you scared the life out of me.'

'Sorry.'

'What's up?'

'Nothing. I was just missing you. I was wondering if you were alright. I heard the weather's bad there.'

'Yeah it is. But it's very late.'

'Sorry I didn't call earlier. I was going to hang up on the next ring. Is the house alright? The trees? I was meaning to look at that gum tree at the side. If it comes down…'

He sounds worried. Peter never sounds worried. If he's worried, I should be worried.

Another message pops up – *Sexybigboy* yet again.

'Go away.'

'Sorry?'

'Sorry. I thought I was just thinking that.'

'Well, if you were I've just become telepathic. What's up?'

'The internet. Those pop-up ads.'

'What are you doing on the net at this time of night?'

'What indeed?'

'That's my job.'

I quickly delete the fourth email. Or was it the fifth, or sixth? Wasn't that a confirmation email and a welcome email? Have I deleted them? 'Are you logged on now, Peter?'

'No. Just about to.'

'I'd better go. Christopher is stirring. Sweet dreams.'

'Thanks. Sweet dreams. Love you.'

'Love you too, Peter.'

God, I do love him. But will he still love me if he sees all these emails. Maybe he won't check. Now, how the hell do I get out of this? I remove the photo from my profile. Without the photo it could be some sort of electronic mix up. But with my face attached, I'm as guilty as hell.

Another email arrives, this time from a *StickyBeak*. Stickybeak? What the hell's that name meant to suggest? That could be Peter. He's a stickybeak. I open the message. This one has no photo. Only words: *You sound like a kindred spirit – I feel lost and alone and away from home. You sound like you're lost and alone at home. You say you have a young child. I know how draining that can be. You have my sympathy. Perhaps we could get together.*

God, it really could be Peter – except that he has no idea how draining his child is.

I check on Christopher; he's still sound asleep. The wind howls and growls and the house rattles and shakes. I feel afraid. I pace around, looking out of all the windows. I think I can see a fat naked man masturbating behind the neighbour's fence – but then I realise it's their mulberry tree moving in the wind.

I ring Peter.

'Hi. Can't you sleep?'

'No. I feel alone. Too alone.'

'Get onto the net again. There are millions of people out there, billions.'

'I'm sure there are. But they aren't necessarily people I'd like to meet.'

Another email pops up. 'Shit!' I delete it immediately. I don't even see who it's from.

'Are you okay, Michelle?'

'Yeah. I just miss you. I wish you were home.'

'Me too.'

Then there's a great howl, like a pack of wolves with toothache.

'Was that the wind?'

'I certainly hope so. But if you come home to a pool of blood and a pile of bones, you'll know it wasn't.'

Then the wind howls again, the house shudders and the power goes off. The lights go out. The computer dies. The fridge stops humming and the phone goes dead.

Shit. How can I unsubscribe now? God knows how many perverts will have tried to contact me by the time the power comes back on. God knows how many of the emails Peter will have read.

I brush my teeth yet again, by candlelight, snuggle into bed with Christopher and sleep fitfully until I'm woken by the humming of the fridge, just after six.

I leap up, turn on the computer and log onto the dating site. Thankfully there are no more messages. I unsubscribe, delete my browsing history and sterilize the mouse and keyboard. I feel dirty – filthy. I shower until the water runs cold, then take Christopher for a long brisk walk, strapped tightly into his stroller. 'Want to walk! Want to walk!' he screams over and over but I ignore him. 'Swings!' he screams as we pass a playground.

I relent. I let him free, buy us ice creams and we play in the park.

While the Cat's Away

I look around at the other mothers. They all look lonely and desperate. And I think of all the lecherous perverts connected to the net, even now – in broad daylight – tapping away at their keyboards, drooling – and worse.

I never got any more emails from that site. I believe my profile has been removed – but I haven't been game to look. The thing that nags at me, though, is that message from *Stickybeak*. I can't help feeling that that was Peter. But I'm not game to ask and he volunteers nothing.

Bring Peace to your Life, the brochure said. I was tossing out the junk mail and for some reason that heading caught my attention. I handed it to Michelle, as she seemed very stressed. 'Yoga, could be just what you need to help you unwind.'

Our son, Christopher, had just started walking and was at that grabbing stage, CDs, knives, razors – suddenly he could get his hands on everything we didn't keep up high.

Michelle read the brochure and turned it over a couple of times. 'Skinny women in flimsy outfits, showing off their tramp stamps. Not my thing.'

A rather strange perspective, I thought.

'Why don't you take it up, Peter? You're always complaining you're stiff and sore.'

'Hmm. Maybe I will.'

Once I'd started, I found it extremely soothing: a very relaxing way to start my weekend. And I felt better for it. I had more spring in my step. I seemed taller and more alert. And it seemed, as I walked the dog, that I saw more of my neighbours' lives over the tops of their fences.

I don't know that my body's really suited to yoga. My arms and legs are too long and they always seem to point in the opposite direction to those of the rest of the class. I'm like a drunken giraffe wearing high heels. But the teacher, Jenny, had such a soft, silky voice that it soothed me into some semblance of the correct poses.

Gradually I'd let go of my self-consciousness and my innate clumsiness and by the end of each class I'd feel relaxed and at peace. Then for the last fifteen minutes Jenny would lie us all down and guide us through a meditation.

Her voice would purr and sigh and I'd feel like I'd gone to heaven. I'd never remember a word of the mediation but when we were done she'd guide us back to the room and leave us with some words of wisdom. 'Be kind to yourselves, drink lots of water, think pure thoughts and do something special for your pets. Namaste.'

'Namaste.'

Michelle and I saw Jenny one day when we were out shopping. 'Wow,' said Michelle. 'She's gorgeous. No wonder you're always so frisky after you get back from doing the down-face dog with her.'

'Is she? I hadn't really noticed.'

And I honestly hadn't. I knew she was young and fit, and very flexible, and that she had a gorgeous voice, but I hadn't really thought about her appearance. Maybe because I always felt so uncomfortable and ungainly at the start of each class or maybe because I kept my eyes closed most of the time. But once Michelle had pointed it out to me I couldn't keep my eyes off Jenny. And even with my eyes closed I could still see her, her buttocks waxing and waning like a pair of moons as she flexed her spine in cat pose.

I'd find my eyes glued to her as she twisted and writhed sensuously. Even away from class, I'd see her. Even sitting watching TV with Christopher, I'd see her. I had to make up a little rhyme to repeat over and over in my head, like a mantra: *Jenny's butt is really stinky, she's got warts on her tinky-winky.*

The Yogi

I think we were watching Teletubbies at the time.

It seemed to work.

One day I was walking Gemma up to the school, with Christopher sitting on my shoulders.

'Undies,' Christopher said, as we passed number 87. 'Red.'

I turned to look. There was a six foot high fence which the owner presumably thought would shield her underwear from view. But I'm 6'5".

I turned to follow Christopher's pointing finger. There were six pairs of the tiniest of red thongs hanging on the washing line. Could you even call them pairs? I think one pair of Michelle's would contain more fabric than the lot of them. They were bright red, Pantone 187, I'm pretty sure, fluttering in the breeze. Then I caught a movement from the corner of my eye. I turned to look and there was Jenny, waving at us from her bedroom window.

God. How embarrassing. *Jenny's butt is really hairy, don't go there it's much too scary.* I waved back and we marched on.

'Who's that?' Christopher asked.

'That's my yogi.'

'Like Yogi Bear?'

'Yes, only not bare. Not quite.'

'Nice undies. Let's get some for Mum.'

'I don't think they're her size.'

'They'd have her size.'

'I don't think Mum would like them. They don't look very comfortable.'

'They're smaller than mine.'

'Yes, they're tiny.' *Stinky, smelly, hairy crack, keep on going, don't look back.*

 'Go back. I want to count.'

'There were six. Six pairs.'

'I want to count myself! Turn around.' He pulled my ears – hard. I hate it when he does that.

'No. We're taking Gemma to the school. Gemma wants to see her friend.'

'On the way back.'

'Maybe.'

Fortunately we found another dog for Gemma to play with and we tossed sticks and ran around until Christopher had forgotten Jenny's underwear. I was less successful and my head was so full of rhymes I could barely think.

When we got home, Michelle's sister was visiting. She met us at the door and Christopher ran straight to her and buried himself in her enormous, misshapen bosom.

'Who's my favourite nephew?' she asked.

'Gemma.'

'No.'

'Dad.'

'No. He's my brother-in-law, and he's not my favourite.'

'Chrispher.'

'Yes!' she screamed,

'Hi Amanda, how are you?'

'Fine thanks, Peter. How are you?'

We pretended to kiss, maintaining a distance of a couple of centimetres. She's not my favourite sister-in-law either, and she's the only one I've got.

'Did you see anything exciting when you were out?' Michelle asked.

'Five dogs,' said Christopher.

'That's great. What else.'

'A fire engine.'

'Wow. Anything else?'

'No,' I answered.

'I wasn't asking you.'

'Some nice undies.'

'Oh. Where did you see them?'

'Over the fence.'

Michelle glared it me. 'It's bad enough that you're a Peeping Tom, now you're teaching our son.'

'It's not my fault I'm tall.'

'No, but it is your fault that you're always looking over people's fences.'

'What did they used to call you at school?' Amanda asked.

I ignored her.

'And we saw the yogi,' Christopher said.

'Yogi Bear?' asked Amanda.

'My yoga teacher.'

'You saw Jenny while you were out perving at our neighbours? I didn't know she lived around here.'

'Neither did I.'

'Who's Jenny?' Amanda asked.

'The Goddess of Erotic Poses.'

'He's perving at goddesses now? You're setting your sights a bit high aren't you, Peter?'

'I've done nothing wrong here, thanks Amanda.'

'Nosey Parker.'

'That's just because I've got a big nose and my surname's Parker.'

'Whatever you say – pervert.'

I don't understand why Amanda dislikes me so much. She claims I saw her once in the shower – completely by accident. I thought it was Michelle. And she did catch me reading some of her mail once.

Somehow, by some miracle, in the chaos of the four-way conversation, the full story of Jenny's underwear never surfaced while Amanda was there.

I told Michelle after she'd left. 'It was so embarrassing. I'll never look her in the eye again. I had no idea she lived there,'

'Hopefully you've learned your lesson. It's nice that you carry Christopher around on your shoulders, but not around here. You get yourself in enough trouble, without making Christopher an accomplice.'

'I promise I will never again let Christopher look over our neighbour's fences and I'll never again even glance over Jenny's fence.'

'Thanks.' We kissed and that was that. End of story. Michelle is so forgiving.

And Jenny was fine. I don't think she even noticed that Christopher and I were admiring, and counting, her underwear. And with the help of my mantras I was able to put it out of my mind until the very end of the class.

'Your homework for this week,' Jenny said, 'Is to awaken your lower chakras. Wear something red and do something naughty. Namaste.'

'Namaste.'

Red! She must be joking. She wears something red every day. *Jenny's undies are so tiny, showing off her gorgeous heiny.* Where did the word heiny come from? That's not part of my vocabulary.

The next morning I was up early and took Gemma for a walk while Michelle and Christopher slept. It was a beautifully clear, still morning, and quite warm. We set off towards the school grounds and as we passed Jenny's place her voice came to me, *Do something naughty.*

I glanced – just glanced – over her fence. Her curtains were wide open. She was bent over in down-face-dog position, her back to me. Her buttocks toward me. Her vagina, I couldn't help notice, was absolutely hairless. As smooth as a baby's bottom. Probably smoother. Whether shaven or waxed I couldn't tell from the distance.

As she pulled back into child position her buttocks swelled beautifully – maybe buttocks are like green grass, they're always shapelier on the other side of the fence – and her labia opened up like a rose in bloom. As she moved forward into cobra position, her gorgeous buttocks waned and her labia closed. I thought I could hear the tiniest kiss. Perhaps that was my imagination.

I meant to turn away. I meant to walk on. But I didn't. I was mesmerised. I watched four or five repetitions. How many did she normally do? I should have paid more attention in class.

I was distracted then by Mister Richardson coming towards me. 'Beautiful morning, isn't it?'

'Yes,' I whispered, dropping down to tie my shoelace. Then I kept my head well below fence level as I scuttled off.

I couldn't go to yoga after that. I just couldn't. And after a few weeks I grew stiff and irritable. I stopped taking Gemma for walks and she grew equally stiff and irritable. And as I couldn't come up with a satisfactory explanation as to why I'd stopped, Michelle nagged me mercilessly. 'You know you'll feel better,' she said.

'I doubt it.'

One morning, while we were out shopping, she dropped me outside the yoga centre. 'Your class starts in five minutes. I'll come back and pick you up after.'

'But, but, but.' She was driving away before I could generate a cohesive sentence.

'Smarter than the abberage bear,' called Christopher.

I would have walked off as soon as Michelle was out of sight but Jenny saw me. I had to go in.

She stood behind a table near the front door. 'Hi Peter,' she said. 'It's been a long time.'

I couldn't look her in the eye. But after a few seconds I realised I was staring at her breasts. I lowered by eyes further and looked at her hands. 'I was hoping, you'd come today,' she continued. 'This is my last class. I'm leaving, moving to Queensland. Maureen's taking over my class.' She gestured with her right hand and I looked up. There was a woman standing next to her. I hadn't even noticed.

This, presumably, was Maureen: frumpy and lumpy, middle aged and grumpy. Everything you could ask for in a yoga teacher.

Jenny sat at the back corner while Maureen took the class. She was very good. Her voice was functional. Her instructions were clear, concise and well enunciated. She barked them out like a drill sergeant, and I found that without the distractions of a gorgeous voice and a heavenly body, I could much more easily align my limbs with the rest of the class.

When our relaxation session was finished, that was it. There were no words of wisdom. Everyone swarmed around Jenny, hugging her and wishing her well, but I made my way to Maureen and shook her hand. 'Thank you, that was great. Fantastic.'

The Yogi

'Thank you.'

'Do you live locally, Maureen?'

'No. I live on the other side of town.'

Good, I thought. That's probably best for both of us.

A White or a Red

As I lay on the table, with Sarah's hands on me, the ghosts of my ancestors howled and wailed. They mocked and berated me, and I felt worthless and weak. But I knew it wouldn't last forever. Sarah moved her hand over my heart and I felt guilty and ashamed but I didn't know why. It wasn't as if I'd done anything.

When her hand moved off my heart and on to my stomach, the sense of panic lifted and I felt soothed. There's something very calming about a woman's hands.

When I think about it, all the practitioners I see are women – my acupuncturist, my osteopath and of course Sarah – my Reikiist. I don't think there's anything sexual about it. That's just the way it's worked out – but I think women are a lot gentler and more caring then men. And for that matter, I think my choices of healing reflect my desire for soft, gentle treatment. The harsh world of packed waiting rooms, cold stethoscopes, unpronounceable diseases and drugs, disinfected hospitals and unfeeling x-rays and CAT-scans does nothing for me. And besides, alternative medicine gives you that feeling of immediate satisfaction. You feel cleansed and whole, and sometimes even euphoric, when you walk out the door.

Not that I'm really sick – I just feel run down. I guess I've felt this way ever since Christopher was born, two years ago. I've got a bad back, aching joints and almost constant headaches – but I can live with these physical symptoms. It's more that I feel drained and flat – that my spirit's crushed and my future stretches ahead of me like a life-sentence of domestic drudgery.

A White or a Red

Our marriage is nurturing and loving. We've had seven good years together. But there's something missing. It's like being served up a plate of microwaved venison every night. I'm well-nourished but I miss the thrill of the hunt. I miss the camaraderie of the campfire. I miss the sensual pleasures of the smoke and the smell and the sounds of sizzling meat. Our sex life has all the excitement of a bowl of cold porridge and our boy, Christopher, although my pride and joy, is sometimes like a millstone around my neck. Sometimes I just long to be free.

Ooooeeeerrrrrghhhhh! groaned my ancestors.

Sarah finished the treatment and turned off the tape. Silence at last.

'Did you like the music?' she asked.

'No. It was awful. What was it?'

'Whales' song. You should have said something. I've got plenty of other tapes.'

'No, it's all right. It seemed appropriate to suffer.'

I had a dream that night. I was walking along a street. I was incredibly tired. My legs ached with the effort of movement but I knew I had to keep going, plodding ever slower – one step after another. I had a big industrial vacuum cleaner strapped to my back. I was sucking up cigarette butts and wrappers and all the crap that people casually discard. An extension cord, several kilometres long, trailed behind me. Each step I took bought me closer to exhaustion but I had to keep going. I could hardly breathe. My heart was thumping in my chest but my blood felt thick, viscous and gluey. Eventually, when I thought I was going to collapse, I reached the limit of the extension cord and could go no further.

How was I going to finish my vacuuming?

I knew I had to go back to unplug the cord.

I woke up in a sweat.

The next day – the very next day – I bumped into an old girlfriend. I was sitting by the river at Southbank, with Christopher, eating ice cream. I hadn't seen Anne years – nine or ten. I didn't even know she was in Melbourne. We'd been living in Brisbane when we went out.

The dream, I thought. I'm still plugged into her.

I've got to go back to that socket and pull out my cord.

She looked just the same as ever. She wasn't obviously beautiful to the casual observer, but I'd been more than a casual observer. Before I knew it, I was mentally undressing her. I could see the fine blue veins through the translucent white skin of her small, round breasts. I could see the dark, plump, firm nipples. I could almost taste them. I could see her flat stomach and the flaming bush of her pubic hair.

'Hi,' she said. 'How's your wife?'

She had a gorgeous voice – a lovely Irish accent.

'She's fine,' I replied, a little taken aback. 'How did you know I was married?'

'The ring around your finger, and the ring around your waist.'

'Yeah, I have put on a bit of weight.'

'And I presume this is your son.'

'Yes,' I said, feeling proud and guilty at the same time. I introduced them to each other.

'Hi Anne,' he said. Shit. We don't know any other Annes. If Christopher mentions her name to Michelle, how will I explain it?

Anne smiled at him and stroked his hair. 'I'd better be on my way,' she said. 'Enjoy your ice creams.' Then, as an afterthought, she added mischievously, 'Give my regards to your wife.' She turned to walk away.

'We must get together sometime,' I called. 'Talk about old times. What's your phone number?'

She pulled a business card out of her purse, wrote her home number on the back and handed it to me. 'You shouldn't be thinking about old times,' she said.

'I'm not,' I said, handing her my card – with my home number on the back.

She walked away, and before I knew it, in my mind's eye, she was naked again. Her buttocks, as shapely as ever, rolling gently as she walked. Every so often, between her cheeks, I'd catch a glimpse of a tuft of flaming ginger.

As soon as she was out of sight, I felt as guilty as hell. I threw her card into the Yarra and watched it for a while as it floated, swirling provocatively, temptingly close.

Three nights later she rang. Christopher and I were watching a Thomas the Tank Engine video and Michelle had just left to play netball.

'I was in the area,' Anne said. 'I thought maybe I'd drop in.'

'Which area?' I asked, panic-stricken. 'How do you know where I live?'

'Have you never heard of a phone book? You could have found me if you'd wanted.'

What could I say? Did I want?

'Toot toot,' called Christopher. 'Here's Gordon.' He pointed at the TV screen. 'Gordon got a lot of carriages.'

'Where are you?' I asked.

'Look out of your kitchen window.'

I did. There was a dark green Commodore parked across the road. The interior light came on. Her hair shone like a golden halo as she waved at me. She smiled.

My intestines twisted and bucked. My palms turned damp and cold. I could feel my heart, like a bicycle pump, going slower and slower while the pressure built up.

Shit, that wasn't my ancestors howling, during my Reiki treatment, it was the ghosts of my ex-girlfriends.

She smiled again. Neither of us said a word.

The Thomas theme music played. 'More?' asked Christopher, coming towards me. 'More Thomas?'

'Yes,' I answered, pointing at the TV. 'Another one coming, you just sit there.'

A White or a Red

'Daddy come too?'

'In a minute.'

My heart pumped more and more slowly. My lungs barely moved, just fluttering gently. All my internal organs ground to a standstill; my penis, meanwhile, had swollen to the size of a whale. It seemed to fill the lounge room and the kitchen and was making its way down the hallway to the front door.

'Is your wife home?' Anne asked.

I looked at my watch and cleared my throat. 'She'll be back in about an hour and a half,' I whispered. 'Do you want to come in?'

'I thought you'd never ask.'

'Hi Anne,' said Christopher. God, he remembers her.

'Hi Christopher,' she replied.

Our dog, Gemma, trotted up and sniffed her. It licked her hand then poked its nose under the front of her skirt.

'That's a friendly dog you've got,' she squealed, then shrieked with laughter as Gemma's snout disappeared between her legs.

'Gemma, blanket!' I shouted at her, and she skulked off to her blanket in the laundry.

'My God,' cackled Anne. 'What a tongue she's got. What have you got to drink?'

'Um, a white or a red.'

'You've not got a drop of Jameson put away for me?'

'No. I don't drink much now.' I'd forgotten how much she used to drink – how much we both used to drink.

'A white would be nice,' she said, sitting down at the dining table.

As I went to fetch a bottle she turned to Christopher. 'And what time do you go to bed?'

'Soon,' I said. 'Very soon.'

'After Thomas,' he said, ignoring the tooting telly and climbing onto the chair next to Anne.

I opened the bottle and took two glasses from the cupboard.

Anne leaned back in the chair and relaxed. 'Nice place you've got,' she said, as she looked around. She rocked back on her seat, slipped off her shoes and let her thighs spread open.

'Orange hair,' said Christopher, pointing at Anne's head.

'Yes, very orange. Orange is his favourite colour,' I explained.

I filled our glasses and we clinked them together. 'Cheers.'

Christopher started to cry. 'Glass for Chrispher,' he whined. I fetched him a glass of water as Anne took a mouthful of Chablis.

'Ah,' she said. 'That's a lovely drop.' She spun the bottle around to read the label.

'Cheers,' said Christopher, repeatedly, as we re-enacted the clinking ritual.

We drank in virtual silence, apart from Christopher. Neither of us knew what to say.

I could hear the clock ticking on the kitchen wall and Gemma's tail beating against the wooden floorboards as she inched closer to Anne. Anne finished her glass and poured herself another. There were so many questions to ask but none of them seemed appropriate – not that our relationship ever had been appropriate. Not that it was really a relationship.

Anne was married when I first met her – we worked together and quickly became good friends. I had no idea that she was having an affair with one of our colleagues, or that she had an affair with one of her husband's friends immediately after that. I had no idea that I was even attracted to her until the night I ended up in her bed. I'd just split up with my girlfriend, Anne had just split up with her husband, we'd been out together with a couple of other workmates, we'd had a few drinks and next thing you know we were at it like a couple of randy rabbits.

She started another affair, with another friend of her husband, while she was seeing me. She preferred having men two at a time – twice the sex and only a fraction of the commitment. She suggested that I get another girlfriend and I complied. The poor girl was heartbroken when she found out about Anne.

'Do you ever see any of the old gang?' I asked.

'No. Those were crazy times – I keep well clear of that lot. It's a time of my life I try to forget.'

I wondered how many more of our workmates had been her lovers. but knew it was pointless to ask.

'I live a very quiet life now,' she continued. 'I keep well away from my past.'

Then why are you here, I felt like asking. But I didn't want to scare her away. I was disgusted by her – I was disgusted by me – but I was excited too. I sipped my wine in silence.

'More Thomas?' asked Christopher. The video had finished.

'No. No more Thomas. Bedtime for Thomas. Bedtime for Christopher.'

'Bedtime for everyone,' murmured Anne. She gulped down her second glass. 'Would you mind opening a red?'

'No, not at all.'

God, how would I explain two opened bottles of wine when I was meant to be babysitting – on my own? I selected one of our cheaper reds. Anne wouldn't notice the difference.

She giggled. 'That wine's gone straight to my cunt. I can feel the juice dribbling down my thighs.' I dropped the bottle on the kitchen floor – fortunately it didn't break.

Did Christopher hear that? Will he repeat it? His vocabulary expands by two or three words every day. *Cunt* used to be one of our favourite words – but it's not one I want Christopher to learn.

'Juice,' he said, holding out his glass.

I poured him a juice, opened the red and handed it to Anne. She poured herself a glass. I poured myself another white, then drank the last drops from the bottle. If I put the empty at the bottom of the recycling, it'll look like I've only had one glass of red. I've got to remember to wash and dry the other wineglass.

Anne rocked her pelvis on the chair, her eyes half closed. I could smell her musk, and so could Gemma. She wagged her tail manically and crept closer.

'Blanket!' I yelled at her and she crept back to her corner.

'How long have we got?' Anne asked.

I looked at the clock. 'Time to brush Christopher's teeth, read him a quick story, then about twenty-five minutes. Not very long.'

'We've done it in less.'

Yes, I thought, as I hurried Christopher to the bathroom. 'Night night, Anne,' he called.

I remember one time we had it off in the toilet at work, at morning tea.

I changed Christopher's nappy as he brushed his teeth. I frantically pulled his pyjamas on. Why is that both legs always go into one? This is madness, I thought. It's too much of a rush. We won't get the most from it. We should do it on a night when Michelle has a late game – when Christopher is already asleep. But that's weeks away. That requires planning. That requires cold-hearted calculation. Spontaneous lust is one thing – deliberate deceit is quite another.

'Mind if I have a look around?' Anne called.

'Sure, make yourself at home.'

I put Christopher to bed, lay down beside him and raced through The Three Little Pigs, stumbling over the words and huffing and puffing at breakneck speed. I couldn't wait to get into Anne, but Christopher won't sleep without a story.

As the familiar words on the page rolled off my tongue, the images that came to mind were all fresh and the focus of the story had changed: it's not about pigs – it's about the wolf. It's a story of lust and seduction.

A White or a Red

The house of straw represents flirtation: smiles, innuendo, suggestive body language and the removal of outer garments – all driven by the wolf's huffing and puffing. The house of wood represents foreplay: the removal of all clothing and the arousal of the genitals and surrounding areas – the licking, sucking and rubbing of the window frames and architraves, to use the analogy of the story. And the house of bricks – where the huffing and puffing reaches its climax – represents full intercourse: the relentless thrusting into the bottomless pit of the gaping vulva. And the shattering of the door – which never happened in the children's story – but which happened so powerfully for Anne and I – is the biting, scratching and howling frenzy when our juices flowed like a tidal wave.

Afterwards, Anne always felt dirty and overcome with Catholic guilt. She'd make me wash my hands and she'd shower for half an hour or more. Then an hour later we'd be at it again.

'I like your bed,' she called from our room.

God, I'll have to change the sheets if she lies on it. 'Spare room bed's better,' I called. 'I'm almost finished.'

'More pigs,' Christopher said. 'Daddy puffing too quick.'

'Okay, more pigs and I'll puff more slowly.'

I read through the pigs at a more leisurely pace, feeling guilty about violating an innocent story with my filthy interpretation. As Christopher started to fall asleep he burrowed his hand down my shirt. It's sweet, the way he does that.

Anne put her head through the doorway. She'd put her shoes on and was carrying her handbag. 'This is crazy; I'd better get going. Give me a call some time.'

'Hi Anne,' said Christopher, sitting upright.

'He's almost asleep,' I said. 'Don't go, please.' I squeezed her hand. 'Just give me two more minutes. Get yourself another drink; he'll be asleep in a second.'

She walked off to the kitchen and refilled her glass. That'll leave about half a bottle. I'll pour that down the sink, hide that bottle, then wash and dry both glasses.

Anne went back to the kitchen and Christopher lay down, burrowed his hand down my shirt and fell immediately asleep.

He's so beautiful when he's sleeping, so innocent. No idea what Daddy's planning. No idea how hurt Mummy would be if she knew. He trusts me completely. She trusts me completely. How can I betray them?

Anne returns with her glass filled to the brim, she dribbles red onto Christopher's doona cover. I pounce on it with tissues and wipes. Shit, there goes my *no wine at all* story.

'Twenty minutes then,' she says, oblivious to my frantic attempts to remove the spilt wine. 'You can do a lot of fucking in twenty minutes.'

God, she's coarse.

Gemma creeps into the room, placing herself between us.

A White or a Red

'Blanket,' I snarl. She hesitates. She puts her head on its side and whines. She does her sad doggy eyes at me. 'Blanket,' I hiss, glaring at her, and she slinks away. Even the dog knows that what I'm contemplating is wrong – that this is no time for bed.

'You can fuck me from behind.' Anne continues, oblivious to everything but her drunken lust. 'Stick your thumb up my arse. You can squeeze my tits, squeeze my nipples – hard – pinch them till I scream. Tell me how hard you're fucking me.'

She always wanted that. She always wanted me to talk dirty, the whole way through the sordid experience. If her flat mate was home I'd have to whisper – but I had to whisper dirty.

'Why do we have to keep quiet?' I'd ask.

'Because he's a Protestant from Belfast and can't be trusted.'

'Then why did you let him move in?'

'He's a good liar and can keep a secret.'

There was no point arguing with her logic. I'd just continue grunting obscenities – quietly.

She finishes her wine and unzips her skirt. She lets it drop to the floor. She's wearing no knickers; her bush exposed for all to see. Shit – did I close Christopher's curtains? Yes I did. 'Where shall we do it?' she asks.

'Not here.'

'In the spare room?'

'Maybe.'

She leaves her skirt on the floor and walks off. Her bottom is much smaller than Michelle's, and nicely rounded. The insides of her thighs are wet with her juice. How can one woman produce so much fluid? Maybe it's the wine.

I pick up her skirt follow her into the spare room, and quickly close the curtains. I hope Dave's not home. I hope he hasn't seen her. She sits down on the bed and leans back. Her glossy, swollen lips peek through the ginger tangle – just like I'd imagined. Only my imagination seemed less sordid somehow. I try to remember what Michelle's lips look like – thin and pale, I think.

'Aren't you getting undressed?' Anne asks.

'No. I don't think so.'

'Lick me,' she moans. 'Lick me.' She grabs my hair and pulls me towards her crotch. The smell is overpowering.

I break away from her and throw her skirt at her. 'I'd like you to leave.'

'Stick your fingers up me.'

'No,' I say, even though my throbbing penis screams *yes!* 'I'd like you to leave, Anne. Michelle will be home soon and I'd like you to be gone.'

She glares at me and grabs her skirt. 'Fuck you,' she snarls. 'Fuck you, and your fat dumpy wife – I've seen her photo – and your whinging little brat. Fuck your respectable suburban lifestyle. Fuck your mid-life morality and your mid-week impotence.'

She storms off to the kitchen, grabs her bag, marches past me and slams the front door. 'Fuck you!' she screams, once more –

loud enough for the whole street to hear. She starts her car, revs the engine and roars off with a squealing of tyres, leaving big black marks on the road.

I hide the second wine bottle, wash, dry and put away the wineglasses, while Gemma gets herself underfoot at every turn, looking up at me pathetically. I turn Christopher's doona over, hiding the wine stain. I search the house high and low for Anne's panties but can't find them. Maybe she took them. Maybe she wasn't wearing any when she arrived. Or maybe they're lurking somewhere: a time bomb waiting to explode in my face.

Lawnmowers

When we first moved here we didn't have a lawnmower. For a while I borrowed our next door neighbour's. 'Any time,' Dave said. 'Any time.' But after a couple of months I realised how frequently I'd need it and figured I should get my own.

So I set off with a pocket full of cash for Laverton Market, and returned home the proud owner of a whipper-snipper, a manual edge trimmer and my first ever lawnmower.

The edge trimmer was rusty and its wheel was bent and blunt. It was probably only good for decoration and the whipper-snipper wasn't much better. The metal bit that fed the line out shot off, practically taking Gemma's eye with it. And as I discovered when I tried to replace it, it wasn't the original part, and original parts were no longer available for that model.

'Are you starting up a gardening museum?' Dave asked, strolling up our drive with a couple of cans of VB in his hand. He offered me one, but I declined.

'Those things are crap,' I said, nodding at the edge-trimmer and whipper-snipper, 'But the lawnmower's good. Started first time.'

Dave eyed it suspiciously. He tilted it on its side and checked the blades. He fiddled with the cables and adjusted levers. He certainly examined it more closely than I had.

'How much did you pay?'

'It was only $80.'

'Shit. They saw you coming.'

'It's a bargain. A new one costs four times that.'

'A new one would work ten times better.'

'It's a Rover. That's a good brand. Isn't it?'

'That bit's off a Rover,' Dave said, tapping the body of the mower with his boot. 'That bit's off a Masport, the handle's off a Victa and God knows where that came from — certainly not a lawnmower. Let's start her up.'

I started it on the driveway and it roared to life after seven or eight pulls. But as soon as I moved it onto the lawn the blades dug into the ground. I hadn't thought of checking the clearance. It was already adjusted to the highest position but Dave somehow managed to force it a little higher. Not too bad,' he commented as I pushed it around the nature strip. It had a tendency to veer off to the left, a bit like a shopping trolley, but I could compensate for that.

He's a small man, Dave, not much taller than Michelle, but very solid and muscular. He's a lovely guy but he always seems to be looking down on me, even though he only comes up to my shoulder. He always makes me feel somehow inadequate as a man.

'Be back shortly,' he said, and returned a couple of minutes later with two more cans of VB, a can of WD40, a hammer and a shifting spanner. He offered me one of the beers but again I refused.

'I could straighten that wheel,' he said, as I wrestled to keep the mower in a straight line.

'Thanks.'

Lawnmowers

'It actually runs better than I thought it would.' He whacked it with the hammer in a few spots and sprayed it with the WD40 in a few different spots. It seemed a little easier to push after that.

'Give me a go,' he said. He opened his fourth can and offered it to me. I took a sip then handed the can back.

He smiled at my dainty sip then he took the can in one hand, the mower in the other and whizzed it around our back yard, one-handed, while he finished off the can. 'Not bad at all. I reckon it'll last six months.'

And Dave's assessment was spot on. *Rover*, as I called it, was fine till it started its winter hibernation, but when spring sprang it wouldn't waken.

Dave introduced me to a product call *Start ya Bastard*, which worked wonders when sprayed into the carburetor. But even that had its limits. It'd take a good spray and a dozen or more pulls to start each time. And when the starter rope broke I figured Rover was probably trying to tell me something. It was retired to the back of the shed and I went back to borrowing Dave's.

A few months later I bought my second mower off this old codger in Altona, who had a whole garage full of them, in various states of restoration. It cost $160 and had several positions, which could cut the grass anywhere between short and long. I tested it on the old codger's nature strip, which was very well mown. I named the machine *Victor*.

Dave nodded his approval. 'Same motor as your old one, Briggs and Stratton. You kept the old one for spares, didn't you?'

'I hadn't thought about that. But yeah, I've still got Rover.'

'I reckon you'll get two years out of this one.' And again Dave was spot on.

After eighteen months I was using *Start ya Bastard* on a regular basis and Michelle was pestering me to buy a new mower.

'No way. There's heaps of life left in this one.'

But one morning it just wouldn't start. I'd pulled out the spark plug and cleaned it. I blew through various bits of the carburetor, as I'd seen Dave do, although I wasn't sure I was blowing through the right bits; and I didn't much like the taste of petrol – although it never seemed to bother Dave. I'd emptied my tin of *Start ya Bastard* into it – but it wouldn't give a single splutter. I wanted to ask Dave for advice but he'd been a bit odd lately. A bit cold towards me.

Then the next morning, while I was out walking Gemma and Christopher, I saw a lawnmower discarded on the nature strip outside number seventy-three. It looked newer and better than both of mine. Surely Dave could build me a decent mower out of the three of them.

I pushed it home and proudly showed it to Michelle.

'You bloody idiot. That's not discarded. Someone just left it on the nature strip while they went inside to get something. Take it back before they call the police.'

'I'm sure it's thrown out,' I protested but Michelle wouldn't have a bar of it. 'It's great that you're not carrying Christopher on your shoulders and teaching him to spy over our neighbour's fences any more, but now you're teaching him to steal.'

We left Gemma at home while Christopher and I pushed the mower back to number seventy-three and up their driveway. I knocked and a woman in her late twenties opened the door.

'I'm very sorry I took your lawnmower. I thought you'd thrown it out but my wife convinced me that I'd actually stolen it.'

The woman looked bemused.

'Did you ring police?' Christopher asked.

She laughed. 'I thought I'd seen the last of it. You can thank your wife for her good intentions, but for God's sake take it away.'

'Thanks.'

'Here, let me get you something.' She walked back into her house returning a minute later with a biscuit for Christopher and a familiar yellow aerosol can for me. 'You'll need this. And if you can get this bastard to start you're a better man than my husband.'

'Thanks. My next door neighbour is a better man than both of us. He'll get it going.'

I pushed the three mowers around to Dave's and knocked on his door. There was mumbling from within and after a minute or so the door opened. Fortunately I'd left Christopher at home. A bleary eyed Dave opened the door wearing only a pair of Y-fronts and smelling like a brewery. I'd never noticed before how hairy he was. He leant on his door post and looked straight past me.

'Jesus Christ, what's this? A lawnmower party? Why wasn't mine invited?'

'I was wondering if I could borrow yours, actually.'

'Help yourself. But don't start it up for an hour or so. I had a few last night.'

'Thanks.'

I'd started to walk away when Dave called after me, 'I need to talk to you.'

'Okay?'

'Later. When you come back.'

'Sure.'

I gave Dave a good two hours before I started mowing and another hour before I took his mower back, trusting that'd give him enough time to dress.

He was in his four car garage when I returned. It's packed full of cars, motorbikes, washing machines, farm machinery and all sorts of unidentifiable stuff. He had my three lawnmowers in bits and was sitting down rolling a cigarette.

'I'm supposing you want me to make these into one mower?'

'Could you?'

'It'll cost you.'

'I'm happy to pay.'

'A slab of VB for the labour and any parts I need to buy.'

'Thanks. Much appreciated.'

'Do you want a can?' He opened a bar fridge that was hiding under a stack of motorbike bits, and handed me a can.

'No thanks. I don't drink beer.'

'Don't drink beer! What sort of a bloke are you?'

'I'm sorry; I'm not much of a bloke at all.' I sat down on an upturned milk crate.

Dave lit his rollie and took a puff. He kicked the latest addition to my collection. 'This one's the best of the bunch. I'll build this one up – but the motor's completely fucked. The Victa's motor's not too bad but the head's cracked, and the head on the Rover's not real good either.' He sucked on his rollie as he surveyed the three piles of machinery, presumably working through various configurations.

'Can't you take the head off this one?'

He laughed. 'That's a two stroke.'

'And that wouldn't work?'

'No. That'd be like putting a sheep's head on a woman's body. Totally unnatural. Unless you're a New Zealander.'

'No. I'm not a New Zealander. Let's not do that.'

Dave finished his smoke and took a swig of beer. 'Who was that woman who came over the other night?'

'Which other night?'

'Driving a green Commodore. Left in a hurry. The redhead.'

'Oh, her.' I hadn't realised Dave had seen her. 'She's an old friend. I worked with her – years ago.'

'She must have been a very good friend. She left her undies behind.'

Shit. I hid my face in my hands but I knew Dave could still see me. Knew he was still looking at me. 'What makes you say that?'

'I found them in the gutter. Right where her car had been.'

'They might be Michelle's.'

'No way. I know undies. These weren't Michelle's. They're the same green as her car, which proves nothing – but, more importantly, they're not a mid-week stay at home pair. These were an *I'm off to see my ex and I hope he rips these off before we've finished our second glass of wine* pair of undies.'

'Jesus.'

'Would you like a beer?'

'Thanks.'

I took the can and gulped half of it down before I could say a word.

'Both these carburetors are shot, but I reckon I've got another one in here somewhere.'

'What makes you such an expert in lingerie, Dave?'

'My sister sells Intimo.'

'What!' I sprayed beer out of my nostrils as I choked, 'You've shown them to your sister?'

'No. I haven't shown them to anyone. But I've learnt a bit from my sister over the years. I'm pretty fluent in the language of lingerie.'

'God, I didn't even know you knew the word, never mind the whole language. You haven't told anyone have you? You haven't told Michelle?'

'No. I haven't told anyone.'

I took another swig of beer. It tasted bitter.

'I'm an innocent victim in this, Dave. She practically raped me.'

'Was that before the third glass of wine, or after?'

'You were spying on me?'

'Sorry, my TV was broken that night. It was three glasses, wasn't it? Or was it four?'

'That was a serious error of judgment on my part.'

'Which glass was the error of judgment?'

'All of them. All of them, Dave. I should go. I don't want to talk about this. If you can fix my mower, that's great. And if you can't, that's great too.' I stood up to leave.

'We need to talk, Pete.'

'We've been talking.'

'I haven't finished.'

I sat down again.

'I've never been married, Pete. But I imagine you get tempted.'

'I wasn't tempted, Dave.'

He sneered.

'Well maybe for a minute or two.'

'Michelle's a good woman.'

'She's the best, Dave. The absolute best.' I finished my beer and wondered if I should ask for another. He nodded at the fridge and I helped myself.

'Who was that woman you were telling me about a few months back? The one that was really hot? Your yoga teacher.'

'Jenny.'

'Jenny, that's right. And the woman from the other night, what's her name?'

'Where are you going with this, Dave?'

'I just want to know her name.'

Dave finished his can, but didn't grab another. He fixed me with a steely eye.

'Her name's Anne.'

'Thanks.'

Dave sat thinking while I sipped my beer.

I'd always thought of Dave as a misogynist yobbo and myself as an enlightened feminist, but now the tables were turned. He was sitting on the moral high ground and I was in the gutter. My beer tasted of bile and the milk crate was digging into my arse.

Eventually Dave spoke. 'She's not a lawnmower.'

'I beg your pardon.'

'Michelle. You can't just shove her in the back of the shed because you've found a better model.'

'I'm not.'

'It seems like you're trying to get the best of all worlds, building the ideal woman out of bits the way you'd rebuild a lawnmower.'

'I'm not.'

'You want to take Jenny's body, Anne's sex drive and Michelle's personality and put them together, so you'll have the perfect woman.'

'Michelle's already the perfect woman.'

'But sometimes you forget that.'

'Only for a moment, Dave. Only for a moment.'

'Have you ever noticed that I hang women's underwear on my clothes line?'

'Yeah, I have actually. Why is that?'

He ignored my question. 'See that green pair?' He pointed through the garage window, 'They're Anne's. I'll leave them up as a reminder. To keep you on the straight and narrow.'

'Okay. That's it?'

'I want a slab of VB and $25 to cover bits and pieces.'

'And that's it?'

'Yep that's it.'

'And you won't tell Michelle?'

'Not a word. Not this time. But if there's a next time…'

'There won't be a next time, Dave.'

'Good. Give me a couple of weeks and I'll make you the best lawnmower you've ever had. I'll guarantee it for five years.'

We shook hands. More accurately, Dave squeezed my hand till it felt like he'd broken every bone.

Dave's a man of honour, a man of his word. And true to his word he kept his silence; he kept Anne's undies waving at me from his line and he built me the best lawnmower any man could ever ask for.

Peter's taken Gemma for a walk, while I listlessly tidy the kitchen with Christopher's half-hearted help. It seems so pointless.

'What happens to them?' Christopher asks.

He's been at me all day but I don't have the answers. I've got my own questions.

'What happens to them?' he asks again.

I wish he'd gone with Peter. I thought it would help keep me calm if he stayed.

'But what happens?'

'What happens to who?'

'The dead people.'

'At the funeral, you mean?'

'Yes.'

'People who love them say things about them. Nice things.'

'Can they hear?'

'I don't know. I don't know, sweetie.'

'Why did Nanna die?'

'Cancer.'

'But why?'

'I don't know why. I don't know.'

'Don't cry, Mum.'

'I didn't know I was.' That's why the table top's so wet. I'm leaking tears onto it faster than I can wipe them up.

Christopher hugs me and I let loose, howling, wailing and bashing my head on the table top. I'm scaring him. He doesn't understand. He's only two. I need to keep control.

'Do you want to watch TV, sweetie?'

'No. I'll stay with you.'

'I'll make us a cup of tea. Amanda's coming soon.'

When I was little I'd sit under the kitchen table while Mum cooked, washed up, wiped, swept and mopped. The kitchen was the centre of her life. In the centre of the kitchen was the table, and under the table was my refuge. I loved all the activity that went on around me. Mum bustled about humming or singing, beating cake mixture or chopping vegies. She didn't like me getting under her feet but she was happy for me to stay under the table all day, drawing, painting, making doll's houses or just watching TV.

It was my favourite place in the house. My sister would try to get under sometimes but I wouldn't let her. It was my place.

'Will you say something about Nanna?'

'What?'

'Will you say something about Nanna?'

'I don't know what to say. Dad will probably say something.'

'My Dad?'

'Both Dads. Your Dad and my Dad.'

Christopher picks up a paint pot from the bench. 'Can I paint something?'

'Not right now.' I put the paint out of his reach.

'Why did you get two black paints, Mum?'

'That's a long story.'

Yesterday I had the urge to paint the kitchen black. The whole kitchen. The walls, the ceiling, the bench tops, the floor, even the windows. I wanted to splatter black all over the appliances, my glasses, my hair.

I drove to Bunnings to buy ten litres.

'That's way too much,' the assistant said, looking at me like I was utterly demented. He talked me down to two litres and said I could come back and get more if I needed – *another day*.

When I got home Peter was here. I left the tin in the car, so I wouldn't have to explain. But he found it. 'For kindergarten, for the kids.' I told him.

'Two litres is way too much. That tin's way too big for little kids. They'll knock it over.'

He put it in the shed and went and bought me two little sample pots.

There's a knock on the door. Amanda calls out, 'Ding dong.'

Christopher races to let her in. I hear her grunting as she picks him up and they chatter away as she carries him up the hall. Sounds like she's handling this much better than I am.

I wipe my eyes and throw the tissues on the table. There are dozens there already. I thought I'd picked them up.

Amanda squeezes Christopher between us while we all hug. He loves that. He laughs like a maniac. Amanda's eyes are red and raw, her cheeks smudged with mascara. She looks awful. I'm not game to look in a mirror.

I make the teas and we sit down. 'How's Dad?'

'He's exhausted. The boys are keeping him so busy, helping him organise the funeral, they say. But they're in denial. They think it's a barbeque, a family get together, a working bee, a whatever. They won't even talk about Mum. I couldn't stand it. I had to get out.'

She rummages in her bag. 'I got you a DVD, Christopher. *Thomas.*' She holds it up to show him. 'Do you want me to put it on for you?'

'I'll do it,' he says, grabbing the DVD and racing off to the TV. Then he runs back to give Amanda a kiss. 'Thanks.'

She gulps her tea down and starts pacing the kitchen, opening cupboards and drawers.

'What are you looking for?'

'I don't know. Peter's not likely to come back is he?'

'No. I told him you were coming. I told him to stay away.'

'Good. For his safety.' She rummages amongst the cutlery. 'I know he's a good man. I know he loves you and he adores Christopher. But if he walked in here right now I'd grab a carving knife and cut his balls off, before I'd even noticed that my hand was in the drawer.'

'I'll send him a text.'

A-m-a-n-d-a-s—h-e-r-e.—D-o-n-t—c-o-m-e—h-o-m-e,— s-h-e-s—a—l-i-t-t-l-e—

Crazy is the word that springs to mind. She glares it me with her panda eyes I'm afraid she's going to snatch the phone from my hand. I try to think of a better phrase.

O-n—e-d-g-e.

'I'm not myself, Michelle. I don't know who I am. I've been doing demented things. The other day Tony Abbott came on TV, he opened his mouth to say something and I kicked the screen in. I wanted to implode the tube and spray shards of glass everywhere.'

'God. Are you okay? Did you get cut up?'

'No. It's a flat screen. There is no tube. No glass. Probably for the best. The picture's a bit distorted now. And Tony Abbott still pops up.'

'Don't kick our TV,' Christopher calls, sitting protectively in front of it.

He doesn't miss much.

Amanda sits down at the table again. 'Have you seen Dad?

'Not yet. I just haven't been up to it.'

Amanda puts her hand on mine and we hold onto each other for life.

'Is he coming to the funeral?' Amanda whispers, nodding at Christopher.

'I'm not sure. Peter thinks he should but I don't know. What do you think?'

'No idea, sorry. I can't even make decisions for myself.'

Then we sit in silence, holding hands, for three or four episodes of *Thomas*, occasionally puffing, in sync with the engines, to let off a little steam.

I stand up to put the kettle on. 'I should go and see Dad.'

'I won't go again. Not for a while. I was so angry. The boys are throwing out all the old furniture, everything that reminds them of Mum. They wanted to toss out the kitchen table – that beautiful battered old table that we used to dribble on, scribble on, paint on; that the boys have all carved their initials into, that we used to hide under.'

'*I* used to hide under it. It was *my* table.'

'That's right. It was only when you went to school that I got to hide there.'

'Over my dead body they're throwing that table out!'

My phone beeps and I read the message. *Can I come home yet?*

Amanda squeezes my hand. 'I should go. It's been great to talk to someone. I'll see you at the funeral.'

'Yeah. Maybe sooner, if I'm up to it.'

Christopher gets up and gives us both a hug. Amanda grabs a handful of tissues for the drive home and I stare at the two little pots of paint on the windowsill. Not even enough to paint the windows.

I'm still staring at them when Peter comes in.

'How was she?' Peter asks.

'As well as can be expected.'

'They say it's better when they go quickly.'

'Better than what?'

'Better than a long drawn out death. She didn't suffer much.'

'Maybe. But it was so sudden. We didn't even know she was sick. One day she's saying she's got a lump and she's going to the doctor, a few days later she's dead.'

I pick up more wet tissues from the table and toss them in the bin. Or maybe I just put them back on the table. 'I've got to get a mammogram.'

'Didn't you get one a couple of months ago?'

'I'm getting another one.'

Peter turns to walk away and I cling to him. 'Hold me, Peter.'

He holds me and strokes my shoulders softly, and again I cry. How can I still have tears?

'I'm not coping, Peter.'

'You don't have to.'

'How did you cope when your mother went? How did you handle it?'

'I didn't. I haven't.' And ever so quietly, ever so softly, he starts to sob.

Christopher comes over and gives us both a hug.

'Do you think we'd all fit under the table?' I ask.

'You can sit under the table,' Peter says. 'I need to do something.'

'Something?'

'Yes.'

Peter walks off and parks himself at the computer to tap senselessly at the keyboard, engrossed in some mindless game, while I sit, tears dripping endlessly onto the table.

Christopher puts his hand on mine. 'Can I come to Nanna's funeral?'

I squeeze his hand. 'Yes. I'd like you to come. And so would Nanna.'

Rabbits

It was winter when Michelle went back to work and Christopher started childcare. He hated it. He screamed when we dropped him off and leapt into our arms whimpering, 'Take me home,' when we came to pick him up. Then he'd whinge and whine and throw tantrums half the night. But after a few weeks he reconciled himself to his fate. I wouldn't go so far as to say that he loved it, although many parents claim their kids do, but he certainly adapted to it. And as winter thawed, I could honestly say that he frequently enjoyed it.

By the time spring had sprung, peace and harmony had returned to our household, and we were surrounded by beauty. Flowers bloomed, birds sang, the lawn went berserk and my sperm swam like Olympic champions. It was no surprise when we discovered that Michelle was pregnant, and for several weeks our hearts bubbled over with love and joy. But at our first ultrasound it was revealed there was nothing there. The child had stopped developing soon after conception.

A blighted ovum, the doctors called it. It was just a part of the body that wasn't fully functional – like a grazed knee or a sprained wrist. But to us it was a dead child – cruelly taken from us. Seeing the radiologist's blank screen was like witnessing our baby being run over by a train or ripped apart by dogs. Our hearts, filled to bursting, were crushed like aluminium cans.

But life goes on. I still had to work, though it seemed utterly pointless. Michelle still had to work, though she could barely drag herself out of bed in the mornings. Christopher still had to go to childcare and we still had to find the time and the energy to drop him off and pick him up.

One day, one beautiful spring day, when the blossoms were at their peak, I walked in the park at lunchtime and just couldn't bear going back to work. I was overcome by the disparity between the beauty surrounding me and the emptiness within, so I went home.

I spent a couple of hours in the backyard, on the verge of tears, before deciding to take the dog for a walk, up to the childcare centre to pick up Christopher. He was really pleased to see us; it was an hour and a half earlier than usual and I'd never taken Gemma there before.

We walked home, hand in hand, enjoying the sunshine and chatting about what he'd eaten and who he'd played with. Gemma pranced around us tangling us in her lead. 'Stop it, you dog,' we shouted at her and we laughed and laughed.

It was such a gorgeous day that when we got to the railway crossing I decided we'd take the track behind the lines so I could let Gemma off the lead.

'This where we used to walk,' said Christopher. 'Daddy, Gemma, Chrispher.'

'That's right,' I said, as Gemma trotted off ahead. 'That was a long time ago, when you were very little.'

'A very long time ago,' said Christopher. 'I'm a big boy now.'

'Yes,' I agreed, so proud of him – my grown-up little two-and-a-half-year-old.

'Look!' shouted Christopher. 'Gemma chasing rabbits.'

Rabbits

It was true; she was indeed chasing rabbits, dozens of them, mummy rabbits, daddy rabbits and lots of baby rabbits. It had been a year or more since the council had stopped putting down baits and the population had exploded.

'Gemma!' I called as she bolted. She was a couple of hundred metres away and disappearing into the undergrowth. 'Gemma!' I screamed again louder, and more sternly – but it was pointless: she was too close to the scent of rabbit; her instincts were far stronger than her loyalty.

'Where Gemma gone?' asked Christopher.

'I don't know, we'll have to find her.'

'She chasing rabbits.'

'Yes, she's chasing rabbits.'

'Why? Why she chase rabbits?'

'She thinks rabbits are food.'

'Rabbits aren't food,' he said laughing.

'Yes, but Gemma thinks they are.' I scanned the scrub, searching for her. I could hear her crashing around and the tag jangling on her collar. Every so often I'd see rabbits darting off, giving some indication of her whereabouts. 'Gemma!' I screamed, but there was no response.

'Why Gemma thinks rabbits are food?'

'I don't know – that's just what dogs think. Come on we'd better find her.'

I took Christopher's hand and dragged him in the direction Gemma had gone. It was hard work once we got off the path: the ground was uneven and weeds and nettles had grown almost waist high – nature gone berserk. I had to pick Christopher up and carry him, watching out for holes and bits of jagged metal and broken bottles – this place used to be a tip. 'Gemma!' I screamed, over and over again. I was getting hot and Christopher was getting heavier and heavier. I carried him for two or three hundred metres, over humps and potholes and a rusty car body.

'Ow,' squealed Christopher, as I accidentally brushed him against a thorny bush. My back was aching with the effort of carrying him, and I was sweating and fuming, and still there was no sign of the bloody dog. I was on the verge of leaving it.

'I have to put you down,' I told Christopher, selecting the clearest spot I could find.

'Ow – spiky!' he yelped.

'Yeah, I'm sorry. It is a bit spiky here but I need a rest.'

A train rushed past in the distance and then, much closer to us, a rabbit, with Gemma in hot pursuit. I grabbed her collar and twisted her onto her back, where she lay, panting and whining submissively – her snout covered in drool and scratch marks. I clipped the lead onto her, picked up Christopher, and headed for the track.

'You dog,' scolded Christopher. 'Rabbits not food.'

He looked to me to back up his statement but I was in no mood to continue the conversation. I ignored his comments, his questions, his protests and his crying, totally preoccupied with task of lugging a fourteen-kilo child and dragging a twenty-five kilo dog through the wilderness.

The council should do something about this place – it's a bloody disgrace.

When we got back onto the walking track, I put Christopher down.

'This where we used to walk,' said Christopher. 'Daddy, Gemma, Chrispher.'

'Yes. This is where we used to walk.'

'Too spiky over there.'

'Yes, it's much too spiky over there.' I sat down on the pipe that runs from the oil refinery, to catch my breath. Gemma nuzzled her saliva-drenched snout into my hand. 'Piss off, dog!' I shouted and unclipped her lead: I didn't want her anywhere near me. I hated her. I felt like kicking her senseless – but not in front of Christopher. She gazed up at me and whined apologetically. She flopped her ears over and crept closer. I growled.

'You dog,' said Christopher.

She turned her head away, caught sight of a rabbit and she was off. I didn't even bother calling her. Let her make her own way home.

I stood up. 'Come on Christopher, let's go.'

We made our way along the path, hand in hand, while Gemma raced around and Christopher prattled on about rabbits not being food. Then Gemma appeared beside us, a baby bunny in her mouth. She dropped it at my feet. A gift: her way of making amends. The bunny twitched its nose in pain; its eyes swung around crazily, desperately searching for its mummy. Its body lay limp, its back broken. Its breathing, rapid and shallow, hissed through its teeth.

'What rabbit doing?' asked Christopher.

'Not much. Let's go.'

'We better bring rabbit.'

'No we can't bring rabbit, let's go.' I clipped Gemma's lead onto her collar and we made our way home, Christopher dawdling behind, constantly looking back.

'What's wrong with rabbit?'

'It's sick.'

'We better take it to hospital.'

'You can't take rabbits to hospital.'

'We better give it some medicine.'

'We can't get rabbit medicine. They don't make it.'

'We better buy some, from the shop.'

'You can't buy it. They don't make it.'

'Yes you can. At rabbit shops.'

'The rabbit shops are closed now,' I snapped. It was a stupid argument and I could see there was no way I was going to win it.

'No they aren't.'

'Yes they are!' I screamed.

Christopher thought for a second or two, looking back at the white spot of fluff behind us. 'We'd better kiss it.'

Rabbits

'We're not kissing it! It's a filthy fucking rabbit. It's vermin; it's full of diseases and parasites. Forget the rabbit.'

'It's dead,' said Christopher.

'Yes,' I agreed. 'It's dead.'

'We better bury it.'

'Yes. We better bury it.'

'With a spade – from the shed,' he continued.

'Yes. With a spade from the shed.'

I picked Christopher up and carried him home; it was only a couple of hundred metres. We dropped Gemma, picked up a spade and made our way back to the spot of fluff. As we drew closer, it seemed like an adult rabbit bolted from its side – its mother, I presumed – but maybe I imagined it.

The poor thing was still alive, when we reached it, but only just. I dug a hole, in a soft looking spot, a little off the path – the baby bunny watching my every move. Maybe I should have knocked it over the head with the spade to put it out of its misery – but how could I with Christopher watching?

I dug a little deeper, then picked up the limp, white body on the end of the spade and dropped it into the hole. Its eyes fixed onto mine, pleading for mercy – to no avail.

Christopher and I sat down by the hole and pushed the soil over the edge, with our hands, until the pleading eyes were covered and the hole was filled. And when we finished tapping down the soil, we stared at the mound we'd made and cried for the life that could have been.

The Tart

Peter's gone away again. I hate it when he's away. The dog gets more neurotic, Christopher won't go to bed, and I turn into a crazy woman. Not that he seems to do much when he's here. I'm the one who seems to have it all together. I'm the one who always knows what's going on, who keeps everything organised and makes the effort to keep in touch with the neighbours. But Peter's a steadying influence. He's the glue that holds our household together. When he's away, the house itself seems to fall apart: the roof tiles scrape against one another, the windows rattle and creak, and the downpipes break free from the gutters.

All our routines break down, but instead of feeling free, I feel like I'm cast adrift in a wild ocean, bobbing up and down, swirling around and around and then flung in whatever direction the winds and tides decide.

I lost my job a few weeks ago. I'd only been back at work for a few months, Christopher had just got used to child care. But it seemed silly to go on sending him when I was at home all day. Maybe we should have continued, anyway. Maybe, maybe, maybe.

I try to keep up Gemma's routine. It calms her down, stops her from digging up the garden. It calms me too. It restores a little sanity to our lives. Peter generally walks her up to the school, so that's the route I follow. Christopher and I dawdle up to the school grounds then let Gemma off the lead. There's a woman we see up there sometimes. Her gate opens into the school and she has a border collie that plays with Gemma. Peter has told me her name but I just call her The Tart.

The Tart

I was hoping we wouldn't see her, hoping she'd have gone to work — but she hasn't. She leans against her gatepost, preening herself. Gemma makes a beeline for her and she bends down to pat her.

'Gemma wants to play with her friend,' says Christopher.

'We don't have time to play today,' I say. 'And her friend's not even there.'

'She can play with her friend's owner.'

'We don't have time to play today,' I persist. I call Gemma, calling her name over and over. Christopher joins in but she ignores us.

We walk towards Gemma; The Tart smiles at us.

'Hello Christopher, how are you today?'

'I'm good.'

'Hi. You must be Michelle.'

'Yes, I am. You must be Ivy.'

She throws her head back and screeches with laughter. 'Ivy! That's a good one. My dog's called Ivy. I'm Ramona.'

She offers me her hand, still giggling. It's warm — too warm — and a little damp. Her sweat is sticky and slippery.

'What sort of name is Ivy for a dog?'

'It's short for Ivories.' She looks at me expectantly.

Ivories? That's an even stupider name for a dog.

'She's black and white. Like a piano's keys.'

'Oh.'

'I find it amusing.'

'I suppose Peter does too.'

'Yes. I suppose he does. He's a good man, isn't he?'

What does she mean by good? Virtuous? Admirable? Satisfying? Good in bed? Good for nothing?

'Gemma's getting a bit grey, isn't she?'

Was that directed at me? Is she suggesting that I'm getting grey? I've got maybe a dozen grey hairs. And she's older than me. I'm sure she is. 'I have to go. Come along, Christopher.'

'I'll see you tomorrow, perhaps.'

'No. Peter's back tomorrow.'

'Oh. Maybe I'll see him then.'

'Yes. Maybe.'

The encounter played on my mind all day, as Christopher and I watched television. Teletubbies, Thomas, Big Blue House, and Play School. All those inane shows that I generally enjoy. Maybe she'll see Peter tomorrow, she said. Maybe she saw him today.

Maybe she saw him last night. No, that's crazy. He was only away for one night. He'll be back again tonight. He doesn't go away often. He's not having an affair with her – with Ramona – otherwise she'd be away too. Unless she met me deliberately this morning, to throw me off the scent. Unless she's catching a later flight. Unless she spent last night with Peter and flew back early this morning, to feed her dog. Unless she's cloned herself and spirited him away to an alternate universe.

The Tart

I need to cook, to clear my mind. I need to bang and crash around the kitchen, to clatter, mash, slice and dice. I need to make soup and quiches, biscuits, bread and scones. I need to make all the meals for the rest of the week. I need to dirty every implement and bring some order to my crazed thoughts.

Christopher wants me to watch telly with him but it's all too sordid for me. Every show is filled with innuendo. Monday is making day, Play School tells us. Let's make an unfaithful husband from pipe cleaners and a milk bottle cap. And let's see what's happening through the round window: it's Big Ted in bed with Jemima. And let's sing a jolly song about bonking your neighbours while your wife has a philosophical discussion with a kitchen appliance.

After Play School, Christopher helps me with the washing up, which is not actually all that helpful. He's only three and he does his best but he splashes water everywhere and he drops the pans and chips the plates. But it's sweet that he tries.

'When's Daddy coming home?'

'Tonight. Late tonight.'

'Will he read me a story?'

'No. It'll be too late. You'll be asleep.'

'No, I won't.'

I can't be bothered arguing. Maybe he's right. He was awake till almost eleven last night.

'Would you like to take Gemma for a walk again?' I ask, hoping it will tire him out.

The Tart

'To the school?'

'Yes. Why not?' I reply, and we stroll up to the school again. It must be half a kilometre; it's a fair way for Christopher.

'That dog, Gemma's friend, it can sing,' Christopher tells me proudly.

'It must be a clever dog.'

'Yes. It's very clever. And it can jump. It can jump very high.'

'Yes. I've seen it jump high.'

'It can jump on her bed.'

'What?'

'It can jump on her bed.'

'How do you know?'

'I seen it.'

'When?'

Christopher thinks hard. 'The day before.'

'You were inside her house?'

'Mmm.'

'Why?'

Christopher is getting agitated. I'm scaring him – but I need to know.

'Why were you in her house?'

'Biscuits.'

'She gave you some biscuits?'

'Mmm.'

'Were the biscuits in her bedroom?'

'I can't remember.'

'Was Daddy in her bedroom too?'

'I can't remember.'

What the hell was he doing in her house? In her bedroom?

We stop in the school grounds, by her back gate. It's a little after five. I can hear her television. I can hear her laughing. I can hear a man's voice. I'm not sure if it's on television, or if there's a man in the house. I thought she lived alone.

'Gemma's friend's not here,' Christopher says.

'No. Gemma's friend's not here.' I'm practically whispering. I don't want her to hear.

'We should go home now.' Christopher looks at me.

'Yes. We should go home.'

Her fence is too high. I can't see over it. I hear her footsteps when she gets up during an ad break. She's got polished wooden floors and she's wearing heels. I hear her toilet flush and water splashing out of her tap and down the plughole. I don't think there's a man in the house but I can't be sure.

'We should go home now,' Christopher repeats. 'I'm hungry.'

'Yes. We'll go home now.'

'Maybe she'll give us some biscuits.'

'No. She won't give us any biscuits. Let's go.'

We walk further into the school grounds, come out on the side street, and walk past the front of her house. Christopher is getting tired so I carry him a little way, but he's getting too heavy for that. We pause out the front of her house and I strain, unsuccessfully, to catch a glimpse of her through her curtains or her frosted glass door. I can't hear her at all from here and her television is very faint. I think her bedroom's at the front, with kitchen, dining area and lounge at the back. There's probably a second bedroom and a bathroom in the middle.

'I'm tired,' murmurs Christopher. 'And I'm hungry.'

I carry him halfway home and let Gemma drag him the other half. He falls asleep before I can get three mouthfuls into him. Usually, it's such an effort to get him to bed that I fall asleep with him as soon as we finish our bedtime story, but tonight he's asleep early and I'm wide awake.

I dye my hair. I normally put it off for months, it's such a hassle. But tonight it's important. And when it's done it looks good. I look better, younger, less frazzled. But still I feel restless.

I start picking up toys, sorting the washing, dusting the ceilings and polishing shoes. My shoes, Christopher's shoes, Peter's shoes. Black shoes, brown shoes, burgundy shoes and blue shoes. I never knew we had so many shoe polishes. I can't even remember when I last polished shoes. I can't even remember when we last wore some of these shoes. I find the shoes we were married in. We've barely worn them since. After I've polished every shoe in the house, I put on my wedding shoes. They still look nice. The heels click on the kitchen floor. I leave Peter's wedding shoes on the table. I open a bottle of Shiraz and sit down to enjoy a glass while I admire my handiwork.

It's so quiet. No television. Christopher's asleep. Peter won't be home for a couple of hours yet. Gemma's asleep, on her blanket. The phone hasn't rung all day. Maybe it's out of order. No, it's all right. The house is the tidiest it's been in months and I won't need to cook another meal till the weekend. I catch my reflection in Peter's shoes. I look peaceful, serene – happy and contented. I look a little fat but that could be distortion from the curve of the shoe.

I'd like to make Peter something special, to welcome him home. A custard tart. He loves custard tarts. But we're out of eggs. I used them all today. I ring our next-door neighbour, Elizabeth, but she's not home. I ring Dave, our neighbour on the other side.

'Hi, it's Michelle. Could I borrow a couple of eggs?'

'Sure, I'll pass them over the fence.'

I open the side door and walk over to the fence. I almost trip. I'm not used to heels.

'Nice shoes,' says Dave.

I wouldn't have thought he'd notice.

'A special occasion?' he asks, nodding at the bottle of wine on our table. You can see straight into our kitchen from his place.

'Would you like a glass?'

'No thanks. I'm starting early tomorrow and I've already had a couple of beers.' He passes half a dozen eggs over the fence.

'I only need three.'

'Take them just in case.'

'I'm making Peter a tart.'

Dave laughs. 'Make one for me too.'

'A custard tart. Would you like one?'

'No thanks. I don't like custard.'

I thank Dave and head back inside to heat the milk and beat the eggs. The phone rings. That'll be Peter. But it's not. It's my friend Irene. She sounds like she's had a few drinks. She was separated a few months earlier, has a very low opinion of husbands, and has an annoying habit of ringing whenever Peter's away.

'Hi, how are you? I was just thinking of you because it's our wedding anniversary today, or would be if Max hadn't been screwing my sister ever since we were engaged, and you're one of the few happily married woman I know, so I thought it would be lovely to have a little chat with someone who's still in love, because you know me, Michelle, I'm a hopeless romantic and I'd love to believe I could be swept off my feet again.'

I never quite know what to say to Irene when she pauses long enough to give me the chance.

'The guy you were going out with last time we spoke, he didn't work out?'

'No. Two-faced bastard. But how are you, and how's little Christian?'

'Christopher.'

'Sorry. And how's Peter?'

'They're fine. They're both fine. Peter's out at the moment but he'll be back soon. I thought that was him ringing.'

'It's a bit late for him to be at work, isn't it?'

'He's travelling – interstate.'

'Oh.'

She sniffs. What does the sniff mean? Derision? Distain? Disbelief?

Holding the phone in the crook of my neck, I beat the eggs till my arm aches. What's the time? It's not that late.

'He goes away rather a lot, doesn't he?'

'He very rarely goes away.' I can feel myself getting flustered. Gemma, sensing my agitation, gets up and walks in front of me each time I move from table to bench to stove.

'Max used to go away a lot.'

The phone cord tangles and twists itself into knots. Why the hell don't we have a cordless phone, like everyone else?

'Peter is not Max.'

'I'm not saying he is.'

'He's not screwing my sister.'

Irene laughs. She brays like a donkey. I can imagine her throwing her head back and tossing her hair from side to side.

'You don't have a sister.'

'I do have a sister. You've met my sister.'

'Sorry. I was thinking of Angela. She doesn't have a sister.'

'Peter is not screwing my sister. He is not screwing the neighbours.'

Dave waves good night to me from next door. I wonder where Elizabeth is tonight. I tread on Gemma's tail. She yelps and I almost spill the hot custard on her. I bang the pan back on the stove top. The pastry isn't straight. If I put the custard in now, it would flow over the top and stick to the tray. It would burn. I hate burning the custard.

'I know Peter's not like Max. But I worry about you, dear. I'm not saying you shouldn't trust him. But keep an eye on him. Even the best men have moments of weakness.'

I pour another glass of wine while I push the pastry around with my thumb. The more I fiddle with it the worse it gets, so I rip it out, squash it into a ball and roll it flat again.

I want to brush Irene off. I don't know why I even talk to her. She needles me and nags me. She twists my words, twists my thoughts and poisons my mind. Forty minutes pass before I can shake her off and my good mood of earlier is long gone.

I untangle myself from the telephone cord, the dog and the tablecloth. I press the pastry into the tray for the fifth time. I need to get this thing into the oven, so that it can cool by the time Peter gets in.

I don't know why I'm even bothering to make it. If he really wants a tart he can buy one himself. In fact he can bloody make it himself. When was the last time he made a dessert? When was the last time he cooked, for that matter?

I am exhausted. I've been at it all day, and my feet are killing me. I kick my shoes off. I turn on the television. A woman laughs. She throws her head back and brays like a donkey. I switch it off. I check the doors. I check on Christopher. I go to the toilet. I brush my teeth, turn off the stove, pour the custard into Peter's wedding shoes, and go to bed.

'Peter, my office now.'

I'd been summoned.

I'm not a star performer. I've never won any awards. But I'm dependable and reliable. I always come up with the goods. I seldom have to work to the manic deadlines that most journalists accept as normal and consequently don't need to collapse into an orgy of nicotine, caffeine and alcohol at the end of a shift. I'm respected by my peers. I doubt that I'm admired, but I'm left to my own devices. I rarely have to take my work home, I frequently get to choose the stories I work on and they're seldom meddled with. All things considered, I'm doing all right.

But occasionally I'm summoned.

'This is a prize assignment, Peter. Three thousand words on men's groups for the Sunday feature.'

I groaned and my editor fixed me with her steely gaze. I hate it when she confronts me when we're both standing. She's a tiny woman and I tower over her but I feel myself slouching and have the urge to drop to my knees. She has the ability to hold my stare without tilting her head more than a few degrees, as though she can see through the top of her skull.

'But every paper and magazine has articles on men's groups,' I protested, weakly. 'They never say anything new. They're shallow, condescending and self-indulgent.'

'Exactly,' she replied. 'That's why I've chosen you. I want something insightful, informative and empathetic. Something with balls but without an overdose of testosterone – I don't want to alienate our women readers. I want the overview and the inside view – something honest and heartfelt – from a man, a father and a husband. I want to touch our readers.'

'That's not me, I don't touch. There are a plenty of guys who could do this story better than I could – and plenty more women. You could write it. You'd be very good, actually.'

Her eyes, magnified by her black-rimmed glasses, burned like lasers.

'Peter,' she said, her voice low and menacing. 'I'm not asking you to track down Osama bin Laden and bring back a personal interview. I'm not asking you to infiltrate a secret society. I'm not asking to risk life and limb. And frankly, Peter, I'm not asking you. I'm telling you. You can write it under a pseudonym, if you like, but you will write it.'

That was that.

I went back to my desk and made a few notes. I trawled the net then took off to the library. I borrowed a few books, took them home and flicked listlessly through them.

There was a guy I'd met a few weeks earlier, who was in a men's group. He'd invited me along and I'd said, maybe some time. He'd given me his number, so I had no excuse not to call.

'Hi, Evan, it's Peter… I've met you a few times, walking the dog… At the school… The brown dog… You belong to a men's group…'

'Ah, Peter. I knew you'd call. We're having a meeting tonight, can you make it?'

'I don't know about tonight.' I was hoping to get more of the overview before getting too intimate with my subject. 'When's the next meeting?'

'Not till next month.'

'Oh.' My deadline was days away. 'I'll try to make it.'

It was a tacky community hall, not far from the school grounds where we walked our dogs. Evan met me at the door and wafted sage smoke over me. 'It's a ritual cleansing,' he informed me.

Evan introduced me to the other members of the group: Barry, Martin, Noel and John, the group's leader. Barry and Martin shook my hand heartily; Noel eyed me suspiciously then offered a limp, pudgy palm.

John embraced me in a bear hug. 'Welcome Peter, Evan has told me so much about you.'

What the hell could Evan have told him? I hardly know him.

It was a bare room with a faded lino floor – used by several groups, judging by the pamphlets and posters on the walls. Vinyl chairs were stacked in the corners and eight of them were arranged in an intimate circle in the centre of the room. John invited us to sit and relax. Barry and Martin took off their shoes and socks and sat opposite me. They were the youngest – late twenties or early thirties. They were athletic and boyish. They could have been brothers, but Martin was dressed in an expensive suit and Barry wore ripped jeans and a tee shirt and was heavily tattooed.

'This is our time of connection, Peter.' John told me, sitting beside me. He was already barefoot when I'd arrived. He was in his late forties and had a thick black beard. 'Let your feet connect to the floor, Peter. Feel your roots growing down into Mother Earth.'

I looked over to Evan, standing at the door – waiting for stragglers and wafting sage smoke over himself. He was about the same age as me – forty. He didn't bat an eyelid at John's spiel. He slipped off his shoes and sheepishly I followed suit, although I left my socks on.

Noel was the oldest; he would have been close to sixty. He had a shiny, bald head and wore the expression of a disgruntled frog. He sat on the other side of John, leaving a space between himself and Barry. There were two empty chairs between Martin and myself.

'We don't have a fixed format,' John told me. 'Sometimes we prepare something, sometimes we don't – we just go with the flow. We've got nothing specific planned for tonight but I sense it's going to be a very special session. There's a lovely energy tonight. We'll just wait a few more minutes; I'm expecting another couple.'

Couple? Did he actually mean *couple*, or did he just mean two more men?

John closed his eyes and began to hum softly. Martin and Barry grinned at each other, sharing some private joke and Noel slipped out of sight behind John.

I caught Barry's eye. 'Have you been coming here long?'

'Yep. Ever since my wife left.'

Noel snorted.

John opened his eyes suddenly. 'Close the door please, Evan, and take out the two spare chairs. Let's begin.'

Evan removed the extra chairs and sat next to me. We moved our chairs in closer, till out knees almost touched.

John put his hand on my thigh and smiled at me. Was that meant to put me at ease?

'We always start the sessions with a clearing,' he said. 'We say who we are and how we feel right now. Just a few words. No long explanations or complicated stories – there'll be plenty of time for further sharing later. And the most important thing, Peter, the single most important thing, is that there is absolute confidentiality. Whatever is said, or done, within these four walls remains here. Are we all in agreement on that?' He looked slowly around the circle, as each man murmured his agreement, finally arriving at me.

'Sure.' I agreed. That would create some severe limitations.

'Good. I'm John. I'm excited. I've had a pretty rough couple of weeks – a lot of conflict at home – but I'm really pleased to be here and looking forward to whatever tonight brings. It feels good to be surrounded by men. I sense there's a lot of hurt in the room tonight and that there will be a lot of healing.'

God. What am I meant to say to that? John looked to Noel, who cleared his throat.

'I'm Noel and I feel grumpy.'

John patted his knee encouragingly.

'I feel angry,' Noel continued. 'Really angry. My wife's a bitch and if I thought I could find someone better, I'd leave her.'

I suspect that he said pretty much the same thing every meeting but everyone listened intently. And once we were all sure he'd finished talking, and been heard, the next man spoke.

'I'm Barry. My wife – my ex-wife – is a bitch too. I was meant to see my kids last weekend – and she took them away. I feel angry – fucking furious. And I feel...'

'Sad.' John finished the sentence for him.

'Yeah. Sad.' Tears rolled down his cheeks and Martin put an arm around him. 'I don't understand why she has to hurt me. Why she has to hurt the kids.'

John let out a big sigh and we all followed suit. We'd stopped breathing.

'Hi, I'm Martin. I feel okay. I feel pretty good. But I'm struggling a bit with my relationship. I starting seeing this girl, as you know, a few months ago and it's great – it's really great. But the honeymoon's over now and it's hard to pass into the next phase. The excitement is starting to fade but there's not enough trust to move into the next stage of intimacy. Each time we get close – really close – she seems to break us apart. I want it to be different but I don't know how to make that happen. I feel frustrated. Confused and frustrated.'

'Mmm,' said John, nodding sagely. 'There seems to be a bit of a theme developing tonight – a lack of understanding between the sexes.'

'Yes. I'm Evan. I'm pleased to be here. I'm glad Peter could make it tonight. I enjoy the company of men, I feel comfortable among men. I think it's sad that it doesn't occur more naturally in my life – that it has to be structured. I miss being young and single. I miss having friends to drink with and socialise with on a regular basis. I miss my father and I wish I had a son. I have two lovely daughters and I love them more than anything. But I'm sad that I don't have a son to pass on to – I don't even know what it is I want to pass on – but I miss that I can't. My father's line is coming to an end. When I go, he's gone – gone for good. My wife just laughs when I say that. She doesn't understand. She doesn't seem to care.'

Evan looked to me. Everyone looked to me. There was a deathly silence in the room. I could hear my watch ticking like blood thumping in my temples. It was my turn.

'Hi. I'm Peter. My reasons for coming here tonight are probably a little different than most of yours. I don't quite know what to say.'

'Say as little or as much as you want, Peter.' John encouraged.

'I don't know what I was expecting tonight. I wasn't really expecting this. I was planning on keeping a very low profile tonight – saying as little as possible – but there's something that's been bothering me for months and I feel that tonight is a good time to share it. I feel…'

'Safe?' John suggested.

'Yes, safe. But also that I owe something to this group. I came here for the wrong reasons and I need to reveal a little more of myself so I can feel worthy to be here.'

I had no idea that I was going to say that – it just popped out of my mouth. I expected John to tell me that was quite all right – that of course I was worthy to be here and that I didn't need to say anything. But he said nothing. Not a word. No one said a word, they just looked at me expectantly and it seemed I had no other choice than to continue.

'Continuing on the theme that John picked up on of our partners not understanding us, my wife did something very strange a few months ago and it's bothered me ever since. I've asked her about it but she won't answer. I feel cheated. I feel she holds all the answers to the mysteries of life but she's withholding them from me. Anyway, that's me. What do we do next?'

'You feel cheated?' John asked.

'Yes.'

'Cheated is rather a strong word. Would you like to tell us more?'

'No not really.'

'Do you think your wife is cheating on you?' Martin asked.

'No!'

'Have you cheated on her?' Noel asked, licking his thin lips.

'No,' I answered, a little less certainly.

'No – but,' John suggested.

'No. No, full stop. There is no but.'

'We're not here to judge you. I sense that you'd like to tell us more, Peter. Would you like to tell us more?'

'No, I wouldn't.'

Again we sat in silence for a minute, while my watch ticked with a manic urgency. I was expecting John to move on to the next stage of the night's activities but he didn't. I'd said I didn't want to say any more but the words were welling up inside me and the silence was oppressive.

'A few months ago I went away, for work, a business trip. I was home late, around eleven. I came in, expecting Michelle to be asleep. The first thing I noticed was the smell of baking – custard tart. I love homemade custard tart. It was a lovely welcome home. The next thing that I noticed was that the house was really tidy. Really tidy. We have a young son and there are generally toys scattered from one end of the house to the other. But the place was spotless – swept, vacuumed, dusted and polished. It was like we'd been visited by housework fairies. I went into the kitchen; I thought I'd have a little bit of tart before I went to bed. The kitchen table had been cleared – it was normally covered in toys and papers and unopened junk mail – but there was nothing on it but a pair of my shoes. My best shoes. The shoes I wore when we got married. They'd been polished. They looked new – they looked better than new. They glowed with love. I opened the fridge, looking for the custard tart, but couldn't find it. There were quiches and cutlets, meatballs and mousse, soups and salads; a sensational selection of culinary delights filled the fridge and freezer to capacity. But no custard tart. Perplexed, I picked up my shoes to put them in my wardrobe. The shoes were full of custard. Full to the brim. It was still warm. Michelle was asleep; I could hear her snoring, softly. I ate a little quiche then brushed my teeth and got into bed. Michelle never woke. In the morning I asked about her about the custard in my shoes. *I don't want to talk about it*, she said. And she hasn't to this day. And she's been distant – there's a barrier between us now.'

'Is this a dream?' Evan asked.

'No it really happened.'

'And you've no inkling of what it's about?' John asked.

'Well, she's asked me several times why our son has been in one of our neighbours' bedrooms. I think that has something to do with it.'

'A female neighbour?' asked Martin.

'Yes, a female neighbour.'

'Hmm,' he said. 'Any other clues?'

'Well, yes. The house being so tidy is a bit strange – but that shouldn't mean anything. And she borrowed some eggs off our next-door neighbour and I'm wondering if he's said anything to her – but I doubt he would have. And yet...'

'I sense there's something you're not telling us, Peter. What exactly do you think your neighbour might have said to her?'

I could have stopped it there. I could have said that I didn't feel safe enough to continue. They would have respected that. They would have moved onto something else. But I didn't.

'There was an incident last year. An ex-girlfriend came around to visit, while my wife was out. She wanted to have sex with me and I almost succumbed to her charms – but I didn't. Nothing happened.'

'There's more, isn't there?' Martin probed.

'Yes there's more. My neighbour saw her – he may have even seen her stripping – and I think she left her knickers behind.'

'So, your neighbour saw her? Your wife found the knickers, while she was cleaning the house. Sexy little frilly numbers, no doubt – and obviously not hers. Your neighbour saw something, maybe heard something as well, and could have passed that onto your wife. Your son's been in a strange woman's bedroom with you, while you're doing something that you can't explain satisfactorily. It's not looking good is it? But it's all circumstantial evidence. It wouldn't stand up in a court of law.'

'I didn't realise I was on trial.' I squeaked.

'You're not on trial,' John reassured me.

'Sorry,' Martin said. That's just the way I think. I'm a lawyer.'

'My neighbour found the knickers. He knows. But I don't think he'd tell Michelle.'

'Your wife's distant though, isn't she?' asked Barry.

'Yes.'

'She's angry.' Barry continued. 'She's angry and she's punishing you. Punishing for something you haven't even done.'

'Maybe,' I answered, not really convinced.

'That stinks, that stinks like shit – and I know shit, I'm a plumber.'

'I'm not sure that she's punishing me. I'm not sure that she's doing anything to me. But…'

'There's a sense of guilt eating away at you, isn't there?' John asked.

'I guess so.'

'You feel bad about what it's perceived you could have done – even though you've actually done nothing wrong.'

'I suppose so.'

'She's not punishing you. You're punishing yourself and it's time to stop. Are you willing to stop?'

'Sure.'

'Are you *really* willing to stop?'

'I think so.'

'Have you heard of psychodrama?'

'I've heard the word before.'

'Do you know what it is?'

'Not really.'

'But you're willing to try it?'

I nodded. I don't know why I agreed. On the one hand I was thinking, I'm a professional – I'll follow this story wherever it goes. But on the other hand I was thinking, I don't know where this story's going but it's certainly not going into print – so why am I still following it?

Evan, Martin, Barry and Noel stood up and cleared the chairs away, while John explained the process to me.

'In psychodrama,' he said, 'The protagonist, in this case you, chooses bit players – or auxiliaries, as they are known – to play out various aspects of an unresolved issue. For example, you could choose someone to be the custard, someone to be the shoes, someone to be your wife, someone your ex-girlfriend and someone else your neighbour – whoever, or whatever, you think plays a key part in this story.'

'And through this I'll work out why my wife poured custard in my shoes?'

'Not necessarily – but it will change your relationship with the incident. It will change your relationship with your wife.'

I explained a little more about the incidents that led to or followed on from the custard in the shoes. There seemed to be several chapters that were connected, even if only in my mind, and I chose men to play out various aspects.

I chose Barry to play my ex-girlfriend, although there was absolutely nothing feminine about him. I chose Evan to play my dog, who had led me into my neighbour's bedroom, and got under my feet and in my way when the ex-girlfriend was trying to get me into bed. He was very good.

With the help of a bunch of virtual strangers, I recreated the scenes that had played in my mind so many times and gave them life and a script. Dialogue that in other circumstances would have been inane and absurd proved to be profound and moving. Part of my mind was amused and bemused and taking notes for the article I was researching, but another part was fully immersed in the drama.

I had Evan, as my dog, saying – *don't do something you'll regret for the rest of your life.*   Barry, as the custard, saying – *I am the oozing pus of perverted love*. And Martin, as my shoes, saying – *I am your honour, I glow with pride*. And for the grand finale, the climax of the final act, I had Noel, as my wife Michelle, sobbing in my arms, *I love you*. God knows why I chose him for that role – but, at the time, he was her. We held each other tight and whispered, over and over, our love for each other.

As we wiped away our tears, John asked me how I felt.

'Embarrassed.'

'Yes. That's a common reaction.'

'I feel sad that I've been dishonest to my wife. I feel ashamed of the lust I felt toward an old lover.'

'That's good. But there's something else. What about proud? Proud to be a man. Proud of the urges that drive you to propagate and to protect to your family. Proud of the courage it takes to stand up and share your innermost feelings.'

'I feel proud,' I repeated, with much less conviction.

'That's good. That's great. You're a good man, Peter.' He put his hand on my heart. It felt warm.

We sat down again in a circle, and each spoke about how we'd been touched by the drama. Then we had biscuits and herbal tea and chatted about dogs and cars and wives and children.

'What a great night,' John said over and over. You must come again, Peter.'

'Sure,' I said.

'How was it?' Michelle asked.

'It was good. It was interesting.'

'Do you want to talk about it?'

'No, not really.'

'Do you want to make some notes? Do you want me to leave you alone?'

'No. I'd like to tell you why Christopher was in Ramona's bedroom.'

And I did.

And Michelle told me why she'd put custard in my shoes. And I told her about my ex-girlfriend coming around, and we drank cups of peppermint tea together and talked half the night. We clung to each other and sobbed on each other's shoulders, and for the second time that evening, I said, 'I love you, I love you, I love you.' But this time it was in the privacy of my own home with a woman I knew very well and respected very deeply.

I made my deadline. My feature was shallow, condescending and self-indulgent. It broke no new ground and revealed nothing of myself. It painted an image of a bunch of immature eunuchs, immersed in a group mid-life crisis, searching for a messiah to stroke their deflated egos. It got a few laughs from my colleagues and a few angry letters from our readers – one of them, I'm almost certain, was from John. And it ensured that I wasn't selected for any more special assignments for several months.

Evan rang me several times and asked me to come back.

Maybe I will one day – but not any day soon.

A Matter of Scale

I was watching Christopher one day playing with his little wooden Thomas trains, and remembered how much pleasure I'd derived from my train set when I was a kid. I was older and my train set was electric but it was the same principle. There's something very satisfying about watching miniaturised life. Playing God; looking over suburban fences with total impunity.

I wondered whatever happened to my old train set.

That weekend I found some model train parts at a garage sale just up the road. The carriages were battered and the wheels were bent or missing. There was an engine that looked pretty good, but the wheels were jammed solid. There were a few bits of rusty track and half a dozen miniature people who were missing limbs or had teeth marks on their torsos. I got the whole lot for $25. A bargain.

Once I'd started the collection more bits and pieces came my way. Almost enough to start a layout, a miniature, mismatched, broken-down little world. I put a few bits of track together and hobbled together a train, to show Christopher.

'I like Thomas,' he said, unimpressed.

'I like Thomas too. When you're older you'll want something a bit more realistic though, a bit more complex.'

'I like Thomas.'

Then I saw an ad in the local paper for a model train fair and I sensed that my little collection was about to grow. And so would Christopher's interest.

The fair was fantastic. There was so much stuff, most of it pre-loved. Lots and lots of old bits and pieces from my childhood.

My favourite loco and a few of my favourite carriages. Strangely, there were very few children there besides Christopher. There were no women and I was one of the youngest men. Apparently it's a hobby for seriously middle-aged men.

Christopher found a few Thomas bits to supplement his collection, and then he helped me find bits for mine. We grabbed cottages and tunnels, carriages, trees, track; whatever caught our fancy – within reason. Most of it was hellishly expensive and even buying mainly second hand bits, many of them pretty shabby, we managed to spend nearly $500. It was great to be doing something with Christopher, something we both enjoyed. Together we'd build our own little world.

Once we got our bits home we tried to assemble them into some sort of sequence. We bought a huge sheet of chipboard and screwed and glued it onto an old table in the spare room. We drew where we thought we'd build mountains and rivers, then placed our collection of bits and pieces where we thought they'd best fit.

Christopher was happy with the layout but I was bothered – deeply bothered. We hadn't thought about scale when we'd chosen pieces and now we had a selection of small, smaller, bigger and almost small. It was aesthetically displeasing. Although Christopher didn't seem at all bothered by having a person standing next to a house that was shorter than them.

'He's a giant,' explained Christopher.

'Then why doesn't he live over there, where the giant houses are?'

'He's visiting his friend.'

'I suppose he could be.'

My discomfort at our little world only increased when Michelle returned from the supermarket. Lugging in bags of groceries she stopped mid-stride when she saw our layout.

'Look,' said Christopher, proudly pointing. 'There's the school, there's the shop, and that's where Thomas goes.'

Wow, that's a hell of a sentence for a three year old to rattle off – but Michelle seemed unimpressed. 'How much did all this cost?'

'Quite a bit.'

She bent down to look under the board. She pushed up one corner and made a sort of grunting noise. Not a good sign.

'What's up, Mum?'

Michelle stood up slowly. She glared at the bottle of PVA, then at me. She spoke in a strangled monotone. 'You can put the shopping away, Peter, I'm going for a walk.'

'What's up?'

'That's my mother's table you've just ruined.'

'We never use it.'

'That's my mother's table.'

'I'm sorry. I'll take the board off.'

'Don't bother,' she shrieked, slamming the door and marching off.

I turned to Christopher. 'Please take all the train bits off while I put the shopping away. We'll find another table to put it on.'

'Mum said don't bother.'

'I know what she said but I don't think she meant it.'

'Nanna's not going to use the table. She's dead. A long time ago.'

'Yes, it was a long time ago but maybe not long enough.'

So we left the layout screwed onto Nanna's table. I wasn't game to ask Michelle again and Christopher's logic seemed much sounder. Christopher and I built some hills together and painted a river but much of the fun had gone from the process. Michelle seemed distant and often explosive.

The *table incident*, as I labeled it, wasn't an isolated case. Something was bothering her and I seemed to be nothing but an irritation. We took to sleeping in separate rooms most nights. We're all restless sleepers and often wander the house at night but it seemed like every morning Michelle would be in a different bed to me. Sometimes Christopher would be in bed with me and sometimes with her. It was almost as though were a divorced couple sharing custody.

I quizzed Christopher, 'Do you think Mum's acting a bit strange lately?'

'No.'

'A bit distant?'

'No.'

'Maybe it's just me.'

We didn't work on our layout much even though I knew where to get all the bits I needed. There were fairs every month, there were a dozen specialist shops to go to and there was a huge amount available on ebay: a massive, monstrous, mind-boggling multitude. But I was bothered by two things.

One, Michelle's mother's table. If I had to retrieve it at some stage I had to do so before I added too much weight to the layout.

Two, the scale. I could go for an N scale, tiny little pieces which would allow me to build a whole suburb or more. That'd be monstrously expensive, but a world in which the people were so tiny that you couldn't see what they were up to in their little houses held a certain appeal.

Or I could go for an HO scale, which seemed the most sensible. The figures were big enough to make out, but small enough that even the naked figures – and why anyone would make naked figures less than an inch tall was beyond me – lacked any eroticism.

Or O scale, the big ones that Christopher liked. People in this scale were big enough to have facial expressions, to live secret lives.

Then there were the pieces didn't seem to be any of these scales. The larger than life and the smaller than life. Where did they fit into the scale of things?

I was leaning towards HO scale. It was close to the OO scale of my childhood set – so close that the two scales could often be mixed on the same layout. Some nights when I couldn't sleep I'd put away all the larger and smaller pieces and arrange an HO layout of sorts. I had dozens of HO items on my watch list on ebay but couldn't bring myself to commit to them. But every time I pruned our layout of the too large and the too small Christopher rebuilt it the next day in its mismatched glory.

What bothered me about the layout also bothered me about our marriage. Small things began to bother me just as much as big things, often more so. Why couldn't everything be just the right size? It seemed Michelle and I had drifted apart almost too far to ever return. Her mother's table was only one of many subjects we could no longer discuss.

Slowly I convinced myself that Michelle was having an affair. There were a few clues, but they seemed contradictory. I'd seen her once on an internet dating site. She became very secretive about her work, at Christopher's kinder. Up until recently she'd always spoken about it: what she'd done, what Christopher had done. New stories every day. But now, nothing. She had this intense on-again, off-again friendship with Elizabeth, our neighbour, and she seemed to be paying an unhealthy amount of attention to our neighbour on the other side.

One morning, after an especially bad night's sleep, I confronted her.

'Fat Rat,' I said. Let's see how she reacts to that. That was the name she'd used on the internet dating site. Or something like that. Something to do with rotund rodents.

'What?'

'You heard.'

'Ungainly Giraffe. The only reason I'm fat is because I'm too fucking exhausted to go to the gym.'

Doh! *Plump Mouse*. That was the name she used. Too late to hit her with that, I'd lost the element of surprise. I'd have to spring it on her another time.

'You can get Christopher ready for kinder. I'm going for a run. Apparently I need to lose some weight.' And with that she stormed out.

She was no plumper than usual. Why so sensitive about her weight all of a sudden? Isn't that what people do when they're having an affair? Get fit? Get their bodies into some sort of shape? And was she really going for a run?

I quizzed Christopher as I helped him dress and breakfast. 'Do you think Mum's acting a bit strange?'

'Maybe. A bit. I think she's sad.'

'Maybe she is. Maybe I'm sad too.'

'Don't be sad, Dad.' He gave me a big hug and I almost burst into tears.

That night Michelle asked me if I'd make dinner.

'Sure. Are you going out?'

'Yes.'

'For a run?'

'No.'

'Where to?'

'Next door, if you must know.'

'Elizabeth's?'

'No.'

'Frodo's?'

'His name's Dave.'

'The dwarf?'

'Frodo was a hobbit, not a dwarf. See you in a couple of hours.' She nipped my cheek, like a savage little dog, and then walked off to give Christopher a proper kiss and a proper goodbye.

'What's a hobbit?' asked Christopher.

'A grubby, hairy, little man, with oil under his fingernails and a fridge completely filled with beer.'

Was I jealous? Surely not.

'But don't call Dave a hobbit to his face. He won't like it,' I warned Christopher.

I made us spaghetti bolognaise while I watched Michelle through the window, wiping down Dave's cupboards and mopping his floor. I looked around our kitchen. We could do with a spring clean. If she's got that much energy she could do our place. But I'll keep that thought to myself. Housework had become a very touchy subject. At least she was in his kitchen, not his bedroom. On cue she disappeared from sight and Dave was nowhere to be seen either. Surely they wouldn't do anything while I'm next door – while Christopher's next door – making her dinner. They couldn't. Could they? The wooden spoon I was stirring the sauce with snapped in my hand and I had to grab another.

Michelle reappeared, looked our way and waved. I held up my hand in the traditional *dinner's ready in five minutes* signal. She signaled back with two hands, closing the fingers then reopening them. Twenty minutes. Hmm.

I caught her attention and signaled *why?*

She waggled her fingers in a way that might or might not mean *party.*

Party? I waggled back. *Why?*

She pulled her blouse off her shoulder and lifted her bra strap. What the hell did that mean? *Strippers?* Why clean the house for strippers? Surely they're used to disgusting bachelor flats?

Michelle did a *walking away* sign then turned her back on me and went back to mopping.

Christopher and I ate our meal while I watched Dave's window. Michelle continued to mop and wipe while Dave did what exactly? Sat on his couch masturbating and swilling beer? He's a nice guy. I know he's a nice guy. And Michelle's loyal and very moral. More than that, she's very discriminating. If she was having an affair it wouldn't be with Dave. Not a chance. Yet still I felt uneasy. Her absence gnawed at me. It scraped at my submerged jealousy like fingernails down a blackboard.

When she did come home, half an hour later, I warmed her dinner and tried not to comment, tried not to ask. But I couldn't help myself.

'Why?'

'Because his place is dirty.'

'So is ours. Why not here?'

She glared at me. Best not go there.

I scanned her clothing for dirty hand prints but couldn't spot any. 'Can't he afford a cleaning lady?'

Actually we could afford a cleaning lady. Why hadn't I thought of that before?

'He doesn't just want cleaning; he wants moral support.'

'I'd like some moral support too.'

'You've got Christopher.'

'I'd like you. I used to have you. And now I've lost you to that beer-swilling dwarf.'

'Hobbit,' Christopher corrected.

'Whatever.'

Michelle laughed.

'I don't think it's funny, Michelle. He's a grubby little man with some nasty little habits. He's always got women's underwear hanging on his line and I've never seen a woman in there once. Never. Except for you.'

'Are you jealous?'

'No. Yes. Maybe. I don't know, Michelle. I just don't know any more. I don't know you anymore.'

'If you must know, I'm helping him clean up for the party on Friday night.'

'Party?'

'Yes party.' Michelle tapped the calendar on the wall: *Intimo party at Dave's.*

That stunned me. It took a while to work out which part I found most offensive. 'You're going, I assume?'

'Of course I'm going.'

'And getting undressed in front of him and all his mates? Why the hell is the party being held there? Why does he need moral support? And why are you so secretive all the time?'

'Which question do you want answered first?'

'All of them.'

'Okay but first let me eat, I'm starving. And can you put Christopher to bed? Thanks.'

I hate it when she's so reasonable when I'm so angry. 'Okay. Come on little feller, time for bed.'

'Bedtime for hobbits?'

'No, not yet. Bedtime for little boys though.'

'I'm a big boy.'

'And big boys.'

I got Christopher to bed, practicing my relaxation techniques, and sat down to a civilised conversation with Michelle.

'The party's being held at Dave's because his sister's place is being renovated.'

'Okay, that makes sense. Sort of. He's a pig though. You know he doesn't even have any food in his fridge, just beer.'

'He has a separate fridge for food. He's actually a very good cook.'

That took me by surprise. Deep breath. Count to five. 'I find the idea, Michelle, of Dave and his mates perving at a bunch of suburban housewives – one of them my wife – a bit disturbing.'

Michelle laughed. 'Dave's mates won't be there and it's unlikely that Dave will be there either.'

That took me by surprise too. 'Why should Dave even bother cleaning up, then? Why doesn't he just let his sister do it?'

'Because he has a new girlfriend and he wants to impress her.'

That really stumped me. The whole tower of outrage I'd built was tumbling floor by floor. 'A real girlfriend? But. But, but. But the underwear on his washing line?'

'He's taken it down. It was just for show. Just so his mates would think he had a string of casual girlfriends who'd stay the night and leave in a hurry in the morning. Now he actually has a girlfriend, he doesn't need to do that.'

I had difficulty imagining Dave with a girlfriend. Even though I'd imagined him with my wife only an hour earlier.

'But you? You're not the same, Michelle. You're distant. You're secretive.'

She melted into my arms, her eyes leaking tiny driblets. 'You're right. I am distant. I am secretive. But it's got nothing to do with you, nothing. I swear. I'm sorry, against my better judgment, I'm sworn to secrecy. One day I'll tell you everything, I promise. But not today.'

We held each other and cried into each other's shoulders.

'Thanks.'

'And the name I think you were searching for this morning was *Plump Mouse*. I was *Plump Mouse* for one deranged night. But I deleted that identity as soon as I could.'

'You'll always be my plump mouse,' I said, squeezing her buttock. 'Sorry, I meant no offence. I didn't mean you were fat.'

She laughed. 'No offence taken.'

'You realise that Intimo's a scam. That the hundred dollar bras are no better than twenty dollar bras you can buy at any department store.'

'I realise that they're overpriced and that the person selling them makes a good commission, if that's what you mean.'

'That's not quite what I meant. You know that I can get you three bras that are probably just as good for ten bucks from Laverton Market.'

'Do you remember the lawnmower you bought from Laverton Market, which you thought was such a bargain?'

'It was fine once Dave fixed it.'

'And you want Dave fixing my $3.33 bras?'

'Probably not.'

'He's a really sweet guy, Peter. And he really likes you. He's got something he wants to give you, something really special. He's just cleaning it up, and he'll bring it over shortly.'

Half an hour later Dave came to our door holding a beautifully cleaned, polished and meticulously oiled, HO scale, 16 wheel steam loco. 'I've had this since I was a kid. I'm not doing anything with it. So I'd like you to have it.'

'Wow, thank you. It's magnificent. How much do I owe you?'

'Nothing. It's yours.'

'A couple of slabs at least.'

'I don't drink much beer these days.'

'I'll just borrow it. You may want it back some day.'

'No. I insist. Keep it. It's yours.'

'Thank you. Do you have any idea what this is worth, Dave? How about a bottle of champagne? A really nice bottle.'

'Sure, Cherie would like that. And thanks for the loan of your wife.'

'Any time, Dave. Any time.'

'I appreciate it. Pete. It's a real sacrifice. A real show of trust.'

'Well I used to borrow your lawnmower…'

'That's not the same, Peter. A wife and a lawnmower are not on the same scale.'

The next night Dave brought his girlfriend, Cherie, over to introduce to us. She was tiny and very cute. Very hobbit-like – although I kept that thought to myself. They made a gorgeous couple. And when they left, Michelle and I started serious work on my layout, giving Dave's loco pride of place. Michelle was fine about using the table as a base: 'It's good to see it being put to use. Mum would approve.'

I made a separate layout for Christopher, in a jumble of different scales. But mine was pure HO. Nothing was too big or too small. It was all just right. I even found an HO scale Goldilocks with three bears.

We've been lucky in some ways with our neighbours. On the one side we've got Dave, a real bloke, who loves his cars, motorbikes and beer. Peter thinks he's rough and crude, and I guess he is a bit. But he's very sweet. And now that he's got a girlfriend – a fiancée in fact – he's even sweeter than ever. I think they're going to move soon, which will be a real shame.

Elizabeth, on the other side, seemed to be a great friend too. She was lively and vivacious and very friendly, although sometimes a little moody. We've been very close, off and on, over the years. But she's secretive, dishonest and very deceitful. I don't want Christopher going over there, or playing with her kids and I don't want Peter spending any time with her. But she shows no signs of moving.

Elizabeth was very kind to me when we moved in. I was pregnant and starting to panic about my ability, or inability, to mother. She was reassuring and made me feel much more confidant. I shared everything with her: all my little secrets, all my little fears, all the uncertainties I felt about things Peter had said or done, or not said and not done. And she shared her life with me, although I did notice there were things she didn't share. Little secrets, or maybe bigger secrets, that she kept to herself.

Her son, Patrick was in prep when we moved in and her daughter, Paula, in grade two. She'd have them over to stay sometimes, although there seemed to be no regular pattern. Her ex lived nearby, only a few streets away, and the separation seemed fairly amicable. She claimed he was a heavy drinker, though I never saw him have more than a beer or two and I saw her rottenly drunk on several occasions.

She claimed he made access really difficult for her, and maybe he did. But I also saw her screwing him around on several occasions while she changed plans or changed them back again at short notice.

But I put my misgivings to one side. We were friends. Good friends. And friends are willing to forgive and to pretend not to notice things. Looking back there was plenty I should have noticed.

She worked at the kindergarten near us and she persuaded me to get a job there too. I had actually trained as a teacher but never did anything with the qualification. I decided I didn't like kids much and would much rather work in retail, selling shoes and clothes to those kids' mothers. But now that I have a child, now that I'm a mother, I realise that kids are really sweet – until we poison them – and that mothers can be pretty awful.

So I started at the *early learning centre*, as they like to be called, a few weeks before Christopher. He'd been on a waiting list for a year but I virtually walked straight in, with no practical experience at all. I can't help thinking there's something wrong with it being easier to get a job at a kindergarten than it is to get your child in.

It was fantastic. I wouldn't even call it work. I spent my days with my best friend, my special boy and heaps of other kids who were all almost as sweet as Christopher. And for the first few weeks I was in heaven. But the more time I spent with Elizabeth the more I noticed things. She'd flirt terribly with some of the fathers that came in. She'd giggle and bat her eyelids and touch them. A couple of times I saw her passing notes to one of the dads. That was unusual. There was an area by the door for notes for parents. Each kid had their own slot. Each slot was labeled with the child's name. There was no need to pass notes directly to the parents.

I asked the other teacher, 'Do you think Elizabeth is a bit too friendly with Mike, Amy's dad?'

'What do you mean by *too* friendly?'

'I'm not sure what I mean.'

'Their kids go to the same school. Mike's wife is Paula's teacher. I guess they've got a lot in common.'

'I guess they have.'

But still I felt uncomfortable. They seemed to have too much in common. I asked Elizabeth, but she got very evasive and stopped visiting for several weeks. She'd barely even speak to me. Then suddenly she changed. She started dropping in again. She bought me an expensive pair of earrings and a beautiful dress – because I was such a special friend – and everything went back to "normal" and I forgot my suspicions.

Then one morning I was up early, unusually even earlier than Peter, and I decided to take Gemma for a walk while Peter slept in. It was six, or maybe a little later – quite dark but light enough to recognise the man sneaking out of Elizabeth's. It was Mike. Not just someone who looked like Mike. It was Mike. There is no doubt in my mind. I would have spoken to him, but I was too embarrassed. I watched him walk around the around the corner and get into his car. I noted his registration number as he drove off.

Once Peter was up I went next door to confront Elizabeth.

'It was an awful mistake,' she said. 'We'd both been drinking. I couldn't let him drive. I offered him the couch to sleep on. But he got up in the night. He must have been disoriented. He ended up in my bed. I'm so embarrassed. I feel awful. Please don't tell anyone. It'll never happen again. Please, I beg you, don't tell a soul.'

'It can't happen again, Elizabeth. It can't. Think of your kids. Think of his wife, his kids. It's not just the two of you.'

'I know. It won't happen again.'

'I have to see Mike and Amy at kinder. I have to talk to them and try to look them in the eye. I don't want to be part of your lies.'

'It won't happen again, Michelle.'

And maybe it didn't happen again, for a little while. Or maybe she was just more careful. We didn't see Mike's car. I gave Peter the registration number and told him to look out for it, saying that it belonged to a shifty looking character I'd seen hanging around. Peter's often out walking early in the morning or late at night and, unlike me, he's very observant.

I didn't notice that Mike had bought a new car or that Elizabeth slipped notes into Amy's slot when she saw it was Mike picking her up. And she bought me more presents, jewelry and clothing. She seemed such a good friend.

Then one day I saw Elizabeth passing a note to Mike, I noticed their hands touching too long, their eyes holding too long, and I knew they were at it.

Again I confronted her.

'You mustn't tell anyone,' she made me promise. My kids would die of shame.'

So I told no one – not even Peter. And that hurt. I built a barrier between us to protect her and to protect her kids. I became an accomplice. And once I knew, Elizabeth didn't have to hide it any more. She could flaunt it, to me, while hiding it from everyone else. It was only then that I realised just how deceitful she was. It became increasingly difficult to look her in the eye and increasingly difficult to work with her.

It was months later that I discovered that Mike wasn't the only kindergarten dad she was shagging or that the presents she gave me – for being such a "special friend" – were unwanted gifts from her lovers.

I was furious. I bundled the gifts together and threw them at her feet. 'I can't be your friend anymore, Elizabeth.'

'Just like that? You just flick a switch and our friendship's over?'

'Yes. Just like that. It's called morals. But you wouldn't understand that.'

'You're right. I don't.'

'And why with someone who's connected to your kids?'

'I guess because it's convenient.'

'Wouldn't it have been more convenient to have stayed with your husband? He lived in the same frigging house as you. What's more convenient than that?'

'He won't put up with it anymore.'

'And neither will I.'

We rarely spoke after that. But we still had to work together and we still had to live next to each other. And she still invited Christopher in for biscuits and still asked Peter to come in to change her light bulbs or help her connect up her new TV.

'Keep away from them,' I warned her.

'I miss our cups of tea together, Michelle. Our little chats. It's such a pity we can't be friends.'

'You've got no shame, Elizabeth.'

'That's where you're wrong. I'm full of shame. Absolutely full of it. There's no room for any other emotion.'

'Except lust.'

'That's just a symptom, Michelle. Just a diversion.'

'I don't care. I don't want Peter diverted. I don't Christopher perverted.'

'Don't be such a fucking prude. Everyone's doing it Michelle. This street's like Wisteria Lane – but without the murders. I could tell you stories that would make your hair curl.'

'I don't want curly hair.'

'You must be about the only faithful spouse in the street, Michelle. Even Peter's at it. I've seen him with that little brunette. The one with the black and white dog. I've seen them cuddling and canoodling. I've seen her melting into his arms.'

'Ramona's a sick woman.'

'Why, because she fancies Peter? He's not a bad catch.'

'No. Because she's dying of fucking cancer.'

'So she says.'

'Fuck off.'

I found it very difficult to continue working with Elizabeth after that. I could have got another job – easily. It was moving Christopher that was the hard part. The waiting lists for all the centres near us were a year or more. And I couldn't leave him there with her.

I couldn't tell Peter. Partly because I'd sworn to Elizabeth that I'd tell no one, and partly because Peter would ask – quite reasonably – why I hadn't told him earlier. And Elizabeth's comments about Peter and Ramona bothered me – bothered me deeply. I didn't know if I could trust him. I didn't even know if I could trust myself. I was lost in a land of lies and deceit and could see no way out.

Then one afternoon I left my purse at work. I didn't realise until after dinner.

'I've got to go back,' I told Peter.

'It'll still be there in the morning. It's a kindergarten, not a pub.'

'It's got my credit cards and everything. I know it'll be safe but I won't sleep. I'll be back soon.'

I let myself in, thinking, that's strange, the lights are on. I'm sure I checked them all when I locked up. And the alarm wasn't set, either. Very odd. It wasn't all the lights, just a few. Not enough that it was obvious from the street but enough that you could walk through the rooms without banging into tables and chairs. I thought I heard voices, very faintly. Not really talking, just mumbling.

I should have left and called the police. Or maybe I should have called out. But I did neither. I picked up my purse, checked the contents and put it in my bag. Then instead of leaving, I made my way towards the voices. They, whoever they were, were in the toilet – the kids' toilet. The one with the tiny little sinks and the tiny little toilets. There, sitting on one of the toilets was one of the kinder dads – Bruce? Bevan? I can't remember his name. His kid hadn't been coming for long. And there, predictably, squatting astride him was Elizabeth, her knickers around one ankle, grunting and moaning amongst the trappings of innocent childhood – finger paintings, clay models and wooden building blocks.

I could never go back there. Christopher could never go back.

I undid the kinder keys from my key ring, threw them on the floor, set the alarm then ran out, slamming the door behind me.

I raced home, way over the speed limit and fumbled with my keys on our doorstep until Peter opened the door.

I fell in bawling my eyes out.

'What's up?' Peter asked, trying to put his arms around me.

I pushed him aside. 'Nothing.'

'Okay.'

Then I walked back to him and collapsed in his arms. 'I'll tell you later. Can you please put Christopher to bed?'

'Are you okay, Mum?'

I picked Christopher up and held him to me. 'Yes, thanks honey, I'm fine. I'm better than I have been in months. I just need to do something then I'll come and check on you. Okay?'

'Okay.'

Then, as Peter put Christopher to bed I sat down and typed. I typed like a mad woman, smashing the keys far harder than was required. Pounding away till my wrists and hands ached; churning out about six hundred words in ten minutes. I printed it off, unchecked, put it on the table for Peter, gave Christopher a goodnight kiss then sat down to a large glass of straight whisky.

'That's my best twelve-year-old scotch,' Peter complained when he came in. 'The Aldi scotch is just as good when you're angry.'

'I'm not angry. I'm elated.'

'Okay.'

Peter read the letter, tsk-tsking softly under his breath as he worked his way through the many typos. When he'd finished, he sat back, his fingers intertwined.

'What do you think?' I asked.

'Hmm. I don't think this is for the local paper. I think you should be aiming higher. Send it to *The Age*, *The Australian*, the big boys. I don't suppose you got a photo of them at it?'

'No. I didn't get a photo. And I wouldn't send it to any paper. It would hurt too many people. Too many innocent people. I just wrote it to vent my rage – and to explain to you what I should have told you months ago.'

'Christopher's happy there. You were happy there. If she leaves…'

'No. I could never go back. Not after what I've seen. I could never let Christopher back there.

'Maybe she should be exposed. She should be stopped.'

'Not by me. I want nothing to do with her. I don't want her in my life. I think we should move.' I took another sip of scotch then handed the glass to Peter. I don't actually drink.

I crumpled the letter, threw it in the recycling then went back to the computer to write, a little more slowly and a little more thoughtfully, my letter of resignation.

When Christopher was two or three he started reading signs. Well not actually reading them – but inferring their meaning from the context.

'Look, Dad, chip shop.' he'd say when we saw a sign for McDonald's.

By the time he was three-and-a-half, he was an expert.

He was a little confused by the *No Trucks* signs we saw in Yarraville.

'Why don't people want trucks?'

'They just don't want hundreds of them driving past their house every day.'

'Trucks are good. Trucks take toys to toy shops.'

'Absolutely. I agree completely. But some people like to buy property cheaply – because of the hundreds of trucks that go past – then complain bitterly to stop the trucks so the value of their property goes up.'

That stumped him. 'But trucks are good.'

'Yes, trucks are good.'

'You don't like trains.'

'I do like trains. I just don't like big goods trains rumbling past our house at three in the morning. They didn't tell us about that.'

'I'm asleep.'

'Yes, so am I until they go past.'

'Let's make a *No Trains* sign. For night time.'

'That's a good idea.'

And it was a good idea. A great idea. Of course it wouldn't actually stop anything, but that didn't seem to bother the residents of Yarraville.

We made a beautiful sign and Michelle helped us paint it. It was fluorescent orange so it would show up better at night. We put it on a pole and hammered it into place, very satisfied.

'We need another one,' said Christopher, 'For the other way.' So we made another. 'What else?' asked Christopher, after we'd hammered it into place. 'What else needs signs?'

'I think that's enough for now.'

'Snakes!' yelled Christopher. 'Let's make *No Snakes* signs.'

'Snakes can't read.' I'd had enough of making signs.

'They might.'

'They might. But it's not likely. And snakes are good. They eat mice. If there were no snakes around here we'd be overrun by mice.'

'I like mice.'

'I quite like mice too.'

'Snakes might bite Gemma.'

'I suppose so.' I'd told him that dozens of times. I'd only myself to blame.

'They might kill Gemma.'

'Yes, you're right. They might.' So we made signs – eight of them – and put them up in the wasteland across the tracks. Then I went to bed. Weekends can be so exhausting.

Snakes and Mice

The next morning when I was emptying our kitchen scraps into the compost I saw movement from the corner of my eye as I opened the bin. A flash of grey with a long pink tail. I put down the bucket of scraps and grabbed a trowel but the mouse was long gone. I was about to tip in the scraps when I noticed a little pile of babies. A litter of seven or eight: tiny, pink and helpless, maybe a couple of days old.

What to do with them? Crush them? Bury them? Or save them? I scooped them onto the trowel as gently as I could, careful not to break their tiny limbs. I carried them across the road and set them down over the fence, in the long grass by the railway lines.

The little bastards would likely turn up in our house within a week. Or maybe they'd be eaten by birds, cats or snakes. Maybe it would have been kinder if I'd killed them. But I couldn't.

The next day they were gone.

Had I done the right thing? It played on my mind for days.

I dreamt of helpless baby mice being gobbled up by an enormous snake. Snakes were on my mind all week. We had a lot of snakes in our area in the summer. Once Gemma walked straight over a tiger snake. It wasn't moving so I thought it must have been dead. Just as I was about to step over it it slithered away. Scared the crap out of me. And the woman who lived behind us lost her dog to a snake a few years back, in their own back yard. Nasty.

And that was a dog – a big dog. What chance would a mouse have?

Snakes and Mice

It seems life is a constant battle between snakes and mice – a battle the mice can never win. And the snake that bothered me most was Elizabeth, the snake next door.

She'd been a good friend to Michelle for a couple of years – or so it seemed. Then she'd turned. She'd crushed Michelle, swallowed her whole, then shat her out.

Michelle and Elizabeth had worked together at Christopher's kindergarten, until Michelle could take no more. Then she'd left, pulling Christopher out. She claimed they liked being at home together – and they did – but I could tell that Christopher missed the social interaction. And so did Michelle.

And now Michelle and Elizabeth wouldn't even acknowledge each other.

Yes, I thought, *No Snakes* signs are very appropriate. But we've put them in the wrong place.

And snakes weren't the only reptile bothering me, there was also a dragon. Michelle's sister, Amanda rang almost every day, always when Michelle was out. She wouldn't leave a message, just, 'Tell her I rang.' And every time Michelle called back, she wasn't there.

I knew something was bothering her but she wouldn't tell me.

'I know you don't like me, Amanda. But you and Michelle keep missing each other. Give me some inkling of what's so urgent and I'll pass it on.'

'Just tell her I rang.'

'You can give the message to Christopher. I'll cover my ears, if need be.'

She hung up.

She was an unpleasant woman – irritating and irritated, poisonous and paranoid. She'd always look at me like I was some kind of pervert, like I was mentally undressing her. That is the last thing I would ever do. She claims I looked at her in the shower once. That was a complete mistake. I heard our shower and assumed it was Michelle. The shower's frosted glass – so it's not like I could actually see her. And I turned away the second she screamed.

God, even if I was stuck on a desert island for ten years, living on nothing but Viagra, I wouldn't look at her naked. She's as ugly as sin. Most human bodies follow a prescribed pattern: two arms, two legs, two breasts – of varying sizes and shapes admittedly – one stomach, and so forth. But not Amanda's. I've no idea how many breasts she has, if I had to place a bet I'd go with either three or one. And she has two stomachs. I can only speculate on what lurks within her ribcage. Five lungs and no heart? The idea that I'd want to perv on her is beyond laughable.

No Dragons, I thought. If only it was that simple.

'Amanda rang – again,' I told Michelle when she returned.

'Thanks. Something's up. I'll ring my brothers. I'm worried about her.'

'We're going to make another sign,' said Christopher. '*No Amandas.*'

Michelle glared at me.

'I didn't say a thing.'

'But you thought it. He's very sensitive. No, sweetie. We won't make a sign like that. Amanda would be very hurt.'

Michelle rang her brothers. It took nearly two hours, she has four and they all like to talk. They all assumed she knew about Amanda but they couldn't just say that once they had to repeat it a dozen times. Three of them said she was in hospital but they couldn't agree on what was wrong with her or which hospital.

Then Amanda called back and Michelle finally got the full story.

'She's very sick,' Michelle said. 'Very sick. Poor thing.'

'They why didn't she say?'

'She doesn't like to be pitied. She doesn't like to be defined by her sickness. I'm going to see her.'

'I'll come too,' said Christopher.

'Sure. She'd like that. She'd love to see you.'

What was Michelle thinking? It was Christopher's bedtime.

'Brush your teeth first, and put your pajamas on.'

'She's always been sick,' Michelle said as she stuffed things into her bag. 'As a baby she practically died, a couple of times. She's been opened up more times than anyone deserves. She's got massive scars.'

'God. I feel awful. I just thought she was ugly.'

'That's why she was so upset by the shower incident. She thought you'd seen her scars.'

'Why didn't you tell me?'

'I probably should have. Half her organs have been removed or tampered with. She can't have children, of course. She's lucky she's lived this long.'

'Poor thing. Give her my love.'

'I will.' And with that Michelle kissed me goodnight and left with Christopher.

I sat down feeling exhausted. I felt like I'd slain the dragon without even lifting a finger, and then discovered that the dragon wasn't dangerous or evil at all. It was just another mouse. A mouse in dragon's clothing.

Michelle and Christopher were gone for hours.

While they were gone I reworked a letter that Michelle had written, exposing Elizabeth's venomous nature. Michelle thought she'd deleted it but I'd kept a copy.

I put it in Elizabeth's letterbox. Like the signs, it would probably have no effect. But it gave me some satisfaction that I was doing something.

For the rest of the week Michelle and Christopher spent more time at the hospital than they did at home. I missed them terribly. One night while they were gone I could hear Elizabeth next door, entertaining one of her "friends". Someone's husband, no doubt. Someone who lived nearby. Someone whose kids went to the same school, or who went to the kindergarten where she worked. That was her style.

Snakes and Mice

I went out, in the dark of night, with an inadequate torch, to the wasteland, tripping over rocks and bits of junk, and wrenched out all the *No Snakes* signs that Christopher and I had planted. I threw them all over Elizabeth's fence, the tallest in the whole neighbourhood, six foot, with another foot of lattice on top. We should have known she was hiding something. The signs made a hell of a noise as they landed. But I didn't feel any better.

A little later I saw a man skulking out of her place, prematurely driven away, I imagine, by the clatter of signs. It was probably the principal of her kid's school.

Still I felt no better. It was time to confront her.

Next day was Saturday and I could hear she was home. Perfect.

Except Michelle decided she wanted to go to the hospital by herself. 'Please,' she pleaded. 'I've been with Christopher twenty-four seven. I need a break. And I thought you'd want to spend time with him.'

How could I refuse? But it meant that Christopher had to be part of the confrontation. It couldn't wait another day.

'You mustn't tell Mum what we're doing.'

'Okay.'

'We're going to see Elizabeth but you have to promise, not to tell Mum.'

'I promise.'

It seemed cruel to expect a kid of less than four to commit to absolute silence – but it had to be done.

Snakes and Mice

We needed an alibi. Just in case Michelle came back early and caught us there. I picked up a gardening fork and we went next door. 'What's that for?' Christopher asked.

'In case we see some snakes. I need this to chase them.'

I opened Elizabeth's gate and we went in. Christopher looked at the pile of *No Snakes* signs scattered in her front garden then looked to me for an explanation.

'Not a word to Mum. No matter what you see or what you hear, not a word.'

'Okay.'

I knocked on her door and she opened it. She'd been drinking and it wasn't even ten o'clock. She looked at the fork in my hand and laughed.

'It looks like you've come to run me out of town.'

'I have.'

'And with little Christopher too. How sweet. How are you, Christopher?'

'I'm okay.'

'Would you like a biscuit?'

'No thanks.'

'He's well trained isn't he? And he has such an amazing vocabulary. What new words have you learnt, Christopher?'

'Venomous.'

'Wow. That's a mouthful. And how about you, Peter? What's new in your world?' Her voice was calm but her eyes were crazed. She looked utterly demented.

'I assume you've read the article I left in your letterbox?'

'No. I always throw out the junk mail unread.'

That threw me. 'Um, I can reprint it.'

'I was joking, Peter. Yes I read it. And I read the signs you threw over my fence. I assume they mean something.'

'I want you to leave, Elizabeth.'

'I like it here.'

'We don't like you here. We want you gone.'

'We!' she snapped. 'Who's *we*? You and Christopher?'

'Me and Michelle. Leave Christopher out of this!'

'You're the one who's dragged him into it.'

I put my hand on Christopher's shoulder. He was scared. He was shaking. But he stood his ground. 'Michelle would never expose you. She's far too concerned about the effect on your kids. But I would. And you know I can get that article published.'

'You're bluffing.' She slammed the door in our face.

I looked at Christopher. 'Are you okay?'

'I'm okay.'

'Okay.'

I knocked. Then knocked again, pounding as hard as I could.

Elizabeth threw the door open, a glass of red wine in her hand. She sloshed it as she spoke. 'You're no better than me, Peter. I've seen your little girlfriend. Little Ramona.'

'Ramona's nice,' said Christopher.

'I bet she's nice. Sweet, sweet little Ramona, she always wants to come over. Isn't that a Ramones song?'

'I've got no idea, and frankly I don't care. We're talking about you, not Ramona.'

'You fucking hypocrite! You're fucking your little Ramona but it's different when I'm at it.'

I took a deep breath.

'Ramona, unlike you, Elizabeth, understands that I'm married and respects that.'

'Bullshit.'

'It's not even about sex, Elizabeth. We don't care if you screw your brains out. It's about the lies and the deceit that you've dragged Michelle into. She's had to face the wives and the kids of your victims.'

'Victims?' She laughed, squawking like a crow. 'They're hardly victims.'

'I just want you gone, Elizabeth. You're only renting, you can move. I'll even contribute to your moving costs.'

I hadn't intended to say that but it made sense. 'Either you're gone by the end of the month or that story goes to print. You'll never work with children again.'

'You're bluffing.'

'Try me.'

'I like it here,' she repeated, then started to cry. Great, just what I needed. 'I'll probably never work with children again anyway. Your wife has made things very difficult for me. They've asked me to leave. The official line is that I'm leaving for personal reasons. But word gets around.'

'Then do something else.'

'Bastard.' She threw the last of her wine in my face then smashed the glass on her path. Christopher hid behind me and Gemma started barking for all she was worth.

'I've got a photo of you at it,' I snarled.

'Michelle deleted every shot she had of me.'

'She thought she had. But I kept one.'

'I don't believe you.'

'You can't see your face. But you can still tell it's you. You can see your tattoo.'

I was bluffing, but Elizabeth didn't know that. There was no photo. I didn't even know what her tattoo was of — but I knew where it was. I'd seen it one day, over our fence, when she was hanging out her washing, half dressed and half drunk, showing off the tattoo on her arse.

'I don't have much money, Peter. I can't afford to move. And I need to stay close to my kids.'

'I can help.'

'How much can you help?'

'I'm sure we can work something out.'

She stood stock still while a succession of emotions flashed across her features. Finally, to my relief, she settled on gratitude. 'Thanks. Thanks, Peter. I appreciate it. It's probably for the best.' She tried to hug me but I backed away.

We went home and Gemma licked Christopher's face, happy to see he was unharmed.

'Why do you want her to go, Dad?'

'Because she's a snake. And Mum's a mouse. And snakes eat mice.'

'That doesn't explain.'

'No. I'm sorry. That doesn't explain. But it'll have to do.'

'Okay.'

'You were fantastic today, mate. You were the best.'

'You too, Dad.'

Elizabeth rang an hour later, from a real estate agent, to check how much I'd contribute. We settled on $1,500. It's more than I'd wanted to spend but her new house was three kilometres away. I figured it was worth it. At some stage I'd have to explain to Michelle where the money had gone. Michelle would likely be outraged but I'd deal with that issue when it arose.

'What happened while I was gone?' Michelle asked, when she returned.

'Not much,' said Christopher. Wow. Where did he learn to lie like that?

'Did you see, Peter, there's a *For Lease* sign up next door?'

'At *her* place?'

'Yes. I can't believe it.'

'Wow. Neither can I. That's great news.'

'And I've heard she's leaving kinder at the end of next week.'

'I've heard that too. Maybe you could go back.'

Snakes and Mice

Fortunately Michelle didn't ask where I'd heard that bit of news.

'Hmm. Maybe. Once she's gone, completely gone.'

'Hey, how's Amanda?' I asked.

'She's good. Really good. She's getting out tomorrow. Do you want to come and see her tonight?'

'Yeah. That'd be nice.'

'I'm going to put the kettle on; I'm dying for a decent cuppa. Would you like one?'

'Sure.'

And once Michelle was out of earshot Christopher whispered, 'See Dad, the signs did work.'

By Myself

Today I'm four. I'm a big boy now. I can do everything myself. I can dress myself. I can make my own breakfast. I can brush my own teeth.

Yesterday we had my presents, because Dad's away today. He went on a plane to Queensland when it was still dark. I got up by myself and got myself ready for kinder all by myself. But Mum says it's much too early. Mum's on the phone. She'll be ages.

Gemma wants a walk. Dad takes her most days but he's not here. He forgot to take her yesterday, so she's extra frisky. Mum said we can take her later. But she's on the phone so I'll take her by myself.

I get a chair to get her lead. Otherwise I can't reach. I clip it on her but that's hard because she's dancing too much. I open the front door, that's hard too. I shut the door so strangers don't come in. I forgot to tell Mum. But she was busy and she doesn't like me talking when she's on the phone.

We have a new person next door. He's an old grandpa. He's a bit deaf, like Gemma. I can hear him in his garden and I say hello but he doesn't hear. Gemma pulls very hard. She likes walks. At the corner Gemma pulls even harder. I smack her and she stops pulling a bit. The ding-dongs are down, there's a train coming. When the train goes past we walk across the tracks and Gemma pulls so hard I fall over. Bad dog. She gets away and runs over the tracks.

I call her, 'Gemma, Gemma, Gemma,' but she keeps running. She still has the lead on. I run after her. I'm scared. Another train is coming and I can't see Gemma. Then I see her. She's a long way, past the pipes and nearly at the end of the horse paddock. I want to go back. I want Mum. But I can't leave Gemma behind.

Bad bad dog. I run after her but she's too fast. I hope a snake doesn't bite her. It's summer and that's when snakes come out.

My knee hurts where I fell over. And my hands. One hand is bleeding. I want a Band-Aid. And I'm tired but Gemma's gone. And it's my fault. I call her, 'Gemma, Gemma, Gemma,' but she can't hear. She's a bit deaf.

I'm tired and it's a long way and I can't leave Gemma. That's what Dad says when she runs away. We can't leave Gemma. She went past the horse paddock to the bunny paddock. She's running to the spiky bit and that's a long way away. And very very spiky. I don't want to go there. I'm crying. I don't want to cry but I am.

I'm four now. I can do nearly everything. But I can't find Gemma.

Then someone calls me. 'Christopher!'

It's Mum. 'Mum!'

But it's not Mum. It's Ramona and Ivy.

'Where's your dad, Christopher?'

'He's in Queensland.'

'Where's your mum?'

"She's at home. She's on the phone.'

'You're by yourself?'

'And Gemma. But Gemma's gone. She's in the spiky bit.'

'Ivy. Go and find Gemma.'

Ivy doesn't go. She just licks my hand. She licks the blood off.

'That works in TV shows,' Ramona says. She gets a phone out of her pocket. 'Do you know your home phone number?'

'No.'

'Do you know your dad's mobile number?'

'Gemma has our phone number, on her tag.'

'That won't help us much. Do you know your dad's mobile number?'

'No.'

'I wish I'd got it. Which is your house?'

I point, 'Over there.'

'That's not far.'

'It is because we have to go to the ding-dongs. We have to go around.'

'I'll take you home.'

'No. We can't leave Gemma.'

'I'm sorry, we have to leave Gemma.'

I cry again. I don't want to but I have to. 'Carry me.'

'I'll carry you a little way but I'm not very strong.' Ramona bends down and I climb on her back. 'You're very heavy,' she says.

'No. I'm only eighteen kilos. That's not much.'

'You're right. That's not much, but it's a lot for me.'

'Are you still sick?'

'Yes. I'm always sick.'

'Are you going to die?'

'Not today.'

By Myself

'What if a snake bites Gemma?'

'We'll get you home first. Then we can look for Gemma.'

Ramona carries me to the pipes. She puts me down and sits on a pipe. 'Are you tired?'

'Yes. I'm very tired. We'll have to rest a minute.'

'But we have to go home.'

'I know.'

'And we have to get Gemma.'

'I know.'

Ramona looks very sick. 'Don't die.'

'I won't.'

I try to sit on the pipe next to Ramona but it's very high. She helps me get up. Then she stands up and says, 'Let's go.' She holds my hand, the sore hand. And we start walking. When we're near our house but across the tracks and the pipes Ramona climbs over the two pipes and helps me over. When we get to the five pipes we can't go over. One pipe is too high.

'Let's go under.'

Under the pipes is a bit spiky and a bit dirty. Ramona doesn't want to go under but she does. I hold her hand. We walk right up to the train tracks. Ramona is very tired. She rests her hand or my shoulder and calls out, 'Michelle. Michelle!' She only calls it twice, she's so tired.

That's a good idea. I call out too. 'Mum! Mum! Mum!' and Mum comes to the door. She's crying but she smiles when she sees me. And I cry too but I'm smiling as well.

Mum runs to the fence and tries to climb over but it's too high. So she runs to the ding-dongs then over the tracks and the rocks and the muddy bits till she gets to us. It's hard for her to run. She cuddles me and laughs and cries and talks at super-speed. 'Are you okay? I didn't even know you were gone. That's very naughty to go out on your own.' She squeezes me and squeezes me. 'My little baby, thank God you're safe.'

'I'm not a baby.'

'No you're not. My big adventurous boy.'

I show Mum my sore hand and she kisses it better. 'Thank God you're safe,' she says again.

'You don't even believe in God.'

'Maybe today I do.' Then she talks to Ramona at super-speed. 'Thank you so much. You must think I'm awful. I didn't even notice he'd gone. You look exhausted. Where's Gemma?'

I nearly forgot about Gemma. 'She's in the spiky bits.'

Mum looks for Gemma but she can't see her. She walks to the pipes and stands on top but she still can't see her. She calls out, 'Gemma!' She whistles really loud. I didn't know she could whistle that loud.

I walk to the pipes again but I'm very tired. And so is Ramona. 'I want a Band-Aid. I want to go home.'

'Okay, let's get you home. I need to ring the police again, to tell them I found you.'

'The police are coming?'

'No. Not yet. You need to be missing for longer.'

By Myself

'How long?'

'They wouldn't say.'

I wish the police would come.

Ramona gives Mum her phone and Mum rings the police while we walk home. Then she rings Dad, but just gets a message.

'Where's Gemma's lead?' Mum asks, when we get home.

'Still on her.'

'God. It's probably caught on something, poor thing. I need to find her. Can you stay here, Ramona, with Christopher?' She gives the phone to Ramona but Ramona gives it back.

'Of course I'll stay here. Take Ivy with you.'

So Mum goes with Ivy. She gives me a big cuddle. She's still crying. 'I was so worried,' she says.

'Me too.'

Mum stays away for ages. Ramona gets me a Band-Aid and a biscuit — a chocolate biscuit. I didn't know we had some but Ramona finds them. Mum hid them up high but now I know where they are. Mum rings up and I answer. She says she found Gemma and we all cry again. Then she talks to Ramona.

Ramona rings the kinder and says me and Mum aren't coming in today. Then Ramona drives Mum's car across the tracks, past the pipes, and along the bumpy path. I didn't know you could drive on it. Mum doesn't like anyone driving her car. Not even Dad. But she lets Ramona drive it.

We see Mum near the spiky bits. She waves her head. She can't wave her hand because she's carrying Gemma. We can't drive all the way. It's too bumpy and there's no path. So we have to wait for Mum to carry Gemma. Ivy runs at us barking and jumps in the car. I hope Mum doesn't mind. Gemma can't walk by herself and she's too heavy for Ramona. She weighs twenty-five kilos. Then we all get in Mum's car, me, Mum, Ramona, Gemma and Ivy. Mum drives.

Ivy barks and barks but Gemma says nothing.

'Gemma's bleeding, Mum!'

'I know. Her lead was caught and she'd been thrashing around. We're taking her to the vet.'

'Tony the vet?'

'Yes, Tony the vet.'

'She's bleeding on the seat.'

'That's okay.'

Mum doesn't even like chocolate on the seat. But today it doesn't matter.

'Mum, you're bleeding too!'

'It's only a scratch.'

'You need a Band-Aid, Mum.'

'I'm okay, sweetie.'

'Everyone's bleeding.'

'I hope I'm not bleeding,' says Ramona. 'I didn't bring a tampon.'

'You can have one of mine,' says Mum.

'Thanks, but it was a joke.'

Mum laughs and Ramona laughs. It's not even funny but I laugh too.

'Sorry, I wasn't thinking. I should have dropped you at home, Ramona.'

'That's fine, Michelle. I'm not doing anything.'

Mum and Ramona both smile. Mum didn't used to like Ramona but today she does.

Tony gives Gemma some medicine and a big needle. He weighs Gemma and says she's only twenty-one kilos now. Soon I'll be more than that. I'm eighteen kilos already and I'm only four and Gemma's ten. Then Tony sews Gemma's paw back together. Gemma doesn't even cry, she doesn't even move.

'Is Gemma dead?'

'No,' says Tony. 'She's just sleeping. But she'll have to stay here till tomorrow.' Then he says to Mum, 'Maybe a few days.' Mum nods.

Then Dad rings Ramona's phone and I tell Dad everything that happened, while we drive home. Dad talks to Ramona for a little while but then I have to talk to him again because I forgot some bits.

When we drop Ramona and Ivy, Ramona gives Mum a piece of paper.

Mum says, 'Thanks, we'd love to come.'

'It's my birthday,' Ramona says, and she puts her fingers up four times. 'But tell Peter I'm thirty-five.'

By Myself

Mum laughs. I try to tell Dad but the battery's gone flat. Even the phone's tired.

'It's my birthday today,' I tell Ramona. 'I'm four.'

'I thought it was soon,' Ramona says. 'I'll have to get you a present.' She kisses my nose; her hair smells like strawberries.

'Happy birthday, Christopher.'

The Last Walk

I guess Gemma was middle aged when we got her. I'd never thought of her as being old, although Michelle had suggested she was *getting on* several times.

As the result of a recent escapade with Christopher, Gemma had a bit of a limp; and she was getting quite deaf but she was still very active. So I thought nothing of taking her for a long walk along the railway lines to Bunnings. It was a couple of kilometres, maybe more, and I'd done it with her before. But by halfway there she was getting very slow and I realised it had been a few years since we'd last done that walk together.

By the time we were three quarters of the way, I realised that she'd be hard pressed just to make it there, never mind walking back. I didn't have my mobile phone with me so I figured the best option was just to keep going. I could ring Michelle when we got there and she could pick us up.

Once we got to Bunning's car park, I put Gemma in a trolley and wheeled her to the door. I noticed how light she was. She was probably lighter than Christopher. She didn't complain or squirm at all. And the trolley can't have been comfortable. I tied her to a post near the main door then bought a bottle of water from the sausage sizzle stand and poured some into my hand for her to lap up. I bought her a sausage but she only ate half, very slowly. That was unusual.

'That's way too far for her, Peter,' Michelle said when she picked us up. I had to help Gemma into the car. 'Haven't you noticed how much slower she's been recently?'

'I just thought I was getting fitter.'

'You're not.'

'Oh.'

'Gemma's like a grandma now,' said Christopher.

'I guess she is. I just hadn't noticed.'

She didn't eat much all week.

'Take her to the vet,' Michelle said. The one in Yarraville – Tony – he's fantastic.'

'Sure.'

'I'd take her myself but I've got an appointment tomorrow.'

So Christopher and I took her to Tony. Tony said, 'She's just old so she can't do so much. And she doesn't need to eat so much. But we can run some tests if you like.'

'Yes please. Then when we get the results…'

'I can't say yet. It's likely we'll find nothing conclusive. We could run more tests if you want. We can run as many tests as you like. But it probably won't make much difference. And it'll be very expensive.'

He wasn't wrong.

'She probably won't last long, will she?' I whispered, so Christopher wouldn't hear. He was playing with a kitten in the waiting room.

'It's hard to say,' Tony whispered back. 'It could be a few weeks or it could be a few years. We may have a better idea when we get the results. Just treat her well. Take her for short walks every day. Half a kilometre, a kilometre at the most. Whatever she feels comfortable with.'

'Thanks.'

I'd spent most of the time we'd had Gemma telling myself that I didn't like dogs. But I'd grown very attached to her. I'd miss her. I'd miss our walks and our adventures. She'd been my companion and my accomplice on many an escapade.

'I want a kitten,' Christopher said, on the way home.

'We can't get a kitten. Gemma would chase it.'

'And eat it?'

'I doubt she'd even catch it. But we can't get a kitten.'

'Okay.'

When we got in Michelle was home. She had a big smile on her face and a big yellow envelope on the table. 'I knew you were pregnant. Why didn't you tell me?'

'You know why. Have a look.'

We hugged and I opened the envelope and slid out the pages. 'Wow. These are so clear, compared to the ones we've got of Christopher. There must have been mayor advances in the technology in the last few years.'

'Possibly. But I think it's just because I'm older. The risks are higher. They gave me the Rolls Royce ultrasound this time.' Christopher looked at the pictures too. 'A little brother or sister for you, Christopher. How would you like that?'

'I'd like a sister.'

'Yes, a girl would be nice. But it will be whatever it will be. It might be a little brother.'

'It's a girl,' Christopher stated.

'And what's the verdict on Gemma?' Michelle asked.

'There is no verdict. But I don't think she'll last till this one arrives.' I patted Michelle's tummy. It was just the tiniest bit big bigger than usual. 'I thought we'd given up.'

'We had given up. But I hadn't quite completely given up.'

Well, that made sense.

Life went on. Michelle got bigger, our little one continued to develop and Gemma got slower. And as Tony had predicted, the test results told us nothing significant.

Everywhere I walked Gemma, never far from home, people came up to her and patted her. And all her doggy friends sat quietly beside her and whined softly.

It seemed she was saying her goodbyes.

Old Mister Richardson, from number eighty-one, got down on one knee beside her one morning and whispered in her floppy ear for several minutes. It almost looked like he was proposing to her. I'd passed him hundreds of times over the years in my morning walks and he'd never said more than a few words, yet here he was reciting poetry or confessing his sins. I had to help him up. 'She's a good dog,' he said. 'She's a really good dog.'

'Yeah. She's the best.'

Michelle invited Christopher and I to her next ultrasound. I found it utterly amazing. I could watch an ultrasound screen all day. Although probably not if it was someone else's.

'Do you want to know the sex?' the radiologist asked.

'Yes,' Michelle said.

'No,' I said.

We both laughed.

'Cover your ears,' said Michelle and the radiologist at the same time. So I covered my ears until they'd stopped talking.

Then when I put my hands down Christopher said, 'I knew it was a girl.'

That had worked well.

When we got home we opened our front door and knew immediately that Gemma was going downhill fast. We'd left her inside the house; she didn't like to be put outside any more. Christopher held his nose. 'Poo. And spew.'

'Yep. Poo and spew.' Both were in the hallway, and likely in other parts of the house too. 'Double prizes.'

'I'll play outside,' Christopher said. 'I don't like spew. Or poo.'

'Good idea.'

'Where is Gemma?' Michelle asked. We called her but there was no response. 'Can you clean this up, please, Peter? I'll look for her.'

'Sure.' Although I'm not a big fan of poo or spew myself.

The Last Walk

I started scooping up the more substantial bits, there was a lot and it smelt foul. Michelle called from our bedroom, 'I've found her. Come and see.'

Gemma was lying on our bed, dribbling a little on Michelle's pillow. She looked at us with her sad doggy eyes. She knew she wasn't meant to be on the bed but she just didn't have the energy to get off. We let her stay there and Michelle softly stroked her muzzle while I continued to clean up. It was in the kitchen, the laundry and lounge room as well as the hall. The poor thing had probably been going frantic wanting to get out.

'Can I come in yet?' called Christopher.

'You can if you want but it's still a bit stinky.'

We let Gemma stay on our bed and we lay down next to her that night. 'Are you sure?' I asked Michelle.

'Yes,' I'm sure.

But when Gemma started throwing up during the night we knew we'd made a mistake. She'd hardly eaten anything. What was she throwing up? We let her stay and we moved to the spare room, which had grown very cramped. My model railway had taken over.

The next morning our room smelt disgusting and Gemma looked worse than ever.

'She's going to die, isn't she?' asked Christopher when he got up.

'Yes. She's going to die.'

'Today?'

'I think today. I think we need to take her to the vet today. Is that okay, Michelle?'

Michelle nodded, tears running down her cheeks. I don't think Christopher understood what I was asking.

'I'll take the day off work.'

Michelle nodded again.

'I'll come too, Dad, to the vet.'

'Okay. What about you, Michelle?'

She nodded again.

'And Ramona too,' said Christopher.

'Yes. I think she'd want to. I'll call her.'

We made a series of phone calls then we wrapped Gemma in her favourite blanket and gathered up her favourite toys. And when it was time we picked up Ramona. She was dressed all in black. I'd never seen her in black before; it suited her. I looked around the car and saw that we'd all chosen to dress in dark tones.

Ramona's dog, Ivy, howled when she realised Ramona was going without her.

'Ivy wants to come too,' said Christopher.

'No, not today sweetie. Ivy can come to Gemma's funeral.'

Michelle looked at me, 'I didn't know she was having a funeral.'

'Neither did I, till just then.'

'Of course she's having a funeral,' Ramona said.

Tony was great. Really gentle, really sensitive and really respectful. He fully understood how much Gemma meant to us.

Each of us held a paw as her dose was administered. She seemed to be smiling. And when she was gone, Christopher just knew. He didn't need to ask.

Tony handed us tissues and left us alone with Gemma for a few minutes. I think he went off to have a private cry himself. When he came back he asked what we wanted to do with her body.

We hadn't actually discussed it but I hoped the others would agree with me. 'I'd like to bury her, in the wastelands across the tracks from us.'

'Near where we buried the baby bunny?' asked Christopher.

'Yes.'

'She'd like that,' Michelle and Ramona said simultaneously.

'I can't pick her up till Saturday,' I told Tony.

'That's fine. I'll keep her here till then.'

'And I want her wrapped in her favourite blanket. Not in a garbage bag.'

'Of course,' said Tony, putting his hand on my shoulder.

I told myself I wasn't going to cry but tears leaked down my cheeks anyway. 'Would you like to come, Tony? To pay your last respects.'

'I'm working till one.'

'Say two o'clock? Is that too early?'

'No, that's great. I'll be there. Thank you.' He shook my hand, then Christopher's. He put his hand out to shake Michelle's but she threw her arms around him and hugged him, as did Ramona. It was very emotional.

As we drove home we told each other stories of Gemma's exploits. She'd touched us all so much. 'If only I hadn't taken her to Bunnings that day,' I lamented. 'Just for a packet of screws. I could have driven. I could have walked by myself.'

'Don't be silly, Peter. She wouldn't have lasted much longer.'

'If only I didn't get her stuck on the spiky bushes,' wailed Christopher.

'It's not your fault, honey.'

On the Saturday morning Christopher and I set off with Dave, with a spade each, to find a suitable resting spot for Gemma. It was a cool crisp morning, and quite misty. A beautiful morning. 'Great digging weather,' Dave said.

Christopher chose a spot, a little off the path – *so people don't walk on her* – and close to where we'd buried the baby bunny. There we dug a hole. More accurately, Dave dug the hole – he was like a digging machine. Christopher and I hardly got a spade in.

Christopher and I went to pick up Gemma a bit before one o'clock and I gave Tony a map I'd drawn of the spot we'd chosen. When we got back with Gemma there was quite a crowd gathered across the tracks, including several dogs.

Michelle and Ramona had wrapped a black blanket around our wheelbarrow, that would be the hearse, and lots of our neighbours had contributed their most prized flowers towards a massive wreath. I placed Gemma in the wheelbarrow hearse and Ivy sniffed her then whined softly.

Michelle's sister, Amanda, had come, as had Ramona's sister. She'd only ever met Gemma once. There was Dave and Cherie from next door, and Ray, our new neighbour from the other side. Christopher called him the deaf old grandpa, but deaf and old though he was, he'd heard enough about Gemma to make the effort. He'd dressed in a suit, with his medals pinned to his jacket.

I checked my watch. Fifteen minutes till the ceremony started. I decided I'd wear my suit, too. Michelle and Ramona were both dressed in black and looked very mournful. My suit was brown – but then so was Gemma. I was sure she'd approve. I asked Christopher if he wanted to get changed.

'Yes,' he said. 'I want to wear a tie.'

Mine were all much too big. Where the hell could we get a kid's tie in ten minutes?

'Do you mind if I cut down one of yours?' Amanda asked.

'Not at all. Please do.'

Christopher chose a tie and Amanda cut it, sewed it and ironed it all in four minutes flat. It was like a bought one. Better than a bought one. Christopher was really pleased.

When we walked out the front the crowd was even bigger. Tony had arrived, so had Mister Richardson and Evan and John from the men's group I'd once attended. Michelle's workmates and my workmates had come, even our ex-neighbour Elizabeth was lurking in the background amongst the dozens of neighbours whose names I didn't even know.

It was huge.

We took Gemma over to her final resting place, in the wheelbarrow hearse; but once we got there we realised that we hadn't worked out what we'd do for the ceremony.

One of the unidentified neighbours spoke up, 'I'm a minister. Would you like me so say a few words?'

'Yes please.'

'Was Gemma of any particular faith?' he asked.

'She was a Buddhist,' replied Christopher, and everyone laughed.

'I hope she doesn't come back as a rabbit,' the minister said.

'No,' said Christopher. 'She's coming back as a cat.' And again everyone laughed.

The minister gave a beautiful service. He'd had very little contact with Gemma but he spoke of her as if she was an old friend.

Dave and I lowered Gemma into the hole then the minister said a few more words and encouraged everyone to throw in a handful of soil before Dave filled in the hole.

As we were milling about, unsure of what came next, Ramona started to sing, softly at first but with each line a little louder.

'Once upon a time there was a paddock,

'Where we used to run when we were young.

'I would always come out here with Peter,

'And Christopher would sometimes come along.

'Oh, oh, oh, oh.'

Then she opened her throat for the chorus and let loose with the most amazing voice.

'Those were the days my friends, we thought they'd never end.'

She sang three or four verses telling Gemma's tale. I was surprised how much she knew. And we all sang along with the chorus. And on the final chorus Ivy joined in with a mournful, and beautifully harmonized, howl. When she was done everyone clapped.

Dave finished tapping down the soil and put a headstone down. It was made of an offcut of marble from the stonemasons nearby. Dave had chiseled into it, just the word *Gemma* in rough letters. 'I was going to write, *Here lies Gemma, a friend to all, 1993 to 2003, Rest In Peace.* But stone's bloody hard to carve.'

'It's perfect, Dave, just perfect.'

'It's a sad day,' Mister Richardson said. 'A sad, sad day.'

'Amen,' said the minister.

'Amen,' we all responded, and the crowd dispersed, passing on their condolences as they left. Most went back to their homes, but a few returned to our place for tea and scones.

'Thank you for that song, Ramona, it was amazing. You have such a beautiful voice.'

'Don't thank me, thank Gemma. I haven't sung like that for years. I didn't think I could. I don't think I could do it again.'

'Well, thank both of you.'

Dave brought beers over for those who preferred something cool.

'Thank you Dave, you were fantastic.'

'My pleasure.'

'It's so good to have such good neighbours. We'll miss you.'

'We'll miss you too. But we want to start a family. We want to get somewhere bigger.'

'With a smaller garage,' added Cherie.

I took one of Dave's beers, then he and I retreated to the spare room to admire my layout. 'That engine looks really happy here, Pete.'

'It sure does.'

'Hey, I've been meaning to ask you, whatever happened with all that drilling they were doing a few years ago in the bunny paddock?'

'Well Ramona guessed it. They were testing the soil for contamination. There was a plan to put up a stack of townhouses. But that was when they were planning on mothballing the refinery. Now it's been upgraded, so the land's safe for a few years.'

Evan and John popped their heads in as they were leaving. 'Wow! Impressive layout,' they said in unison.

'Thanks.'

'You know our next meeting's next week?' Evan asked.

'Yes I know. I'll be there.'

'No hidden agendas?' asked John.

'No. No hidden agendas.'

After everyone had left we sat down exhausted. Technically it was dinner time but we weren't hungry. We'd been grazing all afternoon.

'Sometime soon,' I said to Christopher, 'After the baby's born, we can get another dog if you want.'

'I want a cat.'

'A cat might be nice,' said Michelle. 'You don't like dogs much, remember?'

'But a cat won't come walking with me at seven in the morning.'

'You'll be changing nappies at seven in the morning.'

'I guess so.'

'You could train it,' offered Christopher.

'Yeah, maybe I could. Walking the Cat? That might work.'

Author's Note

It took thirteen years to complete this book, two writing groups and two dogs.

My infant son, who inspired some of these stories, is now a teenager. Our dog Gemma, who inspired other stories, has sadly passed away, and I now have a daughter. Is this life imitating art or art imitating life? A little of each, I think.

I still live in the same house, in the same neighbourhood and wander the same streets with a similar brown dog.

Thank you to my family, and to the many writers who've assisted this project over the years: Mammad Aidani, Jackie Kerin, Bill Marshall, Sarah Berry, Helen Cerne, Margaret Campbell, Louise Swinn Lucinda Ireland and Chris Ringrose, to name but a few.

And thank you Gemma and Coco for the exercise.

Also by Jonathan Griffiths

The Road Behind   **Jonathan Griffiths**

ISBN 978-0-9803500-3-6   RRP $24.95

THE ROAD BEHIND is a journey of self-discovery, an adventure and a picaresque romp. Protagonist Mark Kidman traces a circuitous route from his childhood, to fatherhood and impending middle age. His journey criss-crosses the Tasman, swirls around Australia and circles the globe, as he runs from his past, headlong into his future.

Mark flies into Sydney – as the singer of a punk band – full of expectations of success. But when his girlfriend takes off and the band goes nowhere, he hits the road in search of adventure.

As a bouncer, a taxi driver, a set builder, an actor and a writer, he's constantly on the move. But as he powers along he is often overtaken by his past: his fragmented family, his numerous failed relationships and the ghosts of his brothers and friends.

Again and again the road behind engulfs the road ahead.

'A shaggy propulsive and picaresque novel of misspent youth, it explores the genealogies of damage and self-destruction…'
'Griffiths takes us on a dynamic and humorous ride. He has an outrageously keen ear for dialogue…'
Cameron Woodhead *The Age*

'A wild narrative of energy and brevity.' **John Clarke**

'Lust, loss and redemption collide in a love story like no other.'
Helen Cerne

www.theroadbehind.net

The Bits that Didn't Fit   **Jonathan Griffiths**

ISBN 978-0-9871160-0-0   RRP $15.95

The Bits that Didn't Fit: stories of rock n roll, relationships and the road. These stories are inhabited by the loose nuts, bolts and washers of society. Tales told by the queer, the quirky and the downright demented. The misfits of society. The sad, sick, funny and tragic. The bits that don't fit.

This collection is populated by taxi drivers, punk musicians, and men and women in relationships in various states of disrepair. Lost souls and arse holes, misogynists and terrorists, and, for reasons barely plausible, the cast of Pride and Prejudice.

Some of these stories were intended to be part of the novel, *The Road Behind*, but they didn't fit. Some were written long ago and have been wandering the streets searching for a home ever since. Some were penned especially for this collection and some are made up of odd bits and pieces – patched together like Frankenstein's monster. And why not? Monsters are people too.

Bits of comedy, tragedy and pornography; rock n roll, heart and soul, and a little historical romance to fill in the holes.

The story of Elizabeth Bennett's nymphomaniac sister didn't fit Jane Austen's tale, and doesn't quite fit these bits either. Yet, perversely, it's here.

"A most grotesque and vulgar collection, suitable for neither ladies nor gentlemen." **Jane Austen**

www.theroadbehind.net

Relationships
Taking the Biblical Approach

Steve A. Thomas

Icando Publishing House
England. UK.
www.icandopublishing.com
info@icandopublishing.com

Published by Icando Publishing House
© Steve Thomas, Gold4God Ministries, 2011
Cover design by Peter Oppong-Mensah
Printed in the United Kingdom. All Rights Reserved.

MEN-2-WOMEN SEMINAR

This reference book is for course in the subject area Personal Life and Christian Relationships: Building Spiritual Men and Women for Christ's Kingdom

Order additional copies of this reference book for your seminars or retreats by e-mail: pastorthomas@mac.com or by contacting the South England Conference of Seventh-day Adventists, 25 St Johns Road, Watford, Hertfordshire, WD17 1PZ.

Thomas, Steve A.
Relationship: Taking The Biblical Approach: Discipleship Series 3

1. Relationship   2. Marriage   3. Love   4. Dating 5. Seventh-day Adventists--Belief.

ISBN 978-0-9569381-0-7

Table of Contents

INTRODUCTION

John MacArthur wrote

> Since families are the building blocks of human society, a society that does not protect the family undermines its very existence. When the family goes, anarchy is the logical outcome—and that's where we're headed. Now, more than ever before, is the time for Christians to declare and put on display what the Bible declares: God's standard for marriage and the family is the only standard that can produce meaning, happiness, and fulfillment.[1]

If we are to influence the world with that standard, we must be different. God has called us to be salt and light in this dark and decaying society. Christians' responsibility is to a higher level of living—to a new way of thinking, a new way of acting, a new way of living—to "walk in a manner worthy of the calling with which [we] have been called ... [to] put on the new self, which in the likeness of God has been created in righteousness and holiness of the truth" (Eph. 4:1, 24). We cannot and must not think as the world thinks, act as the world acts, talk as the world talks, or set goals the world sets—we must be peculiar. The ultimate hope of humanity is that in seeing that peculiarity lost people will be drawn to Jesus Christ.

In 1 Corinthians 10, we are told that the experiences of the children of Israel were written for the benefit of the people of God in order to avoid repeating the mistakes ("the people sat down to eat and drink and got up to indulge in… sexual immorality… thereby testing the Lord"). "These things happened to them as examples and were written down as warning for us, on whom the fulfillment of the ages has come."[2]

---

1 *MacArthur, J. F., Jr. (1997, c1994.). Different by Design (49–54). Wheaton, IL: Victor Books.*
2 *1 Corinthians 10:7, 8, 11*

Similarly, my experience as a pastor, counselor, adviser, presenter and preacher has resulted in me having to work with a variety of people with a desire to have a happy, fulfilling marriage, growing old while still in love. However, despite their wonderful desire(s), their relationship and marriage ended in divorce leaving questions, resentment and loneliness.

Ellen, commenting on the importance of being mature enough to get married, said

> Immature marriages are productive of a vast amount of the evils that exist today. Neither physical health nor mental vigor is promoted by a marriage that is entered on too early in life. Upon this subject altogether too little reason is exercised. Many youth act from impulse. This step, which affects them seriously for good or ill, to be a lifelong blessing or curse, is too often taken hastily, under the impulse of sentiment.[3]

Many people enter into a relationship with heart and hopes only to end with brokenness and hopelessness. Their children, without really acknowledging the influences of their parents, enter into life with negative experiences, misapprehension about what true relationship and marriage are. Like the crazy cycle, negatives are added to negatives rolling towards the destruction of values that underpins a Christian relationship and marriage. On the other hand, some relationship and marriages and the dreams and desires are realized, resulting in a happy home, children with a positive outlook on life, relationship and marriage. What makes the difference in the cycle and what determines whether it is a crazy one or not?

In answering the questions, I have, with permission, included several articles as well as my own presentations in order that this reference book may begin to answer the questions of what makes the difference as to whether you have a healthy relationship and marriage, whether it will be one that leaves a positive or negative image on Christian relationships and marriages.

In the selection of areas to be included in this reference book, I have allowed my own personal beliefs and experience to determine the topics, excerpts and biblical approach. I have included the references in the references section (see table

---

3 *Ellen G White, Adventist Home, (Washington, DC: Review and Herald, 1980), 79.*

of content) for the reader to be able to read the excerpts and carry out further studies.

My theological understanding is that the Bible is the authoritative word of God, given by inspiration and is useful for teaching, rebuking, correcting and training in righteousness (right doing), so that the man or woman of God may be thorough equipped for every good work. I believe that God's active involvement in the writing of Scripture, an involvement so powerful and pervasive that word of God is therefore infallible and authoritative. This I believe is the guide for all those who believe in God and wants to do what is right, in His sight.

I also believe that the church is a holy priesthood and a chosen race, a royal priesthood, God's own people (1 Peter 2:5, 6), and in union with Christ, His body shares in His priestly, kingly, and prophetic work. That every member has a part to play and that we, in playing that part, need to follow God's instructions and to avoid relationships and actions that threatens our own personal relationship with Christ.

Therefore, foundational to this reference book is 2 Timothy 3:16,17. I, in following the scripture, have identified areas that will highlight what will make a difference in any relationship. In the same manner, failure to follow the instruction of God and the guide in this reference book will result in your relationship being poor and thereby an unhealthy marriage.

So what does the Bible have to say about the relationship, personality issues, sexuality and the numerous challenges faced within a relationship? In my worldview, a clear thus saith the Lord is necessary in every situation we face. In our postmodern society, where questions are being asked and answers being sort from unreliable sources, is there a word from the Lord? I believe the Bible should be our first point of reference, rather the specialists.

My biblical understanding on relationship, the guide that follows, underline all of the materials/articles and excerpts and reminds us of the richness of the Scripture when seeking help in our moments of searching for answers.

In Your Relationship

EPHESIANS 4:2-3 Always be humble and gentle. Be patient with each other, making allowance for each other's faults because of your love. Make every effort to keep yourselves united in the Spirit, binding yourselves together with peace. (NLT)

ROMANS 12:3-5 Because of the privilege and authority God has given me, I give each of you this warning: Don't think you are better than you really are. Be honest in your evaluation of yourselves, measuring yourselves by the faith God has given us. Just as our bodies have many parts and each part has a special function, so it is with Christ's body. We are many parts of one body, and we all belong to each other. (NLT)

MATTHEW 22:37-39 Jesus replied, "'You must love the LORD your God with all your heart, all your soul, and all your mind.' This is the first and greatest commandment. A second is equally important: 'Love your neighbor as yourself.' (NLT)

ECCLESIASTES 4:9-10 Two people are better off than one, for they can help each other succeed. If one person falls, the other can reach out and help. But someone who falls alone is in real trouble. (NLT)

TITUS 2:7-8 And you yourself must be an example to them by doing good works of every kind. Let everything you do reflect the integrity and seriousness of your teaching. Teach the truth so that your teaching can't be criticized. Then those who oppose us will be ashamed and have nothing bad to say about us. (NLT)

JOHN 13:35 "Your love for one another will prove to the world that you are my disciples." (NLT)

1 PETER 1:22 You were cleansed from your sins when you obeyed the truth, so now you must show sincere love to each other as brothers and sisters. Love each other deeply with all your heart. (NLT)

1 PETER 3:7 In the same way, you husbands must give honour to your wives. Treat your wife with understanding as you live together. She may be weaker than you are, but she is your equal partner in God's gift of new life. Treat her as you should so your prayers will not be hindered. (NLT)

When Faced With Personality Issues

2 PETER 1:5-6 In view of all this, make every effort to respond to God's promises. Supplement your faith with a generous provision of moral excellence, and moral excellence with knowledge, and knowledge with self-control, and self-control with patient endurance, and patient endurance with godliness. (NLT)

PROVERBS 11:11-12 Upright citizens are good for a city and make it prosper, but the talk of the wicked tears it apart. It is foolish to belittle one's neighbor; a sensible person keeps quiet. (NLT)

PROVERBS 11:13 A gossip goes around telling secrets, but those who are trustworthy can keep a confidence. (NLT)

PROVERBS 12:22 The Lord detests lying lips, but he delights in those who tell the truth. (NLT)

PROVERBS 25:19 Putting confidences in an unreliable person in times of trouble is like chewing with a broken tooth or walking on a lame foot. (NLT)

PROVERBS 12:25 Worry weighs a person down; an encouraging word cheers a person up. (NLT)

PROVERBS 17:22 A cheerful heart is good medicine, but a broken spirit saps a person's strength. (NLT)

MATTHEW 6:34 "So don't worry about tomorrow, for tomorrow will bring its own worries. Today's trouble is enough for today." (NLT)

LUKE 6:37 "Do not judge others, and you will not be judged. Do not condemn others, or it will all come back against you. Forgive others, and you will be forgiven. (NLT)

ROMANS 14:12-13 Yes, each of us will give a personal account to God. So let us stop condemning each other. Decide instead to live in such a way that you will not cause another believer to stumble and fall. (NLT)

Sexuality in the Context of Scripture

PROVERBS 5:18-19 Let your wife be a fountain of blessing for you. Rejoice in the wife of your youth. She is a loving deer, a graceful doe. Let her breasts satisfy you always. May you always be captivated by her love. (NLT)

1 CORINTHIANS 7:3 The husband should fulfill his wife's sexual needs, and the wife should fulfill her husband's needs. (NLT)

1 CORINTHIANS 7:4-5 The wife gives authority over her body to her husband, and the husband gives authority over his body to his wife. 5 Do not deprive each other of sexual relations . . . (NLT)

HEBREWS 13:4 Give honor to marriage, and remain faithful to one another in marriage. God will surely judge people who are immoral and those who commit adultery. (NLT)

EPHESIANS 5:28 In the same way, husbands ought to love their wives as they love their own bodies. For a man who loves his wife actually shows love for himself. (NLT)

I CORINTHIANS 6:19-20 Don't you realize that your body is the temple of the Holy Spirit, who lives in you and was given to you by God? You do not belong to yourself, for God bought you with a high price. So you must honor God with your body. (NLT)

In Conflict Within Your Relationship

COLOSSIANS 3:19 Husbands love your wives and never treat them harshly. (NLT)

EPHESIANS 4:26 And "don't sin by letting anger control you." Don't let the sun go down while you are still angry. (NLT)

PROVERBS 14:29 People with understanding control their anger; a hot temper shows great foolishness. (NLT)

ECCLESIASTES 7:8-9 Finishing is better than starting. Patience is better than pride. Control your temper, for anger labels you a fool. (NLT)

1 THESSALONIANS 5:11 So encourage each other and build each other up, just as you are already doing. (NLT)

ROMANS 12:17 Never pay back evil with more evil. Do things in such a way that everyone can see you are honourable. (NLT)

2 TIMOTHY 1:7 For God has not given us a spirit of fear and timidity, but of power, love, and self-discipline. (NLT)

PROVERBS 17:9 Love prospers when a fault is forgiven, but dwelling on it separates close friends. (NLT)

GALATIANS 5:22-23 But the Holy Spirit produces this kind of fruit in our lives: love, joy, peace, patience, kindness, goodness, faithfulness, gentleness, and self-control. There is no law against these things! (NLT)

COLOSSIANS 3:13 Make allowance for each other's faults, and forgive anyone who offends you. Remember, the Lord forgave you, so you must forgive others. (NLT)

In the setting of an immoral world Paul admonished the believers in Ephesus with God's elevated and original divine standard for marriage: "For the husband is the head of the wife, as Christ also is the head of the church, He Himself being the Saviour of the body. But as the church is subject to Christ, so also the wives ought to be to their husbands in everything. Husbands, love your wives, just as Christ also loved the church and gave Himself up for her" (5:23–25). The relationship between a husband and wife is to be holy and indissoluble, just like Christ's relationship with the church.

MacArthur comments holds true when he said "for that type of a relationship to be a reality, Christ must be at its centre. The family can only be what God has designed it to be when the members of the family are what God designed them to be—"conformed to the image of His Son" (Rom. 8:29).

Relationship

1

A Relationship Requires More Than Just Love

Introduction to our aims

Ellen White, in Adventist Home, reminds us of the importance of starting off right, in courtship (dating). Having a right attitude and principles (values) will safeguard a persons' heart and avoid him or her making a shipwreck of their heart and life. White said

The ideas of courtship have their foundation in erroneous ideas concerning marriage. They follow impulse and blind passion. The courtship is carried on in a spirit of flirtation. The parties frequently violate the rules of modesty and reserve and are guilty of indiscretion, if they do not break the law of God. The high, noble, lofty design of God in the institution of marriage is not discerned; therefore the purest affections of the heart, the noblest traits of character are not developed.

Love ... is not unreasonable; it is not blind. It is pure and holy. But the passion of the natural heart is another thing altogether. While pure love will take God into all its plans, and will be in perfect harmony with the Spirit of God, passion will be headstrong, rash, unreasonable, defiant of all restraint, and will make the object of its choice an idol. In all the deportment of one who possesses true love, the grace of God will be shown. Modesty, simplicity, sincerity, morality, and religion will characterize every step toward an alliance in marriage. [1]

Without love, two people could not commit themselves to a relationship. They certainly could never find it worthwhile to become engaged or get married. Love is the catalyst for commitment.

1 White, Adventist Home, 50, 55,

Love is what ensures that a relationship grows and improves. But sooner or later, every good relationship bumps into bad things. And that's when honest people discover that love, no matter how good, is never enough to keep their relationship moving forward.

Let's make this clear. When we decide that we are not simply casually dating someone, but that there is a stronger bond of love, we form a commitment in the confidence that our relationship will not simply survive but thrive. Our confidence is built and bolstered by that love. But here's the kicker: One cannot completely guard one's love against the things that diminish it.

What's more, love in itself is seldom sturdy enough to support a couple when they inevitably run into bad things. Love, while being a good catalyst for a relationship, is not enough to sustain it.

Countless couples out there cling to the sentimental, romantic notion of love expressed in songs, movies, and novels. It is a notion that leads some of us into marriages that are doomed to failure and unhappiness. We believe that everything good in our relationship will get even better in time. But the truth is, not everything gets better. Many things improve in our lives once we find someone special to focus on, but some things become more difficult.

Every successful relationship, for example, requires necessary losses. For starters, forming a commitment with someone means coming to terms with new limits on one's independence. It means giving up a carefree lifestyle. Even to people who have dreamed for years of finding someone to date who they can really connect with and love, and who think of themselves as hating to be alone, a relationship can come as an invasion of privacy and independence. Young people who are still new to the experience of having a relationship are often quite surprised at the sheer intensity of this invasion. And so, for many, they run into their first real challenge to love. But it will not be their last.

Like two weary soldiers taking cover in a bunker, every couple is bewildered by constant assaults to their love life. A relationship is continually bombarded by unpredictable instances that interfere with being the kind of lovers we want to be. We are torn apart by busy schedules, by words we wish we could take back, by not giving all that love demands.

Love asks for everything. And how hard it is to give everything! Indeed, it is impossible. We can tell each other we are in love, we can make a symbolic gesture of commitment, we can even declare it quite dramatically at a wedding ceremony, but even these are just mere messages of intention if based on a feeling of love alone, and not on a knowledge of the work and hardships that must also be traversed. No mere mortal can ever live by romantic love alone.

Dr. Neil Clark Warren believes there are at least 29 personality dimensions, such as our anger management skills, our feelings about children, our energy, and our ambition, that make up who we are and that play a vital role in keeping a relationship together. When we become initially attracted to someone, and even fall in love, often it is more their appearance, their involvement in our lives, or perhaps their interest in a common hobby or occupation that catches our attention and brings us together. Few men ask a woman out because they find her anger management skills enticing! But in the long term, if a couple ignores these traits in themselves and coasts on love alone, eventually their relationship is in deep trouble when a crisis occurs that love cannot solve. Sometimes crises become too numerous and too deep, resulting in a break-up-other times, it just means the couple involved needs to talk and work things out before they can move on. But either way, it is better to avoid coasting through a relationship solely on our feelings of love. We can grow to know each other and to make better decisions about our relationships if we are realistic about the other important factors beside just romantic love.

People get hurt in love. Even after a couple gets married, bad things will still happen. For a couple who understands that not everything good gets better in time, and who share a commitment to learning about each other's faults as well as perfections, love can mature and become something worth devoting their lives toward. The naivety of new love grows into a knowledgeable and confident love, one on which promises and vows can be taken in total confidence. But if a relationship is bandied about by a myriad of bad things, and a couple falsely believes that love alone will eventually lead them away from all pain and conflict, they are in for some terrible times. If they go ahead and get married without dealing with this reality, they are condemning themselves to even worse miseries.

Therefore, it is our hope this reference book will assist you as you develop your relationship, from the point of looking for a companion, dating, marriage and growing gracefully old. We pray that you will find the information (compilation of some wonderful resources, specifically selected because of its' Biblical contents and styles) useful and helpful. Some of the chapters are specifically layout for seminars (in fact the book is really for seminars where there are opportunities for talkback in an atmosphere of trust).

2

What Similarities Between Two People
Are Absolutely Crucial?

I take a strong position on the importance of two people being a lot alike if they're going to try to make a relationship last for a lifetime. There are some similarities that, in my opinion, are just absolutely critical to a long-lasting love relationship. There are also some that are less important.

Amos wrote (Amos 3:3), "do two walk together unless they have agreed to do so." The answer he expects is obviously, 'No'. When two people go for a walk they have to agree the purpose of their walk and the time and place they will meet.

The apostle Paul, in 2 Corinthians 6:14, 15, wrote "be not unequally yoked with ubeliebers. For what fellowship has righteousness with lawlessness? And what communion has light with darkness? And what accord has Christ with Belial? Or what part has a believer with an unbeliever?" In addition, we find in the Old Testament, important commands, which relates to similarities, for the child of God. These provide boundaries for every child of God praying about a relationship or marriage:

- Do not take a wife *(or husband)* from the Canaanites[2] (Genesis 24:3; 37)
- Do not marry a Canaanite woman *(or man)* (Genesis 28:1; 28:6-9)
- Foreign wives *(or husbands)* will turn away your sons from following me (Deuteronomy 7:4)

---

2 Italic added. Canaanite is symbolic for heathen or not worshipper of Yahweh God. The name refers to a nation that worship other gods. Today, this would mean non Seventh-day Adventist, if you are a Seventh-day Adventist. Or non-christian, if you are a christian.

Israel's covenant relationship with God meant that he was their God and they were his people. To safeguard that relationship God commanded them not to intermarry with the surrounding nations who worshipped other gods. However, the children of Israel ignored the command, resulting in it becoming the norm in that society. The writer could safely say the whole nation of Judah had 'profaned' the Lord's institution (his covenant relationship with his people, whom he loved, and that relationship was now being contaminated by the men of the nation treating thier marriages so casually). The postmodern equivalent to a mixed marriage, where the similarities being so visible, is a believer marrying an unbeliever.

Therefore, Similarities or unique relationship strengths and gowth areas of dating or engaged will help couples as they decide whether a life time commitment with their significant other will take place in an atmosphere of trust, happiness and health (free from abuse). For this reason, couples are encouraged to take a couples checkup (Prepare Enrich couples couples relationship assessment), where they will be able to discover their areas of strength and growth.

Similarities between two people are like which denomination or church they both attends, level of education, interests, number of children, marital expectations, role of parents in the marriage and what to do about fincially supporting the church and the work of God. Dissimilarities are like size of house, political party, football (soccer) team, taking office in church and supporting the church through good times and not so good. Every time you have a dissimilarity, a place in which the two of you just don't agree or don't have an interest in common or whatever, you often have to negotiate that dissimilarity. You have to work to try to make that okay in your couple relationship and pre-marital preparation mentoring sessions.

Let's think for an instance about the spending of money. If one of you wants to save money and the other one likes to spend money on important things to you, the two of you are going to come into conflict. You're going to have to negotiate how you deal with your money. That negotiation almost always requires give on both your parts. That giving on both of your parts is okay as long as one of you doesn't always have to give or as long as both of you don't have to give so often that it feels like your relationship is just a constant giving experience.

I want to give you some similarities that in my opinion are crucial to the solidarity of your long-term relationship and I want to tell you why I evaluate them as critical.

1. Spirituality. The reason I think this is so critical is that it involves the way you go about dealing with your life. If one of you is a very spiritual person you will tend to be internally focused. You will think of praying. You will think of meditating, of reflecting on the problem internally. The opposite point of view will tend to look outside of you. You will think of assessing the situation, of coming to a rational understanding of what to do about a situation without involving so much of your internal process. The two of you will come at life in such different ways. I happen to know a lot of people for whom spirituality is a big part of their existence. It influences the way they make virtually every decision in their lives. And then I also know some people who are not at all spiritual and who find individuals who are quite spiritual as a bit, what one man described the other day, as kooky. They just don't think that praying makes any sense. Those two people probably are going to be quite unhappy together over time.

2. Intelligence. Now, I don't know how intelligent you are and it really doesn't matter; you can have a wonderfully happy marital relationship at any intelligence level. But it's important for you to find someone whose intelligence level is about the same as your own. I know persons who are literally geniuses. They're not going to be happy with persons of just average intelligence. Intelligence is not always education driven. However, education will affect the level of intelligence. Here, similarities is important.

Two people need to be able to talk to each other as peers-as equals. I have known persons who had a great deal of difference in their intelligence level. One of them regularly feels frustrated because she has to talk down to him or he has to talk down to her. They just don't feel the other person can understand what they're thinking and feeling. On the other hand, the person who is in the down position regularly feels talked down to. They feel put down. They feel hurt and frustrated on a regular basis. This simply doesn't build a relationship in any meaningful way. I have seen such disparity, in intelligence, leading to a breakdown in the marital relationship, to the point of separation, with divorce on the horizon.

3. Ambition. I know people whose ambition I would describe as "low level." In my culture, we call them "good-for-nothing." I remember a couple that came to me some years ago. She was a counsellor of a local authority (local government). She had tremendous ambition to move ahead. Her husband didn't have the same level of ambition (or maybe vision). He was a sales person who made a fair wage, but he had no desire to make a big wage. He often took the afternoon off to play golf. She was so ambitious, but he didn't have much ambition at all. I'm sorry to have to tell you that in my opinion, their difference in ambition level led to the early demise of their relationship and the break down of thier marriage, leading to divorce. If your ambition level is very high, marry some one who's right there with you with a high level of ambition on their own.

"You know, honey, we really need to pay these bills." Elizabeth just couldn't believe Tom could be so loose with their finances. "If only he'd handle our money the way my father did," thought Elizabeth, "then I wouldn't have to worry so much."

Tom, on the other hand, had a general sense that most of the bills were paid. "If only Elizabeth would stop being such a nag," thought Tom. "This really isn't what I bargained for … does she really think I need her personal coaching?"
As marriage counselors, we often hear, "I'll be happy *if only* my spouse will…." Yet, our experience indicates that when one spouse focuses on the other's performance, it usually leads to the destruction of the relationship.

A Wrong View of Marriage

When coming together in marriage, husbands and wives usually develop their own natural, human plan for marital happiness. The couple's separate plans are based on the unique personalities and personal differences of each partner, including different family influences, role models, books, and often-different church experiences. Because their plans for marriage happiness are different, conflict usually results.

Since each of us is self-centered, we constantly want to know what our spouse has done for us lately. Sadly, as time passes, we subconsciously revert to the "greener pasture syndrome" where we begin to compare our spouse's performance with our own pre-conceived ideas and expectations, making satisfaction with our spouse more and more elusive.

Six Factors That Destroy Marriages

Following are the six primary factors that destroy marriages. They are commonly found in natural, human relationships:
1. Couples fail to anticipate differences resulting from diverse cultural

backgrounds, differing family experiences, gender, and so on.

2. Couples buy into the notion of a "fifty-fifty" relationship, meaning they honestly expect their spouses to meet them halfway.

3. Society has taught us that mankind is basically good. Therefore, couples fail to anticipate their self-centered natures that demand their own way.

4. Couples fail to cope with life's trials. When painful trials come into the marriage, instead of standing together through them, couples tend to blame each other or think something is wrong with the spouse and the way they handle the pain.

5. Many people have a fantasy view of love. They quickly feel stuck with an unloving person and become deceived into believing that the next one will be better.

6. Many people lack a vital relationship with Jesus Christ. It could be that they have never come to a specific point in time when they asked Christ into their lives and therefore He has no impact on the marriage relationship.

God's Solution – The Faith Relationship

The faith relationship is opposite of the performance relationship in two significant ways. First, it is not natural at all – it is supernatural. You will only learn about this kind of relationship from God through His Word. Second, the faith relationship does not focus on the human performance of one's spouse but on God's character, promises, and faithfulness.

This kind of relationship involves God as the Guarantor of the marriage with the specifics of the guarantee found in Scripture. It's long-term hope based on God's character and faithfulness. We know He is good and loves us. His guidance that led us to marry a certain person becomes more important than the initial human attraction that brought us together. You begin to focus more on Him and His Word, rather than your spouse and his or her failure to perform to your expectations.

When considering the faith relationship, one question that often comes up is, "can God fulfill my needs in this marriage despite my spouse's weaknesses?" The answer is yes! If God can meet your needs anyway, then your spouse's weaknesses no longer limit you. This fact frees husbands and wives to love one another unconditionally as they thank God for His gracious provision.

Christ set the example for the faith relationship in 1 Peter 2:21-25. Rather than focus on the failure and weakness of those who unjustly wronged Him, He focused on God and His promises. In 1 Peter 2:23 we read, "but (Jesus) kept entrusting Himself to Him who judges righteously." Jesus believed in God's sovereign plan more than His desire to abandon the cross, more than His disappointment over Peter's denials, and more than His desire for His persecutors to receive instant justice.

Christ based His relationships on faith in God rather than the performance of man. Think about how Christ responded to the failures of others on the cross. Could there be a better example for husbands and wives to model in their own marriage?

For the Christian, similarities are absolutely crucial to them and their families well-being. It affects not only the physical, but also the spiritual. A home with similar values, hopes, dreams and beliefs is like a tower in the time of mismanagement of sexuality and faithfulness.

The story of teh flood that covered the whole earth, and of Noah, the man used by God to save teh world of men and beasts reminds us of how important it is to have someone who shares in your belief, dreams, hopes and values. Genesis 6 speaks of the "sons of God" having relations with teh "daughters of men." The evil that resulted from the unequally yoked was that righteous men and women decreased. God summarises the results of this union by stating that "the earth was corrupt in the sight of God, and the earth was filled with violence." (Genesis 6:11 New American Standard Bible).

3

LOVE & FAMILIES IN THE BIBLE

Love in the Old Testament: In the OT the verb 'to love' (Heb. 'ahab) and its cognates cover the full range of meanings the English word 'love' has, including love for God (Exod. 20:6; Ps. 40:17) and the love God has for his people (Hos. 3:1; Deut. 7:13). This latter sense of love, God's love for his people in the covenant context, is often expressed by the term 'steadfast love' (Heb. hesed). God's steadfast love is a sign of his fidelity.[1]

Examining some texts will indicate the wide range of meaning 'love' has. It can be used to describe physical love between the sexes, as well as sexual concupiscence (Gen. 34:3; Judg. 16:4, 15; 2 Sam. 13:4, 15; see also Song of Sol.). The description of love between the sexes transcending the purely physical is also common (Gen. 24:67; 29:20: 'So Jacob served seven years for Rachel, and they seemed to him but a few days because of the love he had for her'). The Hebrew word can refer to love within a family (Gen. 22:2; 25:28; Ruth 4:15); among friends (Ps. 38:12; Jer. 20:4-6); and between superior and inferior or slave and master (Deut. 15:16). Especially significant is the command that Israel love the foreigner or stranger, and the rationale for such action (Lev. 19:34: 'The stranger who sojourns with you shall be to you as the native among you, and you shall love him as yourself; for you were strangers in the land of Egypt: I am the Lord your God'; also Deut. 10:19). Additionally, Israel is instructed to love the neighbor, namely, the fellow Israelite (Lev. 19:18).

Agape (ah-gah-pay), the principal Greek word used for 'love' in the NT. Of the three words for love in the Hellenistic world, it was the least common. The other two words were eros, which meant sexual love, and philos, which meant friendship, although their meanings could vary according to the context in which

---

1 *Achtemeier, P. J., Harper & Row, P., & Society of Biblical Literature. (1985). Harper's Bible dictionary (1st ed.) (578–579). San Francisco: Harper & Row.*

they appeared. Agape, because it was used so seldom and was so unspecific in meaning, could be used in the NT to designate the unmerited love God shows to humankind in sending his son as suffering redeemer. When used of human love, it means selfless and self-giving love.[2]

Ellen White wrote

> The warmth of true friendship and the love that binds the hearts of husband and wife are a foretaste of heaven. God has ordained that there should be perfect love and perfect harmony between those who enter into the marriage relation.[3]

"Husbands, love your wives, even as Christ also loved the church, and gave himself for it." Dying for someone is the most magnanimous act of submission possible. Husbands are to be submitting to their wives as well. There is beautiful mutuality (cf. 1 Cor. 7:4, 33–34). The husband is to love his wife; that is his act of submission. This standard is infinitely high. However, the text isn't talking about the full capacity of divine love; it's talking about the factors involved in the kind of love Christ manifested. Obviously we cannot match God's love in quantity, or even in quality, but we can love in kind. We may not possess the ocean, but we can have a little of it in our bucket.[4]

The apostle Paul said, "as Christ loved the church." The kind of love Paul is talking about is sacrificial love. MacArthur said

> When Jesus Christ came into the world, He loved the church. In fact, He loved the church before the foundation of the world in eternity past. And He loved us enough to leave heaven, come to earth, take on a human form, be spit on and mocked, crowned with a crown of thorns, nailed to a cross, abused, and have a spear thrust into His side. He loved the church enough to die. That's sacrificial love. And it is sacrificial love that is to mark the love of a husband for his wife. When Christ gave up His prerogative to be equal with God and chose to come to earth in the form of a servant, He was acting in sacrificial love.[5]

---

2 *Ibid.*

3 *Letters to Young Lovers. 1983; 2002 (10). Pacific Press Publishing Association.*

4 *John MacArthur, (1997). The fulfilled family. Chicago: Moody Press.*

5 *Ibid.*

MacArthur went on to say that

> Sacrificial love has nothing to do with whether it's deserved or not. Sacrificial love is undeserved. God is not rescuing people who deserve rescue; He is saving those who don't deserve it because it's His nature to love. An inferior love gives only to those who earn the right to receive it. But God's love is given to those who don't have the right to earn it.[6]

On the other hand, this world loves with an object-oriented love. An object-oriented love says if the object is desirable, "I love you." When people select a partner, they look around and say, "There's a nice one. I'll love that one," or, "Forget that one." Or they go through a group of people and say, "I don't care for those people; they aren't worthy of my love. They don't live up to my expectations. They don't fit into my little group. But those people—oh, I love them." Everything depends upon the form of an object or its personality. We have an object-oriented attraction. However, God's love is different. God doesn't expect the object to be worthy; it's His nature to love *(thank you Jesus!)*. That's the difference. John 3:16 says, "For God so loved the world." This is the kind of love God is expecting His children to have and demonstrate within their relationship and in their homes.[7]

When Paul says in Ephesians 5:25, "Husbands, love your wives," he's not saying "love her because she deserves it"; he's saying "love her even if she doesn't deserve it. Love her enough to die for her, whether she's worth dying for or not." We are commanded to love our wives. It isn't an issue of attraction; whether she is now fat or slim; not about her submission or subjugation; it's an issue of a binding commandment from God.

Love is, therefore, very important for Christians. Jesus taught that the greatest commandments were to love God and to love our neighbors. He said that those two commandments summed up all the commandments that God gave to Moses. In the same way, people like Paul and John wrote how love should be a major part of every Christian's life. Because it is such an important idea to understand, it is helpful to see what the Bible tells us about love.

The true meaning of this significant word is clear in Hosea 2:19-20: "I will make you my wife forever, showing you righteousness and justice, unfailing love and

6 Ibid.
7 Ibid.

compassion. I will be faithful to you and make you mine, and you will finally know me as Lord." The meaning is also clear in Job 6:14-15, where kindness is contrasted with treachery and evil, and in 1 Samuel 20:8, which described a loving-kindness based on a covenant. This unshakable, steadfast love of God is contrasted with the unpredictable moods of the idols that some people worshiped. The Hebrew word hesed is not an emotional response to beauty, merit, or kindness. Instead, it is a moral attitude dedicated to another person's good, even if that other person is not lovable, worthy, or responsive (Deuteronomy 7:7-9).

This enduring loyalty, rooted in an unswerving purpose to do good things, could be stern. In the Old Testament, many of the prophets warned the people of Israel that God, in his love, was determined to discipline his people if they disobeyed him. But even with discipline, God's love does not change. During the years when the people of Israel were in exile, God's love persisted with infinite patience. God did not abandon the Israelites even when they were disobedient. God's love has within it kindness, tenderness, and compassion (Psalms 86:15;103:1-18; 136, and Hosea 11:1-4). However, its chief characteristic is a moral obligation for another person's well being.

Even though God's love was unconditional, he did expect the Israelites to respond to his loving acts. God's law encouraged the Israelites to be grateful for God's redemption of the Israelites (Deuteronomy 6:20-25). God expected the people of Israel to show this by being kind to the poor, the defenseless, the foreigners among them, slaves, widows, and all people who were suffering from any type of cruelty. Hosea similarly expected steadfast love among the people of Israel to result from the steadfast love God had shown for the Israelites (Hosea 6:6, 7:1-7 and 10:12-13).

Because of this, love for God and for "your neighbour as yourself" (Leviticus 19:18) are linked in Israel's law and prophecy. While there are other types of love described in the Old Testament, the most important type of love described in the Old Testament was based around three main ideas: God's love for the Israelites, the moral quality of love, and the close relationship between love for God and loving one's neighbour.

Families play a key role in the New Testament. In his preaching, Jesus used the family as a symbol for the relationship of God to his people (Matthew 19:14; Matthew 23:9; Luke 8:21). From his position on the cross, he gave John the responsibility for the care of his mother (John 19:27). Additionally, the Jerusalem church took fellowship meals in households (Acts 2:46).

Early believers held Christian meetings in their homes due to opposition from authorities. The book of Acts contains examples of entire families being converted at once to Christianity (Acts 10:24, Acts 44:1-48; Acts 16:15, Acts 31:1-32). Additionally, the Bible gives examples of the spiritual legacy many families enjoyed. For example, Timothy learned the gospel from his grandmother and mother (2 Timothy 1:5). In turn, his own family likely inherited his passion for Christ. Although being born into a Christian family does not make one a Christian, growing up with a spiritual heritage is a privilege. Many children suffer from lacking a moral and spiritual example in the home. The Bible stresses the important role a godly family plays in a child's upbringing. In fact, churches often see young couples return to God after they have children because they want their children raised in a Christian home.

<u>My Personal Notes</u>

4

MANHOOD AND WOMANHOOD
The Biblical Pattern
Wayne Grudem

Men and Women Are Equal in Value and Dignity

Very early in the Bible we read that both men and women are "in the image of God." In fact, the very first verse that tells us that God created human beings also tells us that both "male and female" are in the image of God:[1]

So God created man in his own image, in the image of God he created him; male and female he created them.—Gen. 1:27, emphasis added

To be in the image of God is an incredible privilege. It means to be like God and to represent God. No other creatures in all of creation, not even the powerful angels, are said to be in the image of God. It is a privilege given only to us as men and women. We are more like God than any other creatures in the universe, for we alone are "in the image of God."

Any discussion of manhood and womanhood in the Bible must start here. Every time we look at each other or talk to each other as men and women, we should remember that the person we are talking to is a creature of God who is more like God than anything else in the universe, and men and women share that status equally. Therefore we should treat men and women with equal dignity, and we should think of men and women as having equal value. We are both in the image of God, and we have been so since the very first day that God created us. "In the image of God he created him; male and female he created them" (Genesis 1:27). Nowhere does the Bible say that men are more in God's image than women. Men and women share equally in the tremendous privilege of being in the image of God.

---

1 Grudem, W. A. (2002). Biblical foundations for manhood and womanhood. Foundations for the family series (18–19). Wheaton, Ill.: Crossway Books.

The Bible thus almost immediately corrects the errors of male dominance and male superiority that have come as the result of sin and that have been seen in nearly all cultures in the history of the world. Wherever men are thought to be better than women, wherever husbands act as selfish dictators, wherever wives are forbidden to have their own jobs outside the home or to vote or to own property or to be educated, wherever women are treated as inferior, wherever there is abuse or violence against women or rape or female infanticide or polygamy or harems, the biblical truth of equality in the image of God is being denied. To all societies and cultures where these things occur, we must proclaim that the very beginning of God's Word bears a fundamental and irrefutable witness against these evils.

Yet we can say even more. If men and women are equally in the image of God, then we are equally important to God and equally valuable to Him. We have equal worth before Him for all eternity, for this is how we were created. This truth should exclude all our feelings of pride or inferiority and should exclude any idea that one sex is "better" or "worse" than the other. In contrast to many non-Christian cultures and religions, no one should feel proud or superior because he is a man, and no one should feel disappointed or inferior because she is a woman. If God thinks us to be equal in value, then that settles forever the question of personal worth, for God's evaluation is the true standard of personal value for all eternity.

Further evidence of our equality in the image of God is seen in the New Testament church, where the Holy Spirit is given in new fullness to both men and women (Acts 2:17–18), where both men and women are baptized into membership in the body of Christ (Acts 2:41), and where both men and women receive spiritual gifts for use in the life of the church (1 Cor. 12:7, 11; 1 Pet. 4:10). The apostle Paul reminds us that we are not to be divided into factions that think of themselves as superior and inferior (such as Jew and Greek, or slave and free, or male and female), but rather that we should think of ourselves as united because we are all "one" in Christ Jesus (Gal. 3:28).

By way of application to marriage, whenever husbands and wives do not listen respectfully and thoughtfully to each other's viewpoints, do not value the wisdom that might be arrived at differently and expressed differently from the other person, or do not value the other person's different gifts and preferences as much as their own, this teaching on equality in the image of God is being neglected.

Speaking personally, I do not think I listened very well to my wife Margaret early in our marriage. I did not value her different gifts and preferences as much as my own, or her wisdom that was arrived at or expressed differently. Later we made much progress in this area, but looking back, Margaret told me that early in our marriage she felt as though her voice was taken away, and as though my ears were closed. I wonder if there are other couples in many churches where God needs to open the husband's ears to listen and needs to restore the wife's voice to speak.

A healthy perspective on the way that equality manifests itself in marriage was summarized as part of a "Marriage and Family Statement" issued by Campus Crusade for Christ in July 1999. After three paragraphs discussing both equality and differences between men and women, the statement says the following:

In a marriage lived according to these truths, the love between husband and wife will show itself in listening to each other's viewpoints, valuing each other's gifts, wisdom, and desires, honoring one another in public and in private, and always seeking to bring benefit, not harm, to one another.

Why do I list this as a key issue in the manhood-womanhood controversy? Not because we differ with egalitarians on this question, but because we differ at this point with sinful tendencies in our own hearts. And we differ at this point with the oppressive male chauvinism and male dominance that has marred most cultures throughout most of history.

Why do I list this as a key issue? Because anyone preaching on manhood and womanhood has to start here—where the Bible starts—not with our differences, but with our equality in the image of God.

And to pastors who wish to teach on biblical manhood and womanhood in their churches, I need to say that if you don't start here in your preaching, affirming our equality in the image of God, you simply will not get a hearing from many people in your church. And if you don't start here, with male-female equality in the image of God, your heart won't be right in dealing with this issue.

The first step in correcting these mistakes is to be fully convinced in our hearts that women share equally with us men in the value and dignity that belongs to being made in the image of God.

Men and Women Have Different Roles in Marriage As Part of the Created Order

When the members of the Council on Biblical Manhood and Womanhood wrote the "Danvers Statement" in 1987, we included the following affirmations:

1. Both Adam and Eve were created in God's image, equal before God as persons and distinct in their manhood and womanhood.

2. Distinctions in masculine and feminine roles are ordained by God as part of the created order, and should find an echo in every human heart.

3. Adam's headship in marriage was established by God before the Fall, and was not a result of sin.

The statement adopted by the Southern Baptist Convention in June 1998 and affirmed (with one additional paragraph) by Campus Crusade in July 1999 also affirms God-given differences:

The husband and wife are of equal worth before God, since both are created in God's image. The marriage relationship models the way God relates to his people. A husband is to love his wife as Christ loved the church. He has the God-given responsibility to provide for, to protect, and to lead his family. A wife is to submit herself graciously to the servant leadership of her husband even as the church willingly submits to the headship of Christ. She being in the image of God as is her husband and thus equal to him, has the God-given responsibility to respect her husband and serve as his helper in managing the household and nurturing the next generation.

By contrast, egalitarians do not affirm such created differences. In fact, the "statement on men, women and Biblical equality" published by Christians for Biblical Equality (CBE) says:

1. The Bible teaches that both man and woman were created in God's image, had a direct relationship with God, and shared jointly the responsibilities of bearing and rearing children and having dominion over the created order (Gen. 1:26–28)....

2. The Bible teaches that the rulership of Adam over Eve resulted from the Fall and was, therefore, not a part of the original created order....

3. The Bible defines the function of leadership as the empowerment of others for service rather than as the exercise of power over them (Matt.

20:25–28, 23:8; Mark 10:42–45; John 13:13–17; Gal. 5:13; 1 Pet 5:2–3).

The Bible teaches that husbands and wives are heirs together of the grace of life and that they are bound together in a relationship of mutual submission and responsibility (1 Cor. 7:3–5; Eph. 5:21; 1 Pet. 3:1–7; Gen. 21:12). The husband's function as "head" (kephal) is to be understood as self-giving love and service within this relationship of mutual submission (Eph. 5:21–33; Col. 3:19; I Pet. 3:7).

So which position is right? Does the Bible really teach that men and women had different roles from the beginning of creation?

When we look carefully at Scripture, I think we can see at least ten reasons indicating that God gave men and women distinct roles before the Fall, and particularly that there was male headship in marriage before the Fall.

Ten Reasons Showing Male Headship in Marriage Before the Fall

1. The order: Adam was created first, then Eve (note the sequence in Gen. 2:7 and Gen. 2:18–23). We may not think of this as very important today, but it was important to the biblical readers, and the apostle Paul sees it as important: He bases his argument for different roles in the assembled New Testament church on the fact that Adam was created prior to Eve. He says, "I permit no woman to teach or to have authority over men.... For Adam was formed first, then Eve" (1 Tim. 2:12–13). According to Scripture itself, then, the fact that Adam was created first and then Eve has implications not just for Adam and Eve themselves, but for the relationships between men and women generally throughout time, including the church age.

2. The representation: Adam, not Eve, had a special role in representing the human race. Looking at the Genesis narrative, we find that Eve sinned first, and then Adam sinned (Gen. 3:6: "she took of its fruit and ate; and she also gave some to her husband who was with her, and he ate"). Since Eve sinned first, we might expect that the New Testament would tell us that we inherit a sinful nature because of Eve's sin, or that we are counted guilty because of Eve's sin. But this is not the case. In fact, it is just the opposite. We read in the New Testament, "For as in Adam all die, so also in Christ shall all be made alive" (1 Cor. 15:22). The New Testament does not say, "as in Eve all die, so also in Christ shall all be made alive."

This is further seen in the parallel between Adam and Christ, where Paul views Christ as the "last Adam":

Thus it is written, "The first man Adam became a living being"; the last Adam became a life-giving spirit.... The first man was from the earth, a man of dust; the second man is from heaven.... Just as we have borne the image of the man of dust, we shall also bear the image of the man of heaven.—1 Cor. 15:45–49 (see also Rom. 5:12–21, where another relationship between Adam and Christ is developed)

It is unmistakable, then, that Adam had a leadership role in representing the entire human race, a leadership role that Eve did not have. Nor was it true that Adam and Eve together represented the human race. It was Adam alone who represented the human race, because he had a particular leadership role that God had given him, a role that Eve did not share.

3. The naming of woman: When God made the first woman and "brought her to the man," the Bible tells us, Then the man said, "This at last is bone of my bones and flesh of my flesh; she shall be called Woman, because she was taken out of Man."—Gen. 2:23

When Adam says, "she shall be called Woman," he is giving a name to her. This is important in the context of Genesis 1–2, because in that context the original readers would have recognized that the person doing the "naming" of created things is always the person who has authority over those things.

In order to avoid the idea that Adam's naming of woman implies male leadership or authority, some egalitarians deny that Adam gives a name to his wife in Genesis 2:23.[2] But his objection is hardly convincing when we see how Genesis 2:23 fits into the pattern of naming activities throughout these first two chapters of Genesis. We see this when we examine the places where the same verb is used in contexts of naming in Genesis 1–2:

Genesis 1:5: "God called the light Day, and the darkness he called Night."
Genesis 1:8: "And God called the expanse Heaven."

---

2 *According to Wikipedia, "Egalitarianism (derived from the French word égal, meaning "equal"), is a trend of thought that favors equality of some sort. Its general premise is that people should be treated as equals on certain dimensions such as race, religion, ethnicity, political affiliation, economic status, social status, and cultural heritage. Egalitarian doctrines maintain that all humans are equal in fundamental worth or social status.In large part, it is a response to the abuses of statist development and has two distinct definitions in modern English. It is defined either as a political doctrine that all people should be treated as equals and have the same political, economic, social, and civil rights or as a social philosophy advocating the removal of economic inequalities among people or the decentralization of power."*

Genesis 1:10: "God called the dry land Earth, and the waters that were gathered together he called Seas."

Genesis 2:19: So out of the ground the Lord God formed every beast of the field and every bird of the heavens and brought them to the man to see what he would call them. And whatever the man called every living creature, that was its name."

Genesis 2:20: "The man gave names to all livestock and to the birds of the heavens and to every beast of the field."

Genesis 2:23: "Then the man said, 'This at last is bone of my bones and flesh of my flesh; she shall be called Woman, because she was taken out of Man.' "

In each of these verses prior to Genesis 2:23, the same verb had been used. Just as God demonstrated His sovereignty over day and night, heavens, earth, and seas by assigning them names, so Adam demonstrated his authority over the animal kingdom by assigning them names. The pattern would have been easily recognized by the original readers, and they would have seen a continuation of the pattern when Adam said, "she shall be called Woman."

The original readers of Genesis and of the rest of the Old Testament would have been familiar with this pattern, a pattern whereby people who have authority over another person or thing have the ability to assign a name to that person or thing, a name that often indicates something of the character or quality of the person. Thus parents give names to their children (see Gen. 4:25–26; 5:3, 29; 16:15; 19:37–38; 21:3). And God is able to change the names of people when He wishes to indicate a change in their character or role (see Gen. 17:5, 15, where God changes Abram's name to Abraham and where He changes Sarai's name to Sarah). In each of these passages we have the same verb as is used in Genesis 2:23 (the verb qara'), and in each case the person who gives the name is one in authority over the person who receives the name. Therefore when Adam gives to his wife the name "Woman," in terms of biblical patterns of thought this indicates a kind of authority that God gave to Adam, a leadership function that Eve did not have with respect to her husband.

We should notice here that Adam does not give the personal name "Eve" to his wife until Genesis 3:20 ("the man called his wife's name Eve, because she was the mother of all living"). This is because in the creation story in Genesis 2 Adam is giving a broad category name to his wife, indicating the name that would be given to womanhood generally, and he is not giving specific personal names designating the character of the individual person.

The naming of the human race: God named the human race "Man," not "Woman." Because the idea of naming is so important in the Old Testament, it is interesting what name God chose for the human race as a whole. We read: "When God created man, he made him in the likeness of God. Male and female he created them, and he blessed them and named them Man when they were created" (Gen. 5:1–2).

In the Hebrew text, the word that is translated "Man" is the Hebrew word 'adam. But this is by no means a gender-neutral term in the eyes of the Hebrew reader at this point, because in the four chapters prior to Genesis 5:2, the Hebrew word 'adam has been used many times to speak of a male human being in distinction from a female human being. In the following list the roman word man represents this same Hebrew word 'adam in every case:

Genesis 2:22: "And the rib that the Lord God had taken from the man he made into a woman and brought her to the man." (We should notice here that it does not say that God made the rib into another 'adam, another "man," but that He made the rib into a "woman," which is a different Hebrew word.)

Genesis 2:23: "Then the man said, 'This at last is bone of my bones and flesh of my flesh; she shall be called Woman…. ' "

Genesis 2:25: "And the man and his wife were both naked and were not ashamed."

Genesis 3:8: " … and the man and his wife hid themselves from the presence of the Lord God …"

Genesis 3:9: "But the Lord God called to the man and said to him, 'Where are you?' "

Genesis 3:12: "The man said, 'The woman whom you gave to be with me, she gave me fruit of the tree, and I ate.' "

Genesis 3:20: "The man called his wife's name Eve."

When we come, then, to the naming of the human race in Genesis 5:2 (reporting an event before the Fall), it would be evident to the original readers that God was using a name that had clear male overtones or nuances. In fact, in the first four chapters of Genesis the word 'adam had been used thirteen times to refer not to a human being in general but to a male human being. In addition to the eight examples mentioned above, it was used a further five times as a proper name for Adam in distinction from Eve (Gen. 3:17, 21; 4:1, 25; 5:1).

We are not saying here that the word *'adam* in the Hebrew Bible always refers to a male human being, for sometimes it has a broader sense and means something like "person." But here in the early chapters of Genesis the connection with the man in distinction from the woman is a very clear pattern. God gave the human race a name that, like the English word man, can either mean a male human being or can refer to the human race in general.

Does this make any difference? It does give a hint of male leadership, which God suggested in choosing this name. It is significant that God did not call the human race "Woman." (I am speaking, of course, of Hebrew equivalents to these English words.) Nor did he give the human race a name such as "humanity," which would have no male connotations and no connection with the man in distinction from the woman. Rather, he called the race "man." Raymond C. Ortlund rightly says, "God's naming of the race 'man' whispers male headship."

While it is Genesis 5:2 that explicitly reports this naming process, it specifies that it is referring to an event prior to sin and the Fall: "When God created man, he made him in the likeness of God. Male and female he created them, and he blessed them and named them Man when they were created" (Gen. 5:1–2).

And, in fact, the name is already indicated in Genesis 1:27: "So God created man in his own image, in the image of God he created him; male and female he created them." If the name man in English (as in Hebrew) did not suggest male leadership or headship in the human race, there would be no objection to using the word man to refer to the human race generally today. But it is precisely the hint of male leadership in the word that has led some people to object to this use of the word man and to attempt to substitute other terms instead. Yet it is that same hint of male leadership that makes this precisely the best translation of Genesis 1:27 and 5:2.

5. The primary accountability: God spoke to Adam first after the Fall. After Adam and Eve sinned, they hid from the Lord among the trees of the garden. Then we read, "But the Lord God called to the man and said to him, 'Where are you?'" (Gen. 3:9).

In the Hebrew text, the expression "the man" and the pronouns "him" and "you" are all singular. Even though Eve had sinned first, God first summoned Adam to give account for what had happened. This suggests that Adam was the one primarily accountable for what had happened in his family.

An analogy to this is seen in the life of a human family. When a parent comes into a room where several children have been misbehaving and have left the room in chaos, the parent will probably summon the oldest and say, "What happened here?" This is because, though all are responsible for their behavior, the oldest child bears the primary responsibility.

In a similar way, when God summoned Adam to give an account, it indicated a primary responsibility for Adam in the conduct of his family. This is similar to the situation in Genesis 2:15–17, where God had given commands to Adam alone before the Fall, indicating there also a primary responsibility that belonged to Adam. By contrast, the serpent spoke to Eve first (Gen. 3:1), trying to get her to take responsibility for leading the family into sin, and inverting the order that God had established at creation.

6. The purpose: Eve was created as a helper for Adam, not Adam as a helper for Eve. After God had created Adam and gave him directions concerning his life in the Garden of Eden, we read, "Then the Lord God said, 'It is not good that the man should be alone; I will make him a helper fit for him' " (Gen. 2:18).

It is true that the Hebrew word here translated "helper" (*'ezer*) is often used of God who is our helper elsewhere in the Bible. (See Ps. 33:20; 70:5; 115:9; etc.) But the word "helper" does not by itself decide the issue of what God intended the relationship between Adam and Eve to be. The nature of the activity of helping is so broad that it can be done by someone who has greater authority, someone who has equal authority, or someone who has lesser authority than the person being helped. For example, I can help my son do his homework. Or I can help my neighbor move his sofa. Or my son can help me clean the garage. Yet the fact remains that in the situation under consideration, the person doing the helping puts himself in a subordinate role to the person who has primary responsibility for carrying out the activity. Thus, even if I help my son with his homework, the primary responsibility for the homework remains his and not mine. I am the helper. And even when God helps us, with respect to the specific task at hand He still holds us primarily responsible for the activity, and He holds us accountable for what we do.

But Genesis 2 does not merely say that Eve functions as Adam's "helper" in one or two specific events. Rather, it says that God made Eve for the purpose of providing Adam with help, one who by virtue of creation would function as Adam's "helper": "Then the Lord God said, 'It is not good that the man should be alone; I will make him a helper fit for him' " (Gen. 2:18).

The Hebrew text can be translated quite literally as, "I will make for him [Hebrew lo] a helper fit for him." The apostle Paul understands this accurately because in 1 Corinthians 11 he writes, "for indeed man was not created for the woman's sake, but woman for the man's sake" (v. 9, nasb). Eve's role, and the purpose that God had in mind when He created her, was that she would be "for him … a helper."

Yet in the same sentence God emphasizes that she is not to help Adam as one who is inferior to him. Rather, she is to be a helper "fit for him," and here the Hebrew word kenegdô means "a help corresponding to him," that is, "equal and adequate to himself." So Eve was created as a helper, but as a helper who was Adam's equal. She was created as one who differed from him, but who differed from him in ways that would exactly complement who Adam was.

7. The conflict: The curse brought a distortion of previous roles, not the introduction of new roles.

After Adam and Eve sinned, God spoke words of judgment to Eve:
To the woman he said, "I will surely multiply your pain in childbearing; in pain you shall bring forth children. Your desire shall be for your husband, and he shall rule over you."—Gen. 3:16

The word translated **"desire"** is an unusual Hebrew word, *teshûqah*. What is the meaning of this word? In this context and in this construction, it probably implies an aggressive desire, perhaps a desire to conquer or rule over, or else an urge or impulse to oppose her husband, an impulse to act "against" him. This sense is seen in the only other occurrence of *teshûqah* in all the books of Moses (Genesis, Exodus, Leviticus, Numbers, Deuteronomy), and the only other occurrence of *teshûqah* plus the preposition 'el in the whole Bible. That occurrence of the word is in the very next chapter of Genesis, in 4:7. God says to Cain, "Sin is crouching at the door, and its desire is for you, but you must master it" (nasb). Here the sense is very clear. God pictures sin as a wild animal waiting outside Cain's door, waiting to attack him, even to pounce on him and overpower him. In that sense, sin's "desire" or "instinctive urge" is "against" him.

The striking thing about that sentence is what a remarkable parallel it is with Genesis 3:16. In the Hebrew text, six words are the same and are found in the same order in both verses. It is almost as if this other usage is put here by the author so that we would know how to understand the meaning of the term in Genesis 3:16. The expression in 4:7 has the sense, "desire, urge, impulse against" (or perhaps "desire to conquer, desire to rule over"). And that sense fits very well in Genesis 3:16 also.

Some have assumed that "desire" in Genesis 3:16 refers to sexual desire. But that is highly unlikely because (1) the entire Bible views sexual desire within marriage as something positive, not as something evil or something that God imposed as a judgment; and (2) surely Adam and Eve had sexual desire for one another prior to their sin, for God had told them to "be fruitful and multiply" (Gen. 1:28), and certainly in an unfallen world, along with the command, God would have given the desire that corresponded to it. So "your desire shall be for your husband" cannot refer to sexual desire. It is much more appropriate to the context of a curse to understand this as an aggressive desire against her husband, one that would bring her into conflict with him.

Then God says with regard to Adam, "and he shall rule over you" (Gen. 3:16). The word here translated "rule" is the Hebrew term *mashal*. This term is common in the Old Testament, and it regularly, if not always, refers to ruling by greater power or force or strength. It is used of human military or political rulers, such as Joseph ruling over the land of Egypt (Gen. 45:26), or the Philistines ruling over Israel (Judg. 14:4; 15:11), or Solomon ruling over all the kingdoms that he had conquered (1 Kings 4:21). It is also used to speak of God ruling over the sea (Ps. 89:9) or God ruling over the earth generally (Ps. 66:7). Sometimes it refers to oppressive rulers who cause the people under them to suffer (Neh. 9:37; Isa. 19:4). In any case, the word does not signify one who leads among equals, but rather one who rules by virtue of power and strength, and sometimes even rules harshly and selfishly.

Once we understand these two terms, we can see much more clearly what was involved in the curse that God brought to Adam and Eve as punishment for their sins.

One aspect of the curse was imposing pain on Adam's particular area of responsibility, raising food from the ground: "cursed is the ground because of you; in pain you shall eat of it all the days of your life; thorns and thistles it shall bring forth for you.... By the sweat of your face you shall eat bread, till you return to the ground" (Gen. 3:17–19). Another aspect of the curse was to impose pain on Eve's particular area of responsibility, the bearing of children: "I will surely multiply your pain in childbearing; in pain you shall bring forth children" (Gen. 3:16).

A third aspect of the curse was to introduce pain and conflict into the relationship between Adam and Eve. Prior to their sin, they had lived in the Garden of Eden in perfect harmony, yet with a leadership role belonging to Adam as the head of his family. But after the Fall, God introduced conflict in that Eve would have an inward urging and impulsion to oppose Adam, to resist Adam's leadership (the verb teshûqah). "Your impulse, your desire, will be against your husband." And Adam would respond with a rule over Eve that came from his greater strength and aggressiveness, a rule that was forceful and at times harsh (the verb mashal). "And he because of his greater strength will rule over you." There would be pain in tilling the ground, pain in bearing children, and pain and conflict in their relationship.

It is crucial at this point for us to realize that we ourselves are never to try to increase or perpetuate the results of the curse. We should never try to promote or advocate Genesis 3:16 as something good! In fact, the entire Bible following after Genesis 3 is the story of God's working to overcome the effects of the curse that He in His justice imposed. Eventually God will bring in new heavens and a new earth, in which crops will come forth abundantly from the ground (Isa. 35:1–2; Amos 9:13; Rom. 8:20–21) and in which there is no more pain or suffering (Rev. 21:4).

So we ourselves should never try to perpetuate the elements of the curse! We should not plant thorns and weeds in our garden but rather overcome them. We should do everything we can to alleviate the pain of childbirth for women. And we should do everything we can to undo the conflict that comes about through women desiring to oppose or even control their husbands and their husbands ruling harshly over them.

Therefore Genesis 3:16 should never be used as a direct argument for male headship in marriage. But it does show us that **the Fall brought about a distortion of previous roles, not the introduction of new roles.** The distortion was that Eve would now rebel against her husband's authority, and Adam would misuse that authority to rule forcefully and even harshly over Eve.

The restoration: When we come to the New Testament, salvation in Christ reaffirms the creation order.

If the previous understanding of Genesis 3:16 is correct, as we believe it is, then what we would expect to find in the New Testament is a reversal of this curse. We would expect to find an undoing of the wife's hostile or aggressive impulses against her husband and the husband's response of harsh rule over his wife.

In fact, that is exactly what we find. We read in the New Testament: "Wives, be subject to your husbands, as is fitting in the Lord. Husbands, love your wives, and do not be harsh with them" (Col. 3:18–19, niv).

This command is an undoing of the impulse to oppose (Hebrew teshûqah) and the harsh rule (Hebrew mashal) that God imposed at the curse.

What God does in the New Testament is reestablish the beauty of the relationship between Adam and Eve that existed from the moment they were created. Eve was subject to Adam as the head of the family. Adam loved his wife and was not harsh with her in his leadership. That is the pattern that Paul commands husbands and wives to follow.

The mystery: Marriage from the beginning of creation was a picture of the relationship between Christ and the church.

When the apostle Paul discusses marriage and wishes to speak of the relationship between husband and wife, he does not look back to any sections of the Old Testament telling about the situation after sin came into the world. Rather, he looks all the way back to Genesis 2, prior to the Fall, and uses that creation order to speak of marriage:

> *"For this reason a man shall leave his father and mother and be joined to his wife, and the two shall become one flesh." [This is a quote from Gen. 2:24.] This mystery is a profound one, and I am saying that it refers to Christ and the church.—Eph. 5:31–32, rsv*

Now a "mystery" in Paul's writing is something that was understood only very faintly, if at all, in the Old Testament, but that is now made clearer in the New Testament. Here Paul makes clear the meaning of the "mystery" of marriage as God created it in the Garden of Eden. Paul is saying that the "mystery" of Adam and Eve, the meaning that was not previously understood, was that marriage "refers to Christ and the church."

In other words, although Adam and Eve did not know it, their relationship represented the relationship between Christ and the church. They were created to represent that relationship, and that is what all marriages are supposed to do. In that relationship Adam represents Christ, and Eve represents the church, because Paul says, "for the husband is the head of the wife even as Christ is the head of the church" (Eph. 5:23).

Now the relationship between Christ and the church is not culturally variable. It is the same for all generations. And it is not reversible. There is a leadership or headship role that belongs to Christ that the church does not have. Similarly, in marriage as God created it to be, there is a leadership role for the husband that the wife does not have. And for our purposes it is important to notice that this relationship was there from the beginning of creation, in the beautiful marriage between Adam and Eve in the Garden.

10. The parallel with the Trinity: The equality, differences, and unity between men and women reflect the equality, differences, and unity in the Trinity.

Conclusion: Here then are at least ten reasons showing differences in the roles of men and women before the Fall. Some reasons are not as forceful as others, though all have some force. Some of them whisper male headship, and some shout it clearly. But they form a cumulative case showing that Adam and Eve had distinct roles before the Fall, and that this was God's purpose in creating them.

<u>My Personal Notes</u>

5

What God Expects from A Man?

How would you describe the way a male of the human species ought to look, talk, and act? What makes a man different from a womanand not only in biological terms? What is the biblical teaching on man's worth before God; his role in the family, church, workplace, and world at large; his friendships; his singleness? How is a man supposed to treat a woman? How has sin warped the male ideal? What should men be doing to be all that God wants them to be in a less-than-ideal world?[1]

These types of issues will be addressed in this workbook. It is our hope that if you are a man, you will learn more of how you can be all that God designed you to be. If you are a woman, perhaps these pages will help you to better understand and encourage the men in your life.

Does God expect too much from men? Surely He doesn't expect flesh-and-blood beings to duplicate the incredible feats of Superman? The fictional survivor of the ill-fated planet Krypton arrived on earth looking like a human, but he was actually an alien form of life. His super strength, ability to fly, and X-ray vision clearly set him apart from normal men. Superman was too good to be true. No man, single or married, young or old, could ever be like him.

This reference book is not about becoming a superman. It would be of little value to any of us to present a picture of the ideal man that no one could live up to. Real men have limited strength. They stumble and fall. They fail. They can't see

---

1 De Haan II, Martin R. What Does God Exoect Of A Man? (Grand Rapids, MI, USA: RBC Ministries, 1989). Excerpt with Permission. Copyright RBC Ministries 2011

through walls. They can't leap over tall buildings with a single bound, or even short buildings with a running start. But that is not to say that men should be content to be less than what God knows they can be.

God has high ideals for men, but He also knows they need help to achieve those ideals. So He offers His resources and encourages them to learn from Him, draw on His strength, and seek His guidance. To complicate matters, though, many different ideas of what a man should look and act like are being propagated in our world. God's pattern for men has gotten lost in the crowd. Many questions are being asked:

- How does a man express his sexuality?

- How are men supposed to show their emotions?

- How are men supposed to treat women?

- Does God expect all fathers to change diapers?

- How much are men supposed to listen to, and learn from, women?

- Does God's kind of man appreciate beauty?

- Does God expect a man to stop enjoying sports, hunting, or fast cars?

- Does God expect a man to have a lot of friends when he would rather be alone?

The present-day crisis over the male role is evident in several areas of society. The confusion over proper male behaviour has resulted in a variety of symptoms:

- Rampant sexual abuse.

- Marriage and family breakups.

- Male chauvinism and extreme feminism.

- Homosexuality, promiscuity, prostitution.

- AIDS and venereal diseases

- Sex scandals in politics and religion

- Pornography

- Deviant, sex-oriented rock music.

- Media stereotypes and decadence.

- Debate over male/female roles in churches.

- Women in traditionally male roles.

- Violence in sports.

- Ethical dilemmas in the workplace.

With so much confusion about how a man should act in today's world, we need to find answers we can trust and build our lives on. The purpose of this section is to focus on what we can know about men as God wants them to be, and as God can help them to be.

If you were to interview men and women, rich and poor, capitalists and communists, jungle inhabitants and sophisticated urban dwellers, old and young, you would hear so many different ideas on what a man should be that your head

would spin. So many of those ideas are merely expressions of temporary cultural situations. What we need are timeless principles that come from the One who made man in the first place.

It is the Bible that helps us to know what God has said and how He intended men to act. So as you read, keep your Bible open and study the issues carefully for yourself.

Even if you acknowledge the Bible as having come from God, you may wonder how much of what the Bible records was culture-bound and how much applies to today's society. The world has changed a great deal since biblical times. The basic issues, though, are the same. In His wisdom, God has given us guidelines to help us find answers for the confusing questions about man's purpose and place in today's world. The Bible contains principles that cross cultural boundaries.

In the following pages we will look at the plan of God for men as revealed in Scripture. God expects a man to demonstrate:

- Masculine Distinction

- Servant Leadership

- Spiritual Equality

- Strength Of Character

Masculine Distinction

Rambo--the popular, fictional, one-man war machine? Who would dare call him anything but masculine? His bulging biceps can take on an army and leave it in shambles. But is he masculine in the biblical sense?
What does it mean to be masculine? Which of the following are masculine qualities?

- The ability to benchpress your own weight.

- Auto grease under your fingernails.

- An appetite for meat and potatoes (not quiche).

- Scars from street fights.

- A deep voice that utters expletives.

- Treatment of women and children as slaves.

- Loud, opinionated, and bigoted ideas.

- Viewing women as sex objects.

- A fanatical following of sports.

- A refusal to cry.

- A rough and gruff demeanor.

You won't get much help from a dictionary if you want to define masculinity. It will only tell you that males have masculine traits, as opposed to feminine traits. To define masculinity, you must combine the genetic distinctions as well as the God-expected distinctions.

How are men different from women? Some physical traits may come to mind. But the God-designed differences go further than external features. Men and women are different down to each and every cell of their bodies--down to the 23rd chromosome to be exact. Males and females differ physically, emotionally, psychologically, mentally, and relationally.

The male hormone testosterone affects both the way a man's body develops and the way his brain thinks. Compared to a woman, a man generally has a smaller stomach; larger lungs; 20 percent more red blood cells; 50 percent greater brute strength; a shorter lifespan; less ability to stand high temperatures; a lower heart rate; he has greater sensitivity to light but less sensitivity to sound; greater likelihood of being left-handed, dyslexic, or nearsighted; greater tendency to have allergies; greater aggressiveness; stronger sex drive; he is more easily stimulated sexually by sight; less aware of how to develop an interpersonal relationship; more logical and less intuitive.

Men and women are different inside and outside. They look, act, and think differently. Current research is discovering anatomical differences in the brain that may underlie subtle differences in mental abilities that determine verbal skills and spatial perception.

Is masculinity important to God? Or are we making a bigger deal of masculinity and femininity than He cares about? Hardly. From the beginning of human existence, God has had very strong views about masculinity and femininity.

In Genesis 1:27 we are told, "So God created man in His own image; in the image of God He created him; male and female He created them." Masculinity and femininity were part of God's plan. Men were designed for a specific purpose. In Genesis 2:18, God said, "It is not good that man should be alone; I will make him a helper comparable to him." Then after mentioning the animals God had created and that Adam had named, the narrative states, "But for Adam there was not found a helper comparable to him" (v.20).

That comment is followed by an explanation that the man and woman were designed to marry, to cooperate, to "become one flesh" (v.24), to propagate the human race, and rule the natural world together (Gen. 1:27,28; 2:18,21-24). Adam's masculinity was somehow incomplete and undefined without a feminine human presence.

What does our present-day culture say about masculinity? Some people deny the biblical distinctions of purpose and God-designed functions and say that the only difference between masculinity and femininity is the reproductive role. Some males speak as if masculinity is a mark of superiority, while some women speak of males as the enemy.

Sex roles are being confused, and society is paying the price. Many music stars convey an androgynous image of sexuality, with men that look and act more like women. Homosexuals are fighting for acceptance, promoting their man-with-man and woman-with-woman brand of sex as an acceptable alternative lifestyle, and the British Society government have succome to their pressure and granted them that which only God can give.

Another twisted concept of masculinity is expressed by those who are preoccupied with feeding their sexual urges. Pornography is spreading its poison, leaving victims addicted to fantasies, perversions, and violent sexuality. At its most basic level, masculinity has been reduced to mean nothing more than possessing male sex organs with the accompanying sex drive. But that's not the way it's supposed to be.

The Bible contains numerous warnings against sexual perversions that violate both nature and God's laws for the proper expression of our male and female sexuality.

What God expects or allows for men does not include promiscuity (Ex. 20:14; Lev. 20:10; Prov. 6:24-35; 1 Cor. 6:15-20), homosexuality (Lev. 18:22; Rom. 1:26,27), or pornographic lust (Matt. 5:27,28; Col. 3:5). These activities make a male less of a man in God's eyes.

Why has masculinity taken such a beating? Romans 1 details the reason for the problem. Because of sin and idolatry, humanity's relationship with God has been broken. Verse 21 states, "Although they knew God, they did not glorify Him as God, nor were thankful, but became futile in their thoughts, and their foolish hearts were darkened." Verse 24 describes the results of that rebellion: "Therefore God also gave them up to uncleanness, in the lusts of their hearts, to dishonour their bodies among themselves."

Sin has permeated society. The departure from God's revealed truth has resulted in all kinds of perversions in sexuality and relationships.

Does God's idea of masculinity require marriage? Not necessarily. The single life is an acceptable option (1 Cor. 7:1,8). The original ideal in Genesis was for one man to be married to one woman. Although the Bible speaks of married life as the norm, the single life is acceptable and even preferable for some people (Matt. 19:12; 1 Cor. 7:32-35).

Jesus and the apostle Paul are two examples of single men who were in God's will. What else makes a man a man? The remainder of this section will discuss how God has designed men to live out their masculine distinction--by acting with servant leadership, spiritual equality, and strength of character.

Thinking It Over. What kinds of models of masculinity are being presented in today's society for young boys to follow? How have religious groups caved in to the pressures of society and allowed masculine distinctives to be blurred? How do perversions of masculine distinctives affect a woman's view of her own femininity?

Servant Leadership

The title of this section may sound like a contradiction of terms. Servant leadership seems to fit in with the absurd categories of frigid heat, smooth roughness, dry wetness, light darkness, friendly animosity, or ignorant intelligence. The words servant leadership could be contradictory, depending on how they are defined. But in the biblical use of the terms, leadership does not mean dictatorship, nor is a servant someone who is mindlessly subservient to every whim of a master.

What kind of leadership are we talking about? Biblical leadership is responsible, compassionate, understanding, accountable, competent, respectable, authoritative, pioneering, exemplary, and God-fearing. Being a leader does not mean making all the decisions. Nor does it refer to being the "boss" in marriage, the church, or society at large. Leadership implies taking initiative, accepting responsibility, and shouldering the weight of accountability before God.

What kind of servanthood are we talking about? Biblical servanthood is responsive, respectful, willing, loving, self-sacrificing, and submissive. Servanthood does not mean unthinking obedience. What it does mean is a willingness to lower oneself, to humbly serve another person, to put the best interests of someone else above your own enjoyment.

"Wait just a minute!" some men might cry out. "Doesn't the Bible say that wives are to be submissive to their husbands?" Yes, it does (Eph. 5:22). But in a broader sense, it states that men and women are to submit to one another (v.21), and husbands are to love their wives "just as Christ also loved the church and gave Himself for it" (v.25).

How can servanthood and leadership be compatible? It may seem like trying to mix oil and water. In the verses that were mentioned above, Christ is the perfect example of how those two attributes can be combined. He had the power to force us to do what He wanted, but instead He put up with rejection, disobedience, and even crucifixion (Phil. 2:5-11). Jesus described the goal of His life this way: ". . . the Son of Man did not come to be served, but to serve, and to give His life a ransom for many" (Matt. 20:28).

If anyone had the right to dictate by virtue of His authority and power, it was Jesus Christ. But He came to earth and took on human flesh, patiently putting up with imperfect and stubborn people in order to provide exactly what we needed. He provided strong leadership, but His love for people permeated His leadership style. He never forced anyone to follow Him. Rather He earned the respect and obedience of men and women. They willingly followed Him. That's the kind of leadership men need to provide today.

How does servant leadership work out in different roles? The following brief listing offers some examples of how it works.

As a single man. The single male needs to show people of all ages and both sexes that he cares about others, not just himself. He must model a life that is worth following (1 Tim. 4:12-16). Single women should be attracted to him because of his character, stability, and desire to edify others.

As a husband. The husband is said to be the head of his wife as Christ is the head of the church (1 Cor. 11:3), and he is to love his wife as Christ loved the church (Eph. 5:25). A husband must visibly and verbally put love into action if he expects his wife to be willing to follow his lead.

As a father. The father is responsible for the training of his children (Deut 6:6-9; Eph. 6:4), he is to provide for their needs (1 Tim. 5:8), and he is to treat them in a way that does not exasperate them (Eph. 6:4; Col. 3:21).

As a church leader. Men in leadership in the church must lead the people under their care, much as a shepherd leads, feeds, protects, and nurtures a flock of sheep (1 Pet. 5:1-4).

As a member of society. The Old Testament character Daniel demonstrated a willingness to take a stand for the Lord. He did what was right, no matter what the personal risk (Dan. 1,6). He made a difference because he courageously honoured the Lord in a pagan world.

Why is leadership in marriage and in the church a male quality? It's not because males are superior beings (though many men would like to think so). Men and women are equals in Christ (Gal. 3:28). The issue is God-ordained function, not man-ordained bigotry. Somehow we need to get it out of our heads that leadership means superiority and supportive roles mean inferiority. After all, God the Father is the head of Christ, yet they are equal (1 Cor. 11:3).

The first indication of male leadership comes in the creation narrative of Genesis. Adam was created first and Eve was created to complement (complete) the man. God said, "It is not good that man should be alone; I will make him a helper comparable to him" (Gen. 2:18). First Corinthians 11:7-11 and 1 Timothy 2:13 state that men should be leaders in the church because men were designed to lead, as evidenced by Adam being created first and Eve created to be his helping counterpart.

What does headship mean, and where does the term come from? When the topic of headship is introduced, many people suddenly get the mental picture of a Hitler-type dictator who gives orders (often unreasonable). First Corinthians 11:3 uses the word head, as does Ephesians 5:23. This term includes the meaning of "origin" or "source," so some have interpreted headship to mean that woman was created from man. They conclude that as Christ is the source of life for all believers, so man (Adam) was the source of woman's life. However, it hardly makes sense that Paul intended to exclude the concept of leadership or authority from the concept of headship. He uses the term headship to denote God's relationship to Christ, and Christ's leadership over all believers, the church (Eph. 1:22; 4:15; 5:23; Col. 1:18; 2:19).

This concept of leadership in the home is included in the list of qualifications for church leaders in 1 Timothy 3:4,5,12. In Titus 2:5, the apostle Paul told the older women to teach the younger women to be "obedient to their own husbands, that the word of God may not be blasphemed."

Is male headship a result of the fall? And if so, shouldn't we as redeemed people be working to reverse the effects of the fall? Some people have argued that position quite forcefully, but their arguments run against the biblical data. The apostle Paul made the point of headship based on the order of creation (1 Cor. 11:8,9; 1 Tim. 2:13,14). Headship is not a result of the fall; rather it has been perverted by the fall.

When God explained the punishment on men and women because of sin, He said to the woman:

> *I will greatly multiply your sorrow and your conception; in pain you shall bring forth children; your desire shall be for your husband, and he shall rule over you (Gen. 3:16).*

This verse, particularly the phrase "your desire shall be for your husband," has been interpreted in many different ways. Some Bible teachers have taken this to mean that the woman, because of the fall, will be drawn to depend on man. These teachers also believe that the phrase "he shall rule over you" is a positive statement about the man bringing order and security into the woman's life. Others, however, see the man's rule described here as an unnatural domination over women.

There is another possible interpretation that seems to fit the context. Some Bible teachers are convinced that the Hebrew word for desire comes from an Arabic root that means "to urge," "to drive on," or "to seek control." They also point out that the same Hebrew words for desire and rule are used in the same grammatical structure in both Genesis 3:16 and 4:7. In chapter 4, it is sin that "desires" Cain and wants to force him to do what is wrong. But Cain could choose to stay in control and reject the temptation to sin. The word desire in both 3:16 and 4:7 could be understood as a strong desire to control. One result of the fall, therefore, is that women would have an unnatural desire to control men. And the man's proper role as leader would degenerate into a despotic rule.

While this last interpretation is disputed by some, it does accurately describe the battle of the sexes since the fall. Instead of peaceful harmony where man and woman complement each other, each has tried to dominate and manipulate the other for selfish goals. Instead of acting as complements, they have behaved more like contradictions.

Should men expect women to "heel, roll over, and play dead" when men are around? Must men be the initiators of ideas and actions, and must women sit back or follow from a respectable distance? Should we think of women like some people think of children, that they should be seen and not heard? Archie Bunker thought so on the All in the Family television series. But that is not what God expects.

One look at the examples in both the Old and New Testaments shows that godly women were not passive slaves. They made a significant positive difference in their situations and made a valuable contribution to both social and spiritual life (Prov. 31:10-31; 1 Sam. 25:18-44; 2 Kin. 22:14-20; Judg. 4:1-24; Ruth; Esth.; Luke 2:36-38; 8:1-3; Rom. 16:1-15; Phil. 4:3; 2 Tim. 1:5).

Why is a servant attitude so important? Leadership without loving service produces an unbalanced, hideous creature. To be willing to take the role of a servant requires deliberate acts of love. The kind of man worth following expresses the love described for us in 1 Corinthians 13. This love:

• is patient	• is not a grudge-keeper
• is kind	• is not an evil thinker
• is not envious	• is not a fan of evil
• is not boastful	• rejoices in truth
• is not proud	• protects
• is not rude	• trusts
• is not selfish	• hopes
• is not easily angered	• perseveres

Spiritual Equality

"One must utter three doxologies every day: Praise God that He did not create me a heathen! Praise God that He did not create me a woman! Praise God that He did not create me an illiterate person!" (Rabbi Juda ben Elai, circa AD 150). Such has been the view of some men--religious men at that! Women have often been treated as second-class citizens of earthly kingdoms and the heavenly kingdom. Women, though, have not been the only targets of prejudice. Men and women alike have been the victims of discrimination by those who wanted to elevate their own self-interests.

Why has inequality existed? Why is this even an issue? Many people give lip service to the idea that all humans were created equal, but they think and act as if some people were created "more equal" than others. Others come right out and claim some sort of genetic superiority (as did Adolf Hitler). Human beings around the world have had the tendency to try to protect their own interests by denying the rights of others. Bigotry, racism, genocide, abortion, caste systems, financial snobbery, and other expressions of selfish self-interest have flourished at the expense of human dignity and life. But that's not the way God intended the world to be.

One of the expressions of selfish self-interest has been the age-old battle of the sexes. Confusion and debate over male-female equality exists because of prejudice and discrimination; misinterpretation of the Bible; male and female insecurities, failures, and overreactions; men failing to treat women as equals; women doing well in traditionally male roles; women desiring opportunities for service.

Were women created to be the equals of men? In the beginning, "God created man in His own image; in the image of God He created him; male and female He created them" (Gen. 1:27). Notice that both man and woman were created in God's image. One sex does not have an inherent superiority over the other. And because both were created in God's image, both deserve the highest respect for the value of their personhood.

In the verse that follows, God gave man and woman several commands. "God said to them, 'Be fruitful and multiply; fill the earth and subdue it; have dominion over . . . every living thing that moves on the earth.' " The mandate to populate the earth and to rule over it was given to both man and woman. Both men and women are in a position of dominion over the earth. Man is not put on the earth to be ruled by woman, nor is woman put on the same level as the animals to be ruled by man.

Does equality mean sameness? No. When God created Eve, He said that she would be a "helper comparable to him" (Gen. 2:18). Eve was made of the same "stuff" as Adam. She was the necessary companion if Adam was going to reproduce and rule the earth. No sense of inferiority is implied by the word helper. Eve was different. And her abilities would complement Adam's.

Can men and women be considered equals if we make a distinction in their functions? At one time during the civil rights debate in the United States, some people proposed a "separate but equal" policy as a solution. The idea was to provide separate public services, job opportunities, and education to both minorities and the racial majority. It was interpreted by many to be a ploy to preserve segregation and perpetuate a skin-deep sense of racial supremacy. The "separate but equal" policy only served to propagate inequality.

Many women feel that they too have a separate and unequal position in life. No matter how much men talk about equality, some women feel they are treated like second-class citizens. Their feelings are often well-founded. Because of sin, men have tended to gravitate to one of two extremes: they either become passive and withdrawn or they become overly aggressive and domineering. In male-dominated societies, the general tendency has been to suppress women. Their intellectual abilities have been overlooked, their strengths ignored, and their worth unappreciated.

So how do we defend the biblical idea of different roles or functions for men and women? Aren't we perpetuating a self-serving separate-but-equal policy? No. There's a big difference between the racial issue and the sex factor when it comes to leadership in the home and in the church. For one thing, we are talking about a God-created difference rather than a man-imposed distinction. As we saw in the section on masculine distinction, God created male and female with complementary strengths. And as we saw in the section on servant leadership, God created a functional order. This in no way implies that women are viewed as less spiritual by God, nor do they get less attention from God, nor is their role any less important to Him, nor are they less accountable for their actions.

A woman is designed with the capability of bearing and nurturing children. Does that mean that the man is inferior? Of course not. Men are genetically designed to be physically stronger, to be able to do more strenuous work--and that does not make the female to be inferior. The list could go on and on. In each case it is not a matter of superiority but of complementary strengths that God has built into males and females.

What does the Bible say about the equality of male and female? The key verse in the Bible on this topic is Galatians 3:28. In order to get a sense of the context, here are verses 26 through 29.

For you are all sons of God through faith in Christ Jesus. For as many of you as were baptized into Christ have put on Christ. There is neither Jew nor Greek, there is neither slave nor free, there is neither male nor female; for you are all one in Christ Jesus. And if you are Christ's, then you are Abraham's seed, and heirs according to the promise.

Is the apostle Paul saying that no longer should we make any distinction based on a person's gender? No. Paul is discussing the reality of the spiritual unity that believers have in Christ. Racial, social, and sexual distinctions do not make any difference when it comes to becoming a child of God through faith. In Christ, we all have access to God. In Christ, we all become equal recipients of God's grace. In Christ, we all become heirs of everything salvations holds for us.

In a highly prejudiced first-century society, the words of the apostle Paul were quite shocking. Many religious Jews had developed the arrogant attitude that they were spiritually superior to non-Jews. Masters often treated slaves like property rather than people created in God's image. Women too were often considered to be spiritually inferior to men. The words of the apostle Paul struck a nerve when he proclaimed that faith in Christ is the great equalizer. It was a radical, God-inspired thought for Paul's readers.

How should men treat women? Here are several biblical principles:

With purity. Paul told Timothy to treat younger women as if they were his sisters, "with all purity" (1 Tim. 5:2). Impure sexual joking (Eph. 5:3,4) or sexual activity outside of marriage is forbidden (Heb. 13:4).

With understanding. Husbands are to be understanding as they live with their wives (1 Pet. 3:7). Even though the command has primary significance for marriage, the principle would seem to be applicable for the way men, single or married, should treat all women. Men need to invest the time and energy it takes to try to understand how a woman thinks, feels, and acts. Men must not expect women to be like them.

With dignity and honour. The apostle Paul instructed Timothy to treat an older woman as if she were his mother (1 Tim. 5:2). Peter told husbands to honour their wives (1 Pet. 3:7). Though the primary application of this command is to a husband-wife relationship, the same truth should apply to any male-female relationship (Rom. 12:10). Peter said the reason for giving such honour is that Christian women are co-heirs with Christian men of all the spiritual riches in Christ (1 Pet. 3:7; cp. Eph. 1:3,18). Husbands are to honour their wives so their "prayers may not be hindered."

With love. No other command is so demanding or all-inclusive. Love encompasses all the other commands of how men are to act. Husbands are to love their wives with a love that imitates the kind of love Christ has for the church (Eph. 5:25-33). A man should treat a woman as he would want to be treated (Matt. 7:12; 22:39).

With an awareness of their giftedness. The apostle Paul stated that "there are diversities of gifts, but the same Spirit. There are differences of ministries, but the same Lord. And there are diversities of activities, but it is the same God who works all in all. But the manifestation of the Spirit is given to each one for the profit of all" (1 Cor. 12:4-7). Both men and women are gifted by the Holy Spirit.

No one is excluded. And the New Testament gives us many examples of women who demonstrated a giftedness in the church. Romans 16 contains a list of the many women that Paul mentioned who had a notable impact on the spiritual life of the churches.

With submission. "Wait a minute," you might say. "Isn't the man supposed to be the leader?" Yes, but the Scripture also says, "submitting to one another in the fear of God" (Eph. 5:21). That doesn't contradict the headship of the husband, but it does mean that the man is to be self-sacrificing--loving as Christ loved us and gave His life for us. Christ's concept of leadership is not that of a dictator, but it is that of a servant-leader.

Thinking It Over. How do men treat women in your family, your church, your community? Do you agree that complementary functions should not be thought of as being unequal in value? How should a man (as a single, married, or church leader) encourage women to use their spiritual gifts?

Strength of character

What must a man do to develop bulging biceps and perfect pectorals?

It takes a lot of exercise, to be sure, as well as the right kind of diet. As the saying goes, "No pain, no gain." Strength of character doesn't come automatically either. It is developed over time as a person exercises wisdom in following God's will. It comes as a man feeds on a steady diet of God's Word and follows His training program.

The apostle Paul used the analogy of athletics when he wrote to the believers in Corinth. He said, "And everyone who competes for the prize is temperate in all things. . . . Therefore I run thus: not with uncertainty. Thus I fight: not as one who beats the air. But I discipline my body and bring it into subjection, lest, when I have preached to others, I myself should become disqualified" (1 Cor. 9:25-27). And Paul told Timothy, "exercise yourself rather to godliness" (1 Tim. 4:7).

What is strength of character? We've already hinted that to some extent it can be equated with godliness or spiritual maturity. It is that--and much more. But first we need to define character. D. L. Moody said, "Character is what you are in the dark." That's true. Character is what you are really like, not the coverup that you allow others to see. Character is what guides your actions and produces the words you speak. Character is your unique identity, the sum total of your individual characteristics.

Character can be good or bad.

Strength of character refers to strong, good character. A person strong in character is someone who stands for what is right, who has the "backbone" to express and live out his convictions. And those qualities are part of what God expects of a man. So when we talk about "strength of character" as something that God expects of a man, we are talking about the qualities of godliness and spiritual maturity, a consistency of character that reflects a proper self-image, and a life that expresses the character qualities that God wants to develop in every man.

What produces strong character?

- Self-confidence--which comes from being at peace with God and knowing who we are in Christ (Rom. 5:1; Eph. 1,2).

- Consistency (Eph. 2:10; Phil. 3:16; Titus 2:12-14; James 2:14-26).

- Training (Phil. 2:12; 3:12-14; 1 Tim. 4:7).

- Right priorities (Mt. 6:33; 1 Sam. 13:13-14).

- Following the right example (1 Cor. 11:1; Heb. 12:1-3; 13:7; 1 Pet. 2:21).

- Obedience to God's commands (1 John 2:5).

- A steady diet of God's Word (1 Pet. 2:2).

- Relying on the strength of the Spirit (Gal. 5:16-25; Eph. 5:18; Phil. 4:13).

- Right choices--living out the Christian faith, doing what is right no matter what (James 2:14-26).

- Trusting and depending on God (Prov. 3:5,6).

- Learning from others (Eph. 4:7-16).

What are some strong character qualities? A concise list of qualities that are desirable in a man is found in 1 Timothy 3. Although the apostle Paul outlined these character qualities for the purpose of selecting those who were qualified to be church leaders, the characteristics describe what God is looking for in all men. As you read through the list, you will see that they describe character traits and not intellectual ability, education, seminary training, or pulpit expertise. All men should be striving toward these qualities.

Let's look briefly at the characteristics given in 1 Timothy 3:1-7 and apply them in a broader sense to all men.

1. Blameless. God expects men to be above reproach. This is an all-inclusive term that summarizes all the qualities described in 1 Timothy 3. It means that a man must have a pattern of life that is consistent with biblical standards.

2. Husband of one wife. A married man must be faithful to his wife. He keeps his marriage vows and does not toy with any type of sexual immorality. Literally "a one-woman man," this qualification has a broader possible meaning that a man is not to be a "womanizer" or a flirt. His heart is not to be afire with lust (Matt. 5:27,28).

3. Temperate. Gene Getz has stated that "a man who is temperate does not lose his physical, psychological, and spiritual orientation. He remains stable and steadfast, and his thinking is clear." Such a man is balanced in his living, not given to destructive extremes.

4. Soberminded. This term is closely related to the term temperate. It refers to the quality of being sensible in thinking and actions, exhibiting sound judgment.

5. Of good behaviour. A man should be respectable and honourable in his actions.

6. Hospitable. The Greek term behind this word literally means "loving strangers." In a general sense, this term refers to friendliness and a willingness to help those in need.

7. Able to teach. This characteristic carries two possible meanings. It may mean that a man should have the ability to instruct others about the Christian faith. Or it could mean that a man is to be "teachable." If we combine these two elements, the term refers to an ability to teach others without arrogance.

8. Not given to wine. A man of God is not one who is controlled by alcohol (Eph. 5:18). In our day and age, this could be applied to illegal drugs as well. God does not want us to abuse our bodies or cloud our minds.

9. Not violent. The Greek word literally means "not a striker." Temper tantrums do not please God. This includes both violent actions and words.

10. Gentle. A God-honouring man, according to this term, would be gracious, kind, forbearing, and considerate of others.

11. Not quarrelsome. A man is not to be one who is always looking for an argument or stirring up trouble.

12. Not greedy for money nor covetous. Acquiring money and possessions should not be a priority. Jesus and Paul warned against a preoccupation with money (Matt. 6:19-21; 1 Tim. 6:10).

13. Rules his own house well. The man is the head of the home. He is responsible to see that his relationship with his wife and children is good. He is to be a good manager of home life.

14. Having his children under submission. A father is to be a respected leader at home, a man who does all that is in his power to train and discipline his children.

15. Not a novice. A new believer who becomes a leader before he is mature in his faith and practice runs a risk of falling into pride. This is a warning that a man is not to take on responsibilities that he is not mature enough to handle. Men must guard themselves against pride.

16. Good testimony among those outside. A man must develop a good reputation with non-Christians. He is to have a consistent faith that will be a strong witness to unbelievers.

How did Jesus show strength of character?

- He showed compassion (Mark 1:40-42).

- He dared to speak the truth about sin and hypocrisy (Matt. 23; John 8:31-59).

- He hated sin but showed love for hurting sinners (John 8:1-11).

- He took time to pray (Matt. 14:23; Mark 14:32-42; John 17).

- He refused to yield to temptation--drawing strength from the Word of God (Matt. 4).

- He spoke out for God's honour (Matt. 21:12,13).

- He followed through on His commitments (John 12:23-33).

- He humbly served others (Matt. 20:28; Phil. 2:1-11).

- He had His priorities straight (Matt. 5--7).

- He was forgiving (Matt. 18:21-35; Luke 23:34).

How did other men in the Bible display strength of character? Though no man can measure up to Christ's perfection, several men in Scripture do display the type of character traits that all men are to develop in their lives. Here are some examples.

Noah. He was like a beacon of light in the darkness. In a decadent culture, he stood out as a righteous man, willing to obey the Lord and build a ship for 120 years (Gen. 6; Heb. 11:7).

Abraham. Even though he had seniority, he kept the peace by graciously giving Lot first choice of grazing land (Gen. 13).

Joseph. He fled sexual temptation because of his reverence for God (Gen. 39). When he had opportunity for revenge against his brothers, he instead showed compassion, forgiveness, and love (Gen. 42--45).

Moses. He chose to obey the Lord rather than live a life focused on pleasure (Heb. 11:24,25).

David. Even though he was wrongfully accused and relentlessly pursued by Saul, David showed respect for King Saul (1 Sam. 24).

Daniel. As a young man in exile, he would not compromise his standards (Dan. 1:8) nor hide his faith (6:10-23).

Boaz. He protected Ruth's safety and honour, and he assumed responsibility for her (Ruth 2-4).

Stephen. Other believers recognized that he was a man "of good reputation, full of the Holy Spirit and wisdom" (Acts 6:3,5).

Paul. He showed spiritual sensitivity to believers with weak consciences (1 Cor. 9:19-23), and he vigorously guarded his integrity (vv.24-27).

Barnabas. This faithful worker encouraged others (Acts 4:36; 11:23,24), and he took a risk by giving Mark a second chance (Acts 15:36-41).

Thinking It Over. Men, what are you doing to develop strength of character in your life? How do you measure up to the qualities listed in 1 Timothy 3:1-7? What can you do today and in the coming days to be more like Christ? Which would you rather be suffering from: a high fever or hypothermia? Probably neither one, right? Both options are unhealthy extremes. Unhealthy extremes also exist among men. Too many of us men exhibit behavior that does not reflect what God expects of a man.

Listed below are several forms of extreme behavior that men fall into. What biblical principles does each violate? Use this section to review the main points of this reference book:

A Player/playboy. This guy lacks sexual self-control. His sexual appetite controls his life.

Macho man. He seems to think masculine means muscles, meanness, and mastery of women.

Mama's boy. This adult male has never cut the apron strings. Mother still controls his life.

Tinkerer. This guy has a closer relationship with his hobby than he does with people.

Jellyfish. He allows his friends, wife, children, and co-workers to walk all over him.

General. As a boss, husband, church officer, or community leader, he barks orders.

Gymn Rat. This man's thoughts and energies go toward watching or participating in sports.

Gay Guy. He may be male in body but his mind and actions contradict his sexual identity.

Workaholic. The job is number one, the source of his sense of satisfaction and security.

Zombie. He grew up thinking that a man should never show emotions, so he doesn't.

God's expectations are attainable.

God's expectations are attainable. He's not looking for perfection, but He does expect a willingness to allow Him to work in our lives, a readiness to admit wrong attitudes and actions, and an eagerness to aim for Christlikeness every day. Now is the time to stand up and be counted among the men who choose to follow His principles for masculine distinction, servant leadership, spiritual equality, and strength of character. The responsibilities are beyond a man's natural abilities. Sin has badly warped God's plan for man. But the Perfect Man, Jesus Christ, can help. He not only came to earth to show us how to live, but He came to die so we would not have to be judged for our sinful failures. If you have never done so, take a moment right now to talk to God. Use your own words, but admit to Him your sinful failures as a man. Tell Him you know that you do not measure up to His holy standards of right living. Then look to Jesus. Tell God that you believe that Christ died for you and took the punishment you deserved. Accept the new spiritual life He offers. Thank Him for forgiveness of sin and release from the penalty of death, and thank Him for the gift of new life.

<u>My Personal Notes</u>

My Personal Notes

6
WHAT DOES GOD EXPECT OF A WOMAN?

Headline news announced "New Pill (CHILL Pill) makes professional Black women not so bossy."According to 2009 U.S. Census Bureau reports, black females ages 35 to 44 are the only American women in their child-bearing years with lower marriage rates than men of the same race or ethnicity. By their early 40s, 31 percent of black women have never been wives, whereas 9 percent of white women, 11 percent of Asian women and 12 percent of Hispanic women have never been married. Who can use this miracle pill? Only professional black women and they must take it before they get married. Well, the pill is not actually in pill form, it is a CHILL Pill.

Does He expect anything other than He expects of a man? The Scriptures are clear that men and women are equal in Jesus Christ. And they are just as clear that God is no respecter of persons. Is it time to rethink our view of the Christian woman?[2]

Where the Bible is silent, details will have to be worked out according to the consciences of individuals, families, and church congregations. But when and where the Lord has spoken, we must listen and act accordingly.

Today's woman needs more than equal pay for equal work. She needs to be able to come to terms with the complexities of a world that is giving mixed signals about what a woman is to be. A generation that has admired women like, Sojourner Truth (Isabella Baumfree, 1797-1883: Afraican-American abolitionist,

Civil war, Suffragette); Harriet Tubman (1820-1913, underground railroad conductor, Army scout, African-American suffragette), Rosa Parks, Oprey Winfrey, and Corazon Aquino (1933-2009, the 11th President of the Philippines and the first women to hold that office in Philippine history. She is best remembered for leading the 1986 People power Revolution, which toppled Ferdinand Marcos) needs to recover its dignity in the face of pornography, teen rebellion, divorce, and economic disadvantage. A woman needs to cope with fatigue, disillusionment, anger, and depression.

The trouble hasn't surfaced overnight. Thirty years ago, jazz artist Billy Tipton (1914-1989) realized that society would not give a woman opportunity in the field of jazz. Billy lived 30 years as a man. Yet when he died suddenly, he was found by emergency medical personnel to be a woman. Her life reminds us that our world does treat men and women differently. Billy's life also reminds us that women sometimes feel it's necessary to hide their femininity in order to find fulfillment in a "man's world." Sometimes a woman ends up denying something of her own soul just to survive.

What Does God Expect Of A Woman?

In the beginning, woman was created for companionship, conversation, and co-rulership of the earth. Today she is not the person she used to be. Neither is her male counterpart. Both suffer from distortions of gender that limit their ability to give one another the love and help they were made to give. Both are plagued by a twistedness rooted deep in their souls. Both reflect caricatures that betray their inner trouble:

MASCULINE TWISTS

Macho man	Mamma's boy	Tom cat
Gym rat	Gambler	Boarder
General	Lush	Money machine
Workaholic	Fan	Wimp
Closet queen	Archie Bunker	Dirty old man
Good ol' boy	Lone Ranger	Couch potato

FEMININE TWISTS

Tough girl	Daddy's girl	Tramp
Party girl	Gold digger	Primadonna
Witch	Drinker	Shopper
Superwoman	Phone company	Maid
Dumb blonde	Baby machine	Painted lady
Fashion plate	Food service	Door mat

Unfortunately, there is no safe way to be wrong. Both sexes suffer for each other's mistakes, but women seem to feel most acutely the resulting symptoms of poverty, loneliness, boredom, abuse, and depression. Too many women see the damage transferred to their own children, who leave home angry, confused, and wondering whether the life their mother gave them is really worth living.

What's A Woman To Be?

Today's woman needs to look back to go forward. Like her male counterpart, she needs to rediscover the plan of her Designer. Before she can fulfill her distinct feminine identity, she must admit that trying to live on her own terms and by her own strength doesn't work. Before she can find real fulfillment and security, she must be willing to change her mind about where hope is found, and then go back to the pattern and protective shelter of the One who created both men and women for Himself (Ps. 91:1-6).

The Bible offers that plan. It shows a woman how to live with dignity and serenity. It urges her to experience the difference the Lord can make in her life. It encourages her to trust God Himself for the ability to live with:

- Feminine Distinction
- Selective Submission
- Spiritual Equality
- Strength Of Character

These are the main elements of the plan we'll be looking at. As we begin, however, it's important to see that each of these points will be applied to women living under many different kinds of conditions--some ideal, others far from good. The Word of God covers a variety of circumstances with its unchanging principles. The Scriptures introduce us to many women, including a godly woman judge, prophetesses, queens, singles, wives, mothers, and even converted prostitutes. The Bible honours the high calling of women who choose to marry, have children, and nurture them for God. But it also makes it clear that for some the single life is better. Both Jesus and the apostle Paul show that you can remain faithful to your sexual identity while living the single life.

A proper understanding of what is and is not optional can help us to untangle the knotted ropes of tradition and opinion that keep women from coming to terms with the lordship of Christ. To begin, it's important to realize that God expects a woman to live with:

Feminine Distinction

Imagine a sexless race. No maternal order would bear the unequal obligations and responsibilities of childbearing. Modern lawmakers would not have to struggle with the issue of whether or not a woman deserves special legal protection to compensate her for the inescapable physical requirements of having babies. Lady Justice would not have to argue paternity issues with sexually mature males who have never grown up. We would not be faced with the immeasurable problem of teenage promiscuity, or with the specter of children having children.

Yes, our Creator could have avoided the problem of sexuality altogether. He could have devised a different method of reproduction. After declaring that it was not good for man to be alone, He could have developed a method by which genetic information was clipped from Adam's fingernail and planted in the ground. Little Adams could have been raised on a vine and harvested like cucumbers and squash. Yet, the Lord had a better idea. Rather than giving Adam cloned companions who saw and experienced life just as he did, the all-wise God created a woman. Moses told us that after making man, "The Lord God said, 'It is not good that man should be alone; I will make him a helper comparable to him' " (Gen. 2:18).

Interestingly, the Genesis account of human and sexual origins doesn't tell us what made Eve the feminine complement she was. It tells us who made her feminine. It tells us who masterminded the effects of the male hormones and the genetic programming of the 23rd chromosome.

To that original creative pattern, every culture adds its own shaping and detail. Every society develops its own definition of femininity. Yet in spite of all the cultural ad-libbing, the basic biological script is followed. Whether in Britain, Canada, Colombia, or China, girls come into a world that eventually teaches them to walk and talk like a woman. Girls learn early that boys are different. They see the results of genetic and hormonal differences that cause boys to be more muscular and aggressive and loud. They learn that a little girl is to grow up to be a woman who in a special feminine way is to be kind, compassionate, sensitive, and tender.

As a result of these self-evident, yet adaptable differences, there have been many attempts to define the core nature of masculinity and femininity. Some have suggested that hormonally induced male aggressiveness tends to make him an initiator, while women find fulfillment in being responders. Others believe that because of differences beginning in fetal development, men have a statistical edge in objective and spatial reasoning, while women excel in the equally important logic of the heart.

In *His Needs, Her Needs,* author Willard Harley suggests that men and women have a different priority system. Harley says that men tend to desire, in this order, (1) sexual fulfillment, (2) recreational companionship, (3) an attractive spouse, (4) domestic support, and (5) admiration. He says, however, that women's priorities seem to be for (1) affection, (2) conversation, (3) honesty and openness, (4) financial support, and (5) family commitment.

As real as sexual differences are, though, many are not absolute or mutually exclusive. The same Bible that describes our sexual origins and differences also makes it clear that the categories overlap. The Scriptures themselves show that it is foolish to say that a woman should never lead, be strong, or assert herself. Deborah, Abigail, Huldah, Esther, and the daughters of Zelophehad are all examples of women who knew how and when to assert themselves in a godly way. It is just as unthinkable to suppose that a real man should not be sensitive, emotional, compassionate, and responsive to the needs of others. Moses, David, Jeremiah, Jesus, and Paul all expressed emotions of compassion and gentleness.

In short, God made men and women to be much the same, yet significantly and wonderfully different. Even though the scope of these differences is difficult to determine, and even though many are culturally defined, the Bible is very strong in maintaining the distinctions.

Distinctions in appearance (Deut. 22:5). Moses warned against cross-dressing. He said that a woman must not wear a man's clothing, nor a man a woman's clothing. Since both men and women wore flowing robes in Eastern culture, we should not jump to Western conclusions. It's doubtful that the principle of Deuteronomy 22:5 would forbid women from wearing slacks, or men kilts. Yet it certainly means that neither sex should wear anything for the purpose of looking like the other.

To this the apostle Paul added his own God-given conviction that even nature itself teaches that men maintain masculine appearance.

> *Does not even nature itself teach you that if a man has long hair, it is a dishonour to him? But if a woman has long hair, it is a glory to her (1 Cor.11:14,15).*

Here the Scriptures do not provide a basis for "legalistic" criticism. Paul doesn't say how long is too long for a man, nor how short is too short for a woman. Instead he appeals to a higher law. He appeals to nature itself, implying that at some point masculine and feminine distinctions become a self-evident issue.

Distinctions in roles. Is a woman's place in the home? Is that really where she can find her God-given role? The answer depends on whether or not she is married, whether she has children who need her care, and whether or not her husband is able to provide for the basic needs of the home. Women like Ruth, Deborah, and Anna are among many biblical woman who had roles outside the home.

Yet nothing should diminish the honour of the woman who does choose to marry, have children, manage the home and use it as a place of Christian hospitality (1 Tim. 5:10,14). Nothing should be said to discourage the mother who believes she can best serve her children by being there when they need her. The fact that many women don't have that option should not be reason to rule out the ideal. After all, it was the apostle Paul who encouraged older women to:

> *Admonish the young women to love their husbands, to love their children, to be discreet, chaste, homemakers, good, obedient to their own husbands, that the word of God may not be blasphemed (Titus 2:4,5).*

This is not advice for all women. It refers to young wives and mothers. More specifically, it refers to young wives and mothers who have husbands who can and do make it possible for them to work in the home. They are the women who must be encouraged to find fulfillment in the very important profession of raising children and managing the home.

Is this to say that a woman must "stay at home" and honour her husband as head of the house because she, as a woman, is less intelligent or capable than a man? Individual intelligence and competence have nothing to do with it. It's a matter of God's design for families.

Distinctions in sexual relationships. Men who pursue romantic relationships with men, and women who pursue romantic relationships with women dishonour themselves. The apostle Paul lamented such an error when he wrote:

> *Even their women exchanged natural relations for unnatural ones. In the same way the men also abandoned natural relations with women and were inflamed with lust for one another (Rom. 1:26,27 NIV).*

This is not to say that lesbian women do not have reasons for hating and fearing male relationships. Many have never known anything but abusive, arrogant, unloving men. It's understandable that they would retreat from seeking intimacy with a man. But as understandable as it may be, homosexuality is self-destructive. It is not an "enlightened" alternative. A woman caught in such a trap needs to call out to the Lord for His help. She needs to repent of her wrong, appeal to the mercy and love of Christ, and seek the encouragement of a Christian support group that can help her to renew her mind and affections in the Lord.

Selective Submission

The idea of submission is difficult for many women to deal with. But it should help if a woman can know for sure that (1) this is really what God wants, and (2) she has not only an opportunity but also a responsibility to be selective in carrying out such an assignment.

Let's first take a look at what the Bible says about the kind of submission God expects of a married woman. It involves a response that goes beyond the universal principle of Christian submission. After making it clear that mutual submission is a mark of Spirit-filled relationships, Paul went on to say:

> *Wives, submit to your own husbands, as to the Lord. For the husband is head of the wife, as also Christ is head of the church; and He is the Savior of the body. Therefore, just as the church is subject to Christ, so let the wives be to their own husbands in everything (Eph. 5:22-24).*

From God's point of view, this kind of submission is not a negotiable issue. It is not just a question of what a woman committed herself to when she spoke her marriage vows. The Word of God says unmistakably that a wife is to follow the lead of her husband just as her husband is responsible to love her as Christ loved the church (Eph. 5:25). Obedience and recognition of a husband's leadership comes with the territory of being a Christian wife (1 Cor. 11:1-3; Eph. 5:22-24). The apostle Peter wrote that such submission is right even if a husband is not being the kind of godly, loving, sacrificing person he should be.

> *Likewise you wives, be submissive to your own husbands, that even if some do not obey the word, they, without a word, may be won by the conduct of their wives (1 Pet. 3:1,2).*

This is one side of the issue. The other side is that this submission should not be mindlessly servile and passive. This submission should be active and selective. Obviously God does not ask all women to submit to all men at all times and in all places. Neither does the Lord expect a married woman always to obey her husband or church leader, any more than He expects a citizen always to obey the government (Acts 5:29).

The actions of Ananias and Sapphira, as recorded for us in Acts 5:1-11, are a noteworthy example of a wife who foolishly went along with her husband's sin and lost her life in the process. Acts 5:2 says that Sapphira was aware of her husband's attempt to mislead the church of God. Yet, "being aware," she didn't object and refuse to go along with his plan. Instead, she conspired with him to lie to the church about the amount of their contribution. The result was that God struck both of them dead. In retrospect, it is clear that Sapphira should not have gone along with her husband's wishes.

Abigail, on the other hand, is an example of a woman who did just the opposite of Sapphira. She did not submit to her husband's wishes, and by her noncompliance actually saved her life and those of her household (1 Sam. 25:18-

44). Abigail recognized that her "mean and surly" husband was defying David, servant of the Most High God. Showing herself to be an intelligent and godly woman, she acted unilaterally to counteract the foolishness of her husband. He died for his foolishness, and she lived to become the wife of King David.

Yet, having made a point of these two examples, we must acknowledge them as exceptions to the rule of marital submission. The rule is that if a woman chooses to marry, she becomes responsible to follow the lead of her husband. Only when her husband asks something that is in direct conflict with the will of God is she free to do otherwise.

Certainly such submission is made much easier when a Christian husband is the kind of person God wants him to be. Blessed is the woman who has a husband who shows love, gentleness, reasonableness, patience, and fairness to her. That's God's pattern. But keep in mind that neither role is dependent on whether the other partner is doing his or her part. A husband is to serve his wife lovingly whether she is submissive or not. A wife is to be obedient and submissive whether or not her husband is showing her Christlike love.

Such a pattern does not fit the mode of our egalitarian culture. The right kind of submission is a test of faith in God. Submission, however, is not just a feminine challenge. It's a challenge for men in the military, athletics, or business. It's a test of character for children moving through adolescence. It can also be very hard for women in the home or the church.

The idea of any submissive role at all can frustrate and anger a woman. The association might be likened to the uneasiness many people feel while riding in the back seat of a car or taxicab. By being dependent on the judgment and skill of someone else, the passenger feels a loss of any ability to protect himself. When the driver seems negligent, careless, and irresponsible, the rider experiences feelings of resentment, fear, and anger.

Some of that frustration is what a woman can feel in the home or the church. She soon learns that men are far from perfect. How can she then commit herself to their care and judgment? How can she knowingly and voluntarily go along for the ride, especially when it soon becomes apparent that she sees almost everything from a significantly different point of view? With such thoughts in mind, let's take a look at the kind of submission called for in the Scriptures.

A married woman is as responsible to follow her husband as her husband is responsible to follow the Lord (Eph. 5:21-33). Her motive should be to submit to her husband as a way of showing her confidence in the Lord. If that is her perspective, then knowing that the Lord has her best interests at heart will help to minimize any natural resentment or anger that such dependence might elicit. She takes heart in the fact that the Lord understands her. He listens to her, knows her needs, and when necessary will be the judge between her and her husband.

Sarah, wife of Abraham, seemed to understand this. While she is honoured by Peter as a model of respectful submission (1 Pet. 3:5,6), the Genesis account adds some important details, which show what kind of woman Sarah was. We see how two imperfect people can hurt and mislead one another. We also see how after helping to make a mess of things, a woman can still find in the Lord the strength she needs to express her feelings and appeal to her husband's conscience. We may conclude, therefore, that a woman who is known for submissiveness is not necessarily passive.

In Genesis 16:5 we find Sarah confronting Abraham with deep hurt and displeasure. While admitting her own mistake in encouraging Abraham to have a child by her servant, Sarah suggests that the ball is now in Abraham's court to address a bad situation gone worse. After misleading Abraham into having a child by her servant, she says:

> *My wrong be upon you! I gave my maid into your embrace; and when she saw that she had conceived, I became despised in her eyes. The Lord judge between you and me. So Abram said to Sarai, "Indeed your maid is in your hand; do to her as you please" (Gen.16:5,6).*

Notice a couple of things. First, Sarah was not mindlessly passive. She had been deeply hurt, and she let her husband know how she felt. Second, she recognized that she and her husband were being watched. When she said, "The Lord judge between you and me," she showed her awareness that her husband was also accountable to God. Abraham seems to have felt the weight of her appeal, because he again deferred to her wishes.

In light of Sarah's relationship with Abraham, let's ask some questions. What if a husband tells his wife to do something that is in direct conflict with her responsibility to God? What if her husband tells her to lie, or to indulge in his twisted craving for pornography or wife swapping? What if her husband tells her to sign income tax forms that she knows are inaccurate? She must take a firm stand, while trying to maintain her dignity and gracious spirit (1 Pet. 3:1). She must let her husband know that her first responsibility is to remain true to her Lord. The Lord, after all, is the one who holds her security in the palm of His own hand. A husband may die, suffer a stroke, have an accident, or become unfaithful. How then can a woman find her security in a mere man? She can if her submission to her husband mirrors her willingness to submit to the Lord.

A woman, married or single, is to take a supportive role in the church (1 Cor. 11:3-16; 1 Tim. 2:11-15). In many ways a woman in the church can be likened to a member of a football, basketball, or volleyball team that competes under the leadership of a player-coach. As a team member, she is a full participant. But along with the rest of the team, she follows the lead of their team leader.

In a similar way, the women of the New Testament church are pictured as team members--co-workers with men in the gospel.

Paul expressed affection and appreciation to women he acknowledged as co-laborers and spiritual equals in Christ (Rom. 16:1-3,6,13,15; Gal. 3:26-28; Phil. 4:3). He encouraged mature women to teach younger sisters in Christ (Titus 2:3-5). We should be careful not to overlook the strategic need for women to help women in the church. Whether we're talking about one-to-one discipleship, Bible studies, or special-need support groups, women should not overlook the needs of each other. What a tragedy it is when women lose a sense of the unlimited opportunities they have to help one another, to provide hospitality, and to develop outreach! The needs of others, men and women, young and old alike, are too pressing to allow ourselves to become distracted and embittered over the masculine limitation God has placed on the office of elder. In many ways it is a back-to-Eden problem. If we're not careful, we can once again lose sight of a whole garden of opportunities while becoming preoccupied with the one "fruit" that has been put off limits.

We can't overemphasize how much women need the help of other women to think as they should about themselves, about God, about their homes and their families, and about their other relationships. Single women need encouragement. Married women need encouragement too. Older widows and teenage girls need strengthening companionship, phone calls, letters, and other creative expressions of kindness. Women all around us are walking the edge of despair. Without a Christlike embrace, they might give in to the overwhelming crush of their own loneliness and crisis. For lack of strengthening relationships, women young and old are caving in to sexual pressures, reaching out for chemical or alcoholic crutches, or giving in to the materialistic mood of our times.

Spiritual Equality

One of the most self-evident facts of life is that all men are not created equal. Neither are women. In countless ways, there is no justice or fairness on earth. Life as it is usually lived is a struggle of unequals.

What is true, however, is that all persons are equally created. All people are equally dependent on the Lord for every breath and heartbeat. All are equally accountable. Inequalities of roles, material wealth, physical condition, social standing, or education do not change the ways in which all people are equal.

Equal in Honour. Differences of roles do not necessarily imply differences of honour or worth. Being submissive does not imply inferiority of person. Jesus Christ showed us that. He lived on earth "under the law" (Gal. 4:4), under the authority of His parents (Luke 2:51), under the authority of government leaders (Matt. 22:21), and above all, under the authority of His heavenly Father.

The apostle Paul used the Lord Jesus as an example of one who lived under the headship of God just as woman is to live under the headship of man (1 Cor. 11:3). Yet, by assuming such a servant role, Christ did not diminish His honour. Jesus did not become less than God when He temporarily laid aside the expression of His splendor and took on the form of a servant (Phil. 2:2-8). He didn't degrade and dehumanize Himself by humbling Himself and becoming obedient even to the point of death (Phil. 2:8). By such a role, He actually confirmed His honour. By voluntarily accepting His obedient, submissive role, He actually gave the Father reason to exalt Him and give Him a name that is above every name (Phil. 2:9-11).

In this way, Jesus gave woman a precedent for believing that her supportive role does not in any way signal that she is less of a person, less in honour, or less in potential. She is merely different in form and role for the purpose of carrying out the distinct design and purposes of God.

Equal in Nature. While God the Father and God the Son are different and distinct persons, they are equal and co-eternal in nature. So, man and woman, while having different roles in family and church, are made in the image of God. If the Lord had wanted us to believe otherwise, if He had wanted to emphasize sexual diversity rather than unity, He could have made man out of the dust of the ground and woman out of a wisp of cumulus cloud. Instead, the Lord created woman so that Adam would exclaim:

> *This is now bone of my bones and flesh of my flesh; she shall be called Woman, because she was taken out of Man (Gen. 2:23).*

Try to put yourself in the place of Adam and Eve. The emotion would be similar to what a new mother feels as she looks at the miracle and wonder of the newborn that has been formed within her own body.

Equal in Jesus Christ. This is the most important of all emancipation proclamations. The apostle Paul wrote:

> *You are all sons of God through faith in Christ Jesus. For as many of you as were baptized into Christ have put on Christ. There is neither Jew nor Greek, there is neither slave nor free, there is neither male nor female; for you are all one in Christ Jesus (Gal. 3:26-28).*

This puts in marvelous perspective the nature of our temporal differences. Peter declares that men and women are now co-heirs of God's wonderful gift of life in Christ (1 Pet. 3:7). This means that a man has no basis for pride, no basis for presumption, no basis for doing anything but loving, honouring, and serving the woman God made. This truth is like an earthmover knocking down hills and filling in valleys. It says that men and women stand on equal ground before God. Differences of function and form do not signal differences of essence or equality. They reflect differences in roles.

The Strength of Character

The most beautiful women in the world are not those who parade in swimsuits and evening gowns before judges and television cameras. The real finalists and winners are those women who have the inner glow of grace and compassion. No amount of physical beauty can match the spiritual dignity or attractiveness of a mature woman of God. She is a person of serenity because her trust and security is in the Lord. She is a person of dignity because her value and sense of significance is found in God. She will reflect a kind of inner beauty that does more than call attention to herself. It is a beauty that is far more important than anything merely skin deep.

A woman's strength of character is found in the person and example of Jesus Christ. He knew how to live under even the worst kind of authority and still make the best of it. Even though He was the King of kings and Lord of lords, Jesus didn't insist on coming into the world in the role of a king. The apostle Peter described Christ's ability to live under misused authority and then used His example to show what God can do in a woman.

> *Do not let your beauty be that outward adorning of arranging the hair, of wearing gold, or of putting on fine apparel; but let it be the hidden person of the heart, with the incorruptible ornament of a gentle and quiet spirit, which is very precious in the sight of God. For in this manner, in former times, the holy women who trusted in God also adorned themselves, being submissive to their own husbands (1 Pet. 3:3-5).*

Because Peter links this counsel with the example of Christ, who is said to have suffered physical torture without resistance (1 Pet. 2:21-24), we need to be careful with its application. Some might be inclined to say that this also reflects the extent to which a submissive wife should endure the abuse of her husband. Our Lord's example does not mean that a woman should endure any and all physical abuse from a man just because He allowed Himself to be nailed to a cross without going for help. Jesus did not always put Himself at the mercy of the mobs and their governors. He did not take pleasure in being beaten. He allowed Himself to be at their mercy only when He knew His suffering would bring salvation to all men and women. At other times, Christ wisely took evasive action.

What Peter wants us to see, however, is that throughout our Lord's life He showed unparalleled strength of character. He never stopped being godly just because He was living under the shadow of evil authority. He never returned evil for evil or insult for insult. He didn't because He knew that His future, His security, His hope, His provision was not found in men but in His Father.

The result was that Jesus reflected a graciousness and strength that was rooted not in passive aggressiveness but in the strength of His relationship with the Father. It is that same strength of spirit that He can now produce in any woman who chooses to find her security and example in Him.

There is no more beautiful woman than one who is clothed in the Lord Jesus Christ. She is marked by tender kindness, humility, patience, forgiveness, love, peace, joy, and thankfulness (Col. 3:12-17). None of these are sold in a clothing store. None can be bought at any price. Yet all are free to any woman who chooses to live in Christ, even as He Himself lives in her.

A woman's strength of character is found in an ancient formula. The apostle Peter said, "For in this manner, in former times, the holy women who trusted in God also adorned themselves, being submissive to their own husbands" (3:5). A woman who wants to be strong and beautiful will not put her confidence in expensive jewelry, fine clothes, and cosmetics (3:3).

The godly woman puts her real confidence in the graciousness, strength, and integrity that comes from her relationship to Christ. Her beauty will come naturally. Quite unconsciously she will become a model of what God can do in a woman. She will prove that the best-dressed women wear dignity, strength, honour, and quiet confidence in God as unfading sources of beauty. And according to Peter, if she is married, her beauty comes in being submissive to her husband.

A woman's strength of character is made perfect in weakness. In that sense, a woman's strength of character is like a man's. Referring to the inner strength that comes from the Spirit of God, Paul wrote, "But we have this treasure in earthen vessels, that the excellence of the power may be of God and not of us" (2 Cor. 4:7). Then in the twelfth chapter of the same letter he wrote again of his struggle to cope with physical weakness. He found that the Lord wouldn't remove it but would only say, " 'My grace is sufficient for you, for My strength is made perfect in weakness.' Therefore most gladly I will rather boast in my infirmities, that the power of Christ may rest upon me" (2 Cor. 12:9).

Living in a weaker vessel (1 Pet. 3:7) can be an advantage. Relative physical weakness can be an occasion for a woman to become strong in the Lord. An awareness of any weakness gives her a reason to depend on the strength of the Lord.

A woman's strength of character must be channeled through her circumstances. If she is single, she should prayerfully consider all of her options. She should ask whether or not the Lord has given her a deep and abiding desire to devote all of her attention to Him and the service of His people. It's the kind of radical potential Paul had in mind when he wrote (1 Cor. 7:34, 35):

The unmarried woman cares about the things of the Lord, that she may be holy both in body and in spirit. But she who is married cares about the things of the world--how she may please her husband. And this I say for your own profit, not that I may put a leash on you, but for what is proper, and that you may serve the Lord without distraction Paul, himself single, was close to the Lord when he wrote this. He saw the value of being free to devote oneself entirely to the Lord and to the eternal, spiritual needs of His people. Paul also knew that many people are not able to serve the Lord with single undivided attention (1 Cor. 7:17-40). He recognized the obvious--that many women are already thoroughly committed to their husbands and children. To them, Paul pointed out that strength of character means something very different. It was to such already committed persons that he wrote:

> *The older women likewise, that they be reverent in behaviour, not slanderers, not given to much wine, teachers of good things--that they admonish the young women to love their husbands, to love their children, to be discreet, chaste, homemakers, good, obedient to their own husbands, that the word of God may not be blasphemed (Titus 2:3-5).*

Character blooms where it is planted, through the all-sufficient strength of Christ!

Abused Woman

An abused woman should never think that it is her Christian obligation to remain passively silent. When threatened or injured, she should not hesitate to seek protective counsel and shelter. Being a Christian does not mean that she has a spiritual obligation to endure abuse. The Lord doesn't ask a woman to passively endure marital or sexual violence. This kind of violence is not the same as suffering persecution for the sake of the gospel.

If you or someone you know is experiencing such circumstances, please think carefully about the implications of what our Lord Himself said in giving this advice to injured persons:

> *Moreover if your brother sins against you, go and tell him his fault between you and him alone. If he hears you, you have gained your brother. But if he will not hear you, take with you one or two more, that "by the mouth of two or three witnesses every word may be established." And if he refuses to hear them, tell it to the church. But if he refuses even to hear the church, let him be to you like a heathen and a tax collector (Matt. 18:15-17).*

An abused woman needs far more protection than the irate deacon who finds that he has been cheated in business by another brother. It is time for the church to come to the support of our hurting sisters. We live in a day of heartbreaking domestic violence. We must not allow our women to live in bondage and fear. No man has a right to take selfish and heartless advantage of a woman! Furthermore, no woman does a man a favour by allowing him to continue in his sin until finally shaken by an angry God.

We must do to others as we would have them do to us (Matt. 7:12). Christian mother and father, imagine your own daughter suffering at the hands of an abusive husband. Would you want a pastor or counselor to tell your daughter to concentrate on being a more submissive and obedient wife? More likely you would want the Christian support-person to consider seriously your daughter's need for shelter, financial aid, counseling, and family support. I'm sure you would not see the Christian rule of "submission" as applicable if it were your daughter who was enduring unjust, illegal, and inhuman treatment. There is no reason for us to have to make referrals to social agencies until we have first provided the kind of help that we as a church are able to provide. We need to take the same kind of action we would take if it became apparent that one of the deacons were stealing from the Sabbath offering.

Who Are The Biblical Models?

The women of the Bible give us a wealth of information about what God expects of a woman. Let's look at some Old Testament examples:

Abigail was a woman who showed strength of character when she appealed to David to spare the life of her foolish husband and his household. She acted with courage and initiative, independently of her drunken husband (1 Sam. 25).

The daughters of Zelophehad acted with spiritual equality when they went to Moses and the leaders of Israel with the complaint that the inheritance laws were not fair. Because Zelophehad had died in the wilderness without any sons, his family was not going to receive an apportionment of land that they deserved. So his surviving daughters challenged the inheritance laws and had them changed to be more equitable (Num. 27:1-11).

Deborah showed spiritual equality in that God chose her to be a prophetess and judge of Israel. But her feminine distinction was apparent when she deferred to Barak to lead the troops into battle against their oppressors (Judg. 4:1-24).

Esther's feminine distinction was used by God to put her in a place of powerful influence with the king. It was because of her God-given beauty that she was chosen to be the queen. Esther also showed strength of character by putting her own life on the line to save her people (Esth. 2:1-18; 4:10--7:10).

Naomi, while in a foreign land, experienced great loss through the death of her husband and her two sons (Ruth 1:3-5). When she returned to Bethlehem, she was destitute and bitter--feeling that God had caused her hardships (1:20,21). However, she showed strength of character by not allowing her bitterness to blind her to God's hand of blessing. When she saw that God was working circumstances for her good, she immediately praised Him for His kindness (2:20).

Ruth showed selective submission and strength of character by refusing to leave her mother-in-law, Naomi, even though it meant giving up her homeland, her people, and her pagan god and embracing a place and culture foreign to her (1:6-18). Ruth submitted, however, to all of Naomi's instructions about what to say and do in her relationship with Boaz (2:22,23; 3:1-6). She was unselfish (2:14,18), industrious (2:3-7), kind (2:11; 3:10), virtuous (3:11), and "better to [Naomi] than seven sons" (4:15). She used her feminine distinction to be more attractive to Boaz (3:3). And she showed spiritual equality in asking Boaz to fulfill his legal obligation to redeem her (3:9).

The virtuous woman described in Proverbs 31:10-31 has the following characteristics:
- She is a commendable wife and mother.
- She lives for her home and family.
- She is industrious.
- She is self-disciplined and orderly.
- She is a sharp business woman.
- She has good, refined tastes.
- She manifests the grace of hospitality.
- She is charitable in time of need.
- She is spiritually minded.

Virtuous woman

"Please, no more studies on the virtuous woman. I already feel inadequate, and every time I hear a sermon on the 'superwoman' of Proverbs 31, it just makes me feel worse than I already do." Many women feel that way. They know they can't be all that God wants them to be. They are ready to give up before they start.

So what is the answer? Does God expect more than a woman can give? Yes, He does. He requires behaviour that demands superhuman strength. He expects a woman to have attitudes that are beyond her abilities. He maintains standards she can never measure up to. Yet, God is also understanding, loving, and graciously merciful. He doesn't just point demandingly at the mess we've made. He doesn't practice spiritual blackmail with a mile-long list of our sins. Through Jesus Christ, He stoops with love and grace to the most lowly person. Through the inexpressibly painful death of His own Son, He offers forgiveness, complete and irrevocable. Then He offers to do in us everything He asks us to do (1 Thess. 4:1-8). Through the good news of Jesus Christ, God offers hope, life, strength, and status to all women and men who will admit their need and surrender to His mercy.

That's where we must begin. Believe on the Lord Jesus Christ and be saved (Acts 16:31). Begin and end with the God who doesn't ask for anything that He doesn't also freely offer.

My Personal Notes

7

DEFINING YOUR DATING STYLE

The Guided Path

Excerpt by Rick Holland[3]

The approach taken here to dating relationships is called "guided." I call it this because people who follow it are guided through relationships by honouring principles given in the Bible. But I want to make it clear: These are guides, not formulas.

The New Testament addresses a battle for balance between two extreme approaches to godliness: legalism and libertinism. These two extremes have a parallel in the dating debate. Dating without a plan can easily become too loose. Courting without wisdom can easily become legalism. In its extreme, dating becomes an anything-goes free-for-all in which the man and woman concern themselves with the pleasure of the romance instead of the good of each other. Courting in its extreme becomes an infatuation with a process instead of an evaluation using biblical principles.

The Purpose of Premarital Relationships

Premarital relationships should serve one purpose: to test the relationship for marriage. Let me say it another way: There is no good reason to have a girlfriend or boyfriend until a person is ready to get married!

---

3 Taken from "5 Paths to the Love of Your Life" by Lauren Winner, Jeramy Clark and Jerusha Clark, Douglas Wilson, Rick Holland and Jonathan Lindvall. General editor: Alex Chediak. This content is used by permission of NavPress, and the book is available at your local bookstore or at www. navpress.com.

I hope the implications of this statement are obvious. Readiness involves being old enough and mature enough to assume the responsibilities of marriage. No romantic relationship should ever begin unless marriage is the possible – even probable outcome. That said, it is difficult to justify the romances of junior high and high school. If one is not ready to get married, he or she is not ready to date or court.

So what about Jenny and David? They are juniors in high school. They are both Christian and involved in their church. Both get that funny feeling in their stomachs when they are around each other. Add that to their friends' constant nagging about them making a good couple. What should they do? This may not be what they want to hear, but they should forget about it! No romantic relationship should be developed unless the couple can get married if all goes well. If they are not ready to get married, they are not ready to date. Dating without marriage on the radar is an unnecessarily risky business.

Jenny and David should continue to cultivate good, biblical friendships with each other – and with others – as spiritual siblings. But I would encourage them to wait until they are ready to get married before they consider dating.So if you are not ready to be married, how can you get ready? Whether you are too young or too immature to enter into a relationship that could lead to marriage, a path to a God-honouring marriage can be paved if you will look to God's Word.

The following ten principles can help any person in any context honour God's relational values and in turn become godly people ready for godly relationships. In fact, these guidelines can be followed regardless of the model you choose.

The Ten Principles for a God-Centered Relationship

1. The Character Principle

It is the pattern and practice of God to judge a man's or woman's true character by looking inside at what is in the heart. Externals reveal only so much about the true person. If we are to be faithful imitators of our heavenly Father, evaluation of a potential spouse should be based first on character.

The Character Principle is about being the right person more than finding the right person. If your character is being conformed more and more into the image of Christ, you will desire the right kind of person. There are numerous texts informing the believer how to live a life that pleases God. The second chapter of Titus is an exemplary passage that gives a blueprint for training the character of succeeding generations. Because it speaks to both men and women, it provides a succinct summary of what God desires for our lives.

Paul was instructing Titus how to put things in order in the church (see Titus 1:5). An important part of getting the church in order was to ensure that older believers were discipling younger believers to be men and women of godly character. Much of the apostle's instruction to Titus as both a pastor and a young man was directly related to relationships. As he addressed the older men and women, a clear example of godly character came into view. And as he spoke about the next generation, a clear exhortation of godly character emerged:

Older men are to be sober-minded, dignified, self-controlled, sound in faith, in love, and in steadfastness. Older women likewise are to be reverent in behaviour, not slanderers or slaves to much wine. They are to teach what is good, and so train the young women to love their husbands and children, to be self-controlled, pure, working at home, kind, and submissive to their own husbands, that the word of God may not be reviled. Likewise, urge the younger men to be self-controlled. Show yourself in all respects to be a model of good works, and in your teaching show integrity, dignity, and sound speech that cannot be condemned, so that an opponent may be put to shame, having nothing evil to say about us. (Titus 2:2-8)

Notice that godly character is a product of spiritual discipleship. One of the best ways to prepare for a marital relationship is to maintain a mentoring relationship with an older, wiser, and godlier member of the same sex.

In addition to what Paul told Titus, godly character consists of qualities such as humility (see Philippians 2:3-11), holiness (see 1 Peter 1:14-17), godly love (see 1 Corinthians 13:4-8), selflessness (see James 3:14), the fruit of the Spirit (see Galatians 5:22-25), and, of course, Christlikeness (see Ephesians 4:13).

The Character Principle has another dimension: recognition. Not only should godly character be pursued personally, but it should also be recognized in anyone a person might date or court. King Lemuel crystallized the Character Principle with his contrasting words:Charm is deceitful, and beauty is vain, but a woman who fears the LORD is to be praised. (Proverbs 31:30)

2. The Conformation Principle

One of the many potholes of recreational dating is that it often finds affirmation and confirmation from the wrong sources. I know that many who date submit themselves humbly and willingly to the authorities in their lives, but sadly, many others do not. The Confirmation Principal is the commitment to submit one's life and relationships to the spiritual scrutiny of God's authority, care, and protection represented here on earth. Who are these authorities? Let me outline three.

Parental Confirmation. God has given parents authority over their children (see Exodus 20:12; Leviticus 19:3; Deuteronomy 21:18-21; 27:16; Matthew 15:4; Romans 1:28-32; Ephesians 6:1-2; 2 Timothy 3:1-5). Therefore, to ignore this authority is to ignore God. But what does this mean in premarital relationships?

First, parents should be involved from the beginning. Many parents desire to be involved with all aspects of a relationship in the initial stages, including who is to be pursued and considered for marriage. Unfortunately, some do not. Regardless, it should be the heart of a son or daughter to submit his or her decisions about relationships to his or her parents. This involves getting their thoughts, listening to their concerns, proceeding at their pace, and applying the brakes if they say, "Wait" or "stop." But what if you and your parents disagree? Ravi Zacharias shares this wisdom: 'The chances are that if you marry someone in violation of your parents' will, you are playing a high-stakes game as you enter your new future. Any time you violate an authority that has been put in place by God, you need to be twice as sure you are doing the right thing."[45] How can you know if you are doing the right thing? There is another level of authority.

Church Affirmation. One of the most neglected sources of wisdom in the Christian life is church leaders. Pastors, elders, deacons, and other leaders should be intricately involved in any budding relationship. This is especially important if the parents are deceased, far away, or out of the picture for other reasons. It is a curious fact that more is said about the role of church leaders in our lives than even the role of our parents (see Ephesians 4:11-16; 1 Timothy; 2 Timothy; Titus; Hebrews 13:7, 17). Only a fool would disregard this arm of God's authority.

I am often asked what should be done if there is a disagreement among children and their parents about relational issues. Paul answer this in principle in 1

Corinthians 6. Two believers were having a disagreement they could not resolve, and it resulted in a lawsuit. As the apostle shames them for appealing to a secular court, he makes the passing comment that disputes among believers ought to be resolved by wise leaders in the church (see 1 Corinthians 6:4-6). This is true of relational disagreements as well.

What should you do if your plan for your life and romance differs from your parents? Let me offer some guidelines for honouring your parents when you disagree with them. Be prayerful, humble, and ready to be corrected by their concerns. Don't assume that they are wrong and you are right.

Try to be as objective as possible in evaluating the relationship in light of biblical principles instead of your emotional desires. When emotions are high, good judgment is rarely present. Discuss the disagreement in a respectful way. God gives parents – Christian and non-Christian parents – wisdom and instruction. Remember, there are no qualifications in the fifth commandment.

If there is no resolution, seek counsel – with them if possible – from church leaders. When you seek counsel, never speak of your parents in a way that is dishonouring to them. Seek to change your heart rather than your parents! Only go against your parents when all biblical and church resources have been exhausted and the church leadership counsels you in that direction.

We live in a world of Bart Simpson, a world in which obeying and honouring parents is considered uncool and even archaic. But this very fact should bring us all to our knees.

Friend Affirmation. A third source of wisdom to affirm your relationship is godly friends. The book of Proverbs exhorts us to listen to wise counsel around us (see 12:15, 15:22, 19:20-21, 27:9). The insights and observations of mature Christian friends should add yet another layer of accountability in relational decisions. One of the mistakes we often make is listening only to counsel with which we agree. But if we have the right kind of friends, their biblical wisdom, as well as the work of the Holy Spirit in their lives, can be a strong ally to help us make relational decisions, whether it is what we want to hear or not.

The Confirmation Principle invites God's grace into complicated situations. For Steve and Rachel, it could be invaluable. As collegians, they are not living at home. Their families are not only far away, but they are also unbelievers.

93

Yet Steve and Rachel find godly qualities in one another and are attracted to each other. How should they proceed?

Even though their parents are not Christians, seeking their confirmation is wise and obedient. I believe God would honour their efforts to seek their counsel and wisdom. But what if that is not helpful? What if their parents' insights are ungodly and dishonouring to Scripture?

This is where pastoral oversight becomes critical. I would never encourage a couple to go against their parents' counsel (even if the parents are unbelievers) without a serious evaluation and oversight by pastors and elders. And the counsel of other mature believers can also be used by God to put the relationship under the microscope. Steve and Rachel should move forward in the relationship only after they have exhausted the confirmation possible from their parents, pastors, and friends.

3. The Contentment Principle

The foundation for developing a righteous relationship with a member of the opposite sex is the ultimate relationship – your relationship with God. If you are not happy with God alone, you will not be happy with someone else. Paul's walk with Christ was so satisfying that he discovered that contentment was possible regardless of any circumstance (see Philippians 4:10-13; 1 Timothy 6:6-7).

A huge error singles often make is believing that a relationship will make them happy. This is just another form of idolatry. Thinking that anything other than God will bring satisfaction and happiness is to make that object an idol in one's life. Stacy, a friend of mine, used to spend inestimable time dreaming and pining about a relationship. My wife and I spoke to her many times about the fact that a boyfriend would not bring the happiness she thought it would.

Finally, it happened. She met a guy who became her friend and eventually her boyfriend. Stacy put her whole life into the relationship. On the surface, she could have won the girlfriend-of-the-year award. Then something amazing happened: engagement! Everything looked great on the outside. But about two months into her marriage, she began to skip church and slip into despair. When I had a chance to talk with her, her honesty was shocking. She told me, "Rick I really thought a man would bring me happiness. Now I have one. He's a great husband, and I know he will be a loving father. But I am lonelier now than when I was single.

What is my problem?'

Stacy's problem was that her contentment was built on a person rather than on God. If you struggle with discontentment now, you will struggle with discontentment when you are married. Discontentment is a sin. It should be recognized and repented of long before a relationship begins.

But don't misunderstand. Strong desire to have a relationship does not necessarily mean discontentment is present. It is noble and God-honouring to want a godly relationship and marriage. But the line is crossed if you start to feel sorry for yourself because you don't have a relationship, become jealous of those who do have a relationship, compromise or sin in order to obtain a relationship, or become frustrated with God because you are dateless. God is for us! Remember His promise in Psalm 84:11:

> *For the LORD God is a sun and shield; the LORD bestows favor and honour. No good thing does he withhold from those who walk uprightly.*

If we walk with Him, we can trust God's providence to bring us what is good and keep from us what is not. This includes relationships. If you are not currently in a relationship, that means it's not good for you at this time. Marriage is not the solution to the discontentment you feel being single. Matrimony can never replace Jesus as the fulfillment of your heart's desire.

What do you think? How do you feel about Rick's comment, "If you are not currently in a relationship that means it's not good for you at this time"?

4. The Common Ground Principle

A Christian should consider only another Christian for a romantic relationship and marriage. Second Corinthians 6:14-18 teaches that believers and unbelievers mix no better than light and darkness. The Holy Spirit could not have been clearer.

A Christian is not to be yoked with an unbeliever in any spiritual enterprise. And there is no such enterprise more important than marriage. God commands those who are seeking to be married to do so only "in the Lord" (1 Corinthians 7:39).

What do you think? Rick says, "There is no such enterprise more important than major." Do you agree? Why or why not? The point, then, is simple: Don't marry an unbeliever! And if marrying an unbeliever is not God's will, then dating one is also out of bounds. Pursuing a relationship with an unbeliever is the most serious mistake you can make in this area. If you do not choose a person who has a living, breathing relationship in the Lord, there is disaster in your future (see 1 Kings 11:1-3).

I have heard so many justifications for dating unbelievers. But the most creative one is called missionary dating. The idea is that dating an unbeliever is a great way to expose them to Christ. I mean, think about it, how much more access can you have to a person's heart than through a romance? Nice idea, but unwise.

Other Christians enter into relationships with unbelievers because of their desire for a relationship. You know how this one goes. There is a nice Christian girl who is faithful at church, but no Christian guy shows any interest in her. Then it happens. She is sitting in her economics class her freshman year of college, and the cute guy sitting in front of her asks her out. She knows he is not a Christian, but her desire for a relationship elbows her wisdom out of the way – and an unequally yoked relationship is born.

Do you remember what happened to Solomon? He disobeyed God by marrying women from foreign lands with foreign idols. Solomon was considered the wisest man who ever lived. We might expect that if he had unbelieving women in his life, he would have been a good influence on them, right? Surely he would have led them to the Lord and not vice versa. But listen to the tragic consequences of Solomon's relationships with unbelieving women: "For when Solomon was old his wives turned his heart away after other gods, and his heart was not wholly true to the LORD his God" (1 Kings 11:4). If wise King Solomon was ruined by relationships with unbelievers, who do we think we are assuming we can handle it?

This may seem restrictive, but let's face it. As Christian, we'll enjoy our relationships more if we can connect spiritually with our significant other, especially because our faith in Christ is the center of who we are as people. My favorite part of my relationship with my wife, Kim, is that we both love Christ and share His values. We love Him more than each other, and that enhances our love. Our relationship with the Savior brings us closer to one another. It gives us a common bond that nothing else could.

5. The Cultivation Principle

Dating relationships need cultivating. But how do you automatically do that? First, you can cultivate your dating relationship best when you see each other first as spiritual siblings. If you apply the Common Ground Principle, you should be interested only in a brother or sister in the Lord. As such, this person is your spiritual sibling before they are a romantic option.

Also, there is safety in numbers. Getting to know a person of the opposite sex is done best in groups at first. Parents, church leaders, and spiritually mature friends should be in the mix (see the Confirmation Principle). This allows a good view into a person's character and personality. But there are limits to what you can discover and evaluate in this context. There is value in time alone, too. First, let me define "alone." This does not mean that no one else is around. You can eat out together, talk at a coffee shop, go to church, and so forth – these situations provide great opportunities to be alone. In other words, you're interacting only with each other, but you're in a public place. Spending time together with no one else around is asking for trouble. The biggest danger in being alone is the temptation to express inappropriate physical affection (see the Chastity Principle) and inappropriate emotional affection.

The place where many get into trouble is in what I call the all-or-nothing category. What I mean by this is that a romance is started with both knowing little about the other person. They go from nothing to a lot very fast. And then if they break up, they go from a lot right back to nothing. This kind of "all or nothingness" can lay the foundation for future problems and even divorce. How? A pattern begins to emerge that if the relationship is not working, the solution is to bail out. Nothing could be farther from the ideal when it comes to Christians who are pursuing each other. I am not suggesting that you necessarily have to marry the first person you date. We need to be reminded that Christians share a relationship that transcends the arena of romance – that of being spiritual siblings to one another. If you want to cultivate the right relationship you have to understand this.

Christians are spiritually related to every other believer in the world; they are brothers and sisters. Just as parents set rules and standards for their children's interaction, God has set rules and standards for His children to follow. This weighed heavily on the mind of Christ in the final days of His earthly ministry (see John 13:34-35; 15:12, 17). He wanted us to honour each other as spiritual siblings.

The phrase "one another" is a favorite in the Bible to describe the familial relationship that believers share in Christ. There are almost forty commands in the New Testament about believers relating to one another. Romans 12:10 is the fountainhead for all "one anothers": "Love one another with brotherly affection." This is the commitment to do what is best for the other. If Christian couples apply this kind of selflessness, physical and emotional temptations will be held in check.

6. The Complementarian Principle

John Piper observes,

> *"The tendency today is to stress the equality of men and women by minimizing the unique significance of our maleness and femaleness. But this depreciation of male and female personhood is a great loss. It is taking a tremendous toil on generations of young men and women who do not know what it means to be a man or a wo*man."

Contemporary evangelicalism is in the throes of a debate about masculinity and femininity. This is especially evident in the context of preparing for marriage. God has designed men and women to enjoy different roles in marriage. People who disagree with that are called egalitarians. They believe that men's and women's roles in marriage are equal. I disagree, and here's why:

The term complementarity comes from the biblical teaching that men and women have been given different roles so they might complement each other. The complementarian position recognizes the uniqueness in God's creative order with respect to men and women:

> *At the heart of mature masculinity is a sense of benevolent responsibility to lead, provide for, and protect women in ways appropriate to a man's differing relationships.*

> *At the heart of true femininity is a freeing disposition to affirm, receive, and nurture strength and leadership from worthy men in ways appropriate to a woman's differing relationships.*

The biblical data is undeniable for these statements (see Genesis 1-3; Ephesians 5:21-33; Colossians 3:19-19; 1 Timothy 3:4, 12; Titus 2:3-5; 1 Peter 3:1-7). For men and women to be ready for marriage, they must prepare themselves for these roles. Men need to learn to lead with grace. Their leadership is to be as understanding and trustworthy as that of Jesus Himself (see Ephesians 5:22-33). Following the example of Christ, this leadership is not to be heavy-handed or authoritarian. It should be tender and understanding (see 1 Peter 3:7).

To prepare themselves for marriage, women need to learn wise submission to men worthy of this privilege. This is first learned by submitting to their fathers, church leaders, and other authorities in life. But the Bible does not call a woman to submit to a man in a romantic relationship until she is his wife. The process of learning to submit herself to a man in this way – and discerning whether that man is worthy of such submission – should take place during the dating period. I believe God's Word clearly teaches a complementarian design for men's and women's roles that flows out of our understanding of masculinity and femininity. Understanding and developing these roles is an important part of preparing for marriage.

This means that a man should be the initiator in a relationship. Because a wife's role is clearly to follow the leadership of her husband, a single woman should allow a man to pursue her only if he is worthy of her submission.

What do you think? Are you an egalitarian or a complementarian? How do you think this affects your dating relationships? But let's press the issue a bit by looking at our third scenario.

Denise just turned thirty. She is a business professional working in a metropolitan area across the country from her parents. She is active in her local church and busy with friends and activities but has not had any real experience with romantic relationships. She feels her biological clock ticking and wants to get married and have children. What should she do?

> *Ideally, Denise would not have a job away from the care and protection of her parents, especially because she's a single woman. If for some reason she cannot move back to their area, she should first express her desires to God in prayer. Consideration should be given to whether being a wife and mother is becoming an idol in her heart. And if she wants to be found by the right kind of guy, she should focus her time on serving the body of Christ.*

First Corinthians 7 gives wonderful hope for Denise to use her singleness with undivided devotion to Christ (see verse 35) and unhindered ministry for His purpose (see verse 32). Should she move to another church with more single men or even seek to be matched up on a Christian Internet dating service? These questions should be considered with great care and counsel. Speaking with her parents and pastor(s) may provide specific direction. She would be unwise to make such serious decisions without parental and pastoral oversight.

If a single woman such as Denise is attracted to a godly man, but he has not pursued her, it is not her place to be the initiator. She should lay her desires before the Lord and allow Him to direct the man's heart. But if Christian men would learn how to be Christian men, I think situations like Denise's would decrease.

7. The Companionship Principle

God invented marriage because man was alone, not because he was lonely. From the very beginning, God has intended relationships to be about glorifying Him by purposeful companionship. So the purpose of marriage is simple: to serve, represent, and glorify God as a two-in-one team. Dating serves as an arena for testing a relationship to see if it glorifies God enough to warrant marriage. This is the Companionship Principle.

One can use dating as the testing ground for marriage only if one understands marriage. That being true, let's go back to the purpose of marriage. The question that must be asked, then, is this: **Does the relationship move you to serve, represent, and glorify God better or worse than you could alone?**

The best way to find this out is through time – a lot of time. Usually, it's important to go slow. Take as much time as you need to really get to know a person before you decide that he or she is "the one." On the other hand, going too slow can make sexual temptation unbearable. Seek the Lord fervently during this time as you're figuring out whether you should marry this person.

Observe your beauty in as many contexts as possible. A man should not judge a woman solely on how she looks without makeup; in the same way a woman should not consider only whether or not a man has good hygiene. Instead, both should determine if the other has a true heart for the things of God.

Though the ability to serve and glorify God together is of utmost importance, it is also legitimate to ask the question, What about physical attraction? Does it play any part in the decision process? The Song of Solomon clearly – and graphically – illustrates that physical attraction is a part of God's design in marital romance (see 4:1-7, 6:4-7:10). This is a divine gift. Notice that Solomon and his bride were physically attracted to each other before they married (see 1:10, 15-16; 2:13-14). Physical attraction should play a part of premarital attraction, but only a part. When Solomon taught his sons about marital satisfaction, he said,

> *Let your fountain be blessed, And rejoice in the wife of your youth, A lovely dear, a graceful doe. Let her breasts fill you at all times with delight; Be intoxicated always in her love. (Proverbs 5:18-19, emphasis added)*

In other words, physical desire should be satisfied in marriage, but the satisfaction of companionship is more important. And it's amazing how attractive people of godly character can be.

In order to accurately assess a relationship, a thorough understanding of God's design for marriage is crucial. As you consider marriage, it might be a good idea to read more books about marriage than about dating and courting.

8. Commitment Principle

One of the most generic phrases in the English language is "I love you." Love is said to be a feeling unlike anything you have ever felt before. Others say love is like a hole in the ground – you fall into it. If you want to experience biblical love, you need to have the faithfulness and responsibility to love as God loves. The New Testament term for this kind of love is agape. It simply means an unconditional commitment to an imperfect person. Ephesians 5:22-33 describes this as the kind of love a married couple should have. It is not based on emotion, selfish gain, or even attraction. (Note: I am not saying that you should not be attracted to the person you marry!)

But what is the nature of such love? God didn't leave us to our own thinking and hormones to decide. Agape love is the kind of love God has (see John 3:16), and we have been given a very detailed descriptoin of it:

> *Love is patient and kind; love does not envy or boast; it is not arrogant or rude. It does not insist on its own way; it is not irritable or resentful; it does not rejoice at*

wrongdoing, but rejoices with the truth. Love bears all things, believes all things, hopes all things, endures all things. Love never ends. (1 Corinthians 13:4-8)

Love is a commitment. It is a decision to be made and a promise to be kept. It is the way Christians care for one another. And it is the way a husband and wife reflect the glory of Jesus Christ. Real, genuine, sincere, biblical love endures all things and stays committed to an imperfect person. I am not suggesting that you can never break off a dating relationship – even if you have told someone you love him or her. Rather, in a romantic context, those words should be reserved for communicating a permanent relational commitment.

9. The Communication Principle

At the core of every problem in marriage and premarital relationships is prideful selfishness. And nothing solves this problem more than communication. If you want to be successful relationally, learning to communicate biblically is nonnegotiable.

Ephesians 4:25-29 teaches that appropriate, godly communication has at least four elements. Paul encouraged the Ephesian believers to communicate verbally (see verse 25), honestly (see verse 25), regularly (see verse 26), and purposefully (see verse 29). Any relationship, romantic or otherwise, would profit from these principles.

One of the most important skills to evaluate and work on in a dating relationship is communication. Jesus said that a person's heart is revealed by what he or she says (see Luke 6:45). God-honouring communication is the bridge that will take you to relational enjoyment and get you over the inevitable conflicts of relationships.

Men and women communicate differently. Learning to clearly say what you mean and to hear what is really being said is more of an art than a science. But there is a key: humility. If you really want to be a better communicator and listener, put the focus of your communication on the other person. Use wisdom in talking about yourself. Beware of the person who likes to talk only about himself or herself. And especially pay attention to how much that person speaks based on a foundation of Christ's gospel. It's simple. We talk about what is important to us. So let Jesus flavour what you say and how you say it. And listen carefully for the sounds of the Saviour when you listen to that person you are interested in.

10. The Chastity Principle

One question I am regularly asked by people in romantic relationships is, "How far can we go physically?" The problem is that this question is fundamentally wrong. Another way of phrasing it is, "How close can we get to sin without getting into trouble?" The Chastity Principle involves asking another question altogether: "How holy can we be?"

Physical affection is a privilege of the marriage commitment. Said another way, sex is God's wedding gift, and He doesn't want the present touched until after the wedding! So what does that mean? What about holding hands, hugging, kissing and so on? Two important texts need our attention:

> *Flee from sexual immorality. Every other sin a person commits is outside the body, but the sexually immoral person sins against his own body. Or do you not know that your body is a temple of the Holy Spirit within you, whom you have from God? You are not your own, for you were bought with a price. So glorify God in your body (1 Corinthians 6:18-20)*
>
> *For this is the will of God, your sanctification: that you abstain from sexual immorality. (1 Thessalonians 4:3)*

From these passages, God's counsel about physical affection can be discerned. Sexual sin is prohibited, uniquely offensive to God, damaging, against God's will, a violation of the Holy Spirit's presence, and a sinful use of your body that was bought by the blood of Jesus.

These passages raise another rissue that must be tackled: What does it mean to defraud a person in a relationship? First Thessalonians 4:3-7 is a warning against sexual sin. Paul says that immorality is against God's will (see verse 3), a lack of self-control (see verse 4), characteristic of an undredeemed life (see verse 5), sin against a brother (see verse 6), and a lightning rod for God's personal vengeance (see verse 6). Verse 6 says that to commit to sexual sin is to "transgress and wrong his brother in this matter." Some translations use the word defraud for the word wrong (KJV, NASB). The word translated defraud (pleonektein), means "to take advantage of," "to claim more," or "to have more than one's due."[51] Note that the object of the verb is "his brother."

Some people use this verse to encourage singles not to defraud each other by sexual sin. Sexual sin is certainly taking advantage of another. However, the verse is better understood as referring to a future spouse who would be violated by a couple's sin. Leon Morris explains, "Promiscuity before marriage refers to the robbing of the other of that virginity which ought to be brought to a marriage. The future partner of such a one has been defrauded."

These verses are also used to prohibit emotional defraud of a person being dated. Care should certainly be given to avoid violating a person in a relationship (see Romans 12:10), but the point of this pasage is to show love and respect to a future spouse. In other words, you should treat a person you are dating as if they are going to be someone else's spouse. How? By being physically pure (see 1 Thessalonians 4:3). It is far better to hurt the feelings of the person you are dating because of a lack of physcial affection than to defraud a future spouse.

So what constitutes sexual sin? Jesus said even the fantasy of extramarital or premarital sexual intimacy is sin (see Matthew 5:27-30). Paul went so far as to say that we should not even allow ourselves to be in a situation where lust can be fueled (see Romans 13:14). So how much physcial intimacy should an unmarried couple experience? Slim to none. I can hear what you are saying as you read this: "Come on, be realistic. Nobody can be that puritanical." But listen to the logic of that kind of thinking. Are we really willing to say that the power of our fleshly lust is greater than the power of the Holy Spirit? Purity is possible where there is a desire and willingness to be pure.

Ask yourself if being physical is necessary. And by the way, if the person you are dating is putting pressure on you to do more or go farther, you might want to reevaluate if you're with the right person.

First Corinthians 7 contains the most concentrated instruction in the New Testament regarding being single and being married. There are several critical verses in this chapter that need comment: "Now concerning the matters about which you wrote: 'It is good for a man not to have sexual relations with a woman.' But because of the temptation to sexual immorality, each man should have his own wife and each woman her own husband" (verses 1-2).

There is considerable scholarly evidence that the sentence "It is good for a man not to have sexual relations with a woman" is a quotation from a letter the Corinthians had sent Paul. They were asking if he thought it was a good idea for a married couple to abstain from sex. The following verse contains Paul's answer: If sex is withheld in marriage, immorality could result from temptation. Though many use this verse to teach that "it is good for a man not touch a woman"

(KJV, NASB) before marriage, the context of the phrase does not allow such interpretation. I do, however, think that the principle of abstinence is taught other places in Scripture (see 1 Thessalonians 4:3-7).

Singleness has considerable advantages over marriage. However, if sexual desire is a struggle, then marriage is the God-given way to satisfy these God-given desires. Paul taught that both singleness and marriage are good.

The apostle, did not, however, teach that a single person does not have to be self-controlled (see Galatians 5:22-23), nor did he teach that sex is the main reason to get married. He simply urged people to make sure the decision about whether or not to marry is made with godly wisdom. Because 1 Corinthians is an answer to questions the Corinthians sent Paul (see 7:1), he was dealing with specifics unknown to us. But through his answers, the Holy Spirit has provided critical instruction for the church.

So Now What?

We live in a world stained by sin. No relationship system can undo the personal and cultural consequences of our depravity. The only hope for us is in the death of Jesus Christ and the gift of His righteousness.

This guided approach to relationships will be practiced by sinful men and women. Thus, it is easy to be extreme on some points and thereby fall into legalism or to be too relaxed on other points, which results in lawlessness. Because my view is less structured than some of the others, a great degree of maturity is required on the part of the couple. Perhaps the biggest danger in this approach is the possibility of making relationships into a simple checklist or a series of hoops to jump through. However, if the confirmed principle is used with the right people, most of those mistakes can be avoided.

Two important questions are asked repeatedly, "Does God have a specific will for a believer's life with regard to a mate?" and "Is there a 'right one' I am supposed to find?" Yes. But you can't be absolutely sure until you are married! The simple principle is that you choose whom to love and then you love whom you chose. And more important than finding the right person is being the right person.

Conclusion

I believe that honouring these biblical principles is more important than whether you date or court. In fact, they ought to be followed regardless of the system a Christian couple uses. It is possible to have a God-honouring dating relationship if these standards are kept. And anyone who is committed to courtship should not disregard them. Even a betrothal model should include them within its strict guidelines. Again, if we are the men and women God calls us to be and God's Word is honoured in these ten ways, the process we use is secondary.

The time to begin to apply these principles is not when you find yourself attracted to someone. The time is now! Let me say it one more time: God is more concerned that you are the right kind of person than whether you are using the "right" system. Be who He has called you to be and trust that He will honour your passion for Him as well as your desire for a relationship.

No dating system is perfect. But we should still strive to honour God in how we find a spouse. I find it interesting that when I read Christian biographies, how Christian couples got together is rarely emphasized. Their examples teach us that personal godliness – not dating, courtship, or betrothal – is what made their marriages what they were.

The same is true of us. How we respond to the gospel is the primary factor in making us who we are and in guiding how we navigate the road to marriage. The importance of having a biblical plan for relationships cannot be overstated. My prayer is that this book will cause you to evaluate your thinking and become more Christlike as a result. May God grant you His wisdom in your relationships and the satisfaction found only in salvation through Jesus Christ.

So Why Are You Dating?

What are the purposes of dating? The reason many singles have failed in the dating game is that they have never clearly understood their objectives. If you ask a group of singles, "Why are you dating?" the answers would range from "to have a good time" to "to find a mate." In some general sense we know that the end of all this may lead us to marriage, but we are not clear as to other specific objectives. Let me list a few and suggest that you add to the list as you give thought to your own personal objectives.

Developing Wholesome Interactions with the Opposite Sex. One of the purposes of dating is to get to know those of the opposite sex and to learn to relate to them as persons. Half of the world is made up of individuals of the opposite sex. If I fail to learn the art of building wholesome relationships with "the other half," immediately I have limited my horizons considerably. God made us male and female, and it is His desire that we relate to each other as fellow creatures who share His image. Our differences are numerous, but our basic needs are the same. If we are to serve people, which is life's highest calling, then we must know them – male and female. Relationships cannot be built without some kind of social interaction. In Western culture, dating provides the setting for such interaction.

One of the problems is that we have been trained to view each other as sex objects rather than as persons. Years ago psychologist Erich Fromm wrote, "What most people in our culture mean by being lovable is essentially a mixture between being popular and having sex appeal." With a proliferation of cable TV, movies, and now the Internet, this perception of others as sex objects has become deeply ingrained in our thinking. For some single women their unspoken lifestyle objective is to "turn the heads" of the men they encounter. And many single men are happy to turn their heads. Those who proceed further and give their attention to the production or purchase of skin magazines often find themselves addicted to this impersonal, disconnected perception of members of the opposite sex. When this becomes a fixed perception, then one ceases in the truest sense to be human. He or she becomes like an animal playing with his toys or allowing one's self to be a toy with which another animal plays.

Learning about the Person, Personality, and Philosophy

Dating provides an opportunity to break down this perception and to help one learn to see others as persons rather than objects. It is in dating that one discovers names, personalities and philosophies. These are the qualities of personhood. The name identifies us as a unique person. The personality reveals the nature of our uniqueness, and the philosophy reveals the values by which we live our lives. All of these are discovered, not as we stand back and view each other as objects, but as we come close and begin to interact with each other.

It is in dating that we discover that every woman has a mother and a father, and so does every man. Known or unknown, living or dead, our parents have influenced us and thus profoundly affected who we are. The popularity of Alex Haley's book "Roots" and the television series based on it give evidence that we are all connected with our past. In the dating relationship we have the potential for excavating these roots. Every person has a personal history that has also greatly influenced him or her. In the context of dating, these histories are shared.

Why is dating important? Because it gives us a means of connecting with others as persons. Our society increasingly pushes us to live in cocoons, but our isolation has brought us to growing levels of loneliness, emptiness, and sometimes desperation. However, this isolation need not be a permanent prison. Dating is an acceptable way of breaking out of isolation and connecting with others.

Jenny, a very reserved, almost shy single, did not date in high school and only dated twice in college. However, upon graduation and landing her first job, she began to attend a singles group in a local church. She took the opportunity to go out for dessert with a smaller group and in this context met Brent. They had been dating for three months when Jenny said to me, "I don't know why I waited so long to start dating. It feels so good to be getting to know someone else and letting him know me." Jenny has taken a giant step in getting to know people as persons.

Seeing Our Strengths and Weaknesses

A second purpose of dating is to aid in the development of one's own personality. All of us are in process. Someone has suggested that we ought to wear signs around our necks reading "Under construction." As we relate to others in the dating context, we begin to see various personality traits exhibited. This provokes healthy self-analysis and brings greater self-understanding. We recognized that some traits are more desirable than others. We come to see our own strength and weaknesses. The knowledge of a weakness is the first step toward growth.

The fact is all of us have strengths and weaknesses in our personalities. None of us is perfect. Maturity is not flawlessness. However, we are never to be satisfied with our present status of development. If we are overly withdrawn we cannot minister freely to others. If, on the other hand, we are overly talkative we may overwhelm those whom we would help. Relating to those of the opposite sex in a dating relationship has a way of letting us see ourselves and cooperate in God's plan for growth for our lives.

A number of years ago a very talkative young man said to me, "I never realized how obnoxious I must be until I dated Sally. She talks all the time, and it drives me batty." The light had dawned; his eyes were opened. He saw in Sally his own weakness and was mature enough to take steps toward growth. For him this meant curbing his speech and developing his listening skills, a prescription written in the first century by one of the apostles in the Christian church. "My dear brothers, take note of this: Everyone should be quick to listen, slow to speak and slow to become angry." What we dislike in others is often a weakness in our own lives. Dating can help us see ourselves realistically.

Changing personality weaknesses is not always easy. Jenny, whom we met earlier, realized that her shyness was detrimental in building relationships with others. Upon graduation from college, she decided to get personal counseling. It was here that she gained insight and encouragement to take steps in the right direction. The first of those was to attend a singles group at a local church. The second was to push herself to go out with a smaller group for dessert. What was more difficult for Jenny was learning how to share her ideas in that small group, to talk about herself and let people know about her college experience and her present vocation.

It took about six months for her to develop the courage to ask Brent over for dinner, which was the first step in developing their relationship. Once they started dating, Jenny sensed that Brent was someone she could trust. With encouragement from her counselor, she began to share with Brent the details of her history. His interest in listening encouraged her to proceed. In the early stages, her counselor encouraged her to write down the things that she would tell Brent that night and the questions she would ask him about his life. By writing it down beforehand, Jenny had the courage to follow through. Change takes effort, but it is effort well invested.

Practice in Serving Others

A third purpose of dating is that it provides an opportunity to serve others. Service is life's highest calling. History is replete with examples of men and women who discovered that humanity's greatest contribution is in giving to others. Who does not know of Mother Teresa? Her name is synonymous with service. In Africa there are Albert Schweitzer and in India, Mohandas Gandhi. Most people who have studied closely the life of Jesus of Nazareth, the first-century founder of the Christian faith, agree that His life can be summarized by His simple act of washing the feet of His disciples. He Himself said, "I did not come to be served, but to serve, and to give [My] life as a ransom for many." He instructed His followers, "Whoever wants to become great among you must be your servant." True greatness is express in serving. I do not mean to convey the idea that dating should be done in a spirit of martyrdom – "Poor ol' me. I have to do this service as my duty," or "If I serve this guy, maybe he will like me." Ministry is different from martyrdom. Ministry is something we do for others, whereas martyrdom is something others bring upon us.

Dating is always a two-way street. Certainly we receive something from the relationship, but we are also to be contributing to the life of the one whom we are dating. Unmeasured good could be accomplished if we could see service as one of the purposes of dating. Many a reserved fellow could be "drawn out" by the wise questions of a dating partner. Many a braggart could be calmed by the truth spoken in love. Taking ministry seriously may change your attitudes toward dating. You have been trained to "put your best foot forward" so that the other person will be impressed by you. Consequently, you may be have been reluctant to speak to your partner's weaknesses, fearing he or she would walk away from you. Genuine service demands that we speak the truth in love. We do not serve each other by avoiding one another's weaknesses.

Serving by Listening. Fortunately, not all of our service involves pointing out the weaknesses of our dating partners. Often we help them simply by listening as they share their struggles. Empathetic listening is an awesome medication for the hurting heart. Jim was dating Tricia when her father died of a heart attack. They had only been dating a few weeks, but Jim sensed that she wanted him to be with her. So he sat with the family for the memorial service and accompanied Tricia to the burial. The next few weeks he often asked her questions about her father and let her talk freely of her memories.

In so doing, he was helping her work through the grief that so deeply pained her. Had they not been dating, he would have not had this opportunity of service, which was extremely helpful to Tricia.

Discovering the Person We Will Marry

Another obvious purpose of dating is to help us discover the kind of person we will marry. As noted earlier, in some cultures marriages are arranged. Contracts are drawn up between respective families. The choice is made on the basis of social, financial, or religious considerations. The couple is supposed to develop love once they are married. In Western culture the process is left to the individuals involved. Frankly, I prefer this process. Dating is designed to help us gain a realistic idea of the kind of person we need as a marriage partner.

Dating people with differing personalities gives us criteria for making wise judgments. One who has limited dating experience may after marriage be plagued by the thought, What are other women/men like? Would I have had a better marriage with another type of mate? Those questions may come to all couples, especially when there is trouble in the marriage. "But the individual who looks back on a well-rounded social life before marriage is better equipped to answer the question. He is not as likely to build a dream world, because experience has taught him that all of us are imperfect."

What could be more difficult than finding someone with whom we can live in harmony and fulfillment for the next fifty years? The variables are great. The old idea is that opposites attract. There is truth to that, but opposites also may repel. That is why couples can be so attracted before marriage and so disillusioned afterwards. The reality is that the more similar we are, the less conflicts we will have. Similarity is especially important when it comes to the bigger issues of life, such as values, spirituality, morals, whether or not to have children and how many, and vocational goals. Dating provides the context for exploring answers to these questions and determining our suitability for marriage.

What About Love Languages

You have perhaps noticed that to this point we have not discussed love as an element in the dating process. The reason for that should be obvious. Genuine love interfaces with all of the ideas that we have discussed about dating. It is an attitude of love that should motivate one to want to relate to others as persons rather than objects, to develop your own personality so you can reach your potential for good in the world, and to serve your dating partner and seek to encourage that person to reach his/her potential. In seeking a mate, love is the foundational motivation, which not only leads to marriage but to a successful marriage.

If this is true, then learning to express love in a language my dating partner will feel becomes extremely important. When the dating partner feels loved, he or she is much more likely to open to an authentic relationship in which we can each help the other. Therefore, your dating relationships will be enhanced if you learn to speak the primary love language of the person your are dating.

8

MEN AND WOMEN RELATING

Respect and Care

How to Express Heartfelt Commitment to your Spouse

A jealous husband returned home from an evening at the mosque and accused his pregnant wife of having an affair. The wife refuted the allegations, but her unbelieving husband responded by gouging out her eyes.

In the Islamic faith, the Quran encourages the men to beat their wives in order for them to submit to them. There's someone wrong when a holy book condone men behaving badly. In the United Kingdom and the United States of America, such behaviour will result in an arrest of the man and charges will be brought against him.

A husband's or a man's responsiblity is always to love his wife/intimate lady partner. According to the Bile, there are emotional as well as physical differences between the sexes; that is why we read that the woman is 'the weaker vessel' (1 Peter 3:7).

Men need to remember to treat their wives/intimate lady partner with respect and care, for a wife is a man's most precious gift by God.

A man should never beat or injure his wife/intimate lady partner; if he does, he is guilty of breaking the God-relationship guide/his marriage vows, which committed him to protect and caring for her.

The apostle Paul exhorts husbands to 'not be bitter towards them'. Bitterness is a strong emotion that results in coldness, rudeness and harshness. It is sharp, resentful, and can lead to brutality. Bitterness is a root of evil that produces bitter fruit and grieves the Holy Sprit (Eph. 4:30–31).

The Christian man, however, is to 'render to his wife the affection due her' (1 Cor. 7:3ff.). A husband is responsible for the quality and quantity of love in his own home, so if love is lacking, he is responsible. There must be no self-seeking on the husband's part. The man has an excellent guide in 1 Corinthians 13. Here the husband or dating man has the purest love-guide (1 Corinthians 13:4–8a). If husbands or dating man exercises these graces, his relationship/marriages would be stronger and sweeter.

In reexaming the Biblical guide on treating one another, it is important to note that no where in the Bible does the creator God allowed a man or a woman to beat or ill-treat one another. This does not honour the God we serve and will certainly affects the perpetrator's spiritual well-being and salvation.

Domestic Abuse or Violence

In the United States of America, ABC news conducted an experiment by hiring actors to take turns abusing one another within a busy park. They wanted to see whether anyone would intervene and thereby save the person being abused. On a number of occasions, people walked by without intervening in the abusive behaviour when it was the women abusing the man. However, when the actors reversed roles, the response was that several individuals were more than willing to intervene. At the interview, those that walked by the man being abused by the women said they thought he had it coming to him. Others said they thought he had cheated on the women and he deserved what he was getting from her.

Domestic abuse or violence is not an acceptable way to treat your spouse or intimate lady partner in a relationship.

Domestic abuse or violence is defined as any incident or threatening behaviour, violence or abuse (psychological, physical, sexual, financial or emotional) between individuals who are or have been intimate partners or are family members, regardless of gender or sexual.[4]

---

4 *Home Office, United Kingdom*

Domestic abuse and violence against men and women have some similarities and yet are usually different in terms of the outcome. Violences by men against women tend to lead to more serious physical damage in comparison to violences by women against men. However, for both sexes, domestic violence includes pushing, slapping, hitting, throwing objects, forcing or slamming a door, forcing an intimate lady partner or wife to have sex or striking the other person with an object, or using a weapon. In fact domestic abuse can be mental or emotional, leaving a scar that will take years to overcome.

What will hurt a man mentally and emotionally, can in some cases be very different from that which hurts a woman. For some men, being called a coward, impotent or failure can have a very different pyschological impact than it would on a women. Unkind and cruel words hurts, but they can hurt in different ways and remain with a person for long durations and in different ways.

In most cases, both men and women, emotional abuse have had a deeper impact than that of physical abuse.

The Bible provides us with some valuable guides, which if followed, will drastically reduced the chance of there being an abusive and violent relationship. God expects that there should be trust, love (care) and respect.

Using one of my teaching and learning tools, I have developed an acronym, R-E-S-P-E-C-T, to help men and women remember what God calls them to do. Whenever a couple follows the R-E-S-P-E-C-T route, their relationship will grow and will model that which God had originally intended for a God-driven relationship.

R- Rejoice, Respect and Repeating nothing to others about his or her short-comings.

E- Encourage, Esteem

S- Sexual Needs and Self-disciple

P- Prayer Support, Praise, Physical Touch and Put first

E- Elevate, Empowering to serve and Experience love

C- Compliment, Cuddle, Consult, Communicate, Confide, and Cover

T- Treatments, Trust, Time, Togetherness and Touch

Respect is defined as an esteem for or a sense of the worth or excellence of a person, a personal quality or ability, or something considered as a manifestation of a personal quality or ability:[5]

Rejoice (Joy)- Proverbs 5:15-20)

In the Old Testament, the word is translated as joy (Heb. samha, verb sameah). The word covers a wide range of human experiences—from sexual love (So 1:4), to marriage(Pr 5:18), thebirth of children (Psalm113:9), the gathering of the harvest, military victory (Isa 9:3), etc. It implies an outward expression of excitement.

The Bible reminds the husband that his wife is the fountain of blessing for him. that he should "rejoice in the wife of your youth" (Proverbs 5:18). That is to continue to be happy with the wife he married even after being married of numerous years. Even at the age of coming to the end of his life. It further explains what the rejoice entails by saying that "she is a loving deer, a graceful doe. So Let her breasts satisfy you always. May you always be captivated by her love." (Proverbs 5:18,19). These verses gives advice to one who is married. But the author probably does not have in mind a particular individual. These are lessons for anyone to learn, married or not. The main urge here is to find sexual pleasure only in his wife, not in the arms of the immoral woman and be embraced in the arms of a seductress (Proverbs 5:20).

Scholars suggests that the spings/streams refers to the man straying outside of marriage. On the contrary, Song of Solomon (4:12) seems to use the symbolism to suggest that these terms refers to the woman. Therefore, while the husband's job is to rejoice or be excited in the wife God gave him. She is not to be neglected and exposed to seeking consolation elsewhere (Verse 17). In describing the wife as a "hind," and a "doe," the writer is using them to symbolise womanly attractiveness and beauty, as the love language in the Songs of Solomon (3:5). Noting the fact

---

5 *Dictionary.com, http://dictionary.reference.com/browse/respect. 23 May 2011.*

that the man is called "the stage (Song of Solomon 8:14). For the man shows that he has wisdom by being embraced in a erotic passion for his woman/wife rather than being fascinated with the "stranger" who destroys double love: the love for one's wife, and also for wisdom that comes from God.[6]

Respect and Repeat Nothing About him or her (Proverbs 25:19)

There is nothing more embarrassing for a wife, husband or an intimate partner than trying to show who is control in the house. You should never forget that you are dealing with your wife, husband or an intimate partner and not a child. Her or she should be treated with respect at all times, especially in public. It is important to note that whenever trust is betrayed, it is very difficult to regain it. Telling your innermost to someone or another family member is breaking your vows and destroying trust. Your partner's faults and failures should only be discussed between yourself and that person or God. It is not acceptable to place your confidence in another person without the expressed permission of your partner or spouse.

Encourage and Esteem (1 Thessalonians 5:11; Proverbs 12:25; 18:21)

According to Gary Chapman, one way to express love emotionally is to use words that build up.[7] Solomon said, "The tongue has the power of life and death." (Prov 18:21) And "An anxious heart weighs a man down, but a kind word cheers him up." (Prov 12:25) Verbal compliments, or words of appreciation, are powerful communicators of love. They are best expressed in simple, straightforward statements of affirmation, such as:

"You look sharp in that suit." "Dear, you look nice in that dress! Wow!"
"You must be the best cook in the world. I love these potatoes."
"I really appreciate the hard work you put into making our home a delight."

What would happen to the emotional climate of a marriage or a relationship if the husband/man and wife/woman heard such words of affirmation regularly?

6 Murphy, R. E. (2002). Vol.22: Word Biblical Commentary; Proverbs. Word Biblical Commentary (32-33), Dallas: Word, Incorporated.
7 Chapman, Gary D, The Five Love Languages: The Secret to Love that Lasts, Northfield Publishing, Chicago, IL, USA. 37

Chapman goes on to say that giving verbal compliments is only one way to express words of affirmation to your spouse. Another dialect is encouraging words. According to the Oxford Dictionary, the word encourage means to give support, confidence, or hope to someone. In addition it can also mean to help or stimiulate to develop.[8] All of us have areas in which we feel insecure. We lack courage, and that lack of courage often hinders us from accomplishing the positive things that we would like to do. The latent potential within your spouse in his or her areas of insecurity may await your encouraging words.

Love is kind. If then we are to communicate love verbally, we must use kind words. That has to do with the way we speak (1 Corinthians 13:4).

Sexual Needs, Self-dscipline, Share with, Service and Satisfaction (1 Corinthians 7:3; 2 Timothy 1:7; Galatians 6:2; Colossians 3:18,19)

The Message Bible translates 1 Corinthians 7 as follows:
It's good for a man to have a wife, and for a woman to have a husband. Sexual drives are strong, but marriage is strong enough to contain them and provide for a balanced and fulfilling sexual life in a world of sexual disorder. The marriage bed must be a place of mutuality—the husband seeking to satisfy his wife, the wife seeking to satisfy her husband. Marriage is not a place to "stand up for your rights." Marriage is a decision to serve the other, whether in bed or out. Abstaining from sex is permissible for a period of time if you both agree to it, and if it's for the purposes of prayer and fasting—but only for such times. Then come back together again. Satan has an ingenious way of tempting us when we least expect it. I'm not, understand, commanding these periods of abstinence—only providing my best counsel if you should choose them.[9]

While the New Living Translation translates verse 3 in such a way that it gets to the point of what is required in marriage. The translations reads "the husband should fulfil his wife's sexual needs, and the wife should fulfill her husband's needs.

Many married couples struggle with sexual problems. Some women are "willing" to make love (sexual relationship) because they are in love with your

8 *Oxford Dictionary, http://www.oxforddictionaries.com, 23 May 2011*
9 *1 Corinthians 7:2-6, The Message Bible.*

husbands and want to meet his need for sexual fulfilment. At the same time, there are some husbands, with wives having a higher sexual drives. They too, because of love, wants to fulfil their wives sexual desires. However, because they don't always share the same emotional need, they do not always "desire" to make love. This can lead to problems within the relationship. Sex, like other emotional needs, is fulfulled in the truest sense only when both spouses respond to each other enthusiastically. Just going along with your spouse desires is often not enough. There should be mutual sexual desire, which is necessary to provide sexual satisfaction to the one who has the need for sex.

In the Newsweek magazine (29th May 2000), John Leland, commenting on the "Science of Women and Sex," wrote about the challenge many that popularised Viagara as once way to unlock the "mysteries of femal desire."[10] Leland mentioned the problem of many women, that of being sexually satisfied after making love. It is important, here, to echo the Scripture counsel to seek to fulfill each others' sexual needs and to avoid opening the avenues of temptations that a failure in this area can and have led to in many marriages. Here it must also be said that to with hold sex, in marriage, as a way of dominating the relationship, can and will harm the marriage and the sacredness of the bed. Sex ought not to be used as an instrument of control.

D Prime, commenting on 1 Corinthians 7, wrote

> The emphasis in marriage is to be on performing one's duties to one's partner rather than demanding one's rights (v. 3). In a fallen world, we tend to major on our rights and, therefore, within marriage our marital rights. The special perspective the Christian faith gives to human relationships is that it teaches us to emphasize rather our duties. A secret of successful marriage is not to insist upon what our partner owes us but to focus on our duty to our marriage partner. That approach makes a world of difference and promotes harmony instead of discord. When either partner in a marriage asks, 'What are my rights?' seeds of discontent are sown. On the other hand, when, instead, the question is, 'What are my duties?' a good foundation is built and strengthened.[11]

In regards to marital duty and self-discipline, Prime believe

10 John Leland, Newsweek, http://www.newsweek.com/2000/05/28/the-science-of-women-sex.html, 23 May 2011.
11 Prime, D. (2005). Opening up 1 Corinthians (63). Leominister: Day One Publications.

> A clear marital duty is to safeguard and maintain the sexual relationship in marriage (v. 4), something to be achieved by mutual consent (v. 5). As the years pass in a marriage the pattern of life and the sexual needs of a couple may vary and sometimes be different. They need to be sensitive to each other's needs and comfort.

And that

> Self-discipline should be exercised in marriage and often for spiritual reasons, but never so that duty to one's partner is neglected (v. 5). Self-control is part of the Spirit's fruit (Gal. 5:23) to be applied to every area of the Christian's life. Harmony between marriage partners is always a priority in whatever decisions they make, and not least to avoid giving Satan a foothold in their relationship. Married Christians are encouraged to remember that God is concerned and involved in every aspect of their shared life.

Paul, in 2 Timothy (1:7) reminds us that "God has not given us a spirit of fear and timidity, but of power, love, and self-discipline."

Prayer Support, Praise and Physical Touch

Prayer, in a christian marriage, is central to the well being of the relationship. Where prayer exists, God is and where God is, there is hope and help during times of difficulties.

1 Peter 3:7 advise the husband in this area by saying "In the same way, you husbands must give honour to your wives. Treat your wife with understanding as you live together. She may be weaker than you are, but she is your equal partner in God's gift of new life. Treat her as you should so your prayers will not be hindered. This translation should rather be "You husbands in turn must know how to live with a woman."[12]

K Boa wrote

> Spiritual growth is impossible apart from the practice of prayer. Just as the key to quality relationships with other people is time spent in communication, so the key to a growing relationship with the personal

---

12 Michaels, J. R. (2002). Vol. 49: Word Biblical Commentary : 1 Peter. Word Biblical Commentary (167). Dallas: Word, Incorporated.

God of heaven and earth is time invested in speaking to Him in prayer and listening to His voice in Scripture.[13]

I believe that this is also important in the development of a relationship. It is said that a family that pray together, stay together. Whenever there is a problem, in a relationship, it should be approached with prayer, seeking wisdom from God in knowing how to approach and overcome such problems. Couples should seek to spend time both studying teh word of God together as well as praying. Prayer support is essential in a christian relationship. This may be said to be attached to the twin discipline of prayer and Scripture. Prayer and Scripture are essential to our spiritual life. Therefore, it is necessary that time be set aside for scripture and prayer. The prayer life of couples evolves as they learn about prayer, learn from each other adn grow more comfortable together.

God's people, in marriage and dating, need to learn to pray together. We miss so many things necessary for the spiritual victory over relationship problems, that God would gladly provide if we would come to Him in prayer. James 3 ends with a reminder of the need for peace to reign in relationships among Christians (especially in moments of arguments and stresses). James 4 begins with a description of the cause of the conflict that all too often replaces that peace. James 4:2 then provides a most interesting remedy for problems of conflict in marriage/relationship, a remedy called prayer: "You do not have because you do not ask." Yet we fail to use the remedy by not going to God in prayer.

The first stanza of "What a Friend We Have in Jesus states it very well": O what peace we often forfeit, O what needless pain we bear, All because we do not carry Everything to God in prayer.

Why do we seek solutions to our problems so many other ways besides through prayer? Often the first response to a problematic situation in the marriage or relationship is to call a your parent or a close friend to help you to decide how to overcome it. In contrast, when on one occasion Jesus identified a major challenge facing Him and His disciples, "The harvest is plentiful, but the laborers are few" (Luke 10:2), His first action was to instruct the twelve, "pray therefore ..." (RSV).[14]

---

13 Boa, K. (1997). Handbook to prayer : Praying scripture back to God. Atlanta: Trinity House.

14 MacArthur, J., F., Jr, Mayhue, R., & Thomas, R., L. (1995). Rediscovering pastoral ministry : Shaping contemporary ministry with biblical mandates (Electronic ed.). Logos Library Systems. Dallas: Word Pub.

There must also be time for praising each other. Finding things to give credit or praise is important in the development of a relationship. Appreciating the apparent little things by saying uplifting words, praise, will assist in the relationship. Proverbs 31 reminds us that the praise comes from both the husband, as a result of the work of the wife, and the children. Avoiding criticism is vital.

Physical touch is also a powerful vehicle for communicating marital love. Holding hands, kissing, embracing, and sexual intercourse are all ways of communicating emotional love to one's spouse. For some individuals, physical touch is their primary love language. Without it, they feel unloved. With it, their emotional tank is filled, and they feel secure in the love of their spouse.

Sexual intercourse is only one dialect in the relationship. Of the five senses, touching, unlike the other four, is not limited to one localised area of the body. Tiny tactile receptors are located throughout the body. When those receptors are touched or pressed, nerves carry impulses to the brain. The brain interprets these impulses and we perceived that the thing that touched us is warm or cold, hard of soft. It causes pain or pleasure. We may also interpret it as loving or hostile.

Elevate, Empowering to Serve and Experience love

According to the Adventist Review and Sabbath Herald, "those who are associated together in church capacity have entered into a relationship with one another which implies mutual responsibility."[15] In addition, "they have individually pledged themselves to God and to their brethren to build up one another in the most holy faith,--to build up, not to tear down."[16] This also applies to those in an intimate, marriage relationship. In such a relationship, both the man and the woman must take great care to cultivate a continually growing relationship with each other, to build big cisterns and dig deep wells, so that they may "be intoxicated always with each others' love" (Prov. 5:19 NRSV).

In 1 Thessalonians 5, verse 11, we are told to "encourage each other adn build each other up, just as you are already doing." Meaning, and build one another up," i.e. help one another to grow spiritually. We should communicate our knowledge and experiences one to another. We should join in prayer and praise one with another. We should set a good example one before another. And it is the duty of

15 *The Review and Herald; The Advent Review and Sabbath Herald; Review and Herald. 2002.*
16 *Ibid.*

those especially who live together in a relationship and family thus to comfort and edify one another. This is the best means to answer the end of society in regards to marriage.

Compliment, Cuddle, Consult, Communicate and Cover (see chapter 8)

When you live with your wife/husband or visit on a regular basis your intimate lady/man, in an understanding way, which really means "according to knowledge," you will spend time cuddling wiithout any ulterior motive in mind. The man, who is a loving leader, will never view his wife as a sex object. In fact, you should never get to the point where you cuddle simply as a means of foreplay or after-play.

Communication is the third most important element of a relationship, third only to God and trust. Communication is a two-way. If there is going to be good communication, there must a two-way system in place. It is essential that respect is included in the communication. That is talking need to be respectful as well as listening. It is not good for one spouse to dominate teh conversation or refuse to listen to the other spouse. A lack of eye contact, negative facial gesture, or disengaged body language signals poor communication. It is essential that honesty and truthfulness be guarded within the relationship conversation moments. Any spouse that learns that his or her spouse lied about something will find it difficult to believe their spouse and will always wonder whether the truth is being told or not. Here, it most be noted that honesty is crucial in all communication. That is not just avoiding lies, but also sharing information that our spouse has the right to know and would want to know. Good communication in a healthy relationship or marriage does not hide, distort, or evade the truth from the other.

Quality conversation, says Chapman, is a
> sympathetic dialogue where two individuals are sharing their experience, thoughts, feelings, and desires in a friendly, uninterrupted context. Most individuals who complain that their spouse does not talk do not mean literally that he or she never says a word. They mean that he or she seldom takes part in sympathetic dialogue. If your spouse's primary love language is quality time, such dialogue is crucial to his or her emotional sense of being loved.[17]

Quality conversation focuses on what we are hearing. If I am sharing my

---

17 *Chapman, Gary D, Five Love Languages*

love for you by means of quality time and we are going to spend that time in conversation, it means I will focus on drawing you out, listening sympathetically to what you have to say. I will ask questions, not in a badgering manner but with a genuine desire to understand your thoughts, feelings, and desires.

Ecclesiastes 7:8,9 reminds us that "finishing is better than starting. Patience is better than pride. Controling your temper, for anger labels you a fool." In addition, Proverbs 17:9, reminds us that "Love prospers when fault is forgiven, but dwelling on it separate close friends. Therefore, Colossians 3:13, counsel us to "make allowance for each other's faults, and forgive anyone who offends you."[18]

T- Treatments, Trust, Time, Togetherness and Touch

By Time, I mean "quality time," giving someone your undivided attention. Chapman said it "don't mean sitting on the couch watching television together. When you spend time that way, ABC, CNN, or… have your attention—not your spouse. What I mean is sitting on the couch with the TV off, looking at each other and talking, giving each other your undivided attention." It means taking a walk, just the two of you, or going out to eat and look at each other and talking.

Chapman went on to say that
> A central aspect of quality time is togetherness. Togetherness has to do with focused attention. When a father is sitting on the floor, rolling a ball to his two-year-old, his attention is not focused on the ball but on his child. For that brief moment, however long it lasts, they are together. If, however, the father is on talking on the phone while he rolls the ball, his attention is diluted.

Quality time does not mean that we have to spend our together moments gazing into each other's eyes. It means that we are doing something together and that we are giving our full attention to the other person. The activity in which we are both engaged is incidental. The important thing emotionally is that we are spending focus time with each other.

A husband and wife playing tennis together, if it is genuine quality time, will focus not on the game but on the fact that they are spending time together. What happens on the emotional level is what matters. Our spending time together in a common pursuit communicates that we care about each other, that we enjoy being

---

18 New Living Translation

with each other, that we like to do things together. That is why going to church in one way as a family is so important for the sometimes-busy church leader.

Touch

Physical touch can make or break a relationship. It can communicate hate or love. To the person whose primary love language is physical touch, the message will be far louder than the words "I hate you" or "I love you." A slap in the face is detrimental to any child, but it is devastating to ca child whose primary love language is touch. A tender hug communicates love to any child, but is shouts love to the child whose primary love language is physical touch. The same is true of adults.

A note is that fact that there are appropriate and inappropriate ways to touch members of the opposite sex in every society. The recent attention to sexual harassment has highlighted the inappropriate ways. Within marriage, however, what is appropriate and the couples themselves, within certain broad guidelines, determine inappropriate touching. Physical abuse is of course deemed inappropriate by society, and social organizations have been formed to help.

Colossians 3:19 makes it clear what should happen within the relationship. "Husbands love your wives and never treat them harshly. 1 Peter 3:7, Peter said, "Treat your wife with understanding as you live together. She may be weaker than you are, but she is your equal partner in God's gifts of new life. Treat her, as you should, so your prayers will not be hindered. (NLT)

<u>My Personal Notes</u>

9

UNDERSTANDING YOUR SPOUSE

UNDERSTANDING YOUR WIFE

The Mysterious Woman[19]

There are some husbands struggling because the woman he thought he knew last month has seemingly changed this month. In order to effectively love and serve, it is important for the husband to know with whom he is dealing. The more knowledge he has about his wife, the more effective he will be in carrying out his responsibilities as a loving husband. This is what the Bible speaks on in 1 Peter 3:7

Likewise, ye husbands, dwell with them according to knowledge (understanding), giving honour unto the wife, as unto the weaker vessel, and as being heirs together of the grace of life. (KJV)

The Scripture challenges husbands to know what makes her happy on as well as what makes her sad. The husband should understand that even though the wife is made out of the same "stuff" as he, she is still different. The term weaker in 1 Peter 3:7 is not pointed out to suggest that she is on a lower level than the husband. It really points to her delicate nature, which requires special care (noting there are some women who are much bigger, stronger, more financially well off than some men and at times more dependable, reliable. More are leading the church of today while men find themselves in a sleep walk.)

---

19 Dr Myles Munroe, Understanding the Purpose and Power of Woman (PA, USA: Whitaker House, 2001). For further information please see other books by Dr Munroe Myles at http://www.Amazon.co.uk. The presentation was made at the Greater New York Conference Family Ministry Retreat as a part of several talks.

The husband is to treat his wife with special care because of how delicate she is. There is no other human relationship greater than the husband-wife relationship. All human relationships are important, and there are certain "cycles" used to take care of those relationships. But the husband-wife relationship must differ from the employer-employee relationship. The husband-wife relationship must operate on a plane all by itself with a different set of rules based solely on understanding one another. Our wife is a member of a sorority that uses a hilarious term to identify their husbands. Some of us are called "Honey do")." This label is given because it describes what happens in the home of that couple. When the wife needs something done by her husband, she will say, "Honey, do this..." Or, "Honey, do that..."

The following, "Honey Do list," will help in Building up your marital relationship

Do compliment

Every wife needs to hear her husband say something good about the way she does things. The husband should take time to compliment the way she looks and the way she does things. Too often, she does things to get her husband's attention; and he never notices, or he notices and never says a word. She should hear from the husband hat the outfit she is wearing is beautiful or that the smell of that perfume is breathtaking.

Do cover

The word cover, according to Webster, means, "something that protects shelters or guards." One of the basic needs of your wife is that of security. She desires for her husband to be willing t o provide for her as well as protect her. It is usually the husband's responsibility to make sure that the stewardship program at home is operating properly. There must be control placed on the finances. 1 Timothy 5:8 reveals: "If anyone does not provide for his own, and especially for those of his own household, he has denied the faith and is worse than an unbeliever" (KJV).

Whether or not the wife is employed outside the home isn't the point. The husband has been given the responsibility to make sure that he is a provider. The wife should know that the husband has it covered, whet, whether she is employed or not. This of course deals with the basic human needs.

Do continue

Men, do you remember courtship's smiling days? Remember how you would block out everything else to give full attention to your sweetheart? Remember how you did those peculiar and crazy things, just to spend time with her? Remember how you spent hours on a date, dropped her off, and then you'd call her to talk for countless minutes? All of these were connected to a deep companionship that should continue.

Your wife wants and needs companionship. She desires for you to continue providing quality time on your schedule for her. She was made out of relational substance and must continue to feel that she is important to you. When this is done, you are letting her know that she is just as important to you today as she was when she walked down that aisle and you placed the ring on her finger.

Do confirm

Your wife needs to know that you really appreciate her unique contributions. So much of what she does is not visible to the masses. This is why Peter says, "… grant her honour…" When we praise, honour and exalt our wives, it serves as confirmation of her significance and value. If we don't do it, who will? (watch out, your failure can leave empty spaces for others to fill…).

The confirmation of value and significance comes from those who are in that home with her. This is what Proverbs 31:28 speaks of, "Her children arise up, and call her blessed; her husband also, and he praises her" (KJV). Confirm her value by praising her and honouring her.

Do confide

A husband's number one confidant should be his wife. She desires to know what is going on in her husband's life. She deserves to know as well. She has to deal with the problems he is facing, whether he shares them or not. There are many husbands who consider themselves protecting their wives by not confiding in them. As honourable as it may appear from the surface, I've learn that it becomes a tool of Satan, designed to drive a wedge between you and your spouse.

It is better and easier to deal with "us" when the wife is knowledgeable of the things taking place in our lives. Your wife should never have to try to figure out what is wrong with you. She should be told about the trouble on the job.

Do cuddle

When you live with your wife "in an understanding way," which really means "according to knowledge," you will spend time cuddling without any ulterior motive in mind. The husband who is a loving leader never views his wife as a sex object. You should never get to the point where you cuddle simply as a means of foreplay or after-play. Your wife should be cuddled, caressed, and comforted without sex even crossing the corridor of your mind, as difficult as it may mean for men.

Do consult

The last item on the "Honey-do" list is the need to consult your wife. Your wife needs to know that you value her opinion on things. She should be consulted about certain decisions that need to be made. You should always adopt in your union the saying, "Two heads are better than one." When you consult your wife about things, it gives her a sense of value and importance.

Seeking her advice allows her to see that she is not to be a silent partner in the marital relationship. It is important to understand that consultation is designed for confirmation and not confrontation. The reason you want the advice in the first place is for the purpose of confirming whether the decisions you want to make are right or wrong and how it will impact your marriage and family life. If the opinion differs from yours, it is not right for you to blow up. Just try to see it from her point of view. Sometimes it is not so much the decision is wrong, but the way you've presented the information or because of a lack of information. If this is the case, work on it, maybe there are some things you need to re-examine.

"HONEY DON'T" List

Don't neglect

One problem in marriages is the husband that is so caught up in his job and other extracurricular activities that he fails to give his wife the amount of time she deserves (especially for church leaders and Pastors). Sometimes men feel that because their wives are sitting in a mansion and driving a Mercedes that they don't feel neglected. This is not the case at all.

Your wife should never think that your occupation is your life. She should never think that she has to play second fiddle to friends and co-workers. She should never feel that she is competing with your hobbies and the sports channel. We should be careful, because neglecting can lead to regretting later on.

Don't suspect

Satan, the enemy of any institution established by God, loves for the spirit of jealousy to exist in the marriage. He loves for us to listen to others who don't have our best interest in mind regarding the behaviour of women. That person who says, "Listen, man, if I were you, I wouldn't give my wife so much freedom to do as she pleases. If I were you, I would make sure she checks in before leaving to go somewhere. If I were, I would question her about that shopping trip. How do you know she spent all of that time at the mall?"

If you can't trust her, you shouldn't have married her in the first place. Trust is a must in any relationship. If nothing has been done to cause you to distrust her, then you should not suspect her of doing anything wrong. This is one the tricks of the enemy to bring misery in the marriage.

Don't correct (publicly)

There is nothing more embarrassing for a wife than a husband trying to show others that he wears the trousers in his house. You should never forget that you are dealing with your wife and not your child. She should be treated with respect at all times, especially in public. This is not to suggest that there aren't times when one of you needs to be corrected by the other. Those times will come, but make sure that it is done with love and in its proper place.

Don't reject

Don't reject her sexual advance. There are certain times during the month when your wife can accept the fact that you have had a long day and you are tired. There is another time when her body will not even take that as an excuse. It is how God designed her. To reject her during this period can be very damaging to her physically and emotionally.

This is why you should learn all about your wife's makeup as a woman. When you know that time is drawing near, make sure you are ready to take care of it. God has designed it so that you won't regret it.

Don't forget

Don't let anyone fool you. Special days are important to your wife, whether she says anything about them or not. Anniversaries, birthdays, Valentine's day, and others should not be forgotten. Something special should be done. We husband has a tendency to forget anniversary dates after a while, but this is dangerous! She expects you to remember and do something special. You don't need to buy something that will cause you to file bankruptcy, but please don't forget to do something!

UNDERSTANDING YOUR HUSBAND

Meat and Potatoes[20]

When God made Eve, He placed Adam in a deep sleep and removed one of his ribs. After removing the rib from Adam, He began to fashion it into a woman. Can you imagine this event-taking place? God takes a small rib and produces a full-grown woman. After creating this vision of loveliness and beauty with all of the wonderful curves, He decided to breathe life into him. When you compare the way God produced man and woman, the process for creating man doesn't sound as complex and complicated as the process of creating woman. This may be a little far fetched, but the design of man and woman explains the difference in the modes of operation.

God designed woman as one of the most mysterious of all His entire creations. It takes time to figure out the woman because of her physiological makeup. On the other hand, man is not difficult to figure out. The woman is mysterious and the man is Meat and potatoes.

Most men are easy to figure out. You don't have to take a psychology course to understand him. It is difficult to discover a concrete pattern of behaviour for women. One day, she may be the most talkative and jovial person, and the next moment, she may give you the silent treatment with little laughter. When this happens, most men try to figure out what they did wrong. In a lot of those cases, it has nothing to do with the behaviour of the man, but the makeup of the woman.

20 Myles Munroe, Understanding the Purpose and Power of Men (PA, USA: Whitaker House, 2001)

As a matter of fact, the change of behaviour may not symbolize that anything is wrong. She can still be happy and you not know it. God designed her to be this way. God also designed the man to be the way he is. You know when he is happy or sad. You know when he is mad or glad.

With this information in mind, wives can satisfy their husbands by examining some areas that compliment his makeup:

"Sweeteners" List

Admiration

Your husband desires to be admired above all others. He desires to be considered the "king of his castle." A husband who is genuinely admired by his wife will not need to seek the admiration of another person. This admiration is seen when the supreme amount of respect is rendered. When his position of headship is honoured, he feels admired by the family. He needs to know that his absence creates a void in the home. When he believes he is esteemed highly, he will do what it takes to live up to that image.

Admiration causes the husband to have a sense of worth that is not being received by competing. His admiration in other areas is usually based on "what he does." He has to do a better job than others in the workplace, in order to be admired. He has to be more talented than other in organizations to be admired. The admiration received at home should be based on "who he is." When he is admired just because he is the husband and father, it gives him the greatest amount of satisfaction.

Attention

A husband loves to receive his wife's undivided attention. He understands the wife's association with others; however, he does not want to always be the one at the end of the list. He realizes that attention must be given to children, career, and chores, but he desires to have some time given to him as well. I am not dealing with the selfish husband who desires all of the attention. I am not speaking of the husband who expects his wife to jump at his beck and call. The husband who wants all of the attention does not really understand his role as the husband. I am dealing with the husband that feels neglected when his needs are always placed on the back burner.

A perfect example of the lack of attention received by some husbands can be seen when associating with friends. Most men don't spend a lot of time socializing by phone. They make a few calls to handle business and that is usually the extent of it. Women are different. Since women are naturally relational, they can talk for hours to girlfriends. Although this is a natural thing for women, some husbands have problems with their wives' lack of attention given to them when talking to others. When the phone rings and the husbands' say, " I am not going to answer because I know it is for you," it is usually a cry for more attention, or at least, equal attention.

Sometimes little things are done that cause the husband to believe he is receiving extra attention, such as the wife letting the answer machine take the calls so she can spend some time with him.

Appreciation

There are times when husbands and wives take each other for granted. Just as the wife desires to feel appreciated for what she does in the marriage camp, so does the husband. The question should never be: "why should I say thanks for what someone is required to do? The answer to the question is simple. When you express appreciation for what someone is required to do, it becomes more of an opportunity rather than an obligation. The husband desires to be appreciated for the things he does. The appreciation expressed should be done privately and publicly. There is nothing worse than a wife expressing appreciation in the presence of her husband and later had mounting him in his absence. In Proverbs 31:10-12 (KJV)

The husband in Proverbs expresses appreciation for his wife because he feels appreciated by his wife. When he knows that he is appreciated, he will go over and above the call of duty to take care of his family. When appreciation is spoken and shown, it gives him the emotional support needed to continue providing for his family. He recognizes that providing for his family and securing them is his God-given duty. However, when appreciation is not rendered, it becomes a chore rather than a choice. It becomes a burden rather than a blessing.

The wife should not let a week go by without expressing appreciation for something the husband does. Let him know how much you appreciate the way he takes care of the family. Let him know how much you appreciate him adjusting his schedule to accommodate family above everything else. This appreciation should not just cover the big-ticket items. When he says something like, "don't cook this evening," or "Lets' go out to eat," you should express gratitude and appreciation to him for giving you a break from preparing that meal.

Adoration

The husband wants to be adored by his wife. He wants to know that his wife's world is better because he exists. There is nothing more refreshing to the husband than to hear his wife speak of how much she adores him. In real sense, although he may not admit it, he likes for his wife to brag about him. When the wife tells others how much she adores her husband, it gives the husband confidence that he is doing what he is required to do as a husband. The expression of adoration should be spoken to family, friends, and the husband as well. The adoration shown to the husband will cause him to show adoration.

Affirmation

The husband expects his wife to be his most loyal supporter. He needs to know that his wife believes in him. Whenever the husband pursues goals, the wife must continually affirm him. The affirmation shown by the wife creates determination for the husband. She can make him feel like he can conquer the world or she can make him feel like he is wasting his time. When she affirms his abilities, he will try harder to achieve. He becomes more determined to meet that challenge because of the faith that hi wife has in him. The wife can make him feel like he can move mountains.

Even after he fails, she continues to affirm his abilities. She assures him that he still has what it takes to get the job done. She makes it sounds like the company missed their blessings by not hiring him. The more she affirms him, the more confidence he has in his abilities.

Anticipation

The husband anticipates those moments of making love. The sex drive of the man compels him to anticipate having his sexual needs met. His sexual needs differ from his wife. There are times when the sexual desire of the wife is stronger than at other times. The only time when the sex drive is not strong for the average man is usually when he has gone without making love for an extended period.

The problem for some men is that they have learned to combine affection with anticipation. Anticipation focuses in on having the sexual need met. Affection focuses in on the intimacy that leads to the fulfilment of the anticipation. For the woman, the only time when affection is not necessarily required is during that period of the month when she is at her sexual peak. During that stage, she will probably attack you. At all other times, affection is required.

What Lights His Fire?

1. When it comes to food and eating, its...
    a. Carrots, celery, bean sprouts, and tofu
    b. Chez Vicente for fine French dining- the more forks, the better
    c. Just meat and potatoes. What else is there?
    d. Bring on those chocolate-chip pancakes! Extra sausage, please!
    e. Other (explain):

2. When it comes to entertainment, hobbies, and recreation, it's...
    a. Doing fun things alone
    b. Gathering with a bunch of guy friends
    c. Sharing all "fun times" and hobbies with wife and family
    d. Having the occasional "night out: for myself
    e. Other (explain):

3. When it comes to spending money, it's...
    a. "Honey, have you seen the coupon for the cat litter?"
    b. "A penny saved is a penny earned"
    c. "Let the good times roll, Baby!"
    d. "Hey, I work hard; I deserve it. It's just debt, you know"
    e. Other (explain):

4. When it comes to job and career fulfilment, it's...
    a. "Ahhhh... Nothing better than sore muscles and dusty clothes at the end
    b. " I can't believe they're actually paying me for this—just to think up new ideas. I love it"
    c. "Oh no! It's not time to head to the office again, is it?"

5. When it comes to spiritual growth, it's...
    a. Marvelling over a beautiful sunset
    b. Save the blue blue-bellied swamp mouse
    c. Sitting quietly, just to "let God love me."
    d. Other (explain)

6. When it comes to romance and affection (but not sex), it's…
   a. Spending an hour or two at the local hardware store
   b. Bring showered with hugs and kisses for being :My X"
   c. Receiving a great back rub
   d. A black-tie-night out- dinner and the opera would be great
   e. Other (explain)

7. When it comes to the sex, it's…
   a. 10 P.M., sex; 10:05, lights out
   b. "Well, I guess it's that time of year again, Honey"
   c. "How bout you making the first move once in a while?"
   d. "Let's block out three hours tonight…"
   e. Other (explain):

<u>My Personal Notes</u>

10
MARITAL SATISFACTION

According to Peter J. Ward, Neil R. Lundberg, Ramon B. Zabriskie, and Kristen Berrett, satisfaction can be defined as a state of happiness over pain (Collard, 2006). In examining satisfaction, in marriage, one needs to consider all the possible aspects of a person's environment and state of being in order to determine if happiness outweighs pain.[1]

In assessing the level of satisfaction, specifically marital, a person is required to cognitively balance all environmental influences, personal feelings, aspirations, disappointments, and achievement of personal goals and then determine if the positive exceeds the potential negatives. One would therefore view satisfaction as being in a continual state of well-being.

Ward rightly believes that individuals, to some extent, determine their own level of satisfaction and that the process of determining satisfaction is subjective; it is not the same for all individuals. Further, satisfaction is a global assessment of the quality of an individual's situation according to their internally chosen criteria. In addition, it should be said that the criteria for deciding satisfaction is subject to external influences. For example, a situation that may be satisfying for one person may not be satisfying to another, because each person independently chooses his or her own criteria for comparison. Therefore, it is reasonable to conclude that judgments of satisfaction depend largely on a "comparisons of one's circumstances with what is thought to be an appropriate standard" (Diener et al., 1985, p. 71).

---

1 *Peter J. Ward, Neil r. Lundberg, Ramon b. Zabriskie, And Kristen Berrett, (Marriage & Family Review, 45:412–429, 2009).*

Marital Satisfaction

Marital satisfaction is one type of satisfaction that has received widespread attention. It has often been indirectly addressed in the marriage and family literature by implying that marital satisfaction is the state of a non-distressed relationship (Bradbury et al., 2000; Busby et al., 1995; Kinnunen & Feldt, 2004; Spanier, 1976).

Wards definition of marital satisfaction is one which is supported by the biblical principle of Genesis 2, God announcing that man is not complete, not really happy until he has a helpmate, a partner, that can share and care about him and he for her. Resulting in an environment of wellness relating to man's spiritual and physical internal status.[2]

Ward defines it as

An individual's emotional state of being content with the interactions, experiences, and expectations of his or her married life. The first part of the definition focuses on the emotional state of satisfaction. Emotional states are self-contained within the individual and require people to consider all the different elements of marriage based on internal criteria (Collard, 2006). The emotional state of marital satisfaction is being content with the interactions between themselves and spouse.[3]

This, says Ward, "refers back to the original characterization of satisfaction, experiencing overall happiness over pain (Collard, 2006). Thus when individuals experience happiness over pain in their marital relationships, they are in the emotional state of having marital satisfaction."

And

The second part of the definition delimits the emotional state to focus on interactions between the couple. Interactions include all experiences, influences, relationships, and emotions shared between a partner and oneself.[4]

---

2 Peter J. Ward, Neil r. Lundberg, Ramon b. Zabriskie, And Kristen Berrett, (Marriage & Family Review, 45:412–429, 2009).
3 Ibid.
4 Ibid.

Ellen White, commenting, wrote

> The warmth of true friendship and the love that binds the hearts of husband and wife are a foretaste of heaven. God has ordained that there should be perfect love and perfect harmony between those who enter into the marriage relation. Therefore, let bride and bridegroom in the presence of the heavenly universe pledge themselves to love one another as God has ordained they should. Man was not made to dwell in solitude; he was to be a social being. Without companionship the beautiful scenes and delightful employments of Eden would have failed to yield perfect happiness. Even communion with angels could not have satisfied his desire for sympathy and companionship. There was none of the same nature to love and to be loved. God Himself gave Adam a companion. He provided "an help meet for him"—a helper corresponding to him—one who was fitted to be his companion, and who could be one with him in love and sympathy.[5]

It was God's intention that the marital relationship should be one that totally fulfill man and woman needs. Therefore, in order to experience satisfaction in a relationship, specifically marriage relationship, couples have need of friendship, trust and love. These assist in building positive relationship and thereby give a sense of being satisfied. What do we mean by friendship, trust and love in the context of a relationship?

According to Harris, V. William , Skogrand, Linda and Hatch, Daniel

> Trust has been recognized as a foundational component of satisfying, long-term marriage relationships (quoting Hirsch, 2003; Markman, Stanley, & Blumberg, 2001).[6]

> And those components of trusting relationships include individual and couple perceptions of dependability, availability, responsiveness, an ability to negotiate conflict, and a positive sense of the future of the relationship with the absence of infidelity.[7]

---

5 *Letters to Young Lovers. 1983; 2002 (10–11). Pacific Press Publishing Association.*
6 *Harris, V. William , Skogrand, Linda and Hatch, Daniel(2008) 'Role of Friendship, Trust, and Love in Strong Latino Marriages', Marriage & Family Review, 44: 4, 455 — 488*
7 *Ibid.*

In addition to these two foundational components of friendship and trust, it is a vital component of loving and feeling loved in strong and stable marriages. Although sometimes difficult to define, love can be conceptualized as emotion, behavior, and commitment. Love experienced as emotion is often the result of love evidenced through behaviour, such as validation and kind acts, as well as commitment through dedication to the ongoing nature of the relationship. Each is central to stable, strong, and happy marriages.[8]

In conclusion, Harris quotes Wallerstein (1996), as asserting that

Marital happiness can be achieved through finding a perceived balance between individual and couple needs, wishes, and expectations. Specific individual and couple needs, wishes, and expectations that influence happy and stable marriages tend to vary across gender, racial=ethnic, cultural, and socioeconomic lines. Therefore the perceived needs, wishes, and expectations associated with the achievement of friendship, trust, and love in marriage may mean qualitatively different things to different people across cultures. Reciprocally, the achievement of friendship, trust, and love in marriage may influence how needs, wishes, and expectations are both expressed and fulfilled cross-culturally.

According to the Apostle Paul, love champions all things and therefore love is the fulfilling of the law as well as being the greatest of all things (hope, faith and love). Love surfaces in every situation and determines the level of trust and to what extent friendship will be allowed to advance along the pathway of marital love. Therefore it is acceptable to conclude with Paul, that love is the main components of a satisfied relationship.

Love – the main components of Satisfied Relationships

Love, non agape, is defined as

A caring commitment, in which affection and delight are shown to others, which is grounded in the nature of God himself. In his words and actions, and supremely in the death of Jesus Christ on the cross, God demonstrates the nature of love and defines the direction in which human love in all its forms should develop.[9]

---

8 *Ibid.*

9 *Manser, M. H. (1999). Zondervan Dictionary of Bible Themes. The Accessible and Comprehensive*

Human love is ennobled by being patterned on God's love for his people. It is also safeguarded by God's commands. The love between husband and wife, conjugal love, is commanded Col 3:18-19 See also Ge 2:24; Dt 24:5; Pr 5:18-20; Ecc 9:9; Eph 5:22,28,33; 1Pe 3:7. It is patterned on God's love for his people Isa 54:5; Eph 5:25-27 See also Isa 62:5; Jer 3:14; Eze 16:8; Hos 2:19; 2Co 11:2; Rev 19:7

A husband is responsible for the quality and quantity of love in his own home, so if love is lacking, he is responsible. There must be no self-seeking on the husband's part, for the purest love is as described in 1 Corinthians 13:4–8a. If husbands exercised these graces, marriages would be stronger and sweeter.

Therefore 'husbands, love your wives and do not be bitter towards them' (v. 19; cf. Eph. 5:25–29). It is the husband's duty to love his wife and put her interests first. This type of love is more than natural affection and just seeing her as 'a sister in the Lord'. Paul tells husbands that:

Many women pine for words of love and kindness and the common attentions and courtesies due them from their husbands who have selected them as their life companions.[10] It is these little attentions and courtesies which make up the sum of life's happiness. A husband is to love only his wife. There must be no other woman or person substituted in her place. She alone is to be his bride and his lover. No other person is to take her place, not even:

HIS OWN FATHER OR MOTHER, because the Scriptures say he is to 'leave his father and mother and be joined to his wife' (Gen. 2:24). The Hebrew word from which 'joined' comes means 'to glue'! In-laws and money are the two most common sources of trouble in marriages.

HIS CHILDREN, as the man's wife must have first place in his heart (Eph. 5:25).

When a marriage is in trouble couples often stay together for the children's sake—good! But far better is that relationship between husband and wife which is always loving, caring, loyal and fresh.

Tool for Topical Studies. Grand Rapids, MI: Zondervan Publishing House.
10 *In Heavenly Places; Heavenly Places. 1967; 2002 (206). Review and Herald Publishing Association.*

When a marriage is shaky, more time and love must be expended by husband and wife on each other.

HIS BEST FRIEND, as this will damage his marriage. Young men are especially prone to this mistake. A man's wife must be his best friend, and vice versa. Husbands must not neglect their wives to spend time with their mates. I am not, of course, saying that married men cannot have friends or meet up with them ('A man who has friends must himself be friendly', Prov. 18:24). But it is best practice to do things together as a couple.

ANOTHER WOMAN, as this will destroy the marriage. This principle of husbands loving only their wives is especially true when it comes to other women. Adultery is forbidden by the Scriptures, but marriage love is praised (Heb. 13:4) and must be practiced (1 Cor. 13). Platonic relationships must be carefully controlled and they are best avoided, especially in the workplace. A man who looks at another woman with covetous eyes has already committed adultery with her in his heart (Matt. 5:28). Husbands and wives are to be lovers in an exclusive and faithful, monogamous relationship all the days of their life. Wives are given to be loved, protected and cared for. God made one man and one woman and he gave them to each other: 'He who finds a wife finds a good thing, and obtains favour from the Lord' (Prov. 18:22).

How to Keep Love and Marital Satisfaction Alive

Giving thanks always for all things unto God and the Father in the name of our Lord Jesus Christ; submitting yourselves one to another in the fear of God. Eph. 5:20, 21.

In every relationship, love may at times come under stress and strain as couples interact with society and attempt to live up to their responsibilities. However, it is necessary that both men and women continue to cultivate respect, regards, attention, and kind words of appreciation, courtesies, which will keep love alive, and which they felt were necessary in gaining the companions of their choice.

Ellen White believed

> If the husband and wife would only continue to cultivate the attentions, which nourish love, they would be happy in each other's society and would have a sanctifying influence upon their families. They would have in themselves a little world of happiness and would not desire to go outside this world for new attractions and new objects of love.[11]

In addition,

> If the hearts were kept tender in our families, if there were a noble, generous deference to each other's tastes and opinions, if the wife were seeking opportunities to express her love by actions in her courtesies to her husband, and the husband manifesting the same consideration and kindly regard for the wife, the children would partake of the same spirit. The influence would pervade the household, and what a tide of misery would be saved in families! Men would not go from home to find happiness; and women would not pine for love, and lose courage and self-respect, and become lifelong invalids. Only one life lease is granted us, and with care, painstaking, and self-control it can be made endurable, pleasant, and even happy.[12]

Further, White conclude by saying "every couple that unites their life interest should seek to make the life of each as happy as possible. That which we prize we seek to preserve and make more valuable, if we can."

On the other hand, the character and behaviour of a woman or wife can and does make a tremendous difference to the man's feeling of love and thereby being happy. "The influence of the wife over the husband is powerful for either good or evil. Many a man can date his success or failure in life from his marriage day."

---

11 *White, E. G. (1979; 2002). This Day With God (334–335). Review and Herald Publishing Association.*

12 *Manuscript Releases, Volume 10 [Nos. 771-850, 1980-1981]. 1993; 2002 (71). Ellen G. White Estate.*

This is because

> In the companionship of a true, unselfish woman, the man or husband finds peace and happiness, forgetting the cares of the world. But if the one whom he has chosen to stand by his side is self-centered, caring for no one or nothing but herself, requiring his time and attention to be constantly devoted to her, and yet ignorant of her own duties as a wife, and incapable of appreciating his efforts and sympathizing with them, the happiness of the home will be blighted. The wife will be miserable herself, and however well the husband may be qualified to be priest of the household, however energetic and unselfish, she too often lays the foundation for his ruin.[13]

Concluding, she said

> In the marriage contract men and women have made a trade, an investment for life, and they should do their utmost to control their words of impatience and fretfulness, even more carefully than they did before their marriage, for now their destinies are united for life as husband and wife, and each is valued in exact proportion to the amount of painstaking and effort put forth to retain and keep fresh the love so eagerly sought for and prized before marriage.[14]

True love is a plant that needs culture. Let the woman who desires a peaceful, happy union, who would escape future misery and sorrow, inquire before she yields her affections, has my lover a mother? What is the stamp of her character? Does he recognize his obligations to her? Is he mindful of her wishes and happiness? If he does not respect and honour his mother, will he manifest respect and love, kindness and attention, toward his wife? When the novelty of marriage is over, will he love me still? Will he be patient with my mistakes, or will he be critical, overbearing, and dictatorial? True affection will overlook many mistakes; love will not discern them.

Therefore, husbands and young men love your wife/your young lady as Christ love the church and gave Himself a ransom for her. Husbands should be willing to make the necessary sacrifice, even laying down his life, for his wife. And, in a developing (dating/courting) relationship, every women should ascertain whether the man she is dating will be willing to make whatever sacrifice in order to care and

13 *Manuscript Releases, Volume 10 [Nos. 771-850, 1980-1981]. 1993; 2002 (71). Ellen G. White Estate.*
14 *Ibid.*

keep her. Any man not willing to make a sacrifice should be shown the door. At the same time, a man need to ascertain whether his lady will be willing to you make the final decision, even if may lead to disaster. Any woman, who is not willing for her man to have the last say, should be seriously considered whether she is ready for a serious step towards the marital altar. Here, I am not suggestion domination, but rather consultation. Consultation ought to be followed by the man (head of the house and home) making the final decision.

My Personal Notes

11

ELLEN WHITE ON RELATIONSHIP

God's Original Design. God celebrated the first marriage. Thus the institution has for its originator the Creator of the universe. "Marriage is honourable"; it was one of the first gifts of God to man, and it is one of the two institutions that, after the fall, Adam brought with him beyond the gates of Paradise. When the divine principles are recognized and obeyed in this relation, marriage is a blessing; it guards the purity and happiness of the race, it provides for man's social needs, it elevates the physical, the intellectual, and the moral nature.--PP 46. {TSB 13.1}

Approved by God Today. There is in itself no sin in eating and drinking, or in marrying and giving in marriage. It was lawful to marry in the time of Noah, and it is lawful to marry now, if that which is lawful is properly treated, and not carried to sinful excess.--RH Sept. 25, 1888. In regard to marriage, I would say, Read the Word of God. Even in this time, the last days of this world's history, marriages take place among Seventh-day Adventists. . . . {TSB 14.1}

We have, as a people, never forbidden marriage, except in cases where there were obvious reasons that marriage would be misery to both parties. And even then, we have only advised and counseled.--Letter 60, 1900. {TSB 14.2}

A Preparation for Heaven.

Let them remember that the home on earth is to be a symbol of and a preparation for the home in heaven.--MH 363. {TSB 14.3}. God wants the home to be the happiest place on earth, the very symbol of the home in heaven. Bearing the marriage responsibilities in the home, linking their interests with Jesus Christ, leaning upon His arm and His assurance, husband and wife may share a happiness in this union that angels of God commend.--AH 102. {TSB 14.4} A Lifelong Union. Marriage, a union for life, is a symbol of the union between Christ and His church.--7T 46. {TSB 14.5}

In the youthful mind marriage is clothed with romance, and it is difficult to divest it of this feature, with which imagination covers it, and to impress the mind with a sense of the weighty responsibilities involved in the marriage vow. This vow links the destinies of the two individuals with bonds which naught but the hand of death should sever. {TSB 14.6}

Every marriage engagement should be carefully considered, for marriage is a step taken for life. Both the man and the woman should carefully consider whether they can cleave to each other through the vicissitudes of life as long as they both shall live.--AH 340.

From an Elevated Standpoint. Those professing to be Christians should not enter the marriage relation until the matter has been carefully and prayerfully considered from an elevated standpoint, to see if God can be glorified by the union. Then they should duly consider the result of every privilege of the marriage relation, and sanctified principle should be the basis of every action.--RH Sept. 19, 1899. {TSB 15.1}

Examine carefully to see if your married life would be happy or inharmonious and wretched. Let the questions be raised, Will this union help me heavenward? Will it increase my love for God? And will it enlarge my sphere of usefulness in this life? If these reflections present no drawback, then in the fear of God move forward.--FE 104, 105. {TSB 15.2}

All in the Name of the Lord Jesus.

One about to marry a wife should stop to consider candidly why he takes this step. Is his wife to be his helper, his companion, his equal, or will he pursue toward her such a course that she cannot have an eye single to the glory of God? Will he venture to give loose rein to his passions and see how much care and taxation he can subject his wife to without extinguishing life, or will he study the meaning of the words, "Whatsoever ye do, in word or deed, do all in the name of the Lord Jesus"?--Ms 152, 1899. {TSB 15.3}

The Necessity of Careful Preparation.

Before assuming the responsibilities involved in marriage, young men and young women should have such an experience in practical life as will prepare them for its duties and its burdens. Early marriages are not to be encouraged. A relation so important as marriage and so far-reaching in its results should not be entered upon hastily, without sufficient preparation, and before the mental and physical powers are well developed.--MH 358.

God forbids marriage between believers and unbelievers.

With Believers Only. The wife of Lot was a selfish, irreligious woman, and her influence was exerted to separate her husband from Abraham. But for her, Lot would not have remained in Sodom, deprived of the counsel of the wise, God-fearing patriarch. The influence of his wife and the associations of that wicked city would have led him to apostatize from God had it not been for the faithful instruction he had early received from Abraham. The marriage of Lot and his choice of Sodom for a home were the first links in a chain of events fraught with evil to the world for many generations. {TSB 17.1}

No one who fears God can without danger connect himself with one who fears Him not. "Can two walk together, except they be agreed?" (Amos 3:3). The happiness and prosperity of the marriage relation depend upon the unity of the parties; but between the believer and the unbeliever there is a radical difference of tastes, inclinations, and purposes. They are serving two masters, between whom there can be no concord. However pure and correct one's principles may be, the influence of an unbelieving companion will have a tendency to lead away from God. . . . The marriage of Christians with the ungodly is forbidden in the Bible. The Lord's direction is, "Be ye not unequally yoked together with unbelievers." 2 Corinthians 6:14, 17, 18.--PP 174, 175.

Let not unholy bonds be formed between the children of God and the friends of the world. Let there not be marriages made between believers and unbelievers. Let the people of God take their stand firmly for truth and righteousness.-- RH July 31, 1894.

Great care should be taken by Christian youth in the formation of friendships and in the choice of companions. Take heed, lest what you now think to be pure gold turns out to be base metal. Worldly associations tend to place obstructions in the way of your service to God, and unhappy unions, either business or matrimonial, with those who can never elevate or ennoble, ruin many souls. Never should God's people venture upon forbidden ground. God forbids marriage between believers and unbelievers. But too often the unconverted heart follows its own desires, and marriages unsanctioned by God are formed. Because of this, many men and women are without hope and without God in the world. Their noble aspirations are dead; by a chain of circumstances they are held in Satan's net.--RH Feb. 1, 1906.

God's Claims First. Though the companion of your choice were in all other respects worthy (which he is not), yet he has not accepted the truth for this time; he is an unbeliever, and you are forbidden of heaven to unite yourself with him. You cannot, without peril to your soul, disregard this divine injunction. . . . To connect with an unbeliever is to place yourself on Satan's ground. You grieve the Spirit of God and forfeit His protection. Can you afford to have such terrible odds against you in fighting the battle for everlasting life? **You may say:** "But I have given my promise, and shall I now retract it?" I answer: If you have made a promise contrary to the Scriptures, by all means retract it without delay, and in humility before God repent of the infatuation that led you to make so rash a pledge.

The Lord has in His Word plainly instructed His people not to unite themselves with those who have not His love and fear before them. Such companions will seldom be satisfied with the love and respect which are justly theirs. They will constantly seek to gain from the God-fearing wife or husband some favour which shall involve a disregard of the divine requirements. To a godly man, and to the church with which he is connected, a worldly wife or a worldly friend is as a spy in the camp, who will watch every opportunity to betray the servant of Christ, and expose him to the enemy's attacks. Satan is constantly seeking to strengthen his power over the people of God by inducing them to enter into alliance with the hosts of darkness.--ST Oct. 6, 1881. {TSB 19.1}

1. Cautions and Counsels

Importance of Family Backgrounds. Let time teach you discretion, and what the genuine claims of love are, before it is allowed to step one inch further. Ruin, fearful ruin, is before you in this life and the next, if you pursue the course you have been following. Look to the family history. Two families are to be brought into close and sacred connection. Perfection in all these relations is not, of course, to be expected, but you would make a most cruel move to marry a girl whose ancestry and relatives would degrade and mortify you, or tempt you to slight and ignore them.

Counsel From Parents and Close Friends. It is safe to make haste slowly in these matters. Give yourself sufficient time for observation on every point, and then do not trust to your own judgment, but let the mother who loves you, and your father, and confidential friends, make critical observation of the one you feel inclined to favor. Trust not to your own judgment, and marry no one whom you feel will not be an honour to your father and mother, [but] one who has intelligence and moral worth. The girl who gives over her affections to a man, and invites his attention by her advances, hanging around where she will be noticed of him unless he shall appear rude, is not the girl you want to associate with. Her conversation is cheap and frequently without depth.

No Marriage Preferable to a Mismatch. Nellie A will not be as much prepared by cultivated manners and useful knowledge to marry at twenty-five as some girls would be at eighteen. But men generally of your age have a very limited knowledge of character, and no just idea of how foolish a man can make himself by fancying a young girl who is not fit for him in any sense. It will be far better not to marry at all than to be unfortunately married, but seek counsel of God in all these things. Be so calm, so submissive to the will of God, that you will not be in a fever of excitement and unqualified for His service by your attachments.--Letter 59, 1880.

Faithfulness in the Parental Home. It is by faithfulness to duty in the parental home that the young are to prepare themselves for homes of their own. Let them here practice self-denial and manifest kindness, courtesy, and Christian sympathy. Thus love will be kept warm in the heart, and he who goes out from such a household to stand at the head of a family of his own will know how to promote the happiness of her whom he has chosen as a companion for life. Marriage, instead of being the end of love, will be only its beginning.--PP 176.

2. Individuality

Individuality of the Wife. A woman that will submit to be ever dictated to in the smallest matters of domestic life, who will yield up her identity, will never be of much use or blessing in the world, and will not answer the purpose of God in her existence. She is a mere machine to be guided by another's will and another's mind. God has given each one, men and women, an identity, an individuality, that they must act in the fear of God for themselves.--Letter 25, 1885.

Separate Identity of Husband and Wife. I was shown that although a couple were married, gave themselves to each other by a most solemn vow in the sight of heaven and holy angels, and the two were one, yet each had a separate identity which the marriage covenant could not destroy. Although bound to one another, yet each has an influence to exert in the world, and they should not be so selfishly engrossed with each other as to shut themselves away from society and bury their usefulness and influence.--Letter 9, 1864.

A Passive Wife. Let the wife decide that it is the husband's prerogative to have full control of her body, and to mould her mind to suit his in every respect, to run in the same channel as his own, and she yields her individuality; her identity is lost, merged in that of her husband. She is a mere machine for his will to move and control, a creature of his pleasure. He thinks for her, decides for her, and acts for her. She dishonours God in occupying this passive position. She has a responsibility before God, which it is her duty to preserve.

When the wife yields her body and mind to the control of her husband, being passive to his will in all things, sacrificing her conscience, her dignity, and even her identity, she loses the opportunity of exerting that mighty influence for good which she should possess, to elevate her husband.--RH Sept. 26, 1899.

Love for Christ, Love for Each Other. Neither the husband nor the wife should merge his or her individuality in that of the other. Each has a personal relation to God. Of Him each is to ask, "What is right?" "What is wrong?" "How may I best fulfil life's purpose?" Let the wealth of your affection flow forth to Him who gave His life for you. Make Christ first and last and best in everything. As your love for Him becomes deeper and stronger, your love for each other will be purified and strengthened.

The spirit that Christ manifests toward us is the spirit that husband and wife are to manifest toward each other. "As Christ also hath loved us," "walk in love." "As the church is subject unto Christ, so let the wives be to their own husbands in everything. Husbands, love your wives, even as Christ also loved the church, and gave Himself for it."

No Arbitrary Control. Neither the husband nor the wife should attempt to exercise over the other an arbitrary control. Do not try to compel each other to yield to your wishes. You cannot do this and retain each other's love. Be kind, patient and forbearing, considerate and courteous. By the grace of God you can succeed in making each other happy, as in your marriage vow you promised to do.--RH Dec. 10, 1908.

Importance of Love and Tenderness. You have no right to dictate to your wife as you would a child. You have not earned a valuable reputation of goodness that would require reverence. You need, considering your failures in the past, to take a humble position and divest yourself of a dignity you have not earned. You are too weak a man to require submission to your will without an appeal. You have a work to do to govern yourself.

You should never set yourself above your wife. She needs kindness and love, which will be reflected back to you again. If you expect her to love you, you must earn this love by manifesting love and tenderness in your words and actions for her. You have in your keeping the happiness of your wife. Your course says to her, In order for you to be happy, you must yield your will up fully to mine; you must submit to do my pleasure. You have taken special delight in exercising your authority because you thought you could do so. But time will show that if you pursue the course your own temperament would lead you to do, you will not inspire in the heart of your wife love, but will wean her affections from you, and she will in the end despise that authority, the power of which she has never felt before in her married life. You are certainly making hard and bitter work for yourself, and you will reap what you are sowing.

When Ages Widely Differ

Another cause of the deficiency of the present generation in physical strength and moral worth, is, men and women uniting in marriage whose ages widely differ. It is frequently the case that old men choose to marry young wives. By thus doing, the life of the husband has often been prolonged, while the wife has had to feel the want of that vitality which she has imparted to her aged husband. It has not been the duty of any woman to sacrifice life and health, even if she did love one so much older than herself, and felt willing on her part to make such a sacrifice. She should have restrained her affections. She had considerations higher than her own interest to consult. She should consider, if children be born to them, what would be their condition? It is still worse for young men to marry women considerably older than themselves. The offspring of such unions in many cases, where ages widely differ, have not well-balanced minds. They have been deficient also in physical strength. In such families have frequently been manifested varied, peculiar, and often painful, traits of character. They often die prematurely, and those who reach maturity, in many cases, are deficient in physical and mental strength, and moral worth.

3. Family

Importance of the Home Atmosphere.--The atmosphere surrounding the souls of fathers and mothers fills the whole house, and is felt in every department of the home. {AH 16.1} To a large extent parents create the atmosphere of the home circle, and when there is disagreement between father and mother, the children partake of the same spirit.

Make your home atmosphere fragrant with tender thoughtfulness. If you have become estranged and have failed to be Bible Christians, be converted; for the character you bear in probationary time will be the character you will have at the coming of Christ. If you would be a saint in heaven, you must first be a saint on earth. The traits of character you cherish in life will not be changed by death or by the resurrection. You will come up from the grave with the same disposition you manifested in your home and in society. Jesus does not change the character at His coming. The work of transformation must be done now. Our daily lives are determining our destiny. {AH 16.2}

Creating a Pure Atmosphere.

Every Christian home should have rules; and parents should, in their words and deportment toward each other, give to the children a precious, living example of what they desire them to be. Purity in speech and true Christian courtesy should be constantly practiced. Teach the children and youth to respect themselves, to be true to God, true to principle; teach them to respect and obey the law of God. These principles will control their lives and will be carried out in their associations with others. They will create a pure atmosphere--one that will have an influence that will encourage weak souls in the upward path that leads to holiness and heaven. Let every lesson be of an elevating and ennobling character, and the records made in the books of heaven will be such as you will not be ashamed to meet in the judgment. {AH 16.3}

Children who receive this kind of instruction will . . . be prepared to fill places of responsibility and, by precept and example, will be constantly aiding others to do right. Those whose moral sensibilities have not been blunted will appreciate right principles; they will put a just estimate upon their natural endowments and will make the best use of their physical, mental, and moral powers. Such souls are strongly fortified against temptation; a wall not easily broken down surrounds them. {AH 17.1}.

God would have our families' symbols of the family in heaven. Let parents and children bear this in mind every day, relating themselves to one another as members of the family of God. Then their lives will be of such a character as to give to the world an object lesson of what families who love God and keep His commandments may be. Christ will be glorified; His peace and grace and love will pervade the family circle like a precious perfume. {AH 17.2}

Much depends on the father and mother. They are to be firm and kind in their discipline, and they are to work most earnestly to have an orderly, correct household, that the heavenly angels may be attracted to it to impart peace and a fragrant influence. {AH 17.3}

Make Home Bright and Happy.--Never forget that you are to make the home bright and happy for yourselves and your children by cherishing the Saviour's attributes. If you bring Christ into the home, you will know good from evil. You will be able to help your children to be trees of righteousness, bearing the fruit of the Spirit. Troubles may invade, but these are the lot of humanity. Let patience, gratitude, and love keep sunshine in the heart though the day may be ever so cloudy. {AH 18.1} The home may be plain, but it can always be a place where cheerful words are spoken and kindly deeds are done, where courtesy and love are abiding guests. {AH 18.2}

Administer the rules of the home in wisdom and love, not with a rod of iron. Children will respond with willing obedience to the rule of love. Commend your children whenever you can. Make their lives as happy as possible. . . . Keep the soil of the heart mellow by the manifestation of love and affection, thus preparing it for the seed of truth. Remember that the Lord gives the earth not only clouds and rain, but the beautiful, smiling sunshine, causing the seed to germinate and the blossom to appear. Remember that children need not only reproof and correction, but encouragement and commendation, the pleasant sunshine of kind words. {AH 18.3}

You must not have strife in your household. "But the wisdom that is from above is first pure, then peaceable, gentle, and easy to be intreated, full of mercy and good fruits, without partiality, and without hypocrisy. And the fruit of righteousness is sown in peace of them that make peace." It is gentleness and peace that we want in our homes. {AH 18.4}

Tender Ties That Bind.--The family tie is the closest, the most tender and sacred, of any on earth. It was designed to be a blessing to mankind. And it is a blessing wherever the marriage covenant is entered into intelligently, in the fear of God, and with due consideration for its responsibilities. {AH 18.5}

Every home should be a place of love, a place where the angels of God abide, working with softening, subduing influence upon the hearts of parents and children. {AH 18.6} Our homes must be made a Bethel, our hearts a shrine. Wherever the love of God is cherished in the soul, there will be peace, there will be light and joy. Spread out the word of God before your families in love, and ask, "What hath God spoken?" {AH 19.1}

Christ's Presence Makes a Home Christian.--The home that is beautified by love, sympathy, and tenderness is a place that angels love to visit, and where God is glorified. The influence of a carefully guarded Christian home in the years of childhood and youth is the surest safeguard against the corruptions of the world. In the atmosphere of such a home the children will learn to love both their earthly parents and their heavenly Father. {AH 19.2}nFrom their infancy the youth need to have a firm barrier built up between them and the world, that its corrupting influence may not affect them. {AH 19.3}

Every Christian family should illustrate to the world the power and excellence of Christian influence. . . . Parents should realize their accountability to keep their homes free from every taint of moral evil. {AH 19.4} Holiness to God is to pervade the home. . . . Parents and children are to educate themselves to co-operate with God. They are to bring their habits and practices into harmony with God's plans. {AH 19.5}

The family relationship should be sanctifying in its influence. Christian homes, established and conducted in accordance with God's plan, are a wonderful help in forming Christian character. . . . Parents and children should unite in offering loving service to Him who alone can keep human love pure and noble. {AH 19.6}

The first work to be done in a Christian home is to see that the Spirit of Christ abides there, that every member of the household may be able to take his cross and follow where Jesus leads the way.

Common Courtship Practices

Wrong Ideas of Courtship and Marriage.--The ideas of courtship have their foundation in erroneous ideas concerning marriage. They follow impulse and blind passion. The courtship is carried on in a spirit of flirtation. The parties frequently violate the rules of modesty and reserve and are guilty of indiscretion, if they do not break the law of God. The high, noble, lofty design of God in the institution of marriage is not discerned; therefore the purest affections of the heart, the noblest traits of character are not developed. {AH 55.1} Not one word should be spoken, not one action performed, that you would not be willing the holy angels should look upon and register in the books above. You should have an eye single to the glory of God. The heart should have only pure, sanctified affection, worthy of the followers of Jesus Christ, exalted in its nature, and more heavenly than earthly. Anything different from this is debasing, degrading in courtship; and marriage cannot be holy and honourable in the sight of a pure and holy God, unless it is after the exalted Scriptural principle. {AH 55.2}

The youth trust altogether too much to impulse. They should not give themselves away too easily, nor be captivated too readily by the winning exterior of the lover. Courtship as carried on in this age is a scheme of deception and hypocrisy, with which the enemy of souls has far more to do than the Lord. Good common sense is needed here if anywhere; but the fact is, it has little to do in the matter. {AH 55.3} honoured and recompensed of God. {AH 59.2}

The Great Decision

A Happy or Unhappy Marriage?--If those who are contemplating marriage would not have miserable, unhappy reflections after marriage, they must make it a subject of serious, earnest reflection now. This step taken unwisely is one of the most effective means of ruining the usefulness of young men and women. Life becomes a burden, a curse. No one can so effectually ruin a woman's happiness and usefulness, and make life a heartsickening burden, as her own husband; and no one can do one hundredth part as much to chill the hopes and aspirations of a man, to paralyze his energies and ruin his influence and prospects, as his own wife. It is from the marriage hour that many men and women date their success or failure in this life, and their hopes of the future life. {AH 43.1} I wish I could make the youth see and feel their danger, especially the danger of making unhappy marriages. {AH 43.2}

Marriage is something that will influence and affect your life both in this world and in the world to come. A sincere Christian will not advance his plans in this direction without the knowledge that God approves his course. He will not want to choose for himself, but will feel that God must choose for him. We are not to please ourselves, for Christ pleased not Himself. I would not be understood to mean that anyone is to marry one whom he does not love. This would be sin. But fancy and the emotional nature must not be allowed to lead on to ruin. God requires the whole heart, the supreme affections. {AH 43.3}

Make Haste Slowly

Few have correct views of the marriage relation. Many seem to think that it is the attainment of perfect bliss; but if they could know one quarter of the heartaches of men and women that are bound by the marriage vow in chains that they cannot and dare not break, they would not be surprised that I trace these lines. Marriage, in a majority of cases, is a most galling yoke. There are thousands that are mated but not matched. The books of heaven are burdened with the woes, the wickedness, and the abuse that lie hidden under the marriage mantle. This is why I would warn the young who are of a marriageable age to make haste slowly in the choice of a companion. The path of married life may appear beautiful and full of happiness; but why may not you be disappointed as thousands of others have been? {AH 44.1}

Those who are contemplating marriage should consider what will be the character and influence of the home they are founding. As they become parents, a sacred trust is committed to them. Upon them depends in a great measure the well-being of their children in this world, and their happiness in the world to come.

To a great extent they determine both the physical and the moral stamp that the little ones receive. And upon the character of the home depends the condition of society; the weight of each family's influence will tell in the upward or the downward scale. {AH 44.2}

Vital Factors in the Choice.--Great care should be taken by Christian youth in the formation of friendships and in the choice of companions. Take heed, lest what you now think to be pure gold turns out to be base metal. Worldly associations tend to place obstructions in the way of your service to God, and many souls are ruined by unhappy unions, either business or matrimonial, with those who can never elevate of ennoble. {AH 44.3} Weigh every sentiment, and watch every development of character in the one with whom you think to link your life destiny. The step you are about to take is one of the most important in your life, and should not be taken hastily. While you may love, do not love blindly. {AH 45.1}

Examine carefully to see if your married life would be happy or inharmonious and wretched. Let the questions be raised, Will this union help me heavenward? Will it increase my love for God? And will it enlarge my sphere of usefulness in this life? If these reflections present no drawback, then in the fear of God move forward. {AH 45.2}

Most men and women have acted in entering the marriage relation as though the only question for them to settle was whether they loved each other. But they should realize that a responsibility rests upon them in the marriage relation farther than this. They should consider whether their offspring will possess physical health and mental and moral strength. But few have moved with high motives and with elevated considerations which they could not lightly throw off--that society had claims upon them, that the weight of their family's influence would tell in the upward or downward scale. {AH 45.3}

The choice of a life companion should be such as best to secure physical, mental, and spiritual well-being for parents and for their children--such as will enable both parents and children to bless their fellow men and to honour their Creator. {AH 45.4}

Qualities to Be Sought in a Prospective Wife

Let a young man seek one to stand by his side who is fitted to bear her share of life's burdens, one whose influence will ennoble and refine him, and who will make him happy in her love. "A prudent wife is from the Lord." "The heart of her husband doth safely trust in her. . . . She will do him good and not evil all the days of her life." "She openeth her mouth with wisdom; and in her tongue is the law of kindness. She looketh well to the ways of her household, and eateth not the bread of idleness. Her children arise up, and call her blessed; her husband also, and he praiseth her," saying, "Many daughters have done virtuously, but thou excellest them all." He who gains such a wife "findeth a good thing, and obtaineth favor of the Lord."

Here are things which should be considered:

1. Will the one you marry bring happiness to your home?
2. Is [she] an economist, or will she, if married, not only use all her own earnings, but all of yours to gratify a vanity, a love of appearance?
3. Are her principles correct in this direction?
4. Has she anything now to depend upon?

I know that to the mind of a man infatuated with love and thoughts of marriage these questions will be brushed away as though they were of no consequence. But these things should be duly considered, for they have a bearing upon your future life.

5. In your choice of a wife study her character.
6. Will she be one who will be patient and painstaking? Or will she cease to care for your mother and father at the very time when they need a strong son to lean upon? And
7. Will she withdraw him from their society to carry out her plans and to suit her own pleasure, and leave the father and mother who, instead of gaining an affectionate daughter, will have lost a son? {AH 46.3}

Qualities to Be Sought in a Prospective Husband

Before giving her hand in marriage, every woman should inquire whether he with whom she is about to unite her destiny is worthy.

1. What has been his past record?
2. Is his life pure?
3. Is the love which he expresses of a noble, elevated character, or is it a mere emotional fondness?

4. Has he the traits of character that will make her happy?

5. Can you find true peace and joy in his affection?

6. Will you be allowed to preserve your individuality, or must your judgment and conscience be surrendered to the control of him?

7. Can continue to honour the Saviour's claims as supreme?

8. Will body and soul, thoughts and purposes, be preserved pure and holy?

These questions have a vital bearing upon the well-being of every woman who enters the marriage relation. Let the woman who desires a peaceful, happy union, who would escape future misery and sorrow, inquire before she yields her affections,

9. Has my lover a mother?

10. What is the stamp of her character?

11. Does he recognize his obligations to her?

12. Is he mindful of her wishes and happiness? If he does not respect the honour his mother, will he manifest respect and love, kindness and attention, toward his wife?

13. When the novelty of marriage is over, will he love me still?

14. Will he be patient with my mistakes, or will he be critical, overbearing, and dictatorial?

True affection will overlook many mistakes; love will not discern them. {AH 47.2}

Accept Only Pure, Manly Traits.--Let a young woman accept as a life companion only one who possesses pure, manly traits of character, one who is diligent, aspiring, and honest, one who loves and fears God. {AH 47.3}

Shun those who are irreverent. Shun one who is a lover of idleness; shun the one who is a scoffer of hallowed things. Avoid the society of one who uses profane language, or is addicted to the use of even one glass of liquor. Listen not to the proposals of a man who has no realization of his responsibility to God. The pure truth which sanctifies the soul will give you courage to cut yourself loose from the most pleasing acquaintance whom you know does not love and fear God, and knows nothing of the principles of true righteousness. We may always bear with a friend's infirmities and with his ignorance, but never with his vices. {AH 47.4}

Easier to Make a Mistake Than to Correct It.--Marriages that are impulsive and selfishly planned generally do not result well, but often turn out miserable failures. Both parties find themselves deceived, and gladly would they undo that which they did under an infatuation. It is easier, far easier, to make a mistake in this matter than to correct the error after it is made. {AH 48.1}

Better to Break Unwise Engagement

Even if an engagement has been entered into without a full understanding of the character of the one with whom you intend to unite, do not think that the engagement makes it a positive necessity for you to take upon yourself the marriage vow and link yourself for life to one whom you cannot love and respect. Be very careful how you enter into conditional engagements; but better, far better, break the engagement before marriage than separate afterward, as many do. {AH 48.2}

You may say, "But I have given my promise, and shall I now retract it?" I answer, If you have made a promise contrary to the Scriptures, by all means retract it without delay, and in humility before God repent of the infatuation that led you to make so rash a pledge. Far better take back such a promise, in the fear of God, than keep it, and thereby dishonour your Maker. {AH 48.3}

Let every step toward a marriage alliance be characterized by modesty, simplicity, sincerity, and an earnest purpose to please and honour God. Marriage affects the afterlife both in this world and in the world to come. A sincere Christian will make no plans that God cannot approve. {AH 49.1}

True Love Versus Passion.--Love . . . is not unreasonable; it is not blind. It is pure and holy. But the passion of the natural heart is another thing altogether. While pure love will take God into all its plans, and will be in perfect harmony with the Spirit of God, passion will be headstrong, rash, unreasonable, defiant of all restraint, and will make the object of its choice an idol. In all the deportment of one who possesses true love, the grace of God will be shown. Modesty, simplicity, sincerity, morality, and religion will characterize every step toward an alliance in marriage.

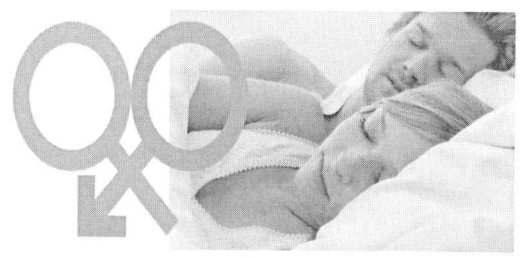

12

SEX

BIBLICAL TEACHINGS AND ITS' SACREDNESS

Biblical Teachings

The Bible addresses human sexuality from a holistic perspective of God's intention and design. In contrast to both pagan sex rituals and modern obsession with sex, the Bible places sex within the total context of human nature, happiness, and holiness.[1]

Gender and Relation God created human beings as male and female, both in His own image (Gen. 1:27). Thus, gender is not a mere biological accident or social construction. The contrast and complementarity between the man and the woman reveal that gender is part of the goodness of God's creation. Modern efforts to redefine or redesign gender are directly contrary to the Bible's affirmation of maleness and femaleness as proper distinctions. This pattern of distinction is affirmed and enforced by liturgical orders and restrictions on dress, hair length, etc. Any effort to confuse or deny gender differences is expressly forbidden and opposed by Scripture, especially as seen in OT legal codes.

Throughout the Bible a complementary pattern of relation between man and woman, particularly within the institution of marriage, is presented as the divine intention. Both are equal in dignity and status, but a pattern of male leadership in the home and in the church is enforced by both descriptive and prescriptive passages (1 Tim. 2:8–3:7; 1 Cor. 11:2–16; 14:34–38).

---

1 Brand, C., Draper, C., England, A., Bond, S., Clendenen, E. R., Butler, T. C., & Latta, B. (2003). *Holman Illustrated Bible Dictionary* (1469–1471). Nashville, TN: Holman Bible Publishers.

Sex as Gift and Responsibility

The Bible places sex and sexual activity within the larger context of holiness and faithfulness. In this regard, the Bible presents an honest and often detailed explanation of God's design for sex and its place in human life and happiness.

First, the biblical writers affirm the goodness of sexuality as God's gift. The Song of Songs is an extended love poem with explicit erotic imagery and language. Sex is affirmed as a source of pleasure and shared intimacy between husband and wife.

Second, the gift of sexual activity is consistently located only within the context of the marital covenant. Joined to each other within this monogamous covenant, the man and the woman may be naked and not ashamed (Gen. 2:25). The consistent witness of the biblical writers is that sexual relations are limited to this covenant relationship. All forms of extramarital sexual activity are condemned, including premarital sex (fornication) and adultery (Exod. 20:14; Deut. 22:22; 1 Cor. 6:9–10). At the same time, the husband and wife are ordered to fulfill their marital duties to each other and not to refrain from sexual union (1 Cor. 7:2–5).

Third, though pleasure is one of the goods biblically associated with sexual union (Prov. 5:15–19), the Bible consistently links procreation with the marital act (Ps. 128:3). Sexual pleasure and procreation are linked in a healthy and natural approach that avoids the denial of either. Modern contraceptive technologies were unknown in the Bible, and the contemporary "contraceptive mentality" that champions sexual pleasure completely severed from procreation is foreign to the biblical worldview.

Fourth, the biblical writers address human sexuality honestly. Paul acknowledged the reality of sexual passions (1 Cor. 7:9) and admonished those who have not been given the gift of celibacy to marry, rather than to allow their passions to turn into sinful lust.

The reality of sexual brokenness is also addressed. The pain and shame of adultery, for example, are demonstrated in the account of David's sin with Bathsheba. Paul's horror in learning of sexual sin among the Corinthians occasioned some of his clearest teachings on sexuality and holiness.

Sex, Holiness, and Happiness

The biblical writers affirm sexuality as a part of our embodied existence. As human beings we are sexual creatures, and as sexual creatures we are called to honor God with our bodies (1 Cor. 6:15–20). Within the context of the marital covenant, the husband and wife are free to express love for each other, experience pleasure, and join in the procreative act of sexual union. This is pleasing to God and is not to be a source of shame.

The biblical writers link holiness to happiness. True human happiness comes in the fulfillment of sexual holiness. The attempt to enjoy sexual happiness without holiness is the root of sexual deviance.

Sexual Deviance

Just as the biblical writers present marital sex as holy and natural, all other forms of sexual activity are presented as condemned and sinful. In addition to adultery and fornication, the Bible expressly forbids homosexuality, bestiality, incest, prostitution, rape, pederasty, and all other forms of sexual deviance (Exod. 22:16–17, 19; Lev. 18:6–18, 22–23; Prov. 7:1–27; Rom. 1:26–27; 1 Cor. 5:1–13).

The Bible presents sexual deviance as intentional rejection of God's authority as Creator and Lord (Rom. 1:18–25). As Paul warns, those who practice such sins will not inherit the kingdom of God (1 Cor. 6:9–10). Both OT and NT writers warn that the people of God are to remain untainted and uncorrupted by such sins. Interestingly, the sexual practices of the various pagan nations described in the OT and the sexual mores of the Roman Empire of the first century are remarkably like the obsessions of our own day.

Sexuality is one of God's good gifts, and the source of much human happiness. At the same time, once expressed outside its intended context of marital fidelity, it can become one of the most destructive forces in human existence.

Marital sexual love is expressed in the intimacy of sexual union and the marital act of conjugal union is the source of both pleasure and procreation. Both are goods of the marital act and relationship that are to be welcomed and accepted with thankfulness. The biblical writers instruct that true sexual happiness is inextricably linked to sexual holiness as believers live their lives before God.

Sex is Sacred[2]

The Place for Sex

Not that Scripture is squeamish about sexual joy, as Christians have sometimes been. Passages like Proverbs 5:18ff. and the Song of Songs show that God, who invented it, is all for it—in its place! But sexual activity is often out of place—when, for instance, it is directed by such motives as the quest for kicks, or for relief from mental or physical tension, or loneliness or boredom, or the desire to control or humiliate; or mere animal reaction to someone's sex appeal. Such motives cheapen sex, making it (despite the short-term excitement) trivial and ugly, and leaving behind, once the thrill is over, more of disgust than delight.

What then is the place and purpose of sex?

God intends, as the story of Eve's creation from Adam shows, that the "one flesh" experience should be an expression and a heightening of the partners' sense that, being given to each other, they now belong together, each needing the other for completion and wholeness (see Genesis 2:18–24). This is the "love" that committed couples are to "make" when they mate. Children are born from their relationship, but this is secondary; what is basic is the enriching of their relationship itself through their repeated "knowing" of each other as persons who belong to each other exclusively and without reserve.

So the placefor sex is the place of lifelong mutual fidelity, i.e. marriage, where sexual experience grows richer as the couple experiences more and more of each other's loving faithfulness in the total relationship.

False Trails

It follows that casual sex outside marriage (called "adultery" if either partner is married, "fornication" if not) cannot fulfill God's ideal, for it lacks the context of pledged fidelity. In casual sex a man does not strictly love a woman, but uses and so abuses her (however willing she may be). Nor can solitary masturbation fulfill God's ideal; sex is for relationships, not ego trips. And the relationships intended

---

2 Newheiser, J. (2008). Opening up Proverbs (80–84). Leominster: Day One Publications

are heterosexual only; God forbids and condemns homosexual practices (Leviticus 18:22; Romans 1:26ff.). In these days it needs to be said, indeed shouted, that accepting as from God a life without what Kinsey called "outlets" (i.e., physical sex acts) does one no harm, nor does it necessarily shrink one's humanity. After all, Jesus, the perfect man, was a celibate, and Paul, whether bereaved, deserted, or never married, lived single throughout his ministry. Not all who wish for a sexual partner can have one, but what God by circumstances calls us to he will also enable us for.

Sex is a Signpost

In the jungle of modern permissiveness the meaning and purpose of sex is missed, and its glory is lost. Our benighted society urgently needs recalling to the noble and ennobling view of sex which Scripture implies and the seventh commandment assumes: namely, that sex is for fully and permanently committed relationships which, by being the blend of affection, loyalty, and biology that they are, prepare us for and help us into that which is their archetype—"the happiness of being freely, voluntarily united" to God, men, and angels "in an ecstasy of love and delight compared with which the most rapturous love between a man and a woman on this earth is mere milk and water" (C. S. Lewis).

Will that be fun? Yes, that is one thing it will be, so no wonder God has made its earthly analogue fun too. Nor may you despise it, any more than you may deify it, on that account. The sweetness of affection between the sexes, linked (as it always is) with the sense that a couple's relationship, however complete, is never quite complete, is actually a jeweled signpost pointing us on to God. When folk in the Romeo-and-Juliet state of mind say "this thing is bigger than us," they speak more truly than they sometimes realize. But a signpost only helps those who will head the way it directs, and if you insisted on camping for life beside a lovely signpost, you would be daft; you would never get anywhere.

Find sexual happiness with your spouse (Proverbs 5:15–17)

The answer to sexual desire is not mere abstinence but marital delight. Sex itself is not evil but rather is a gift of God when enjoyed by two people who have entered into the covenant of marriage. The New Testament also teaches that marriage, including the sexual union, is honourable before God (Heb. 13:4). This is in stark opposition to some in Christendom who have taught that sexual desire is inherently evil and that those who want to serve God in significant ways must be celibate. The apostle Paul warned that false teachers would arise who would 'forbid marriage' (1 Tim. 4:3). Scandals throughout church history and in recent years demonstrate that efforts to suppress human sexuality often result in secret and wicked sexual expression. One of the great advances of the Reformation was the recovery of consistent biblical teaching on the wholesomeness of marriage, including the marriage bed (Eccles. 9:9).

Sex within marriage has been given by God to help both the husband and the wife to fulfil sexual desire. Paul tells those who are single that it is better to marry than to burn with sexual desire (1 Cor. 7:9). He also exhorts husbands and wives to fulfil their marital duties to each other so that they will not be tempted to sin (1 Cor. 7:3–5). Some married couples fail to fulfil this duty to each other because of selfishness or perhaps because one or both spouses have an unbiblical view of sex as being merely a necessary evil for procreation. Husbands and wives should not focus upon their own wants and desires (or lack of desire) but must selflessly give themselves to each other sexually as an expression of love and commitment.

A man is to drink exclusively from his 'own cistern' (5:15), which means that all of a man's sexual energy is to be directed to his wife. She is his exclusive source of sexual refreshment. Negatively, he is not to disperse his sexual energy outside his marriage (vv. 16–17). Any sexual act or thought which is not directed towards his wife is sinful and destructive. This truth is reinforced by our Lord Jesus, who makes it clear that even looking at or thinking (fantasizing) about someone other than your wife is adultery (Matt. 5:27–28). Paul tells men that their bodies, including their minds and eyes, belong exclusively to their wives for their joy (1 Cor. 7:3–4). This is why solo sex is wrong. Your body is not your own, and sex isn't primarily about pleasing yourself. Sex is meant to be relational, an expression of love to bring happiness to your spouse.

The exclusivity of sex within marriage also implies that sex is a private matter. The Song of Solomon speaks of marital love as a garden (S. of S. 4:12–15; 5:1) for the exclusive enjoyment of the married lovers. It is wrong to violate the privacy of marital love through immodesty or voyeurism.

Marital sex is exhilarating (Proverbs 5:18–19)

The greatest possible sexual happiness is to be found with your wife, not with a strange woman. A husband and his wife should fully enjoy pleasures which thrill all of their senses. The Song of Solomon describes how the man and his bride are thrilled by the sights, the sounds, the smells, the touches, and the tastes of marital love (S. of S. 1:2–3; 2:3, 6, 14; 4:9, 14; 5:1). Within the garden of marital love, all five sense gates can be opened wide for mutual enjoyment. You can let yourself go with your spouse. Waltke speaks of this text's 'biblical eroticism of male virility and female sexual beauty and charm'. Husband and wife can forget the cares of life, legitimately enjoying being 'intoxicated' (another possible translation of 'exhilarated' in 5:19c) with their love for each other. The man who has to look away from all the other female breasts put on display in our culture can freely enjoy his wife's breasts (5:19b). The wife may delight in being desired and being overwhelmed by the love of her husband. Their sexual thirst can be quenched in a way that pleases God.

Practise 'safe sex' (Proverbs 5:20–23)

Safe sex is sex with your spouse. If you are sexually exhilarated with your wife, the harlot's seductions won't affect you. Why would anyone who is fully enjoying the blessings of marriage be so foolish as to ruin everything by going to a strange woman who will ruin his life?

Some caveats

This beautiful portrayal of marital joy assumes a godly marriage. Sexual union is meant to be an expression of love between a husband and a wife who are committed to each other and to God. As both fulfil their God-given roles in marriage and sacrificially care for each other, the sexual union takes place naturally and joyfully. The selfish man who treats his wife badly all day should not be surprised when his evenings don't fully meet his hopes and expectations. If you are married, tend your (sexual) garden. Spend time together promoting personal intimacy. Take care of yourself physically. Pull up the weeds of unresolved conflict and sinful patterns of communication. Don't take each other for granted but cultivate romance.

If you are single, protect and preserve your garden. Your sexuality belongs to your future spouse. Keep it locked until the day of your wedding, when you and your spouse can enter and enjoy God's gifts without shame or regret. As wonderful as married love can be, Wisdom must still be your first love. If you are not wise, a wife will not deliver you from sexual temptation.

Proverbs 5–7 tells us about three women. The adulteress can kill you. Wisdom will save you. Your wife can help you.

Conclusion: Christ is our true love

Probably none of us is without sin in the area of moral purity. We have all, at times, been unfaithful and unwise. On a spiritual level, we have all been guilty of loving the world too much (1 John 2:15), which is unfaithfulness to God. Because God is a holy and jealous God, we deserve his wrath. Thank God for the Lord Jesus, who cleanses us from our sin and makes us wise. Though we prostituted ourselves with the world, he has bought us with his blood and cleansed us by his grace. He purifies and transforms us (1 Cor. 6:9–11; 2 Cor. 5:17). He quenches our spiritual thirst and provides the ultimate satisfaction for our souls (Prov. 14:27; Isa. 12:3; Zech. 13:1; John 4:14). He rejoices over us just as a bridegroom rejoices over his bride (Isa. 62:5). Make him your first love!

Further Bible Study
- Sex mishandled:
- Proverbs 6:20–7:27
- 1 Corinthians 6:9–20
- The joy of sexual love:
- Song of Solomon 1–8

Questions for Thought and Discussion
- What is the biblical concept of marriage?
- What does sex outside marriage lack in terms of God's ideal?
- What is God's primary purpose for sex?
- What does the expression "one flesh" indicate about this?
- How would you counsel a person who confessed to homosexual inclinations?2

Sexual health and aging: Keep the passion alive

Sexual health is important — at any age.

Though movies and television might tell you that sex is only for the young and beautiful, don't believe it. The need for intimacy is ageless. Sex may not be the same as it was in your 20s, but it can still be as fulfilling as ever.

What aspects of sexual health are likely to change as you and your partner get older? How can you both adapt? Janice Swanson, doctor of psychology, licensed psychologist and sex therapist at Mayo Clinic in Rochester, Minn., has some answers.

How can you maintain a satisfying sex life as you age?

When confronted with the physical and emotional changes of aging, you may feel as ill-prepared and awkward about sex as you did during your first sexual experiences. To maintain a satisfying sex life, talk with your partner. Set aside time to be sensual and sexual together. When you're spending intimate time with your partner, share your thoughts about lovemaking. Tell your partner what you want from him or her. Be honest about what you're experiencing physically and emotionally.

Many couples want to know how to get back to the sexual arousal and activity levels they experienced in their 20s, 30s and early 40s. Instead, find ways to optimize your body's response for sexual experiences now. Ask yourselves what's satisfying and mutually acceptable.

How does aging affect men's sexual health?

Testosterone plays a critical role in a man's sexual experience. Testosterone levels peak in the late teens and then gradually decline. Most men notice a difference in their sexual response by age 60 to 65. The penis may take longer to become erect, and erections may not be as firm. It may take longer to achieve full arousal and to have orgasmic and ejaculatory experiences. Erectile dysfunction also becomes more common. Drugs such as sildenafil (Viagra), vardenafil (Levitra) and tadalafil (Cialis) can help men achieve or sustain an adequate erection for sexual activity.

How does aging impact women's sexual health?

As a woman approaches menopause, estrogen production decreases. As a result, most women have less natural vaginal lubrication, which can affect sexual pleasure. Women may experience emotional changes as well. While some women may enjoy sex more without worrying about pregnancy, naturally occurring changes in body shape and size may cause others to feel less sexually desirable.

What medical conditions can cause sexual health concerns?

Any condition that affects general health and well-being also affects sexual function. Illnesses that involve the cardiovascular system, high blood pressure, diabetes, hormonal problems, depression or anxiety — and the medications used to treat these conditions — can pose potential sexual health concerns.
High blood pressure, for instance, can affect your ability to become aroused, as can certain medications used to treat high blood pressure.

What can you do if medications negatively affect your sexual health?

Certain medications can inhibit your sexual response, including your desire for sex, your ability to become aroused and your orgasmic function. If you're experiencing sexual side effects from a medication, consult your doctor. It may be possible to switch to a different medication with fewer sexual side effects.

Don't let embarrassment keep you from asking your doctor for help — and don't stop taking prescribed medication before discussing it with your doctor. If you take several medications, each of which can have a different effect on your sexual function, try varying the type of sexual activity you engage in and how you approach it.

What is testosterone?

Testosterone is a hormone produced primarily in the testes. For men, testosterone helps maintain:
- Bone density
- Fat distribution
- Muscle strength and mass
- Red blood cell production

- Sex drive
- Sperm production

If you have an unusually low level of testosterone (hypogonadism), your doctor may prescribe a synthetic version of testosterone. You may be able to choose from testosterone injections, patches or gels.

What happens to testosterone level with age?

Testosterone peaks during adolescence and early adulthood. As you get older, your testosterone level gradually declines — typically about 1 percent a year after age 30. Does a naturally declining testosterone level cause the signs and symptoms of aging?

Some men have a lower than normal testosterone level without signs or symptoms. For others, low testosterone may cause:

- Changes in sexual function. This may include reduced sexual desire, fewer spontaneous erections — such as during sleep — and infertility.
- Changes in sleep patterns. Sometimes low testosterone causes insomnia or other sleep disturbances.
- Physical changes. Various physical changes are possible, including increased body fat, reduced muscle bulk and strength, and decreased bone density. Swollen or tender breasts (gynecomastia) and hair loss are possible. You may experience hot flashes and have less energy than you used to.
- Emotional changes. Low testosterone may contribute to a decrease in motivation or self-confidence. You may feel sad or depressed, or have trouble concentrating or remembering things.

It's important to note that some of these signs and symptoms are a normal part of aging. Others can be caused by various underlying factors, including medication side effects, thyroid problems, depression and excessive alcohol use. A blood test is the only way to diagnose a low testosterone level.

Testosterone therapy: Key to male vitality?

Can testosterone therapy promote youth and vitality?

Testosterone therapy can help reverse the effects of hypogonadism, but it's unclear whether testosterone therapy would have any benefit for older men

175

who are otherwise healthy. Although some men believe that taking testosterone medications may help them feel younger and more vigorous as they age, few rigorous studies have examined testosterone therapy in men who have healthy testosterone levels — and some small studies have revealed mixed results. For example, in one study healthy men who took testosterone medications increased muscle mass but didn't gain strength.

What are the risks of testosterone therapy for normal aging?

Testosterone therapy has various risks. For example, testosterone therapy may:
- Contribute to sleep apnea — a potentially serious sleep disorder in which breathing repeatedly stops and starts
- Cause your body to make too many red blood cells (polycythemia), which can increase the risk of heart disease
- Cause acne or other skin reactions
- Stimulate noncancerous growth of the prostate (benign prostatic hyperplasia) and possibly stimulate growth of existing prostate cancer
- Enlarge breasts
- Limit sperm production or cause testicle shrinkage

Should you talk to your doctor about testosterone therapy?

If you wonder whether testosterone therapy might be right for you, work with your doctor to weigh the risks and benefits. A medical condition that leads to an unusual decline in testosterone may be a reason to take supplemental testosterone. However, treating normal aging with testosterone therapy remains controversial.

The following article came from the National Institute on Aging: Sexuality in Later Life. NIH Publication Number 05-7185

Sex and Aging for Men: Main Changes

Primarily due to a drop in testosterone, men will experience changes in their sexual function as they age. These changes include :
- Fewer sperm are produced
- Erections take longer to occur

- Erections may not be as hard
- The 'recovery time' (time between erections) increases to 12 to 24 hours
- The force of ejaculation decreases
- Sexual desire decreases are due to emotional reasons or health problems

Coping Strategies

1. Talk Openly With Your Spouse

Good sex always relies on open communication with your spouse. As both of you age, things will change. These changes will require patience, understanding and experimentation. Emotions can greatly impact sexual health. By maintaining good communication and intimacy, you and your spouse will be able to adapt to changes as necessary.

2. Manage Your Health Conditions

Health conditions like high blood pressure and chronic pain can make a healthy sex life difficult. By aggressively managing any health conditions, you can greatly reduce their impact on your sex life. A good approach is to follow your doctor's advice and make lifestyle changes.

3. Talk To Your Doctor

Your doctor cannot help you with your sexual concerns unless you mention them. Some sexual problems are actually medication side effects, which can be handled by adjusting medications that you are already taking or changing the time of day that you take medications. Many medications also directly treat sexual problems.

4. Experiment With Positions and Times

Sometimes changing the time of day or the position used in sex can relieve sexual problems. If a health condition is interfering with your sex life, you may notice that your symptoms are better at a certain time of day. Try having sex then. Varying the sexual positions that you use can help too, especially if pain from arthritis or other condition interferes with sex.

5. Expect Difficulties

As you age, you will experience certain changes in your sexual function. When these changes occur, don't panic. Rather, think of them as problems to be solved. If you react emotionally to these problems, you can make them worse. By expecting some degree of sexual change as you age, you can react calmly and troubleshoot your situation.

6. Eat Healthy and Lose Weight

Being overweight puts a strain on your body that can result in high blood pressure, heart disease, diabetes and other health conditions, all of which can interfere with a normal sex life. By eating healthy foods and losing excess weight you can prevent sexual problems.

Sex and Aging for Women: Main Changes

Sex and aging are topics most older women do not want to talk about. The most obvious changes in a woman's body as she ages come with menopause. During menopause, decreasing estrogen levels cause physical changes that may impact sexual function. Aging may also bring emotions that can interfere with sex (see these sex tips for the older women for some help).

Menopause and Decrease in Estrogen

During menopause, the levels of estrogen are reduced. These estrogen decreases alter the thickness and size of a woman's reproductive organs. These changes include:

- Loss of elasticity and a thinning of the vaginal tissue
- Decrease in the amount of lubrication
- Decrease in the size of the clitoral, vulvar and labial tissues
- Decreases in the size of the cervix, uterus and ovaries
- The Impact on Sex
- These changes alter the experience of sex in the following ways:
- The anticipation before orgasm decreases
- Orgasms may be less intense
- Sexual desire may be reduced

However, the sensitivity of the clitoris remains the same

Medical Procedures and Sexual Desire

Emotions can impact both sexual desire and sexual satisfaction. As women age, the changes in their bodies can trigger powerful emotions. Surgical procedures can also change how a woman feels about her own body. Some examples of how aging impacts sex through emotions include:

Hysterectomy (removal of the uterus and sometimes ovaries): This surgical procedure does not change a woman's ability to have sex, though both strong emotions about this procedure and changes in hormones can impact sexual desire.

Mastectomy (removal of a breast due to cancer): A mastectomy can radically alter how a woman perceives her own beauty and sexual attractiveness. Open communication with your sexual partner can help tremendously.

Health Conditions and Sexual Function

Many chronic health conditions can interfere with sex. Conditions such as arthritis can make sex painful. Heart disease, can make the physical activity of sex difficult. By aggressively managing your health conditions, you can improve the quality of your sexual experiences.

Perception of Aging

How women perceive themselves as they age greatly impacts sexual desire. In our culture, we are constantly exposed to images of youth. As we age, there is little to reassure women that they are still sexually attractive and beautiful. Because of this, women may lose interest in sex as they age. Talking about these emotions with your sexual partner can help relieve some of the stress around body image and aging.

Coping Strategies

1. Talk With Your Spouse

Open communication has always been essential for good sexual activity. Talk with your spouse about any sexual difficulties you might be having as a couple. Try to treat the difficulties as problems to solve and work together on finding creative solutions.

2. Lubricate

As a woman ages, natural lubrication for sexual activity decreases. This is easily fixed by using a water-based lubricant. At first, applying a lubricant for sexual activity may seem awkward, but you and your partner will quickly become used to it.

3. Experiment with Positions and Times

Pain caused by arthritis or other condition can interfere with sexual activity. Experiment with different sexual positions, and you may find one that works much better. Also, arthritis and other pain conditions are often less severe at certain times a day, which will vary for each person. Try having sex when your pain is the least severe.

4. Deal with Erectile Problems

For men, trouble having an erection is an expected part of aging. If this happens to your partner, gently help him troubleshoot this problem. Lifestyle changes and medications that can help.

5. Feel Beautiful

We live in a culture that is constantly showing us images of youth and beauty. As women age, they may feel less sexually attractive, which can interfere with sexual desire. Try not to be influenced by these cultural messages. Sure, your body changes as you age, but that does not reflect on your worth or desirability. Ignore messages and stereotypes from television, magazines and other media sources and embrace your body at every stage of your life.

6. Take Care of Your Health

Poor health can interfere with sexual satisfaction. If you have a health condition, be sure to the manage it. Follow your doctor's orders and make the lifestyle changes you need to be healthy. Losing weight, exercising and eating well will not only improve your health, your sex life will also improve.

7. Sex After Surgery

As women age, they may need to undergo surgical procedures that alter the reproductive organs. The most common are mastectomy (the removal of a breast or part of a breast to treat cancer) or hysterectomy (the removal of the uterus and sometimes the ovaries). These surgeries do not interfere with a woman's ability to have sex. However, these procedures can dramatically change how a woman perceives her own attractiveness. Open communication with your spouse both before and after these procedures can help reduce anxiety and negativity.

Sexual Problems in Men

Many men will notice that their sexual activity motivation (libido) goes up and down over time. They may be less interest when they are tired, distracted, ill, or depressed. Relationship issues can also affect sexual activity. Fortunately, it tends to return to normal when these problems go away.

However, some men can experience a lasting decrease in sexual activity drive that they found worrisome or bothersome. Low sexual activity drive itself can also affect a man's relationship with his spouse.

In the majority of cases, persistent low sexual activity drive comes from stress or other psychological issues. In some cases, there may be underlying medical conditions, including
- side effects from medications
- alcohol or drug use
- certain hormone problems
- chronic medical conditions
- major psychiatric problems including depression and anxiety.

Let's start with medications. A variety of medications can affect sex drive, including drugs used to treat the following conditions
- heart disease
- high blood pressure
- heartburn or ulcers
- depression and other psychiatric conditions
- chronic pain
- certain types of cancer, especially prostate cancer
- an enlarged prostate gland certain hormonal conditions, including thyroid problems and pituitary tumors.

<u>My Personal Notes</u>

13

THE BIG QUESTIONS

Should I Get Married?

The answer to this question is often assumed by our culture. From early childhood most of us absorb the idea that marriage is a natural and integral part of normal life. From the fairy-tale characters Snow White and Prince Charming, the romantic plays of Shakespeare, and the mass media heroes and heroines, we receive signals that society expects us to be numbered among the married. Should we fail to fulfill this cultural expectation, we are left with the nagging feeling that perhaps something is wrong with us, that we are abnormal.

If a young man reaches the age of thirty without getting married, he is suspected of having homosexual tendencies. If a woman is still single by thirty, it is often tacitly assumed that she has some defect that makes her unattractive as a marriage partner, or worse, has lesbian preferences. Such assumptions are by no means found in the Scriptures. From a biblical perspective the pursuit of celibacy is indicated in some instances as a legitimate option. Under other considerations it is viewed as a definite preference. Though we have our Lord's blessing on the sanctity of marriage, we also have his example of personal choice to remain celibate, obviously in submission to the will of God. Christ was celibate not because of homosexual leanings or from a lack of the masculine traits necessary to make him desirable as a life partner. Rather, his divine purpose obviated the destiny of marriage, making it crucial that he devote himself entirely to the preparation of his bride, the church, for his future wedding.

The most important biblical instruction that we have regarding celibacy is given by Paul in a lengthy passage from 1 Corinthians 7:25-40.

Now concerning the unmarried, I have no command of the Lord, but I give my opinion as one who by the Lord's mercy is trustworthy. I think that in view of the present distress it is well for a person to remain as he is. Are you bound to a wife? Do not seek to be free. Are you free from a wife? Do not seek marriage. But if you marry, you do not sin, and if a girl marries, she does not sin. Yet those who marry will have worldly troubles, and I would spare you that. I mean, brethren, the appointed time has grown very short; from now on, let those who have wives live as though they had none, and those who mourn as though they were not mourning, and those who rejoice as though they were not rejoicing, and those who buy as though they had no goods, and those who deal with the world as though they had no dealings with it. For the form of this world is passing away.

I want you to be free from anxieties. The unmarried man is anxious about the affairs of the Lord, how to please the Lord; but the married man is anxious about worldly affairs, how to please his wife, and his interests are divided. And the unmarried woman or girl is anxious about the affairs of the Lord, how to be holy in body and spirit; but the married woman is anxious about worldly affairs, how to please her husband. I say this for your own benefit, not to lay any restraint upon you, but to promote good order and to secure your undivided devotion to the Lord.

If any one thinks that he is not behaving properly toward his betrothed, if his passions are strong, and it has to be, let him do as he wishes: let them marry—it is no sin. But whoever is firmly established in his heart, being under no necessity but having his desire under control, and has determined this in his heart, to keep her as his betrothed, he will do well. So that he who marries his betrothed does well; and he who refrains from marriage will do better.

A wife is bound to her husband as long as he lives. If the husband dies, she is free to be married to whom she wishes, only in the Lord. But in my judgment she is happier if she remains as she is. And I think that I have the Spirit of God.

The teaching of the apostle Paul in this matter of marriage has been subjected to serious distortions. Some observe in this text that Paul is setting forth a contrasting view of marriage that says celibacy is good and marriage is bad, particularly for Christians called to service in the interim period between the first advent of Christ and his return. However, even a cursory glance at the text indicates that Paul is not contrasting the good and the bad, but rival goods. He points out that it is good to opt for celibacy under certain circumstances. Moreover, it is also good and quite permissible to opt for marriage under other circumstances. Paul sets forth the pitfalls that a Christian faces when contemplating marriage. Of prime consideration is the pressure of the kingdom of God on the marriage relationship.

Nowhere has the question of celibacy been more controversial than in the Roman Catholic church. Historically Protestants have objected that the Roman Catholic church, by imposing upon its clergy a mandate beyond the requirements of Scripture itself, has slipped into a form of legalism. Though we agree that Scripture permits the marriage of clergy, it indicates, at the same time, that one who is married and serving God in a special vocation does face the nagging problems created by a divided set of loyalties—his family on one hand; the church on the other. Unfortunately the dispute between Protestants and Catholics over mandatory celibacy has become so heated at times that Protestants have often reacted to the other extreme, dismissing celibacy as a viable option. Again let us return to the focus of Paul's word which sets forth a distinction between rival goods. His distinction, in the final analysis, allows the individual to decide what best suits him or her.

Paul in no way denigrates the honorable "estate" of marriage, but rather affrrms what was given in creation: the benediction of God over the marriage relationship. One does not sin by getting married. Marriage is a legitimate, noble, and honorable option set forth for Christians.

Another aspect regarding the question, Should I get married? moves beyond the issue of celibacy to whether a couple should enter into a formal marriage contract or sidestep this option by simply living together. In the last thirty years the option of living together, rather than moving into a formal marriage contract, has proliferated in our culture. Christians must be careful not to establish their precepts of marriage (or any other ethical dimension of life) on the basis of contemporary community standards. The Christian's conscience is to be governed not merely by what is socially acceptable or even by what is legal according to the law of the land, but rather by what God sanctions.

Unfortunately, some Christians have rejected the legal and formal aspects of marriage, arguing that marriage is a matter of private and individual commitment between two people who have no further legal or formal requirements. These view marriage as a matter of individual private decision apart from external ceremony. The question most frequently asked of clergymen on this matter reflects the so-called freedom in Christ: Why do we have to sign a piece of paper to make it legal?

The signing of a piece of paper is not a matter of affixing one's signature in ink to a meaningless document. The signing of a marriage certificate is an integral part of what the Bible calls a covenant. Biblically, there is no such thing as a private marriage contract between two people. A covenant is done publicly before witnesses and with formal legal commitments that are taken seriously by the community. The protection of both partners is at stake; there is legal recourse should one of the partners act in a way that is destructive to the other.

Contracts are signed out of the necessity spawned by the presence of sin in our fallen nature. Because we have an enormous capacity to wound each other, sanctions have to be imposed by legal contracts. Contracts not only restrain sin, but also protect the innocent in the case of legal and moral violation. With every commitment I make to another human being, there is a sense in which a part of me becomes vulnerable, exposed to the response of the other person. No human enterprise renders a person more vulnerable to hurt than does the estate of marriage.

God ordained certain rules regulating marriage in order to protect people. His law was born of love and concern and compassion for his fallen creatures. The sanctions God imposed upon sexual activity outside of marriage do not mean that God is a spoilsport or a prude. Sex is an enjoyment he himself has created and given to the human race. God, in his infinite wisdom, understands that there is no time that human beings are more vulnerable than when they are engaged in the most intimate activity known to human beings. Thus he cloaks this special act of intimacy with certain safeguards. He is saying to both the man and the woman that it is safe to give one's self to the other only when there is a certain knowledge of a lifelong commitment behind it. There is a vast difference between a commitment sealed with a formal document and declared in the presence of witnesses before family, friends, and authorities of church and state, and a whispered hollow promise breathed in the backseat of an automobile.

Do I Want to Get Married?

Paul states in 1 Corinthians 7:8-9: "To the unmarried and widows I say that it is well for them to remain single as I do. But if they cannot exercise self-control, they should marry. For it is better to marry than to be aflame with passion." The distinction is between the good and the better. Here Paul introduces the idea of burning, not of the punitive fires of hell, but of the passions of the biological nature, which God has given us. Paul is speaking very candidly when he points out that some people are not made for celibacy. Marriage is a perfectly honourable and legitimate option even for those who are most strongly motivated by sexual fulfillment and relief from sexual temptation and passion.

The question, Do I want to get married? is an obvious, but very important one. The Bible does not prohibit marriage. Indeed it encourages it except in certain cases where one may be brought into conflict with vocation; but even in that dimension, provisions are left for marriage. So, to desire marriage is a very good thing. A person needs to be in touch with his own desires and conscience.

If I have a strong desire to marry, then the next step is actively to do something about fulfilling that desire. If a person wants a job, he must seriously pursue employment opportunities. When we decide to attend a college or a university, we have to follow the formal routine of making applications, of evaluating various campuses. Marriage is no different; no magic recipe has come from heaven that will determine for us the perfect will of God for a life partner. Here, unfortunately, is where Christians have succumbed to the fairy-tale syndrome of our society. It is a particular problem for young single women who feel that if God wants them to be married, he will drop a marriage partner out of heaven on a parachute or will bring some Prince Charming riding up to their doorstep on a great white horse.

One excruciating problem faced by single women is caused by the unwritten rule of our society that allows men the freedom actively to pursue a marriage partner while women are considered loose if they actively pursue a prospective husband.

No biblical rule says that a woman eager to be married should be passive. There is nothing that prohibits her from actively seeking a suitable mate. On numerous occasions, single women had insisted that they have no desire to be married, but simply want to work out the dimensions of the celibacy they believe God has imposed upon them. After a number of years, the scenario usually changes when a nice young man starts to show some interest or when the biological clock kicks in and not many months afterwards, there are talks about setting a wedding date.

Wisdom requires that the search be done with discretion and determination. Those seeking a life partner need to do certain obvious things such as going where other single people congregate. They need to be involved in activities that will bring them in close communication with other single Christians.

In the Old Testament Jacob made an arduous journey to his homeland to find a suitable marriage partner. Isaac did much the same thing. Neither of these patriarchs waited at home for God to deliver them a life partner. They went where the opportunity presented itself to find a marriage partner. The fact that they were men does not imply that such a procedure is limited to males only. Women in our society have exactly the same freedom to pursue a mate by diligent search.

What Do I Want in a Marriage Partner?

A myth has arisen within the Christian community that marriage is to be a union between two people committed to the principle of selfless love. Selfless love is viewed as being crucial for the success of a marriage. This myth is based upon the valid concept that selfishness is often at the root of disharmony and disintegration in marriage relationships. The biblical concept of love says no to acts of selfishness within marital and other human relationships. However, the remedy for selfishness is nowhere to be found in selflessness.

The concept of selflessness is originally one that proceeds from Oriental and Greek thinking where the ideal goal of humanity is the loss of self-identity by becoming one with the universe. The goal of man in this schema is to lose any individual characteristic, becoming one drop in the great ocean. Another aspect of Oriental absorption is the notion of the individual becoming merged with the great Oversoul and becoming spiritually diffused throughout the universe. From a biblical perspective the goal of the individual is not the annihilation or the disintegration of the self, but the redemption of the self. To seek selflessness in marriage is an exercise in futility. The self is very much active in building a good marriage, and marriage involves the commitment of the self with another self based on reciprocal sharing and sensitivity between two actively involved selves.

If I were committed to a selfless marriage, it would mean that in my search for a marriage partner I should survey the scene to find a person for whom I was willing to throw myself away. This is the opposite of what is involved in the quest for a marriage partner. When someone seeks a mate, he or she should be seeking someone who will enrich their life, who will add to their own self-fulfillment, and who at the same time will be enriched by that relationship.

What are the priority qualities to seek in a marriage partner?

One little exercise that many couples have found helpful is based upon freewheeling imagination. While finding a marriage partner is not like shopping for an automobile, one can use the new car metaphor. When one purchases a new car, he has many models from which to choose. With those models there is an almost endless list of optional equipment that can be tacked onto the standard model.

By analogy, suppose one could request a made-to-order mate with all the options. The person engaged in such an exercise could list as many as a hundred qualities or characteristics that he would like to find in the perfect mate. Compatibility with work and with play, attitudes toward parenting, certain skills, and physical characteristics could be included. After completing the list, the person would have to acknowledge the futility of such a process. No human being will ever perfectly fit all the possible characteristics that one desires in a mate.

This exercise is particularly helpful for people who have delayed marrying into their late twenties or early thirties. Such a person sometimes settles into a pattern of focusing on tiny flaws that disqualify virtually every person he meets. After doing the made-to-order mate exercise, he can take the next step: reduce the list to the main priorities. The person involved in this exercise reduces the number of qualifications to twenty, then to ten, and finally to five. Such a reduction forces him to set in ordered priority the things he is most urgently seeking in a marriage partner.

It is extremely important that individuals clearly understand what they want out of the dating and eventually the marital relationship. They should also find out whether their desires in a marriage relationship are healthy or unhealthy. This leads us to the next question regarding counseling.

From Whom Should I Seek Counsel?

Many people resent the suggestion that they seek counsel in their selection of a marriage partner. After all, isn't such a selection an intensely personal and private matter? However personal and private the decision might be, it is one of grave importance to the future of the couple and their potential offspring, their families, and their friends.

Marriage is never ultimately a private matter because how the marriage works affects a multitude of people. Counsel can be sought from trusted friends, pastors, and particularly from parents.

In earlier periods of Western history, marriages were arranged either by families or by matchmakers. Today the idea of arranged marriages seems primitive and crass. It is totally foreign to our American heritage. We have come to the place where we think that it is our inalienable right to choose one whom we love.

Some things need to be said in defense of the past custom of arranged marriages. One is that happy marriages can be achieved even when one has not chosen his own partner. It may sound outrageous, but I am convinced that if biblical precepts are applied consistently, virtually any two people in the world can build a happy marriage and honor the will of God in the relationship. That may not be what we prefer, but it can be accomplished if we are willing to work in the marital relationship. The second thing that needs to be said in defense of arranged marriages is that in some circumstances, marriages have been arranged on the objective evaluation of matching people together and of avoiding destructive parasitic matchups. For example, when left to themselves, people with significant personal weaknesses, like a man having a profound need to be mothered and a woman having a profound need to mother, can be attracted to each other in a mutually destructive way. Such negative mergings are repeated daily in our society.

It is not my intention to lobby for matched or arranged marriages. I am only hailing the wisdom of seeking parental counsel in the decision-making process. Parents often object to the choice of a marriage partner. Sometimes their objections are based upon the firm conviction that "no one is good enough for my daughter [or son]." Objections like these are based upon unrealistic expectations at best and upon petty jealousy at worst. However, not all parents are afflicted with such destructive prejudices regarding the potential marriage partners of their children. Sometimes the parents have keen insight into the personalities of their children, seeing blind spots that the offspring themselves are unable to perceive. In the earlier example of a person with an inordinate need to be mothered attracting someone with an inordinate need to mother, a discerning parent can spot the mismatch and caution against it. If a parent is opposed to a marriage relationship, it is extremely important to know why.

When Am I Ready to Get Married?

After seeking counsel, having a clear understanding of what we are hoping for, and having examined our expectations of marriage, the final decision is left to us. At this point some face paralysis as the day of decision draws near. How does one know when he or she is ready to get married? Wisdom dictates that we enter into serious premarital study, evaluation, and counseling with an ordained pastor or a qualified Christian counselors (according to guidance given by the Seventh-day Adventist Church) so that we may be warned of the pitfalls that come in this new and vital human relationship. Sometimes we need the gentle nudge of a trusted pastor or counselor to tell us when it is time to take the step. With the breakdown of so many marriages in our culture, increasing numbers of young people fear entering into a marriage contract lest they become "statistics."

What things need to be faced before taking the actual step toward marriage? Economic considerations are, of course, important. Then understanding the expectations (roles and responsibilities), and Communication. The second greatest reason given for divorce is conflict over finances, sometimes sparked by misunderstandings or disagreements. Financial pressures imposed upon a relationship already besieged with emotional pressures of other kinds can be the straw that breaks the proverbial camel's back. That is why parents often advise young people to wait until they finish their schooling or until they are gainfully employed so that they can assume the responsibility of a family.

It is not by accident that the creation ordinance of marriage mentions that a man shall leave his father and mother and "cleave unto" his wife and the two shall become one flesh. The leaving and cleaving dimensions are rooted in the concept of being able to establish a new family unit. Here economic realities often govern the preparedness for marriage.

But entering into marriage involves far more than embarking upon new financial responsibilities. The marriage commitment is the most serious one that two human beings can make to each other. I am ready to get married when I am prepared to commit myself to a particular person for the rest of my life, regardless of the human circumstances that befall us.

In order for us to understand the will of God for marriage, it is again imperative that we pay attention to God's preceptive will. The New Testament clearly shows that God not only ordained marriage and sanctified it—but he also regulates it. His commandments cover a multitude of situations regarding the nitty-gritty aspects of marriage. The greatest textbook on marriage is the sacred Scripture, which reveals God's wisdom and his rule governing the marriage relationship. If someone earnestly wants to do the will of God in marriage, his first task is to master what the Scripture says that God requires in such a relationship.

What does God expect of his children who are married or thinking about getting married?

God expects, among other things, faithfulness to the marriage partner, provision of mutual needs, and mutual respect under the lordship of Christ. Certainly the couple should enhance each other's effectiveness as Christians. If not, something is wrong.

Now, while celibacy is certainly no less blessed and honourable a state to be in than marriage, we do have to recognize Adam and Eve as our models. God's plan involved the vital union of these two individuals who would make it possible for the earth to be filled with their "kind."

Basically I cannot dictate God's will for anyone in this area any more than I can or would in the area of occupation. I will say that good marriages require hard work and individuals willing to make their marriages work.

Ultimately what happens in our lives is cloaked in the mystery of God's will. The joy for us as his children is that the mystery holds no terror—only waiting, appropriate acting upon his principles and direction, and the promise that he is with us forever.[1]

---

1 Sproul, R. (1996). Following Christ. Wheaton, IL: Tyndale House Publishers.

Questions Couples Should Ask (Or Wish They Had) Before Marrying

Melinda J Hill, a Family and consumer Science agent, Wayne County, Ohio State University Extension, The Ohio State University, wrote

When the love bug strikes and two individuals begin to plan their lives together, what kind of questions do they ask? "What month do we want to get married in? Who should be invited to the wedding? What colours are we going to use? What kind of food do we want to serve?" The list goes on with details that will help make this day a very special memory for years to come. But, sometimes the planning for the wedding overshadows the preparation for the marriage and important issues get ignored. "How do we manage conflict? Who is going to handle the money? How will the roles and responsibilities be divided? Where are we going to spend the holidays?" These are all questions that should be considered and discussed with your partner at some time during the courtship and before you both commit to marriage.

According to the New York Times, December 17, 2006, Relationship experts report that too many couples fail to ask each other critical questions before marrying. Here are a few key ones that couples should consider asking:

1) Have we discussed whether or not to have children, and if the answer is yes, who is going to be the primary care giver? How many children do we want?

2) Do we have a clear idea of each other's financial obligations and goals, and do our ideas about spending and saving mesh?

3) Have we discussed our expectations for how the household will be maintained, and are we in agreement on who will manage the chores?

4) Have we fully disclosed our health histories, both physical and mental?

5) Is my partner affectionate to the degree that I expect?

6) Can we comfortably and openly discuss our sexual needs, preferences and fears?

7) Will there be a television in the bedroom?

8) Do we truly listen to each other and fairly consider one another's ideas and complaints?

9) Have we reached a clear understanding of each other's spiritual beliefs and needs,

and have we discussed when and how our children will be exposed to religious/moral education?

10) Do we like and respect each other's friends?

11) Do we value and respect each other's parents, and is either of us concerned about whether the parents will interfere with the relationship?

12) What does my family do that annoys you?

13) Are there some things that you and I are NOT prepared to give up in the marriage?

14) If one of us were to be offered a career opportunity in a location far from the other's family, are we prepared to move?

15) Does each of us feel fully confident in the other's commitment to the marriage and believe that the bond can survive whatever challenges we may face?

16) Do my parents, friends, peers, or co-workers support my choice or are they concerned for my welfare? How do I feel about their apprehension? Have I really made a good choice for me or have I compromised my values because I hope things will get better?

17) What does commitment mean to me? Do I have a spiritually matured role model to follow who helps me see how to navigate through the tough times? What changes do I expect to see after the wedding?

18) How do I handle conflict? Am I willing to face the situation and discuss options, or do I ignore the facts and hope they will go away? Can I talk about my anger or disappointment with my partner and can we reach a compromise? Can we come to an agreement about how to deal with our problems—a way to communicate that does not include violence, put-downs, or walking away without resolving the issues?

19) What are the common goals and dreams we want to achieve? Where will we live? Who will clean the toilet and take out the trash (put out the bins)? Who will handle the money? How many credit cards will we have? How much money will we save from each pay? What colour will the bedroom be? Where will we spend the holidays?

20) What kind of marriage relationship do I want? How happy am I in this relationship? Who is responsible for my happiness? How much fun do we have on our dates? Do I have fond memories of our courtship?

Take Your Time

Every person and every relationship is different. Slow down and take time to think through these and other issues you may not have considered. Give yourselves the gift of time and the reassurance that you are the right person for this commitment. If the above questions raised concerns or issues that you and your partner haven't discussed or thought about (or your premarital counselor forgot to discuss with you), maybe the relationship and the counseling sessions needs more time before you say "I do." In fact, you should first go through the counseling and subject your final decision to the outcome of the counseling sessions.

<u>My Personal Notes</u>

14

The Christian Family and Lifestyle

The Bible attaches great importance to the formation of a human family. Christian family lifestyle reflects this significance in the standards of family life.

(1) General principles. The principle of childbearing (Gen. 1:28) assures the propagation of the human race and calls for an adequate home for children. God gave the command to be fruitful and multiply to both Adam and Eve, not only because both were needed for procreation, but also because the best sanctuary for the weak, vulnerable, and totally dependent newborn is the home of a godly couple. Marital harmony must predate the arrival of the child and should be independent of it. When childbearing is considered a means of keeping the marriage together, the children may become victims of tensions between the parents. The principle of nurturing the child (Gen. 18:19; Eph. 6:4) encompasses several tasks. First, and most important, is love for every child. Partiality in parent-children relations inflicts deep wounds on those who are neglected and often incapacitates those who are coddled excessively. Based on impartial love parents can engage in education and discipline. The Bible insists that discipline is also an eloquent expression of love when administered appropriately (Prov. 13:24). The principle of support of children in financial and physical needs (1 Tim. 5:8) molds the Christian lifestyle. Parents are responsible not only to provide everyday necessities, but when circumstances allow they should furnish education, vacations, cultural activities, and even some inheritance (2 Cor. 12:14).

The principle of respect for parents (Ex. 20:12) creates a context in which family responsibilities can be adequately discharged. Parents cannot fulfill the parental duties listed above if they hold no authority over their household. The age, the greater maturity, the education, the experience, are all advantages from which children can and should profit with gratitude. The necessary but unpleasant lessons and tasks may never be learned or accomplished when due respect is wanting. The principle of care for the elderly (Lev. 19:32) completes the human life cycle. Christians consider respect and care for elderly parents or grandparents as a Christian duty and privilege. In a civilization where the value of a human being tends to be measured by usefulness, success, and contributions, the weak and elderly are discounted. Often loving parents feel pushed aside, away from the warmth of their children's homes into institutions where infrequent visits by children create inexpressible anguish. The Bible enjoins proper respect for those who are older.

(2) **Normative models**. The Creation account presents an example for spouses contemplating parenthood. First of all, God planned the creation of man and woman: "Let us make man" (Gen. 1:26). Childbearing must be purposeful and planned, not a thoughtless incident of insignificant consequence. Second, God prepared everything needed for the human creature: air for the lungs, food for the stomach, light for the eyes, work and sleep for the muscles, mysteries and laws of nature for the mind, and the Sabbath for communion with God. A Christian lifestyle beckons modern parents to imitate our heavenly Father in upholding the principles of care and support of the family.

In the household of Isaac and Rebekah there was a serious neglect of the principle of impartial love. Isaac preferred Esau and Rebekah favored Jacob (Gen. 25:28). Sibling rivalry and even hatred tore this family apart. Jacob also showed a preferential bias toward Joseph; identical consequences followed (Gen. 37:3, 4). These two negative examples only support the principle of proper nurture of children, indicating how important it is for parents to be impartial.

Abraham and Isaac stand as a beautiful example of mutual respect and love. On Mount Moriah the son trusts his father to the point of death because he has learned to trust his father's God (Gen. 22:1–14). A very different example is given by Eli, a father who lost control over his sons, as well as their respect (1 Sam. 2:22–25). Just as Isaac reaped blessings, so the sons of Eli the priest harvested personal ruin and death, and caused national decay and collapse of the moral order.

Finally, many other examples can set norms for family behaviour. Among them we mention Hannah and Elkanah (1 Sam. 1; 2), Joseph and Mary (Matt. 1:18–25; 2:1–23), and Lois and Eunice, grandmother and mother of Timothy (2 Tim. 1:5).

(3) **Rules of action.** For more direct guidelines on family life, a Christian may refer to passages such as Exodus 21:15, 17; Leviticus 19:3; Deuteronomy

27:16; Proverbs 1:8; 6:20; 23:22; Ephesians 6:1–4; 1 Timothy 5:1–8; Titus 2:3–6; and Hebrews 12:7–11. Many positive values emanate from following Christian standards of family life. Identity, the sense of self, is among the most important. Its basis rests on dialogue with oneself and others (Gen. 2:18). The dialogues may take a form of self-appraisal (Rom. 2:15) or self-encouragement (Ps. 5:11; 116:7). In addition, the need for belonging urges us to dialogue with and imitate those who are important to us. Thus our self-concept receives its social dimension. At birth, humans have no instincts to guide them autonomously as do animals. They need caring, coaching, modeling, forgiving, accepting, and affirming in love. The family is the God-given environment in which humans receive a healthy sense of self-worth and identity.

In the same way, the family provides the context that encourages and facilitates the development of habits and values. The examples that children observe, the opportunities offered to them, the kind of music, books, food, social climate, and religious orientation to which children are exposed, determine in large measure their habits and value preferences. Ellen G. White writes: "Every one in the family is to be nourished by the lessons of Christ … . This is the standard every family should aim to reach … ."
"Religious instruction means much more than ordinary instruction. It means that you are to pray with your children, teaching them how to approach Jesus and tell Him all their wants. It means that you are to show in your life that Jesus is everything to you, and that His love makes you patient, kind, forbearing, and yet firm in commanding your children after you, as did Abraham" (AH 317).

Experience confirms that religious and spiritual formation cannot be left to the child alone. It takes parental dedication and a loving environment to overcome the pressures that lead humans in the wrong direction. The Christian family seeks to uphold divine standards and thus provides society with men and women who live with integrity and in the fear of God.

ISSUES IN THE FAMILY

Christians cannot be satisfied with merely describing ideals and identifying shortcomings. The grim reality of troubled and broken marriages and homes cries out for help. Before focusing on the biblical guidelines for dealing with marriage and family problems, it is necessary to highlight briefly the preventive features inherent in the Christian marriage and family lifestyle.

Preventive lifestyle. The premarital period is of crucial importance. A Christian lifestyle urges careful self-examination, patient study of the possible marriage partner, sufficient time to know each other before emotional attachments overpower reason, seeking advice from more experienced and trusted people, maintaining a high standard of sexual purity, and most of all constant prayer and searching for God's will. No one can be too prudent and wise for the choice of a marriage partner (5T 106, 107), but the above-mentioned precautions can reduce the risk of serious tragedies.

The Christian lifestyle aims at harmony and permanence in a marriage relationship. For that reason the mutual care and romance from the premarital period should survive the wedding day, the arrival of children, and the coming of the golden years. Both spouses need to nurture their mutual love and work with tenacity to reach their common potential. In a Christian marriage there must be consistent communication of feelings, goals, fears, and hopes to prevent the onset of disillusionment, alienation, and the estrangement that may mar the marriage.

The Christian family lifestyle centres on people within the family. Togetherness must be practiced intentionally around games, outings, or in simple cuddling. Traditions unique to every family further enhance the sense of identity of each member; these may include special celebrations, vacations, regular spiritual activities, and other creative family customs. Acceptance of each member as he or she is will require tolerance of mistakes and affirmation of the personal talents and unique characteristics of each. Discipline will protect each member from immediate harm and from the eventual danger of developing harmful habits. And finally, regular worship will strengthen the sense of divine presence in the home, bringing a feeling of security to all. When, in spite of intentional efforts to implement this Christian way of life, troubles set in, the Bible presents guidance for the Christian experiencing problems in marriage and family life.

(1) General principles. The principle of redemptive confrontation taught by Jesus in Matthew 18 applies to marital and family problems as well. As soon as a distance in attitude becomes evident, Jesus entreats, "go" and confront, to redeem your "brother." If there is no opening of communication it may be necessary to seek help elsewhere. Sharing the problem with one or more skilled helpers often brings good results. In case such efforts fail, the church that witnessed the marriage vows engages in a healing ministry. The p 694 principle of separation for a period of time may be another redemptive step (1 Cor. 7:5, 10, 11). This might provide time to lessen the tension, think, counsel, and pray through the issues that separate. But Paul cautions that such disassociation might bring temptations to the spouses and advises a short separation for prayer. The principle of sacredness of marriage sets the marital union above human touch and beyond vulnerability to the will or desires of any person. The words of Jesus are clear: "What therefore God has joined together, let no man put asunder" (Matt. 19:6). Death is the only inescapable reason for the dissolution of marriage (1 Cor. 7:39). Even adultery, the most serious infraction of marriage law, does not provide automatic cause for divorce. Jesus treats it as an exception to the principle of sacredness or inviolability, not as another rule opposing or alongside the main principle (Matt. 19:9). Malachi speaks of God's rejecting His people "because the Lord was witness to the covenant between you and the wife of your youth, to whom you have been faithless, though she is your companion and your wife by covenant … . So take heed to yourselves, and let none be faithless to the wife of his youth. 'For I hate divorce, says the Lord the God of Israel' " (Mal. 2:14–16). A Christian spouse faced with a faithless companion opts for divorce only when there is no possibility for reestablishing communion (1 Cor. 7:15).

(2) Normative models. The experience of the prophet Hosea illustrates the conduct of the husband of an adulterous woman (Hosea 1:2, 3; 3:1–3). The restless spouse runs away but he buys her back, forgives her unfaithfulness, and treats her with respect and love. The prophet's predicament presents only a dim picture of the relationship between God and His people. "They are all adulterers," says God (Hosea 7:4), yet He does not "divorce" them. "How can I give you up! … How can I hand you over!" He exclaims (Hosea 11:8), moved by a love that transcends faithlessness. Thus we hear in the Bible the call to faithfulness in marriage (Mal. 2:14–16), as well as an example of model behavior in the divine example of forgiveness of adultery.

Family problems cannot be totally prevented through faithful conformity to standards alone. Even the home of Adam and Eve faced jealousy between brothers and the insubordinate behavior of Cain. In the parable of the prodigal, Christians can find inspiration for patience and forbearance in dealing with prodigals; they also find encouragement to uphold the principles of redeeming family relations (Luke 15:11–32).

Family problems may result from wrong actions of parents as well. Jonathan sets a worthy example of a son who respected his father, King Saul, but refused to cooperate or submit to his way of life (1 Sam. 19:1–7). Unfortunately, Jacob cooperated with the dishonest scheming of his mother, which resulted in family disturbances for generations (Gen. 27).

(3) Rules of action. Among the biblical passages containing direct rules of action on marriage and family problems we note Deuteronomy 21:15–21; Matthew 5:32; 19:5–9; Mark 10:11, 12; Romans 7:2, 3; and 1 Corinthians 7.

A distressing fact is that good Christians do not always make good marriages and not all Christian families are good families. This may happen because God is not invited or because His will is not discerned aright, not to mention our reluctance to forsake our self-centered ways. Furthermore, since harmonious relationships stand as a bulwark against sin, Satan attacks marriages and families with fury. So we ask, what is the Christian way through fatal relational disintegration?

My Personal Notes

15

COMMUNICATION
Men and Women under the microscope

There is biological evidence that women and men are different. Men are generally taller and have deeper voices than women. Men have hair on their chest and face; women do not. Agreed? But dare to suggest that the brains of males and females may be different, and the world will condemn you as a brutish fool. In January 2005, Lawrence H. Summers, president of Harvard, offended women at an academic conference of the National Bureau of Economic Research by

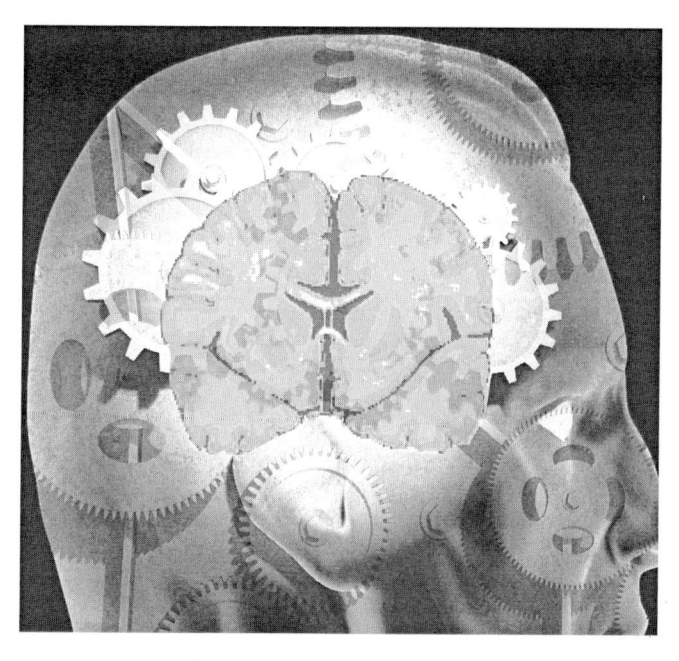

suggesting that innate differences between the sexes may explain why fewer women succeed in science and math careers. He further noted that such differences might stem from biological roots. Female academics were furious—as demonstrated by Nancy Hopkins, a biology professor at MIT who walked out of in the middle of Summer's speech saying, "I felt I was going to be sick." Front page news stories threw rocks, and intellectuals around the United States of America wondered aloud why Summers felt women were so inferior. All the man did was note that there is research supporting the idea that the brain of a male is different from that of a female. Many people are not yet ready to accept this idea.

According to Dr Scott Haltzman, a psychiatrist and Brown University professor, and author of the book *"The Secrets of Happily Married Men,"* "men's social roles do not focus on relationship development as a primary objective; improving a relationship is a means to an end. When two men get together, they establish a hierarchy of interaction based on one-upping the other."

Men aren't as Emotional as Women

Men are emotionally different, or at lease reacts differently to emotional situations. It is a common belief and acknowledged that "men don't cry" or find it difficult to show their emotions, publicly.

Deep within the brain, the centre that controls respiration, temperature, balance, and activities that are thought of as "instinctual," lies a section called amygdala. The amygdala is in charge of making emotional connections to life events.

Emotional arousal following the learning event influences the strength of the subsequent memory for that event (Wikipedia). Greater emotional arousal following a learning event enhances a person's retention of that event. According to Haltzman,

> The amygdala scans the signals that enter the brain and stands sentry, ready to light up in recognition of a friendly smile, or send out an alarm if it perceives any threats. When triggered, the amygdala releases a flood of stress hormones into the bloodstream. This flooding shuts down the "thinking" part of the brain, freezes the body to prepare for assault, and prepares the memory centers to retain any necessary information for future reference.

Studies have shown that females are more sensitive and responsive to social cues, including threat signals, than are males (in fact most females responses are heighten when they feel their child or children are at risk. This can be seen in most mammals). Haltzman believes that

> This difference between men's less responsive reaction to threat signals and a women's more sensitive alarm system may be one reason why women don't think we are as emotional. Another reason is that even when our emotional reactions are equally strong, men tend to be better able to shut down their amygdala and redirect their brain activity back to the cortex -- the place where logical thought takes over. This may seem like emotional coldness to women, but to men it may be a way of making sure our emotions don't get in the way of getting the job done.

That

> Men may also have internal mechanisms to dampen the seriousness of frightening thoughts. MRI scans have shown that when given two sets of words, one neutral and the other designed to stimulate intense negative emotion, men relied on their left brains and didn't discern a difference between the two sets of words. In contrast, women's right and left brains were involved in recalling both sets of words, and emotional centers were activated when the intense words were recalled. Moreover, women (not men) had an increase in blood flow to the area of the brain that stores memory when negative emotions were triggered. Apparently, women are not only deeply hurt by words, but they implant those slights in their memory for . . . who knows how long?

That's not to say that men can't, or don't, experience negative emotions. In fact, studies show his amygdala is much more responsive to sadness than his wife's. But unlike women, men will shut down the amygdala to keep the cortex in control and thus appear ever confident and emotionally stable. This variance contributes to the way men communicate and what they communicate. What they say and how much they actually say. Many a times a man will say something seemingly innocence, but the woman will become annoyed or upset by his comments. Men need to realize that a woman's brain and ability to read into messages are far more sensitive than what he will ever be able to achieve.

Men are not Good Housewives

The change in society and change in who is the breadwinner (main provider) as well as how much money is brought to the family table has resulted in a shift in men's role of the dominating, leader of the home and society. More and more men are now opting for the home-maker (housewives) role rather than being the main provider. The result is that men are now taking care of the home. They bath the baby, do the laundry, comb their daughters' hair in preparation for preparatory school, clean the house, cook the dinner and feed the dog. Yet still some of us never achieve that ultimate level where our wives can say well done, I don't have to send you a reminder or give you a shopping list. Some men will burn the toast, mix colours in doing the laundry and if all fails, purchase ready-made meals.

If you are one of those men who burns dinner while the baby is screaming for change, you'll be happy to know that it's the way you were made. Your brain structure is to be blamed.

Haltzman reason, based on his research, that

Women on average have more gray matter in their brain than men. Gray matter is composed of nerve cells that make connections between other cells to move information around in the brain. Scientists have found that besides having more of these important cells, women also have a greater number of connections between these cells than men do. No, there's not a direct correlation between the number of nerve connections and how easily a person can attend to many demands at one time, but scientists do theorize that one reason a woman can manage better is because there are many more areas of her brain that process information at once.

Men also find it difficult to be a good housewife because of his ability to multitask. This ability is affected by his ability to transfer information from his right side of the brain to the left.

When the man's well-endowed right hemisphere—the visual-spatial area— is hard at work, you will notice he is not talking. That is because the right side of the brain is slow in moving information over to the left side of the brain, where the verbal centers are nestled. One of the reasons men have to turn off the car radio when they are lost is to cut down on interference between the (right) side of the brain that says, "If I turn left here, will I be able to detour around the construction?" and the (left) side of the brain that is trying to decipher the lyrics to "Bennie and the Jets."

Men Think A Lot About Sex

Men and women are biologically different in the area of sex. The distinctions comes from gender-based differences in hormone levels. Hormones are a regulatory substance produced in an organism and transported in tissue fluids such as blood or sap to stimulate specific cells or tissues into action. This causes changes in the delicate balance of our behavior—and our desire for sex. For men, it's testosterone that fuels the drive. This is produced in the testes and flows through the blood to affect the functioning of nearly every other organ system, fro cholesterol levels to muscles strength to brain function. This hormone is the reason why your wife is right: you do think about sex far more often than she does (usually)—because you have ten to twenty times more testosterone flowing through your system than she does, causing you to have more thoughts of sex and a greater desire for sex (most of the time) than your wife.

Testosterone[1] tends to contribute to an increase tendency to be competitive and even aggressive. It also affects energy levels, motivation, and drive, which have a large influence on the sex drive (the most pronounced). It was discovered that married men and other men in committed relationships have a 20 percent drop in their testosterone, which is to help them from straying.

Haltzman believes certain body chemicals influences the way men act and the way they see the world.

Communication—Key to Healthy relationship

Playful Communication in Relationships

It is said that playful communication is one of the most effective tools for keeping relationships exciting, fresh, and vital. Laughter and play enrich interactions and give your relationships that extra feeling that keeps them interesting, light and enjoyable.

---

1 *A steroid hormone that stimulates development of male secondary sexual characteristics, produced mainly in the testes, but also in the ovaries and adrenal cortex.*

This leads to a sense of intimacy and connection—qualities that define solid, lasting relationships.

Laughter draws others to you and keeps them by your side. When you laugh with one another, a positive bond is created. This bond acts as a strong buffer against stress, disagreements, and disappointment. And laughter really is contagious—just hearing laughter primes your brain to smile and join in on the fun.

The benefits of playful communications are
- Connect to others. Your health and happiness depend, to a large degree, on the quality of your relationships—and laughter binds people together.
- Smooth over differences. Using gentle humor often helps you broach sensitive subjects, resolve disagreements, and reframe problems.
- Feel relaxed and energised at the same time. Laughter relieves fatigue and relaxes your body, while also recharging your batteries and helping you accomplish more.
- Overcome problems and setbacks. A sense of humor is the key to resilience. It helps you take hardships in stride, weather disappointment, and bounce back from adversity and loss.
- Put things into perspective. Most situations are not as bleak as they appear to be when looked at from a playful and humorous point of view.
- Be more creative. Humor and playfulness loosen you up, energizing thinking and inspiring creative problem solving.

The health benefit of laughter, in playful communication:

- Boost your mood
- Decreasing stress hormones
- Improving oxygen flow to the brain
- Reducing physical pain
- Relaxing your body

Conversation, not just communication, is the Premium

Conversation (interrelation communication) is involved in almost every aspect of our interactions with others; for this reason, communication and relationships are inseparably connected. You cannot have a relationship with someone without communicating with him or her.

Communication includes how we express our thoughts, ideas, and feelings to others, including what we say and how we say it and the attitude (dressing) that conveyed it. When we communicate with others, we also communicate attitudes, values, priorities, and beliefs. No matter what we actually say to other people in words, we also send messages about what we think of them, what we think of ourselves, and whether or not we are being sincere and genuine in what we say. Our non-verbal communication -- those things we do not say with words, but with our gestures, our facial expressions, and our attitude -- speak volumes. This communication can be good (clear, open and honest) or bad (vague, guarded and dishonest). Communication is both verbal and non-verbal (spoken and unspoken). In fact, everything we do in the company of others involves communication. Our body language, facial expressions, tone of voice, and level of interest (or disinterest) communicates something to the receiver.

The number one secret to maintaining a healthy relationship is having good conversation-communication skills. If you are in an intimate relationship and feel that you could improve in this area, here are some ways to keep the communication — and the relationship — flowing.

Communication in Important Relationships

Effective communication is essential in day-to-day life, extremely important in developing a relationships. Establishing good communication, it is advisable that you:

- Put a premium on openness. Find ways to be honest, express your feelings, and share ideas.
- Share your problems. Sharing the good times and the bad times is important in relationships, and serves to deepen and strengthen relationships and communication within them.

- Share your daily life. Share those things in your life that are mildly interesting, funny, sad, or affect you in some way. Find a way to connect with others, sharing your life with them and allowing them to share their lives with you.
- Avoid verbally bruising other people. Refrain from insults, put-downs, and expressions of disgust, and avoid generalizations, which are not only stereotypes, but often hurt.
- Boost self-esteem, don't crush it. When it comes to relationship building, naming someone's deficiencies or failures is rarely as effective as praise. Focus on each other's positive traits. Find something good to say, catch each other doing something right, and help build self-confidence and self esteem.
- Avoid controlling. Whenever one person seeks to always be right, always be the agenda-setter, and always be the virtuous one, he or she may feel like a winner - but it is the relationship that loses.

Where there are many factors involved in healthy relationships, the ability to communicate effectively is one important route to mutual satisfaction within any relationship. And once again, there are two ways to communicate with others: effectively and ineffectively.

The Key: Communication

In order to have a healthy, relationship and a successful marriage, each party to must work on their communication skills. Good communication is at the heart of every healthy relationship. Relationships and marriages are struggling; usually suffering from poor or bad couples communication. In fact, most communication difficulties, usually centres around man's inability to relate or communicate at a level that stimulates his wife or partners emotion, resulting in a lack of feelings of value and appreciation.

Men communications are reasonable, deliberate, and intentional during the chasing and dating stages of the relationship. However, once a man has won his darling's heart and hand in marriage, the level of communication commence the slow death march, an ultimate destination of no return, unless arrested and place on witness stand by his wife/partner. One reason maybe that men are task oriented. Once a man set his heart and mind on something, he focuses his attention and effort until he accomplished his task. Once accomplished, once rewarded, his interest wane, unless kept alive by further and future rewards.

Women's level of communication differs to that of a man. Her need for quality conversation (communication that goes beyond providing her with mere facts and figures, but rather inclusive of emotions) drivers her world and affects her sense of value and appreciation. Quality conversation is the door to her heart. A switch that lights up her room and that allows a man to sit on her inner furniture's of her private room. It sends a message of interest, care, well-being and answers the question of whether her husband/partner is still interested in her and her happiness.

For some women, sharing bed, having a meal together, nor being in the same room means nothing if there is no quality conversation with her husband/partner. Communicating says more than spending days in her presence. Love is the fulfilling of the law of God and quality conversation, for a woman, is the fulfilling of her heart's desire.

How To Treat A Lady

Biblical treatment

In our postmodern society, understanding how you treat a lady will have a great impact on your quality of life. So how should a man treat a lady?

1. Don't treat her like your mother
   a. Ignore her talks
   b. Say yes, when you mean no
   c. Don't listen to her
   d. Say she is getting on your nerves
   e. Calling her only when you need something
2. Don't treat her like your little sister
   a. Argue with her
   b. Put her down
   c. Talk about her short-comings
   d. Say she don't know much
   e. She's second to you in importance

3. Don't treat her like a doormat
   a. Walk on her
   b. Walk over her
   c. Fill her life with dirt
   d. Mess up her life
   e. Change her after many years of good times

4. Don't treat her your Pet
   a. Insider waiting for you
   b. She follows you around
   c. She on a leash tied to our hand and move at your every will
   d. Give her what you think she needs instead of consulting her

Rather treat her

1. Like your equal
2. Your copilot
3. Your lover
4. Your football (soccer) team
5. Your best friend
6. Your partner in victories, and your advisor in tragedy
7. Your applie pie
8. Your sugar dumpling
9. Your everything

So what does the Bible have to say about the relationship roles and numerous challenges faced within a marriage or serious dating:

Relationship

EPHESIANS 4:2-3 Always be humble and gentle. Be patient with each other, making allowance for each other's faults because of your love. Make every effort to keep yourselves united in the Spirit, binding yourselves together with peace. (NLT)

ROMANS 12:3-5 Because of the privilege and authority God has given me, I give each of you this warning: Don't think you are better than you really are. Be honest in your evaluation of yourselves, measuring yourselves by the faith God has given us. Just as our bodies have many parts and each part has a special function, so it is with Christ's body. We are many parts of one body, and we all belong to each other. (NLT)

MATTHEW 22:37-39 Jesus replied, "'You must love the LORD your God with all your heart, all your soul, and all your mind.' This is the first and greatest commandment. A second is equally important: 'Love your neighbor as yourself.' ECCLESIASTES 4:9-10 Two people are better off than one, for they can help each other succeed. If one person falls, the other can reach out and help. But someone who falls alone is in real trouble. (NLT)

TITUS 2:7-8 And you yourself must be an example to them by doing good works of every kind. Let everything you do reflect the integrity and seriousness of your teaching. Teach the truth so that your teaching can't be criticized. Then those who oppose us will be ashamed and have nothing bad to say about us. (NLT)

GALATIANS 6:10 Therefore, whenever we have the opportunity, we should do good to everyone—especially to those in the family of faith. (NLT)

JOHN 13:35 Your love for one another will prove to the world that you are my disciples." (NLT)

GALATIANS 6:2 Share each other's burdens, and in this way obey the law of Christ. (NLT)

JAMES 3:18 And those who are peacemakers will plant seeds of peace and reap a harvest of righteousness. (NLT)

1 PETER 1:22 You were cleansed from your sins when you obeyed the truth, so now you must show sincere love to each other as brothers and sisters. Love each other deeply with all your heart. (NLT)

1 PETER 3:7 In the same way, you husbands must give honor to your wives. Treat your wife with understanding as you live together. She may be weaker than you are, but she is your equal partner in God's gift of new life. Treat her as you should so your prayers will not be hindered. (NLT)

Personality Issues

2 PETER 1:5-6 In view of all this, make every effort to respond to God's promises. Supplement your faith with a generous provision of moral excellence, and moral excellence with knowledge, and knowledge with self-control, and self-control with patient endurance, and patient endurance with godliness. (NLT)

PROVERBS 11:11-12 Upright citizens are good for a city and make it prosper, but the talk of the wicked tears it apart. It is foolish to belittle one's neighbor; a sensible person keeps quiet. (NLT)

PROVERBS 11:13 A gossip goes around telling secrets, but those who are trustworthy can keep a confidence. (NLT)

PROVERBS 12:22 The Lord detests lying lips, but he delights in those who tell the truth. (NLT)

PROVERBS 25:19 Putting confidences in an unreliable person in times of trouble is like chewing with a broken tooth or walking on a lame foot. (NLT)

PROVERBS 12:25 Worry weighs a person down; an encouraging word cheers a person up. (NLT)

PROVERBS 17:22 A cheerful heart is good medicine, but a broken spirit saps a person's strength. (NLT)

MATTHEW 6:34 "So don't worry about tomorrow, for tomorrow will bring its own worries. Today's trouble is enough for today." (NLT)

LUKE 6:37 "Do not judge others, and you will not be judged. Do not condemn others, or it will all come back against you. Forgive others, and you will be forgiven. ROMANS 14:12-13 Yes, each of us will give a personal account to God. So let us stop condemning each other. Decide instead to live in such a way that you will not cause another believer to stumble and fall. (NLT)

Sexuality

PROVERBS 5:18-19 Let your wife be a fountain of blessing for you. Rejoice in the wife of your youth. She is a loving deer, a graceful doe. Let her breasts satisfy you always. May you always be captivated by her love. (NLT)

1 CORINTHIANS 7:3 The husband should fulfill his wife's sexual needs, and the wife should fulfill her husband's needs. (NLT)

1 CORINTHIANS 7:4-5 The wife gives authority over her body to her husband, and the husband gives authority over his body to his wife. 5 Do not deprive each other of sexual relations . . . (NLT)

HEBREWS 13:4 Give honor to marriage, and remain faithful to one another in marriage. God will surely judge people who are immoral and those who commit adultery. (NLT)

EPHESIANS 5:28 In the same way, husbands ought to love their wives as they love their own bodies. For a man who loves his wife actually shows love for himself. (NLT)

SONG OF SOLOMON 7:10-12 I am my lover's, and he claims me as his own. Come, my love, let us go out to the fields and spend the night among the wildflowers. Let us get up early and go to the vineyards to see if the grapevines have budded, if the blossoms have opened, and if the pomegranates have bloomed. There I will give you my love. (NLT)

I CORINTHIANS 6:19-20 Don't you realize that your body is the temple of the Holy Spirit, who lives in you and was given to you by God? You do not belong to yourself, for God bought you with a high price. So you must honor God with your body. (NLT)

My Personal Notes

16

SINGLENESS

The Misunderstood World of Single Adults

SINGLENESS TODAY

It's Saturday night--date night for many singles. Ken, a 29-year-old computer analyst who lives in Toronto, knows where the action is and that's where he's headed. He's looking for a girl and a good time. He's also hoping for something special that will lead to a satisfying long-term relationship. He goes out almost every Saturday night. Perhaps tonight that lasting relationship will begin.

Jill, a 33-year-old graphic designer who lives in Kansas City, is attending a concert with a new male friend. She'll go slowly, though, because she's been through all this before. Jill watches her diet and works out at the health center. She is attractive and smart. But no relationship has "clicked," and she sometimes wonders if there's something wrong with her. She chooses not to date as often as she used to, but deep inside she still hopes to find someone.

Across town, 28-year-old Debra is also getting ready to go out. She is actively looking for a husband, and her datebook is always full. "Finding a husband is my parttime job," she says. "I sell clothing during the week, and on the weekend I look for a man." But Saturday night is not date night for every adult single. Steve, for example, prefers to stay home, prepare his own gourmet dinner, and strum his classical guitar.

Sandra, a 32-year-old single parent, doesn't have time to go out. Her husband deserted her after their second child was born, and the divorce was final a year ago. Sandra has sole responsibility for herself and her girls, ages 4 and 1. Her job, the children, cooking, and laundry leave her with little energy and even less money. On Saturday night she rents a movie, eats popcorn, and crashes.

For Marguerite, it's a night for memories. She and Frank had enjoyed so many wonderful Saturday nights together and with friends. But after 43 years of marriage his weak heart finally stopped. Now she's alone. Oh, she goes out to dinner with friends sometimes, and gets together to play Yahtzee, but mostly she is content to be alone.

For James, a retired preacher, it's a night to look forward to. He knows that one of his children will call and ask if he can babysit his grandchildren while Mom and Dad go out for the evening. His grandchildren love his jovial spirit, his hearty laugh, and his entertaining stories. Besides, when they play games they always win. Being with the grandkids helps James to get over losing his wife, whom he loved so deeply.

Singleness includes people of all ages and stations in life. They may be 22 or 38 or 67. They are engineers and chefs and typesetters and convenience store clerks and executives and salespersons. They drive Escorts, pickup trucks, old Chevys, and Lincolns. They wear Nikes and wingtips, Calvin Kleins and Levis. They shop at Brent Cross, Primark and Asda. Some of these singles offer a multitude of gifts and talents and experiences. Many of them are carrying deep hurt and going through intense struggles. Few match the media stereotypes. And chances are, they are misunderstood.

A MISUNDERSTOOD WORLD

Many factors contribute to the misunderstanding of singleness today. Two that deserve special attention are the media and the church.

1. Media Misrepresentation. The media, in conjunction with high-impact marketers, presents an inaccurate caricature of singleness. Television and magazine ads often portray singles as shallow, pleasure-seeking, impulsive, and materialistic. They show them as flitting from one relationship to another amid an endless round of parties, good times, and hedonistic experiences. Even a casual observer can see the connection between that kind of image and the high-ticket products these advertisers want single adults to spend their money on.

While this profile does describe many single adults, it is an exaggerated view. Being single does not automatically mean that someone is extravagant, self-centered, or promiscuous. Being single today involves asking hard questions about life and looking for answers that work. But singles are not finding them in the mixed messages of the media. On one hand, they are encouraged to follow a free-spending, drink-it-up, sexually unrestrained lifestyle. But on the other, they are warned about the dire consequences of financial excess, drunk driving, and AIDS. It reveals a misunderstanding--and some manipulation.

2. Insensitivities in some Churches. The church is equally at fault when it is not sensitive to the struggles of today's single. It's important to recognize that single adults are the same sensitive human beings as anyone else, with similar joys, hurts, cares, and need for God and His people. They come to the church for God, for fellowship, and for a sense of family. And they expect to find more love and concern among believers than they get in their workplace and society. But all too often, single adults tell about experiences like these:

Jane, who is 31 and never married, agreed to be a bridesmaid for a younger friend. She dreads going to the church shower because these are the kinds of comments she'll hear:

- "I've been noticing that new guy Kevin. Have you tried to make friends with him? He looks so lonely. He needs a girl like you."

- "You've got your sights set too high. Time to lower them. After all, you're 31 aren't you? The odds are turning against you."

- "Well, we're all waiting. When's it going to be your turn to be the bride?"

Remarks like that add to feelings of inadequacy and inferiority. And they hurt--even though they may not be intentional.

Brian is 34. He finished his schooling a number of years ago and is working for a military aircraft contractor. He capably heads a department that has 32 employees and he programs anti-missile guidance systems for F-18 jet fighters. He has a good sense of humor and is one of the first to volunteer for church work projects. He has generously given of himself on two short-term mission trips. But when some of the men decide to get together for an early breakfast, a round of golf, or an occasional Canadian fishing trip, Brian's name is overlooked. For some reason, the married guys don't even consider him. If you asked them, they'd say they just don't think they have that much in common with Brian. After all, he has his own single friends.

A similar problem develops when nominations are taken for the church board. Married men without children are readily considered. But no one has ever really talked about whether Paul's qualifications in 1 Timothy 3 and Titus 1 rule out singles.

219

Marcie, an attractive 27-year-old divorced woman with a child, was feeling that she must have leprosy. Sabbath after Sabbath she ended up sitting in church alone. It was quite a while before she "overheard" this loudly whispered comment: "I'm not going to let her take my husband away from me!"

The church has a great opportunity to reach into the world of adult singles with the gospel of grace, a message of hope, and warm family acceptance. But for the most part it's not trying. Singleness remains, in all too many churches, a misunderstood and unconsidered world.

A PATH TO UNDERSTANDING

Many of today's television shows portray the changing place of singles in society. Although they are often exaggerated and obviously fictional, they do show flashes of the real world of single adults today. Beneath the casual intensity, sexual allusions, and persona of confidence are very real emotions and needs that are part of singleness. Loneliness, hardness, discontentment, insecurity, brittleness, desire, and fear are all covered by a mask of self-sufficiency and composure.

One woman in her thirties, who could have been speaking for many singles when she responded to some questions about being unmarried, said, "I love my career. I adore my apartment and my friends. I'm basically content. But deep inside I have a desire to be part of something bigger than myself. Sometimes I feel so wrapped up in my own world. I guess I'm saying that I'd like to be part of a family."

Single adults need to be a part of a family. And the church can help to provide for that need. Unfortunately, there are certain unseen barriers that hinder effective fellowship between single and married people in the church. These barriers are primarily due to misunderstandings about today's single life. The purpose of this booklet is to clear up some of these misunderstandings by:
- Getting the Facts

- Exploding the Myths

- Searching the Scriptures

- Facing the Issues

Getting the Facts

As the number of single people continues to grow, it has an increasing impact on our society. Retailers, advertisers, housing developers, legal entities, government agencies, and the church are finding that they have to consider the concerns of adult singles more than ever. In Western society, more than 40 percent of the adult population is single. Think of it--at the minimum, 4 out of every 10 adult Americans, Canadians, and Europeans are single! These singles fall into four categories:

- Never married

- Divorced

- Separated

- Widowed

Around six out of ten men and women in the UK live in a couple. Five in ten men and women are married and one in ten are cohabiting. Men are more likely than women to be single (never married), while women are more likely than men to be divorced or widowed. There are over three times as many widows as widowers in the population as women ten to live longer than men.

Statistics indicate the growing place adult singles have in today's world. The following figures are taken from the 2001 census:

The pattern of partnership formation has changed over the last 30 years. The proportion of married people has fallen, while the proportion of single and divorced people have increased. The average age at marriage in England and Wales increased by seven years from 1971 to 2001 for both men and women, to nearly 35 years of age for men and 32 years for women.

Cohabitation has increased over the past twenty years as marriage has declined. Single women are more likely than single men to be cohabitiing. However, separated and widowed men are around twice as likely to cohabit than women of the same marital status.

With the long-term rise in divorce, the number of divorced people in England and Wales has also increased, adding to the number of singles in society and in the church. There were 1.5 million divorced men and 2.0 million divorced women in 2001, compared with 187,000 and 296,000 divorced men and women, respectively, in 1971.

There has been a doubling in the proportion of households headed by a lone parent with dependent children in the UK since the early 1970s, to 6 per cent in 2002. More recently, the number of single, lone mothers has grown at a faster rate, because of the rise in the proportion of births outside of marriage. Lone mothers headed the majority of lone parent families in spring 2002, with just one in ten headed by a lone father.

Older women are more likely than older men to live alone and the proportion increases with advancing age. Among women aged 75 and over who live in private households in Great Britain, 60 per cent lived alone in 2002 compared with 29 per cent of men of the same age.

Cohabitation is becoming more common among people in their 50's, and again the proportion declines with age. In 2002, 5 per cent of men and 4 per cent of women aged 50-59 lived witih a partner without being married to them.

These adult singles are impacting society as never before. They have enormous buying power, with their total spending estimated at £ billions per year. This greatly influences the marketing techniques of those who sell automobiles, clothing, beverages, and sports equipment.

The entertainment industry, fitness centers, ski resorts, and other enterprises are directing more and more of their ad dollars to singles. Some restaurants and bars appeal to singles exclusively.

Today's single adults are more self-analytical and introspective than those of the past. They are taking the time to know themselves. They are looking at the multiple options society offers them before making life commitments--vocational, marital, or residential. One woman said, "We are the first 'wait and see' generation of singles."

More single people are choosing not to marry, more single women are purchasing homes and adopting (or having their own) babies, and more professional singles are turning to dating services to help them find companionship. They have turned it into a multimillion dollar business.

Another factor is important in understanding singleness today. In 1970 the median age for women getting married was 20.8 years of age; in 2000 it was 25.1. For men in 1970 it was 23.2; in 2000 it was 26.8. An increasing number of men and women are choosing to live together before marriage, and at a younger age than those who marry. When those who chose to "play house" do marry, they have a significantly higher incidence of divorce than those who did not. This seems to indicate that the primary argument given for cohabitation-- to avoid divorce--is not valid.

Another interesting fact is that singleness is concentrated in urban areas. For example, 61 percent of the people who live in the city of Chicago are single. When they marry, they move away from "where the action is" to the suburbs.

How about singleness among Christians? In a survey taken by Carolyn Koons and Micheal J. Anthony (Single Adult Passages, Baker, 1991), 1,300 Christian single adults were asked about the advantages and disadvantages of singleness. They indicated that the following advantages of singleness, in order, were:

Women	Men
1. Mobility and freedom	1. Mobility and freedom
2. Time for interests	2. Time for interests
3. Social life in general	3. Privacy
4. Privacy	4. Social life in general

The disadvantages of being single were:

Women	Men
1. Loneliness	1. Loneliness
2. Financial insecurity	2. Restrictions on sex life
3. Self-centeredness	3. Self-centeredness
4. Restrictions on sex life	4. The dating grind

The point of listing all these facts and statistics is to get a better context for understanding the world of single adults in today's church--those adult single men and women who identify themselves as followers of Jesus Christ. They are more apt to be looking for moral and spiritual peace and direction. Many of them are serious about knowing the Bible, walking in the Spirit, and pleasing the Lord Jesus in their jobs, their leisure time, and their social activities. They need the fellowship, interaction, and encouragement that can come only from other members of the body of Christ--both married and single.

Exploding The Myths

Singleness today is misunderstood in part because of some myths about single adults that are accepted as facts. A second step to clearing away the misunderstandings about singleness is to identify and reject some of those wrong assumptions. These myths are not just believed by married people about singleness, but also by singles about married life. Let's look at several of them.

MYTH #1: Singles are more unfulfilled than married people. Marriage is not the basis for a fulfilled life. Fulfillment comes from a close relationship with Christ. Many of today's singles know that marriage does not carry with it a guarantee of happiness and fulfillment. One reason people give for staying single or delaying marriage is that they saw their parents go through a divorce and they know the pain it produces. They also hear horror stories from their friends who married young, and they are waiting until they feel they can make a mature choice for a lifelong mate.

In addition, an unmarried person today has a wide range of choices for a fulfilled life apart from marriage. Women especially have educational, vocational, and financial opportunities that were not available a few decades ago. Women and men are choosing to find fulfillment through employment or service to society or other ways that bring them into relationships with people.

Married people need to be aware that some of the single men and women sitting next to them in church can choose to remain single and be just as fulfilled as those who are married.

MYTH #2: Marriage solves all the problems of singleness. The reality is that marriage brings with it many new problems. Even at best, two people who marry can expect a period of marital adjustment. The first few years can be filled with turbulence as they go through the period of communication and compromise--no matter how well they thought they knew each other. "Moonlight and roses" becomes "daylight and dishes," and the adjustment, as any married couple will attest to, continues for a lifetime.

God never promised anyone a life without pressure or difficulty. Everyone must learn to grow in relationships. The thing to remember is that the better a person can manage life as a single, the better chance that person will have of establishing a successful marriage relationship.

MYTH#3: Marriage is God's highest calling for men and women. Some contented married adults today may sincerely believe that a single person could not possibly be living a fulfilled, satisfying life. This concept is fostered by a couples-centered society. The Bible, however, does not teach that marriage is a higher calling than singleness. Consider Jesus' words to His disciples in Matthew 19. In response to Jesus' teaching about divorce, the disciples said, "If such is the case of the man with his wife, it is better not to marry" (v.10). Jesus replied:

> *Not everyone can accept this word, but only those to whom it has been given. For some are eunuchs because they were born that way; others were made that way by men; and others have renounced marriage because of the kingdom of heaven. The one who can accept this should accept it (vv.11-12 NIV).*

In other words, not everyone can or should be single, but those who can, should. In 1 Corinthians 7, the apostle Paul added:

> *For I wish that all men were [single] even as I myself. But each one has his own gift from God, one in this manner and another in that. But I say to the unmarried and to the widows: It is good for them if they remain even as I am . . . . I want you to be without care. He who is unmarried cares for the things of the Lord--how he may please the Lord. But he who is married cares about the things of the world--how he may please his wife (vv.7-8,32-33).*

While it's true that the majority of people get married, it's actually a higher calling to be single "for the kingdom of heaven."

MYTH#4: Singles struggle with loneliness more than married people. There's no question about it: Loneliness is a major element of singleness. The survey cited previously indicated that loneliness is one of the major disadvantages of being single. But it's not accurate to assume that all adult singles struggle with loneliness more than married people do. A recent study identified young wives, college students, the elderly, and prisoners as being among the most lonely people in society.

In reality, singleness gives ample opportunity to be with people and create strong friendships. One 26-year-old single said, "Find a good friend. That's the best thing if you're single." She's right. Adult singles can form strong networks of friends of all ages that can help them face times of loneliness.

A 35-year-old single man said, however, that it became increasingly difficult for him to develop strong male friendships as he grew older. That's because eventually his friends would find a woman they liked, date, then marry. His friends always promised that they would maintain the friendship after the wedding, but it seldom happened. The loss of a good friend can be like losing someone in death. This man got tired of the mourning. Sometimes, single adults (especially those who have been previously married) are seen as threats by those who are married. For example, a divorced woman may be treated coldly by some of the married women in the church because they view her as a threat to their marriage. These women simply do not realize that singleness can include strong friendships, and that taking someone else's spouse is probably the farthest thing from the single person's mind.

It is possible, and even healthy, for couples to befriend singles. Strong guidelines of propriety and communication must be followed, of course, and the result can make life richer for everyone.

MYTH #5: Singles have more time and money than married people. Some adult singles do have more discretionary time and income than their married counterparts. But many singles are kept extremely busy by family, friends, and church commitments. And some singles who choose to purchase their own homes will probably have less discretionary income than married people with two incomes.

Further, when the single person is divorced or widowed and there are children involved, expenses can be overwhelming. Many single mothers do not have job training or experience, and they face the additional burden of child-care costs.

In terms of spare time, a single mom has almost no time for herself. Widows may find every minute filled with responsibilities they are not used to. And the never-marrieds can fill their lives with family, friendships, and meaningful activity. In other words, busy people are going to be busy regardless of their marital status.

MYTH#6: Singles are more self-centered than married people. This myth is based on the belief that single people do not marry because they want to spend their income on themselves and be free to do whatever they want whenever they want. While that is true of some singles, the fact is that all adults can choose to live selfishly, married or single, and all too many do.

The advertisers don't help. Those singles who buy into a carefree, high-flying, materialistic and hedonistic lifestyle, committing themselves to expensive cars and pampering themselves, are headed for disappointment.

Many adult singles are selfless, giving people, inside and outside the Christian community. Much volunteer work is done in hospitals and other agencies by widows and other adult singles. Where would the cause of missions be without the adult single? How many singles are in your church orchestra? Your choir? The staff of your Sunday school and children's programs? These volunteers are certainly not selfish. They're wonderful examples of those who faithfully serve their church and community.

MYTH #7: Singles are more sexually frustrated than married people. When Koons and Anthony surveyed Christian adult singles, they discovered the following issues to be ranked above sexual frustration: (1) proper entertainment, (2) managing money, (3) making good friends, and (4) raising children.

True, some singles are promiscuous, but so are some marrieds. Married adults are subject to sexual frustration too. But both married and single people have to learn how to control this part of their lives.

Singleness means susceptibility to certain temptations, especially the way society sends sexually charged signals today. Married people are receiving those same signals. One of the important challenges for the church is to help its entire adult congregation deal with the sexual pressure of today's world.

Myth #8: Singles can't lead as effectively as married people. This myth probably arises out of an interpretation of the qualifications for church leadership in 1 Timothy 3. Paul stated that church elders and deacons must be husbands of one wife (vv.2,12) and it's assumed that they have children (vv.4,12). This probably is a restriction against unfaithful husbands and irresponsible fathers. But even if it is thought to disqualify single men from these two offices, that doesn't mean singles can't lead effectively in other areas. What about Jesus? And what about the leadership ability of one of the greatest leaders of the Christian church, the apostle Paul?

Married people are often placed in positions of leadership over adult singles. But singleness does not automatically mean immaturity and irresponsibility--just as marriage doesn't mean maturity. Adult singles can lead, and they do it very well.

These eight myths contribute to a misunderstanding of singleness in today's society. They need to be replaced by the truth of God's Word.

Searching The Scriptures

A third way to understand singleness is to search the Scriptures. The Bible gives some direct teaching to the issue of adult singles (1 Cor. 7 for example). But most of what it tells us about the subject is spoken through the example of godly single adults, who include no less than the apostle Paul and Jesus Christ Himself.

The Old Testament.

The Old Testament gives us some examples of godly adult singles that speak volumes to singleness today and in every age. Consider Joseph, whose conduct in Egypt as an adult single was exemplary (Gen. 37-41:44).

Look at Elijah, a bold and dedicated prophet of God who stared down the likes of Ahab and his prophets.

Look at Daniel, who was highly respected as a man of God. He was a governmental leader for many years during the exile in Babylon. Numerous prophecies were revealed through him.

Look at Hagar, a single mother. She and her child were taken care of by the Lord.

Look at Naomi, a resourceful widow who followed the Lord and cared for her daughter-in-law.

Look at Ruth, who showed faith, courage, and loyalty as an adult single.

Yes, the Old Testament gives stirring examples of how the Lord strategically used adult singles to do His work. He showed no partiality to married people, and there is no hint that He considered adult singles to be of any less value in His eyes.

The New Testament.

The New Testament gives additional insight into God's mind regardingsingleness. Consider the teachings of Christ and Paul.

In His important discourse about divorce, the Lord Jesus said that singleness is a gift from God (Matt. 19:11-12). A person who marries is to leave his or her parents and remain married (vv.5-6), but the person who remains single does not carry the pressures and responsibilities of marriage.

An adult single looking for a model needs look no further than to Jesus, who obeyed the Father in everything He did (John 15:10). Even though He was God, in His humanity He was our example (1 Cor. 11:1). His selflessness, His compassion, His purity, and His contentment with doing the will of God in everything are especially relevant to singleness today.

In his first letter to the believers at Corinth (see chapter 7), Paul clarified and expanded on what the Lord Jesus said. What Paul taught about singleness may be summarized as follows:

• Singleness can be a gift from God (v.7).

• A married person is concerned about serving God and pleasing a spouse (vv.26-35).

• Celibacy brings the freedom to serve God unencumbered (vv.32-35).

• Unmarried persons can develop a deep relationship with God because they have fewer distractions (v.35).

Some New Testament singles we can study and admire are the sisters who were good friends of Jesus--Mary and Martha--along with their brother Lazarus. The sisters were as different as night and day, yet both served Christ faithfully and were His good and loyal friends.

Mary Magdalene was an adult single with a past, and her devotion to Jesus was unquestioned.

Paul gave his life in complete dedication to the gospel. He suffered unbelievable hardship as he went into Europe with the story of Christ. Could he have done it as a married person? Probably not. As a single he was free to do the great pioneer work of taking the gospel to the Gentile world.

The biblical teaching about singleness can be summarized by the following statements:

1. We need one another. We need companionship and relationships--whether single or married.

2. God accepts and respects singleness. Nothing in the Bible indicates that a person who chooses not to marry has any less worth than a person who marries.

3. Singleness has advantages for the person who wants to give his or her life to God's service.

4. God gives wonderful gifts. One of them is the ability and choice to be single for many years or for a lifetime.

5. God is all-sufficient. His sufficiency sustains the adult single. It's okay to want to be married, but it's far more important, single or married, to lean on the sufficiency of Christ and walk in obedience to Him.

Facing The Issues

Now that we have looked at the facts and some myths about singleness in today's society, and we have examined the Scriptures, we are ready to identify and speak to the primary concerns adult singles are facing today. What are the struggles? The pressures? The needs? And what can be done to produce understanding and acceptance? If you are single, here are two principles to follow in facing the issues of your singleness.

Principle 1: Accept Your Singleness. It's not a sin to be single. A man or woman is free to choose singleness and should find full acceptance by the community and the church. An increasing number of adults are choosing to remain single. Others have been left single by an unwanted divorce or the untimely death of a spouse. Singles must work in cooperation with married people to remove any barriers of prejudice or fear that might hinder acceptance.

Look around you. Think about the place where you work, your neighborhood, your church. How many adult singles can you identify? One pastor was amazed to discover that 28 percent of his children's workers and 33 percent of his adult choir were singles.

You may be dealing with deep and painful issues. If you have never married, you may have experienced a number of disappointments and you may have a dismal self-image. If widowed, you may still feel deep sadness, and you may need help to work through your grief. If you are divorced, your dreams have been shattered and you may have been rejected. Perhaps your trust and love have been betrayed. You may be facing crushing financial burdens, especially if you have the children, and you may have housing needs. You are probably working through difficult emotional issues. If you are a single parent--managing a household while working and rearing children alone--you probably feel unbelievable tension and anxiety. If you are separated, it may be because you could no longer take the physical and emotional abuse you or the children were subjected to again and again.

You know all too well that you're not perfect. You've made mistakes and you fear that you may make them again. You need the solace and grace and help that only God can give. He gives it, but in large measure it comes through His people. You need people of God who are willing to accept you where you are. You need to be free to grow from that point. Sure, you'll have to make yourself vulnerable. Sure, you'll have to let some people enter into your pain. It will take patience and love and understanding and, most of all, being accepted for who you are right now.

You need to find a church where people make an effort to open their arms and hearts and accept you as you are--without prejudgment or suspicion. Help them form small groups for grief recovery or single parents or divorce recovery. Encourage them to offer social activities that welcome singles into fellowship with married couples, and to give them opportunities to serve the Lord with their God-given gifts.

It would be wonderful if you could see your church as a sanctuary--a place of safety and healing and service to God. Singles need to be welcomed in, not legislated out by suspicious attitudes or legalistic, nonbiblical limitations. You may have trouble accepting yourself as a single. You may let attitudes around you undermine your confidence and sense of self-worth.

Stop! Don't let yourself feel inferior or incomplete! As we have seen, it's okay to choose not to marry or remarry. Yours is not an "alternate lifestyle." So you're widowed or divorced, or you've been forced to separate. God is willing to accept you where you are and go from there. You should be willing to do the same. No apologies!

Principle 2: Face Up to Your Needs. Singleness carries with it certain needs. You have to face those needs and not dodge them. We will look at six of them: a sense of purpose, loneliness, sexuality, contentment, service, and ministry.

1. A sense of purpose. As an adult single, you may be struggling with seeing God's purpose for singleness. You may have put your life on hold until Mr. Right or Miss Wonderful comes along. You say to yourself, "When I get married I'll become serious about God," or, "After I'm married I'll look for a steady job and get out of debt." "After marriage I'll purchase a home." So you are wandering aimlessly, waiting for something to happen.

You must see the importance of formulating a strong life-plan right now. Set realistic and specific personal goals. Some of those goals should be spiritual. It's wise and necessary to forge ahead with life--to get established in the church and community, to move ahead with a career, to purchase a home. The Bible makes it clear that we are all to be watchful (1 Tim. 4:16), to make good use of our time (Eph. 5:16), to use our gifts for the glory of God (1 Cor. 10:31). Seek opportunities for growth and service to Christ. Form and follow a clear and satisfying life-plan.

2. Loneliness. Billy Graham once said that loneliness is the greatest problem facing humanity today. Two recent national surveys identified loneliness as the number one issue in singleness. It ranked ahead of managing time, for example, and sexual issues. Closely linked is the need for companionship and intimacy. You may be lonely because you're in school or have long hours of employment or shyness or the untimely loss of a mate. Face your loneliness and do something about it. Don't deny those feelings; acknowledge them, and take action.

You might begin by finding a church that has established a healthy atmosphere where friendships can develop. Look for opportunities to fellowship in smaller groups. Find a church that sees the importance of mutual trust and respect, privacy, toleration of differences, and realistic expectations of one another. You'll fit right in!

Help your church become a safe place where single adults can risk making friends. At the same time, do not forget the advantages of solitude. Jesus went often to be alone. How many mothers would give anything for "a moment's peace"? Singleness gives you an opportunity for solitude.

You might also make friends with couples who have a healthy marriage. You need to learn about the struggles they face. At the same time, married people need exposure to you and your needs. If you can find a church where singles and marrieds can walk beside one another, bearing one another's burdens and doing good to one another, your loneliness will be significantly eased.

But remember, the greatest deterrent to loneliness is an intimate relationship with Christ. No amount of involvement with people will ever take the place of fellowship with God. When loneliness assails you, acknowledge your feelings to the Lord and draw close to Him. The apostle James said, "Draw near to God and He will draw near to you" (4:8).

3. Sexuality. As an adult single, you need solid biblical teaching about sexuality that takes your situation into account. Look for a church that does not accept the myth that all singles are living sexually frustrated lives, or that there "must be something wrong with them." Rather, a wise church will reinforce healthy sexual attitudes for its entire congregation by:

- Standing up to the liberalization of sexual attitudes in today's society.
- Showing what is wrong with the media's view of sex and obsession with it.
- Differentiating between intimacy and sex.
- Realistically warning of the heartbreaking results of cohabitation.
- Teaching the biblical truth about human sexuality.

This last recommendation is of primary importance. But how can it be accomplished? Some of it can be done from the pulpit and in the Sunday school classroom. Seminar speakers, Christian videos, and discussions in appropriate small group settings are also effective.

The church can help in another, more painful way. When it learns that one of its singles has embarked on an unwise sexual relationship, it must have the love and courage to confront that person, lead him or her to repentance, then forgive and restore. Sure, it's difficult. The church might lose that person. But single people, as

233

well as the entire congregation, will know it's a church that really cares and means business spiritually.

4. Contentment. Contentment is a key issue of singleness. You may long for a mate. You yearn for children. You want affection and acceptance and love--just someone to hold you. You want a nice home in the suburbs, not a shared apartment. Contentment is not a singles' issue exclusively. Everyone wrestles with dissatisfaction and envy. The Bible teaches that contentment begins and ends with God (1 Tim. 6:6).

Living by two key principles will help you deal with the issue of contentment. First, contentment is not an end in itself. No one can begin to let himself believe that he will be content if he purchases a certain sports car, achieves a certain rank, marries a certain woman, or earns a Ph.D. Those things simply do not guarantee contentment. Besides, before they are even achieved, the person has gone on to set new goals for contentment.

The second principle is that contentment is found in enjoying God. Paul had the secret (Phil. 4:11-12). He said, in essence, that he could be content in prison or out, in rich garments or rags, surrounded by friends or alone. Why? Because for Paul, contentment was found in obeying and enjoying Christ.

It does us little good to live in the "if only's" of life. How much better to find our contentment in God rather than in something we decide will make us happy! You must have the courage to ask yourself, "Have I ever thought that I should accept my circumstances as coming from a loving, caring, good God?"

You also need to train yourself to think more about the things you have than what you do not have. Remind yourself that "godliness with contentment is great gain" (1 Tim. 6:6).

5. Service. Look for opportunities to serve. Avoid the tendency to seek respect and recognition as an unmarried person. Look instead for ways to help others see Christ at work in a godly single adult. Be an example and an advocate for others who tend to be overlooked in the church planning process.

Karen, a single, was concerned about her church. It had a growing number of singles, and they were enjoying the teaching and fellowship of the church. But Karen felt more was needed. So she went to the pastor and expressed her feeling that the singles needed to give as well as receive. This meeting led to a food distribution program that bonded the singles, brought blessing to the whole church, and helped the community.

6. Train for discipleship and ministry. Singleness is not a good reason for inactivity or uninvolvement. As a child of God, you can be actively involved in the ministry of your church and community. Get some leadership training. Connect with areas where you can serve--children's work, music, drama, teaching, the elder or deacon board. You may even feel called to accept the chairmanship of a key committee or board. The Bible places no limits on what you can do in your church or the community.

A CHALLENGE TO SINGLE

If you're single, perhaps you're saying, "I wish my church would start a ministry for adult singles." Or you may be thinking, "All this sounds good, but it will never happen in my church."

Why not? Do you really know it won't happen? You may be the one God uses to increase the sensitivity in your local congregation to its singles. He may want you to take the lead in creating single awareness. More and more churches are ministering directly to singles. An increasing number are creating a staff position for a pastor to singles. Some excellent publications, available through most Christian bookstores, tell what is being done in some churches and give good advice for getting started with a ministry to singles.

Even if your church is not large, you can do some things to bring more single people into your church and encourage an understanding ministry.

In a proper attitude and spirit, and after prayer and knowing you are led by the Spirit of God, begin by talking with the pastor or Christian education director. You might even go to the church board. Perhaps two or three of you could present your burden and ideas.

Indicate your need. Tell of your love for Christ and your desire to grow and reach others. Without criticizing or judging, offer some suggestions for getting started. Volunteer to serve on committees. Offer assistance in any way you can. That kind of action has led to a better singles' ministry in many churches, and it can in yours as well.

JESUS: FRIEND OF SINGLES

What kind of person are you? Athlete? Musician? Outdoors man? Administrator and organizer? Computer whiz? Mystery reader? Automobile mechanic? Painter? Decorator? Volunteer? And what about inside? Is your heart empty? Do you sometimes look at others and long for what they have? Is there an ache, a longing? Is your life definitely "on hold"?

Jesus Christ is the friend of singles. A single Himself, He walked through life with a sense of purpose and mission. It took Him to the cross, where He died for you. Sin is a universal problem. "All have sinned" (Rom. 3:23). Jesus died to pay the penalty for your sin. Start by inviting Him into your life. Receive Him as your Saviour.

But Jesus does more as the friend of singles than just save them. Perhaps you have trusted Him, but you still struggle with feelings of inadequacy, envy, frustration, and loneliness. A wonderful verse says, "Our sufficiency is from God" (2 Cor. 3:5). We have the assurance that Christ will give us all the grace we need to serve Him and live happily (see 2 Cor. 9:8;12:9).

Make friends with the friend of singles. Trust Jesus. Put your hand in His hand. Draw His sufficiency into your heart and life. Give yourself to Him. You will discover that He is a friend who will never desert or betray you - a friend who will satisfy your heart's deepest need.

SAMPLE EXERCISES

PRE-MARITAL COUNSELLING WORKBOOK

With
Subjects that ought to be included by
Counselors
During pre-marital counselling sesssions

From

PREPARE-ENRICH

Note. The full material should be available from any duly registered
and qualified Prepare-Enrich Counselor

1. SHARING STRENGTH AND GROWTH AREAS

2. COMMUNICATION: Assertiveness and Active Listening
   Creating a Wishg List Using Assertiveness and Active Listening
   Daily Dialogue and Daily Compliments

3. PERSONAL STRESS PROFILE
   Identifying Most Critical Issues
   Balancing your Priorities
   Wedding Stress

4. CONFLICT RESOLUTION
   Ten Steps for Resolving Conflict
   How to take a Time-Out
   Seeking and Granting Forgiveness

4. FINANCIAL MANAGEMENT
   The Challenges of Money
   Importance of Financial Goals
   Budget Worksheet
   The Meaning of Money

5. LEISURES ACTIVITIES: The Dating Exercise

6. SEX AND AFFECTION: The Expression of Intimacy

7. RELATIONSHIP ROLES: Sharing Roles

8. SPIRITUAL BELIEFS: Your Spiritual Journey

9. MARRIAGE EXPECTATIONS: Managing Your Expectations

10. CHILDREN AND PARENTING
    Couple Discussion about Children
    Planning a Weekly Family Conference
    StepFamilies: Choosing Realistic Expectations

11. COUPLE AND FAMILY MAPS
    Mapping Your Relationship
    Closeness Exercise

12. PERSONALITY: Scope Out Your Personality

13. GOALS: Achieving Your Goals...Together

SHARING STRENGTH AND GROWTH AREAS

But the Holy Spirit produces this kind of fruit in our lives: love, hoy, peace, patience, kindness, goodness, faithfulness, gentleness, and self control." Galatians 5:22, 23

Check what areas you agree on or disagree most with your partner.
Select three Strength Areas (most agreement and positive aspect of your relationship)
Select three Growth Areas (most disagreement and areas you want to improve)

Areas	Strength Areas	Growth Areas
1. COMMUNICATION: We share feelings and understand each other		
2. CONFLICT RESOLUTION: We are able to discuss and resolve differences		
3. PARTNER STYLE AND HABITS: We appreciate each other's personality and habits		
4. FINANCIAL MANAGEMENT: We agree on budget and financial matters		
5. LEISURE ACTIVITIES: We have a good balance activities together adn apart		
6. SEXUALITY AND AFFECTION: We are comfortable discussing sexual issues and affection		
7. FAMILY AND FRIENDS: We feel good about our relationships with relatives and friends		
8. RELATIONSHIP ROLES: We agree on how to share decision-making and responsibilities		
9. CHILDREN AND PARENTING: We agree on issues and related to having and raising children		
10. SPIRITUAL BELIEFS: We hold similar religious values and beliefs		

COUPLE DISCUSSION:
1. Take turns sharing what each of you perceive as your relationship strengths. Verbally share one strength at a time, until you each have shared three.
2. Use the same procedure to share and discuss growth areas
3. Now have a discussion around these questions:
        a. Did any of your partner's response surprise you?
        b. In what areas did you mostly agree with your partner?
        c. In what areas did you mostly disagree with your partner?

COMMUNICATION

Understand this, my dear brothers and sisters: You must all be quick to listen, slow to speak, and slow to get angry. - James 1:19

ASSERTIVENESS AND ACTIVE LISTENING

ASSERTIVENESS

Assertiveness is the ability to express your feelings and ask for what you want in the relationship.

Assertiveness is a valuable communication skill. In successful couples, both individuals tend to be quite assertive. Rather than assuming their partner can read their mind, they share how they feel and ask clearly and directly for what they want. Assertive individuals take responsibility for their message by using "I" statements. They avoid statements beginning with "you." In making constructive requests, they are positive and respectful in their communication. They use polite phrases such as "please" and "thank you."

> **Example**
> "I'm feeling out of balance. While I love spendibg time with you, I also want to spend time with my friends. I would like us to find some time to talk about this."
> "I want to take a ski vacation next winter, but I know you like to go to the beach. I'm feeling confused about what choice we should make."

ACTIVE LISTENING

Active listening is the ability to let your partner know you understand them by restating their message.

Good communication depends on you carefully listening to another person. Active listening involves listening attentively without interruption and then restating what was heard. Acknowledge content AND the feelings of the speaker. The active listeniung process lets the sender know whether or not the message they sent was clearly understood by having the listener restate what they heard.

> **Example**
> "I heard you say you are feeling 'out of balance,' and enjoy the time we spend together but that you also need more time to be with your friends. You want to plan a time to talk about this."

"If I understand what you said, you are concerned because you want to go skiing next winter. But you think I would rather to go to the beach. Is that correct?"

Note: When each person knows what the other person feels and wants (assertiveness) and when each knows they have been heard and understood (active listening), intimacy is increased. These two communication skills can help you grow closer as a couple. And if developed in your marriage, then you will have a rich marital relationship.

CREATING A WISH LIST

In this exercise, you will each individually make a Wish List of things you would like more or less in your relationship. Next, take turns sharing your Wish List with each other.

In sharing your wish list with your partner, you will be demonstrating your assertiveness skills. In giving feedback to your partner about their Wish List, you will be demonstrating your Active Listening skills.

Make a Wish List of three things you would like more or less of in your relationship

1._____

2._____

3._____

COUPLE DISCUSSION
Take turns sharing your Wish List with each other.

SPEAKER'S JOB:
1. Speak for yourself ("I" statements eg "I wish...")
2. Describe how you would feel if your wish came true

LISTENER'S JOB
1. Repeat/summarise what you have heard
2. Describe the wish AND how your partner would feel if the wish came true

After completing the Wish List Exercise, discuss the following questions:

a. How good were each of you at being assertive?

b. In what ways did you each effectively use active listening skills?

Some people make cutting remarks, but the words of the wise bring healing. - Proverbs 12:18

DAILY DIALOGUE AND DAILY COMPLIMENTS

Daily Dialogue is an intentional effort to talk about your relationship, rather than discussing your activities that day. The focus of this dialogue should be on your feelings about each other and your lives together. Set aside fi ve minutes per day to discuss the following:
- What did you most enjoy about your relationship today?
- What was dissatisfying about your relationship today?
- How can you be helpful to each other?

Daily Compliments help you focus on the positive things you like about each other. Every day give your partner at least one genuine compliment. These can be general ("you are fun to be with") or specific ("I appreciate that you were on time for the concert").

COMMUNICATION SKILLS TO INCREASE INTIMACY

1. Give full attention to your partner when talking. Turn off the phone, shut off the television, make eye contact.
2. Focus on the good qualities in each other and often praise each other.
3. Be assertive. Share your thoughts, feelings, and needs.
   A good way to be assertive without being critical is to use "I" rather than "You" statements. (e.g. "I worry when you don't let me know you'll be late" rather than "You are always late").
4. Avoid criticism.
5. If you must criticize, balance it with at least one positive comment.
   (e.g."I appreciate how you take the trash out each week. In the future can you remember to also wheel the trash can back from the end of the driveway?") .
6. Listen to understand, not to judge.
7. Use active listening. Summarize your partner's comments before sharing your own reactions or feelings.

8. Avoid blaming each other and work together for a solution.
9. Use the Ten Steps approach. For problems that come up again and again, use the Ten Steps for Resolving Couple Confl ict.
10. Seek counseling. If you are not able to resolve issues, seek counseling before they become more serious.

WHAT THE BIBLE SAYS ABOUT COMMUNICATION

PSALM 19:14 May the words of my mouth and the meditation of my heart be pleasing to you, O LORD, my rock and my redeemer.

PROVERBS 17:27 A truly wise person uses few words; a person with understanding is even tempered.

PROVERBS 12:18 Some people make cutting remarks, but the words of the wise bring healing.

MATTHEW 7:3 And why worry about a speck in your friend's eye when you have a log in your own?

PROVERBS 20:19 A gossip goes around telling secrets, so don't hang around with chatterers.

JAMES 1:19 Understand this, my dear brothers and sisters: You must all be quick to listen, slow to speak, and slow to get angry.

PROVERBS 18:13 Spouting off before listening to the facts is both shameful and foolish.

MARRIAGE EXPECTATIONS

Can two people walk together without agreeing on the direction? — AMOS 3:3

MANAGING YOUR EXPECTATIONS

Expectations about love and marriage have a powerful impact on relationships. To a large degree, you will be disappointed or happy in life based on how well what is happening matches up with what you think should be happening. All married couples start out hoping for and believing they will experience the very best. Problems arise when these hopes and beliefs are not based on reality.

The following statements are common fantasies couples have about marriage. Read them and select the ones you believe are true. Take turns sharing and discussing these with each other.

1. My partner will meet all my needs for companionship.
2. Time will resolve our problems.
3. If I have to ask, it is not as meaningful.
4. We should live 'happily ever after' with no major problems.
5. Keeping secrets about my past or present is acceptable if it would only cause pain for my partner.
6. Less romance means we have less love for one another.
7. Our relationship will remain the same.
8. My partner's interest in sex will be the same as mine.
9. Our relationship will be better when we have a baby.
10. We will do things just like my family did.
11. Nothing could cause us to question our love for one another.
12. I believe I know everything there is to know about my partner.
13. Love is all you need for a great marriage.
14. It is better to keep silent about something bothering me than to cause unnecessary problems in our relationship.

COUPLE DISCUSSION:

1. Which of these statements have you been tempted to believe?
2. If you agree with these statements, how might they set you up for being disappointed later on?
3. How does believing or living out these statements keep you from fully loving and/or honoring yourself and your partner?

WHAT THE BIBLE SAYS ABOUT MARRIAGE

GENESIS 2:18,24 Then the LORD God said, "It is not good for the man to be alone. I will make a helper who is just right for him." This explains why a man leaves his father and mother and is joined to his wife, and the two are united into one.

MATTHEW 19:4-6 "Haven't you read the Scriptures?" Jesus replied. "They record that from the beginning 'God made them male and female.' And he said, 'This explains why a man leaves his father and mother and is joined to his wife, and the two are united into one.' Since they are no longer two but one let no one split apart what God has joined together."
ECCLESIASTES 4:9-11 Two people are better off than one, for they can help each other succeed. If one person falls, the other can reach out and help. But someone who falls alone is in real trouble. Likewise, two people lying close together can keep each other warm. But how can one be warm alone?

PROVERBS 31:10-11 Who can find a virtuous and capable wife? She is more precious than rubies. Her husband can trust her, and she will greatly enrich his life.

EPHESIANS 5:25 For husbands, this means love your wives, just as Christ loved the church. He gave up his life for her.

EPHESIANS 5:31-33 As the Scriptures say, "A man leaves his father and mother and is joined to his wife, and the two are united into one." This is a great mystery, but it is an illustration of the way Christ and the church are one. So again I say, each man must love his wife as he loves himself, and the wife must respect her husband.

GENESIS 2:23-24 "At last!" the man exclaimed. "This one is bone from my bone, and flesh from my flesh! She will be called 'woman,' because she was taken from 'man.'" This explains why a man leaveshis father and mother and is joined to his wife, and the two are united into one.
MATTHEW 18:19 "I also tell you this: If two of you agree here on earth concerning anything you ask, my Father in heaven will do it for you.

AMOS 3:3 Can two people walk together without agreeing on the direction?

RELATIONSHIP ROLES

Always be humble and gentle. Be patient with each other, making allowance for each other's faults because of your love. Make every effort to keep yourselves united in the Spirit, binding yourselves together with peace. — EPHESIANS 4:2-3

SHARING ROLES

List your responsibilities and your partner's responsibilities related to the household and/or children. Your partner should also separately create the same two lists. Note: For couples who are not yet sharing a household, complete these lists as things you expect to do in your future household.

Things You Do (or plan to do) for your Household	Things Your Partner Does (or plans to do) for your Household
a.	a.
b.	b.
c.	c.
d.	d.

COUPLE DISCUSSION:

1. After you have each completed your lists, compare and discuss them. Any surprises?
2. Are roles mainly divided by interests and skill, or by more traditional male/female roles?
3. Consider for a moment how similar or dissimilar these lists are compared to what you witnessed in your parents' roles growing up.
4. Discuss what each of you would like to adjust in your lists of roles. If needed, agree on how you might revise your current lists.
5. Revise your current lists, finalizing an agreement about tasks you will each do in the future. Set a time to review the new lists.

Relationship Roles Exercise: Switching Roles for a Week

After you have each completed your Household Tasks lists, plan a day (or a week) when you can perform each other's household responsibilities. This Role Reversal experiment will help you gain a new appreciation for one another.

For further information, please contact Dr Steve Thomas or a Prepare-Enrich counselor within your church or your pastor.

Excerpt References
Permission Granted

Chapter 4
Grudem, Wayne A. (2002). Biblical foundations for manhood and womanhood. Foundations for the family series (18–68). Wheaton, Ill.: Crossway Books.

Chapter 5
De Haan II, Martin R. *What Does God Exoect Of A Man?* (Grand Rapids, MI, USA: RBC Ministries, 1989). Excerpt with Permission. Copyright RBC Ministries 2011

Chapter 6
Martin R De Haan II, *What Does God Exoect Of A Woman?* (Grand Rapids, MI, USA: RBC Ministries, 1989). Excerpt with Permission

Chapter 7
Holland, Rick . *Defining Your Dating Style: The Guided Path* - Excerpt from Lauren F Winner, Douglas Wilson, Rick Holland, Jonathan Lindvall, Jeramy & Jerusha Clark, 5 Paths to the Love of Your Life: Defining Your Dating Style (Colorado Springs, Colorado, USA: TH1NK, 2005).

Chapter 9
Munroe, Myles. *Understanding the Purpose and Power of Woman* (PA, USA: Whitaker House, 2001)

Chapter 10
Brand, C., Draper, C., England, A., Bond, S., Clendenen, E. R., Butler, T. C., & Latta, B. (2003). *Sex: Biblical and Sacredness,* Holman Illustrated Bible Dictionary (1469–1471). Nashville, TN: Holman Bible Publishers.

Chapters 13
Covey, Stephen R. *The 7 Habits of Highly Effective People* (London, United Kingdom:Simon & Scuster UK Ltd, 2004).

Chapter 14
Dave Egner, *Singlenes: The Misunderstood World of Single Adults.* N.P

Additional References Used in context

Armstrong, Alison A. *Keys to the Kingdom,* (Sherman Oaks, CA: PAX Programs Incorporated, 2003).

Arp, David & Claudia. *10 Great Dates to Energize Your Marriage* (Grand Rapids, Michigan: Zondervan, 1997).

Arthur, kay, David & BJ Lawson. *Building A Marriage That Really Works.* N.P

Arthur, Kay. *A Marriage Without Regrets* (Eugene, Oregon: Harvest House Publisher, 2000).

Chapman, Gary. *The Five Love Languages: How to Express Heartfelt Commitment to Your Mate* (Chicago: Northfield Publishing, 2004).

Covey, Stephen R. *The 7 Habits of Highly Effective People* (London, United Kingdom:Simon & Scuster UK Ltd, 2004).

Garland, Diana R. *Family Ministry: A Comprenhsiven Guide* (Downers Grove, Illinois: InterVarsity Press, 1999).

Garland, Diana R and Betty Hassler. *Covenant Marriage: Partnership and Commitment (Nashville, Tennessee: LifeWay Press, 1999).*

Hegstrom, Paul. *Angry Men and the Women Who Love Them: Breaking the Cycle of Physical and Emotional Abuse* (Kansas City, Missouri: Beacon Hill Press of Kansas City, 2004).

National Online Statistics. *Census 2001, http://www.ons.gov.uk (25 January 2006)*

Smalley, Gary. *Hidden Keys of a Loving, Lasting Marriage* (Grand Rapids, Michigan: Zondervan, 1988).

_____ . *If Only He Knew: Understanding Your Wife* (Grand Rapids, Michigan: Zondervan, 1988).

Wesley, Karry D. *If This Marriage Was Made in Heaven, Why Am I Going Through Hell?* (Emumclaw, WA: WinePress Publishing, 2000).

White, Ellen G. *The Adventist Home* (Review and Herald Publishing Association, Washington DC, 1980).

_____ . *Child Guidance* (Review and Herald Publishing Association, Washington DC, 1980).